THE BLOOD ENCHANTRESS

BEATRICE B. MORGAN

AUTHORS 4 AUTHORS PUBLISHING

Marysville, WA, USA

Published by Authors 4 Authors Publishing
1214 6th St
Marysville, WA 98270
www.authors4authorspublishing.com

Library of Congress Control Number:

E-book ISBN: 978-1-64477-195-2
Paperback ISBN: 978-1-64477-196-9
Audiobook ISBN: 978-1-64477-197-6

Edited by Lisa Borne Graves
Line edited by Renee Frey
Copyedited by Rebecca Mikkelson
Formatted by Rebecca Mikkelson

Cover design ©2025 Practically Perfect Covers. All rights reserved.

Authors 4 Authors Publishing branding is set in Bavire. Titles and headings are set in Garcedo. All other text is set in Garamond.

BEATRICE B. MORGAN

THE BLOOD ENCHANTRESS

Authors 4 Authors Content Rating

This title has been rated XS, appropriate for adults, and contains:

- graphic sex
- strong language
- graphic violence
- moderate alcohol use

Please, keep the following in mind when using our rating system:

1. A content rating is not a measure of quality.

Great stories can be found for every audience. One book with many content warnings and another with none at all may be of equal depth and sophistication. Our ratings can work both ways: to avoid content or to find it.

2. Ratings are merely a tool.

For our young adult (YA) and children's titles, age ratings are generalized suggestions. For parents, our descriptive ratings can help you make informed decisions, but at the end of the day, only you know what kinds of content are appropriate for your individual child. This is why we provide details in addition to the general age rating.

For more information on our rating system, please, visit our Content Guide at:
www.authors4authorspublishing.com/books/ratings

DEDICATION

To anyone who once claimed to hate vampires, and one day
realized they didn't.

To those who hold on to those they love most, through thick and
thin, through hell and high water, because love will conquer all.

Works by Beatrice B. Morgan

Stars and Bones Series
Thief in the Castle
Mage in the Undercity
Dreams in the Snow
Nightmares in the Ice
Witch in the Wylds
Archmage in the Ruins

Hard as Stone Trilogy
Hard as Stone
Thick as Blood
Strong as Steel

TABLE OF CONTENTS

1

BLOOD ENCHANTRESS

Ryn

Ryn stalked the drunk guard for three blocks before he staggered into an alley to piss.

Finally.

Dawn would soon warm the eastern sky. She needed to finish this job before the shopkeepers opened their stalls and stores, before the guard switched shifts, before the shadows vanished under the glaring light of the sun. Her dark layers of clothing wouldn't blend in with the daylight. She was dressed for the deep shadows of a Calcurta night.

Ryn exaggerated her swagger to that of a drunk waddling home after three too many drinks at one of Calcurta's shoddy low town taverns. As the male swiveled into the alley, his glazed eyes didn't even stray in her direction. She hesitated a step, putting space between the drunk guard and her, just in case he wasn't as drunk as he acted.

She'd been fooled by that before and wouldn't be again.

Hopefully, this would go smoothly. If not, well… Ryn would worry about that *if* it didn't go smoothly.

Horse hooves clomped a street over, and Ryn glanced over the drunk's head. Across the street and through the next alley over, a dark horse and its armored rider passed in and out of sight. The armor wasn't City Watch or Hunter, so it didn't matter. Mercenary or other such sword for hire. They were a copper a dozen on this side of town.

Ryn glided a step past the alley, as if she meant to walk by it. The drunk guard paused halfway down the alley, one hand propping his body against the stone wall, the other fighting with the ties of his trousers. A grumbled curse seethed on his breath. Without a sound, she eased into the alley, the ends of her black tailcoat trailing like her own personal shadows. She slid a dagger free. The blade was narrow and deadly sharp, a gift from Nobel.

The male didn't notice her. They never did.

One jab—the drunk guard let out a surprised grunt, but it was too late. One drop of blood, one cut, was all Ryn needed. As it beaded on his arm, her magic seized him—enchanting the whole of his blood supply in less time than it took for his heart to beat. Her magic flowed through his bloodstream, touching every organ, vein, and tissue; she silenced the protest in his lungs and the rush of adrenaline to his heart.

THE BLOOD ENCHANTRESS

Her magic recoiled at the astringent, cheap alcohol lingering in his blood and the grim in his soul—oily and sticky, moldy and corroded.

She didn't know how her blood magic could feel people, but it did. When she touched their blood, she felt their being, their soul. This guard was not the upstanding male he portrayed himself to be in front of his squad and the people. He was dirty. Whatever this male had done, it had layered darkness into his soul, blackening it like frostbite, burning it to a char.

A dirty soul made her job easier to stomach.

Despite the stillness of his organs, Ryn felt his panic rise. Hot and fluid, it coursed through his addled mind, twisting with his entitled, drunken fury, turning rabid and wild. A drunken rage and wounded pride. Typical male.

Ryn reached for one of several green glass bottles on her person and held it to the nick on the guard's arm. She enchanted the blood to flow into the bottle without touching his skin. The impurities and oil would ruin it. As the blood filled the bottle, she laced her magic within it. Blood, once it left the body, started to dry and clot. Her enchantment kept it fresh until uncorked.

In Calcurta, magic was perverse and wicked. Ryn didn't know where her magic came from. Legends said magic once ran deep in fae blood until vampires hunted them to extinction, until they stole every drop of that blood for themselves, until magic belonged only to vampires. Ryn wasn't a vampire. Her parents were dead, so she couldn't ask them about her lineage.

She had spent the last fifty years learning to enchant on her own, how to feel blood and the soul it belonged to. It was her little secret.

Bottle full, she corked it and replaced it in the special holder on her back, hidden by her cloak. She reached for the twin bottle on her other side.

The typical male contained a considerable amount of blood. Two jugs would carry it all, but she couldn't exactly walk around the dark streets with two jugs of blood. With the two large bottles on her back, smaller bottles on either thigh, and vials tucked into the leather belts across her chest and waist, all secured into holsters designed for this exact purpose, Ryn could carry the blood of the average male under her cloak without being obvious.

The male started to lose consciousness. With her magic threaded in his organs, she felt his body giving out. Using her command over his blood, she eased his body to the alley floor. A meaty thud would signal a problem. She slumped him against the wall, flaccid dick still in his hand, and continued to coax blood from the wound.

His lungs shuddered. His heart hesitated. His muscles seized. She felt the moment the blood loss became irrevocable—when death was unavoidable.

His heart gave one last pitiful beat, then stilled.

With the last vial filled and corked, the dirty guard was dead. His clothes hid most of his shriveled skin, but even in the dark, Ryn saw his face. Mouth gaping, eyes bulging and listless, cheekbones jutting, cheeks sunken. Gray skin pulled tight over his face, throat, and fingers, exposing the bones underneath. In life, he hadn't looked older than fifty, but with the long lifespan of the fae and the sprinkling of human blood, it was impossible to tell. He might have been fifty or one hundred and fifty.

It was a nightmarish sight. No matter how many times she saw it, each face triggered primal fear in her bones—a desperate, instinctual need to run.

Ryn stalked out of the alley. Dawn would reveal the dead guard soon enough, and she needed to be as far away from the body as possible.

Getting caught was bad for her health.

The only fate for magicians in Calcurta was execution.

2
VILE AS A COILED SNAKE
Ryn

Ryn made her way through Calcurta's tittering morning streets. Dawn came sooner than she'd expected, and to an unforgiving, clear sky. Sunlight bared down on the city's twisting, spiderweb-like streets with unnecessary exposure. The nicer parts of the city weren't so winding or narrow; they were cleaner and better guarded. The rich and important warranted such protection from the guard, whereas Ryn's side of the city was where thieves went to hide until nightfall.

The sun banished the worst of the night's chill. A small consolation for losing the shadows. A cool wind slithered through the streets, whispering of the incoming winter and the frigid cold that would soon descend upon the city. Rotted autumn leaves clogged gutters, waterlogged and trampled. Ryn didn't care for winter. Snow turned to mush, and ice clung to the cobbles and waterways and didn't melt until spring.

Despite the chilly autumn air, sweat gathered along Ryn's spine. As much as she wanted to shed her outer layers, she would rather sweat than explain why she carried blood-filled bottles on her person.

It wouldn't be long and she wouldn't be able to keep warm, even during the brightest hours of day.

With the sun came people. By the time Ryn reached the market, the streets teemed with people, readying ovens for bread, throwing open windows, sweeping dust through doorways, tossing dirty water into the alleys. Faded advertisements, sun-worn banners, dusty windows with half-ass displays, and weathered stone blurred together in dismal shades of brown and sage. A few shops were legal and straight-laced, the rare honest citizen trying to make a living the old-fashioned way, but most shops dipped their toes into the black market. The people were the same breed; a few strived to do the best with what they had, but others survived any way they could. This side of Calcurta teemed with thieves, mercenaries, and criminal guilds always pushing against one another for straws of power and territory and profit.

People wandered from shop to shop, others marched with intention. Ryn stepped carefully. She would rather be home by now. Far too many people to bump into. One wrong shuffle, one clumsy asshole, one accidental clink was all it took. Unsoiled blood would raise questions. One shout to the guards, and her head would be on the line.

Typical City Watch, she could handle. But Hunters? Hunters trained to hunt vampires, and by extension, magic. She didn't know if she could hide her magic if they caught her with bottled enchanted blood. It was King Victor's constant hunt for magic that kept Ryn living in the slums, hiding in the shadows and lies that held the black market and criminal guilds together.

Thankfully, fresh blood was a rarity for alchemists, potion masters, and the occasional vampire—rumor said they lurked in the darkest corners of the city where the sun didn't reach. She didn't care enough to find out for certain.

Hers was not a glamorous life, but Ryn could exist in the slums far easier than anywhere else.

She turned onto a busier street lined with shops and stalls opening for the day. Already, the smell of fresh rosemary bread, buttery rolls, and poppy buns wafted into the air. Her stomach twisted with hunger, and her mouth watered. Fresh brewed coffee and tea spiced the air with the bittersweet combination of milk and honey. Already, people gathered to buy their bread and goods.

Ryn stepped down a less crowded alley. Clotheslines left it mostly in shadow, dotted with bits of sunlight.

There was a certain comfort in being alone. It was familiar. Safe.

Halfway down the alley, a weaselly little male stepped from a dark alcove and latched onto the edge of her cloak. Panic seared through her body, and she grabbed it before he revealed the bottles beneath.

"Please, fair maiden, spare a coin?" His words reeked of cheap whiskey and rotting teeth.

"Get off me, you worm." She tried to yank her cloak out of his hands, but his grip stayed firm. Anger seared against her skin. One bottle of blood was worth more than every coin this weasel of male had ever held.

She fueled that freezing anger into the nasty hand clutching her cloak, turning the blood within cold as frostbite.

"Please, fair lady. My children are sick—" He wrenched his hands from her cloak and held them against his chest. His wide eyes narrowed. "Witch."

Her heart pounded at the accusation. Panic flashed under her skin, but she leaned into her anger at the male's interruption, at his audacity to touch her, and banished the panic and fear from her heart. She could not afford to be afraid, not in the shadows, not before others. Not ever. Fear got you killed.

"You're lucky you still have hands," Ryn spat. She stormed away from him.

He mumbled another obscenity under his breath, but she ignored it. Not worth it. She didn't have the time or patience to deal with him. Maybe later if he was unlucky enough to cross her path a second time.

THE BLOOD ENCHANTRESS

By the time Ryn approached Leander's Wares, her anger had calmed. Her heart, however, continued to pound. She could hear his sneering little voice. *Witch. Witch. Witch.*

She had done well to keep her magic to herself. One pointed finger, and the Hunters would descend like hounds. Eager to sever heads from shoulders.

The dimly lit storefront boasted dusty oddities and repurposed furniture and jewelry. It had a bit of everything, eclectic and common, stacked on the floor and piled on floor-to-ceiling shelves, in boxes and barrels. The shopkeeper stood behind the counter, wearing a bright green vest with dull copper buttons, an off-white tailcoat, and powder blue trousers. A velvet hat perched on top of his blond head. The dulled points of his ears stuck out of his hair.

At the sight of Ryn, his eyes went wide, and a nervous, knowing smile stretched over his face. Well-worn wrinkles pushed into his cheeks. Ryn had rarely seen the male not smiling.

"Leander," Ryn said in greeting.

"Ah, my little hooded friend," he said in his charmed, easy tone. He leaned onto the counter and wiggled his eyebrows. "Here to buy or sell?"

"Sell." She carefully withdrew the two large bottles from her back and set them on his counter.

The smile vanished from Leander's face. He swallowed as she unloaded the smaller bottles, then the vials. Without the extra weight, Ryn rolled her shoulders.

Leander's brother, Nobel, was the guild master of a well-off den of thieves and assassins, including Ryn. Leander managed the storefront and fencing side of the business, and while a formidable haggler, he had the unfortunate problem of being squeamish.

He swallowed again, notably paler than before, and let out a slow, forced chuckle. "I would hate to see the poor sop these came from."

"He wasn't attractive," Ryn said. "Before or after."

Leander paled further, looking a bit too pasty. He tugged at his collar.

"You good?" Ryn lifted her brows. She enjoyed nudging his squeamish side, even though she would never admit out loud how the first several bodies she'd left had made her retch.

Leander took a deep breath. From under the counter, he took out a brown bottle. After a healthy swig, he released a sigh. Color returned to his cheeks.

"Yes, yes." Another swig. "I assume this means the contract is complete?"

"He's dead as dead gets."

"Fantastic." Leander forced a smile. "I will inform my brother and take these off your hands. Nobel delivered your payment last night. Give me a moment. Have a look around the shop." Leander began the odious task of taking the bottled blood into the back room.

Hot items went into the back room. Ryn had never been back there and didn't care to. She didn't want to muck any deeper into the guild than she already was.

Leander took his time, so Ryn strolled about the shop. There was plenty to see. The store constantly changed, and it never looked the same. Ryn eyed an assortment of steel-plated leathers with matching gauntlets and a sword belt. The emblem of the blacksmith had been worn away to hide the theft. She meandered through an archway made from baskets and bolts of fabric and into a little space packed with jars of buttons, colored thread, and a cup full of differently sized seam-rippers.

Ryn ran her fingers down the skirt of a maroon gown with brocade silk and amber lace. Beautiful, yes, but utterly useless. Dresses were for females who attended tea parties and balls, who had suitors to impress or a spouse to do the work. Ryn didn't attend parties or have friends who hosted them, and she had no need to attract or impress anyone. She did what work needed to be done. She had more use for sturdy boots and trousers with deep pockets.

Her stomach rumbled, reminding her of what needed to be bought with her blood money.

"Here we are." Leander set a bag of coins on the counter. Without the bottles between them, he looked better. "Nobel knew he could rely on you. You're quite the asset to the business."

Ryn divided the coins among her three purses, one of which was visible, two were hidden. She left the empty bag on the counter.

She didn't know how she felt about being an asset for murder. It left her feeling dirty, the kind of dirty that never washed away. She often wondered what her soul looked like after eight years of playing blood-thief. She suspected it darkened with each bottle of blood she stole and sold.

Ryn couldn't see what a soul had done, only the result. Nobel had told her a few of the dead guard's crimes, including turning children into orphans when their parents couldn't pay made-up fines for made-up crimes, skimming from the guard, and twisting the laws for himself and his friends. He wasn't innocent. His soul was molted and wilted.

Knowing the pain and suffering he'd inflicted had helped Ryn accept the contract. Feeling the grime of his soul helped her not feel guilty when his heart stopped, or when she accepted coin afterward. She had gotten revenge for all the people caught in his web.

Or that was how Nobel explained it. She accepted his reasoning—she had to, or else the darkness would swallow her whole.

"Anything else he needs of me?" Ryn asked, voice flat.

Leander shook his head. "Not right now. He'll send word if he needs you. Go celebrate your victory. You've earned yourself a nice drink and a good fuck, maybe two."

Ryn left the shop with the market in mind, though a drink would not be her first purchase. Neither would pleasure. Her stomach growled, reminding her that her own needs were not the only ones relying on her blood money.

RATS IN A NEST
Ryn

In the short time Ryn had been in Leander's, the market crowd had doubled. People swarmed like rats to the fresh bread and coffee, bartering for their day's needs, dressed in varying states of poverty. Living one day to the next. Ryn kept her hood up as she navigated through, eyes open for pickpockets. She'd learned to pickpocket young—she knew the tricks. She'd caught a few of them, snatching their tiny wrists before they neared her pocket or purse.

She didn't blame the kids. She had once resorted to petty theft to survive, and she had since graduated from pickpocket to bloodletter.

A horn sounded a street over. A second horn sounded. Not the warning horn of danger, but the horn of the City Watch for people to get out of the way of someone more important. Ryn's curiosity won over caution. She joined nosy onlookers in an alley between a bakery and a spice vendor. City Watch formed a blockade on the street, forming a protecting wall between the city's scum and whoever warranted their attention.

"Who's so important they've shut down the street?" asked a female as she marched out of the bakery in a flour-spotted apron. Her scowl pulled at the deep wrinkles across her face and neck. "This is cutting into my profits."

A younger female appeared beside her with dusting sugar on her cheek. Her eyes widened at the crowd. "It must be Lady Aurora!"

A squeal sounded from within the bakery, and a girl, no older than twelve, ducked back the two older females and climbed onto a crate beside the bakery's entrance. "I don't see anyone, just guards. Are you sure it's Lady Aurora?"

"Who the fuck is Lady Aurora?" spat a gray-streaked male as he stepped out of the bakery's door.

The young female scoffed. "She is here to court Prince Zain. She is the only daughter of Lord Banach. He's that wealthy merchant from the south. They say he's as rich as a king and has connections all over the continent."

"With ten thousand servants," said the girl in a dreamy voice. "And a castle with a thousand rooms!"

Ryn fought to not roll her eyes. She barely remembered being as starry-eyed and childish over the nobility.

"Oh, I see a carriage!" squealed the young female. She rose onto her tiptoes and clung to the wooden facade of the bakery to keep from tumbling.

THE BLOOD ENCHANTRESS

The crowd thickened. City Watch stood nearly shoulder to shoulder, glaring at the common scum. Ryn shrank into the shadows of the alley. Crowds tickled her nerves, especially those overseen by the City Watch.

A carriage approached, drawn by white horses with golden rigging. Guards in lilac and deep brown uniforms surrounded it on horseback. They wore an unfamiliar house crest over their breasts. The carriage was open, and nestled between a plainly dressed servant and a guardswoman sat a painted doll of a female.

"Oh, that must be her!" The girl on the crates squealed.

"She looks unpleasant." The older female turned up her nose. "Like someone shat in the carriage."

"If you'd trekked across the kingdom to marry that monster of a prince, you'd be unpleasant-looking too," spat the male with a scowl to match the female's. "Don't forget what happened to Princess Lucia. You can't tell me that prince didn't kill her."

Lady Aurora's carriage came closer, and Ryn took her leave. She cared not for the politics of the rich, especially with an empty stomach and three full coin purses. Lady Aurora wasn't the first female suitor for the terrible prince, and Ryn would bet gold she wouldn't be the last.

Prince Zain was a sickly prince with the personality of barren soil and all the charm of a rotting carcass: mean, arrogant, and unpleasant. He had scared away every female suitor, and rumors told of noble females refusing to court the prince. Due to his fragile health, Zain spent most of his time shut away in Nightshade Keep. He was the complete opposite of his brother, Crown Prince Esben, whom the public adored.

Five years ago, Princess Lucia had come from the south to meet with the princes. Rumors whispered that they fought over her, and she vanished from Nightshade Keep. Her body was never found. It was common gossip that Prince Zain killed her after she chose Prince Esben over him.

But Ryn didn't care about the princes and their gossip. Following the scents of fresh bread and sugared rolls, Ryn let her eyes pass over the iced cookies, cinnamon-dusted pastries, and the delicate chocolate truffles. Her mother used to buy her a single piece of chocolate on her birthday, and Ryn tried so very hard to make that one piece last as long as possible. Just the sweet scent of the chocolatier's small shop made her mouth water and her memory horde those precious moments of innocence.

She passed carts of shriveled produce with wilting stems. Harvest had ended a month prior. Only the gourds looked decent, but the vendor wanted twice as much as they were worth. She passed vendors selling jars of fruit preserves, the closest thing they'd get to real fruit until late spring. The upper markets still had apples and berries and melons, grown in greenhouses under the protection of supervision of the Sun Council. As much as Ryn loved blackberries, she wouldn't venture close to the sun monks on purpose. Those berries were not worth her life.

The food market blended together in the most intoxicating aroma, all the scents twisting and mingling. A feast of every flavor imaginable.

Like most things, the feast was always out of her reach.

She bought a loaf of day-old bread, half the price of fresh, and fought the urge to tear into it with her teeth. She perused the market and picked up a few necessities, then with a enough coin left over, she paused by a weather-worn cart selling fruit preserves.

The person to Ryn's left shifted, and a flash of plum caught at the corner of her eye.

The slums consisted of muted shades of brown and beige and gray. For the most part, everything was a shade of dust or dirt. Vibrant colors stood out like the moon against the stars. Especially that shade of plum, rich as a sunset, striking as amethyst, and as alarming as crimson against white.

Hunters. Only they wore that shade of plum. Just the glimpse was enough to make Ryn's heart skip and a cold sweat break over her skin. Hunters never came to this part of town unless they were looking for something. Unless they were after someone.

As gracefully as she could, Ryn tilted her head to see. A cluster of hunters stood half a block down the street, their dark leather armor spotted with steel plates, plum capes catching the sunlight as if woven with golden thread. Five or six Hunters. Here. In the slums.

Ryn felt the color drain from her face. Why were there so many?

"Need something, dear?" said the shopkeeper, an older female with silver streaks in her brown hair. She wore it braided back, proudly displaying the soft points of her ears.

The angle of the ears signified how much fae blood a person had. On these streets, it hardly mattered. Just thinking about it made Ryn's pointed ears prickle under the safety of her hood. Both of her parents had had the sharply pointed ears of the fae, but they hadn't been concerned with bloodlines or lineages like the nobles.

The shopkeeper smiled as if she heard the guilty beating of Ryn's heart.

Ryn schooled her features into a calm mask. "Do you have blackberry?"

The female grabbed a jar of dark berries spotted with little seeds. A black ribbon hugged the wide neck.

People were noticing the Hunters. Curious whispers slithered around her, fingers pointed, hands gestured. A few people made quick exits down side streets and alleyways.

Because the vampires of old had stolen magic from the fae, the very idea of magic had been warped into folklore full of witches and deadly curses and bloodless monsters. It was a common superstition that, where there was magic, there were also vampires, because they were both evil and thus interchangeable. The Sun Council came after anyone suspected of housing, helping, feeding, employing, or associating with magic in any capacity. It made having magic difficult, even among shadows and criminals.

Ryn quickly paid for the preserves. The stupid female took her time making change, all the while the Hunters remained on Ryn's left. She couldn't look without being suspicious, though others were looking, and not looking could also be suspicious.

"There you are." The old female handed the change and the blackberry preserves across the rough wooden cart to Ryn, who hastily slid the coins into her purse and the jar into her satchel.

Her hands shook.

Easy, easy. Ryn had avoided and outrun several Hunter patrols. She could dodge another. All she had to do was slip down the nearest alley, and she'd be out of their sight. Hunters might have skill and training on their side, but she knew these alleys. She knew where the shadows resided, where the sun never touched.

A large male approached her right shoulder, and turning that way would have her turning awkwardly into him, and within a breath, she turned to the left. As she turned, one of the Hunters shifted, giving her a straight line of sight to where a Hunter spoke to the weaselly little beggar. As if sensing her gaze, the weaselly man looked up. His gaze locked with Ryn's.

Oh, shit. *Shit. Shit. Shit.*

The weaselly man's entire face brightened, almost madly so, and he pointed a dirty finger at Ryn. As one, the patrol of Hunters followed that finger to her.

Nobel instructed his thieves to never run. It made one look guilty. *Unless you've been spotted, then run like your fucking life depends on it. Because it does.*

The Hunters started toward her, plum capes flashing behind them. Ryn sidestepped, bumping into the shoulder of a female. She cast Ryn a sharp glare and opened her mouth, but she hesitated at Ryn's dark attire and deep hood that left most of her face in shadow. The female averted her eyes and went on about her business.

Others noticed the Hunters' approach. Some stared; others scattered like rats. No one wanted to be involved or noticed. Ryn tried to flow with the swarm, but there were far too many people.

She ducked into an alley but hadn't taken one step before a fierce grip closed around her upper arm and yanked her around. She came face-to-face with a brown-eyed Hunter. Unfeeling, pissed-off brown eyes set into a soft brown face with a strong jaw and a no-nonsense expression.

Ryn panicked, then realized the other Hunters hadn't yet passed through the throng of shoppers. One Hunter, she could handle.

She reached for the small vial of blood she hadn't sold Leander. In one motion, she uncorked it and threw it; it struck the Hunter's side. Fresh blood splattered her leather armor and the alley beside her. The vial shattered against the cobblestones.

The blood sparkled in the sun, unmistakable as it streaked against the dirty stones and pieces of bloody glass. The Hunter's eyes widened—she thought she'd been struck. She loosened her grip on Ryn to grab for her side. Ryn twisted her arm out of the Hunter's grip and bolted down the alley, across the busy street, and down another alley. She paused to glance back—and locked eyes with the brown-eyed Hunter, in pursuit.

Shit. Ryn bolted down the alley, elbowed her way through the crowd on the sidewalk, and half fell into the street—right into the path of a pristine white horse. One of two pulling the carriage of Lady Aurora.

Ryn let out a shriek of surprise, as did the horse. The horse started and clamored back, and in fear of being hit with a hoof, Ryn threw herself back—the preserves slipped from her satchel and smashed onto the ground. Glass and blackberries pounded underfoot, the ribbon stained and bent.

"Shit," Ryn muttered.

The other horses panicked, and the two of them lurched the carriage to the side. With an unladylike screech, Lady Aurora pitched forward, into the floor of her carriage, her brown boots sticking straight into the air and fluffy white and pink skirts fluffed around her legs, ivory bloomers exposed.

Laughter erupted on either side of the street, and it might have been the only thing that saved Ryn; the guards were too distracted by the lady's undergarments to worry about Ryn, the crowd too thick and shaking with laughter.

Ryn used the panic and madness to slide away from the guards and the brown-eyed Hunter. Authority dissolved in the face of panic, and Ryn had used it more than once to her advantage. Or, in this case, undergarments.

4

LUELLA

Ryn

One alley, then another, Ryn twisted her way through the uneven streets of Calcurta's low town, evading Hunters and the weasel who'd tattled. That weasel better pray he never saw Ryn again. He wouldn't survive the encounter, and his blood would be extra gold in her pocket.

A few words to Nobel, and someone would take care of the weasel. The vindictive rage seething through her bones wanted her to be the one to carry out the sentence, to make sure the weasel knew whom he wronged. Nobel wouldn't let her be his assassin for the sake of vengeance. According to him, it would darken her soul.

Begrudgingly, she knew Nobel was right.

Ryn slowed, hand against the stitch in her side, to catch her breath. No one followed. Once her erratic heartbeat slowed, she continued—keeping her eyes alert for plum. The streets narrowed as she wound through the residential district. Stacked homes grew taller and uneven. Clotheslines strung between windows, leaving most of the streets spotted with shadow. The stench of life and laundry filled the air, along with the murk of the canal and chimney smoke.

Ryn lived on the third floor of a stacked house. The canal rushed by a block over, dousing any sound she might have made as she climbed a makeshift staircase and then a ladder to the window. They barred the door with a dozen deadbolts and a bookcase—they never used it.

Ryn set her few purchases on the small kitchen table.

Light footsteps sounded against the rough wooden floor, and then Luella appeared from the curtain leading to the washroom. Honey-brown hair hung over her shoulder in a loose braid. Her threadbare dress swallowed her.

"Ryn?" Luella blinked, and tension evaporated from her features. She put a hand over her heart and took a breath. "You're late."

Ryn shrugged it off. "Morning, Lu."

Lu shared Ryn's pale brown skin and dark hazel eyes, both features inherited from their mother. Lu inherited their mother's wavy honey-brown hair that gleamed like gold in the summer, whereas Ryn's hair was so dark a brown, it appeared black. Like their father's.

"I didn't get preserves," Ryn said casually. She set her satchel on the table to unload what remained of her purchases. "Not because there wasn't any, but Hunters showed up, and there was this parade, and I didn't want to get kicked by the horse, and the jar fell out of the bag."

"Hunters? Parade?" Lu stormed to Ryn's side with the grace of a dove. "Sabryn Evern, you tell me what happened. Right now."

Lu's protective nature reminded Ryn of their mother, ten years gone to the winter sickness, despite her being only five years older. Ryn sometimes suspected that their father's death the winter before—infection from a skirmish in the market and a rusty knife—had accelerated their mother's illness.

In the days following their mother's death, Ryn overheard a shopkeeper say that one lovebird cannot live long without its mate.

Ryn banished the memories. She had no time for them now. To Lu, she said, "I did my job, and then, on the way to Leander's, this nasty little beggar grabbed me, and I shoved him off. He tattled on me to the Hunters, who decided to wander low town this morning." Ryn busied herself with sorting their groceries into the cabinets. "While running from said Hunters, I accidentally ran into a parade for some female coming to court Prince Zain, and I spooked the horses." She snorted at the memory. "You should have seen it. This lady was all high and mighty until her bloomers were on display for all to see. Damn dress was so puffy, she couldn't get up."

Ryn laughed. She'd been too busy running from the Hunter to laugh at the time.

A beat of silence, and Ryn glanced over her shoulder. Lu's gaze pierced hers. Not the slightest bit humored by the lady's plight.

"You used magic," Lu whispered.

Ryn sighed through her nose. Her hope to distract her sister with the rest of the story hadn't worked. In a single breath, she muttered, "I might have chilled the blood in his grimy little fingers."

Lu's eyes widened, her lips slackened, and then her fury returned. Her nostrils flared, and she stomped her bare foot. "Ryn! What would we do if the Hunters found you?"

Ryn didn't answer. The Sun Council took magicians, and they were never seen again. No one knew what happened to them or where they went. Dead, everyone assumed. Or worse.

Without the income of Ryn's bloodletting, Lu would be left destitute. She would work herself to the bone with her sewing to make ends meet.

Ignoring her sister's gaze, Ryn unclasped her cloak and hung it by the door they didn't use. She had braided her dark hair the night before into two neat braids, but the events of the morning loosened them, and hairs stuck out all over her head.

"There's water for a bath," Lu said sharply. "It was warmer. I expected you home sooner."

"Thank you, I need one." Ryn vanished into the tiny washing room tucked behind the kitchen. A few buckets of water sat beside the narrow tub, as did a bottle of wine.

Lu knew Ryn all too well.

They didn't have functional plumbing like the wealthy did. Ryn and Lu, like most on this side of the city, hauled buckets of water from the canal for their needs, either to be boiled and strained clean for cooking and drinking or dumped into the tub for washing themselves and clothes.

Ryn peeled back her layers and left them in a pile by the curtain. She ran her fingers down the faded brocade of her black tailcoat. It needed a wash too. It had belonged to their father, who had thankfully been slender enough for his daughters to wear his old clothes. Lu and Ryn kept most of their parents' clothing and shared it between themselves. The nicer pieces were sold, others repurposed.

All her clothes needed a wash. Without a contract waiting for her that night, she would have time. They hadn't been washed in a good week, maybe two, and they were starting to smell.

She poured just enough water to wash herself into the tub.

What would it be like to have hot water available on tap? Enough to fill a tub? To have a tub large enough to lounge in? To have clean clothes every day? To have soap that didn't suck the life out of her skin?

If not for Ryn's cursed magic, they might have been able to leave the slums. Either she or Lu could have married into money, or found work as servants in a wealthy household. Most servants lived in the homes of the nobles they served, and likely lived like royalty compared to those by the canal. Lu was everything a man could want in a wife. She was beautiful, demure yet stern, with the loving personality of a mother. She should have suitors fighting for her hand. But nice men did not look for wives in low town. Ryn refused to let Lu whore herself out, and so Ryn used her magic to provide for them both.

As Ryn washed the grime from her skin and hair, she stopped worrying about it. She and Lu had what they needed. Ryn was an enchantress, a vile creature by the Sun Council's decree. The slum was her home, and it would be until death came for her like it did everyone, be it by blade or sickness. In her line of work, someone was bound to snatch the chance for revenge the moment she slipped up.

Until then, she might as well enjoy it. She took a swig from the wine, letting the warmth surge down her throat and into her limbs.

Filling a tin cup with the lukewarm water, Ryn poured it over her head, washing the soap from her hair, flooding it over her eyes. A chill worked over her scalp. Soon, winter would set in, and it would be too cold to wash.

Lu's footsteps sounded from the other room. She paused by the curtain. "So, this Lady Aurora. You think she can tame our wicked prince?"

Ryn snorted. "If the rumors about Prince Zain are true, I doubt it."

"What did she look like?" Lu asked, trying to hide the thirst for gossip.

"She was beautiful, but she looked like she had no desire to be here." Ryn recalled the snobbish, bored look on her painted face.

Lu hummed. "Maybe she and Zain are perfect for each other. Maybe they will bring out the good in each other and fall in love."

Ryn doubted it. More likely, they would live the rest of their lives hating one another while pretending otherwise. She took a long swig of the bottle. Not that she didn't think love existed. Her parents were proof that it did.

However, Ryn also knew she had a better chance at being stabbed in her sleep than finding it for herself.

5

THRILL OF THE HUNT
Ryn

Ages ago, the Abrani vampire clan had ruled northern Sovann. They thrived in the Red Forest and the foothills, preying upon anyone, fae or human, foolish enough to wander too close. Ryn didn't know how or when the war began, only that it ended when Prince Victor Casiano led his newly formed Hunters against the home of the Abrani clan, ultimately decimating it. The land was annexed into Sovann, and when Victor became king, he transformed the vampire's home into his own, renaming it Nightshade Keep.

Three hundred years later, King Victor's legion of Hunters were unrivaled in the realm. Their stupid plum capes and sun sigil were known in every corner. Ryn knew, because her father had told her and Lu stories of heroic Hunters, fearless and selfless warriors, who tracked ruthless and cruel vampires all over the snowy north and rid the world of their sinful existence. In the stories, Hunters tracked and killed not only vampires, but all manner of magic-twisted beings. Ghosts. Werewolves. Pixies.

As a child, Ryn had thought of those plum capes as a symbol of good. Hunters were heroes, good-hearted and strong-willed and chivalrous. Then her magic manifested, and she grew to hate the shade. It instilled a deep-rooted fear that she could not shake. She became the evil the Hunters sought to eradicate from the world.

Ryn's body ached for sleep, but she refused to go to bed until Lu returned. She combed the tangles out of her hair by the window, watching the people passing by below as they carried buckets to and from the canal, chatting and laughing with each other, carving out an existence. She didn't see that damned shade of plum anywhere. Hair combed, Ryn paced to stay awake. Lu worked as a seamstress, and she'd taken an order back to a client. If her sister did not return, Ryn would go find her. If someone had hurt her, Ryn would add another death to her soul.

Ryn understood why Lu was anxious when Ryn came home late. People vanished in the slums. People were stabbed and left in alleys. People were arrested for whatever reason the guard made up. People just…didn't come home.

Midday slid across the sky, stretching the late autumn shadows across the floor, and when Ryn was about to go find her, Lu appeared in the window.

"Where have you been?" Ryn said in a single breath.

"Sorry. I was talking." Lu set her basket on the floor. By the excess of faded red fabric, she'd brought home another project. By the dreadful look on her face and breathlessness in her words, something had happened. Before Ryn could ask, Lu added, "A body was found this morning. Bloodless. Shriveled like a raisin."

Ryn's panic subsided. "Oh."

Lu's stern expression and fearful eyes didn't change. "Ryn, where did you go last night?"

She hesitated to answer. They rarely talked about Ryn's work.

Lu stepped closer. "The body the Hunters found this morning was a block south of the dam. In an alley between Blackwall and Humphrey."

Ryn's heart plummeted. That was two blocks from their home. She whispered, "That wasn't mine."

Fear cracked Lu's stern expression, and she sank to the floor beside her basket. "That's what I was afraid of. Everyone's talking about the body. They say it was vampires, because no one else could've drained a body. I spent the walk back here telling myself it was you."

Ryn fisted her hands in her shirt. Icy cold dread coiled under her skin and sank like stones in her gut. For a bloodless body to have been found, it meant that there was either another blood enchantress, or more likely, there was a vampire.

A vampire in the slums. Within walking distance of where she slept.

"That would explain why there were so many Hunters in the market," Ryn said, her voice weak.

"They're saying Hunters are sweeping the streets for the vampire," Lu whispered.

"I'll be careful. I promise." Ryn sat beside Lu and grabbed her sister's cold, shaking hand in her own. "Nobel understands the risk Hunters pose, and he won't send me out on a job that puts me in danger. I promise, Lu, I'll be careful."

"No more using your magic to spite beggars." Lu's hand tightened on Ryn's.

"I promise not to use my magic to spite anyone." Not that she ever did. She knew the risks, and she used her magic only when working for Nobel.

Ryn waited to see if Lu added a clause to the promise, and when she didn't, she released her death grip on her sister's hand.

"You should get some sleep," Lu said. "You look awful, and I've got work to do. I'll wake you if anything exciting happens."

Ryn retreated into the tiny bedroom she and Lu shared and collapsed onto the thin mattress. It had room for two, but they rarely slept at the same time. Ryn worked nights; Lu worked days.

Sleep felt impossible. She kept thinking of the bloodless body in the slums. A vampire's victim.

THE BLOOD ENCHANTRESS

It wasn't the first drained body found in Calcurta, but the first so close to home. Bloodless bodies had been found sporadically over the past three hundred years, and a few of the more recent ones belonged to Ryn. But not all. Like Ryn, the vampires hid in the city's shadows. Because of them, her crimes went unnoticed—everyone believed her bloodless bodies left by vampires, not an enchantress.

Ryn rolled onto her side and pulled the thin blankets over her head. The Hunters wouldn't find the vampire responsible for this body either. They would wander the slums for a few days, the trail would go cold, and then life would return to normal.

With no contract to keep her busy that evening, Ryn opted for a night out. She donned a red dress—a gift from Nobel when she needed a disguise for a higher end con of his—and headed north to a midtown tavern. The Smoking Barrel wasn't the finest tavern, but it was far from the seediest. Low town folk went there to pretend they were richer than they were, and the wealthy folk went there because they didn't want to go to their own dives. Ryn had picked many a rich man's pocket in its dim light, and spent plenty of nights tangled with a stranger in the upstairs rooms.

Candles filled the tavern with warm, flickering light. Laughter and chatter mingled with the stench of ale and burned meat. Hanging her cloak by the door, Ryn took a deep breath of the familiar space and surveyed the tavern's crowd. She found her target immediately. Leaning on the bar was a beefy male with arrogance she could feel across the room. He wore decent clothes and new boots. He had money, which pegged him as someone coming to a tavern below his normal station to gamble or fuck without his regular society knowing. He was talking to a rat-faced male half his size, meaning he needed to feel in charge. An easy, predictable target.

Ryn sauntered toward the beefy male. Eyes snagged on her as she passed. Her red dress was inappropriate in all the right ways, low cut to show off the swell of her breasts, close-fitted to hug the curve of her hips, and the perfect material to show off the swagger in each step.

She tried to catch his eye, but he seemed more interested in the conversation. The rat-faced male noticed her approach, and a grin stretched his thin lips as he took her in head to toe. Then the big male noticed her, but Ryn pretended to ignore him. Males like him hated to be ignored, and jealousy made her job easier.

Ryn leaned on the bar and signaled for a drink, and as the tankard of ale landed on the counter, the rat-faced male set down a coin.

"A drink for the lady?" asked the rat-faced male.

Ryn pretended gratitude. "I never turn down a gift, especially a drink."

Rat-Face grinned. Behind him, the beefy male scowled at Ryn, like she had interrupted something. Ryn sipped the ale—lukewarm and frothy but free—and reassessed the two strangers. Rat-Face wasn't badly dressed. While dirty, his clothes were decent quality. A gold bead adorned his left ear. It screamed poorly managed money.

Beef was better dressed and well kept, yet scars dotted his hands and the bit of his forearms she could see. He had money for nice clothes, but he knew how to fight.

Interesting. Had she interrupted someone else's con?

"We were getting ready for a game of cards." Rat-Face looked Ryn up and down. "I could use a good luck charm."

She flashed him a wicked grin. "I just so happen to feel incredibly lucky tonight."

Rat-Face guided Ryn to the table. It looked as if a game had recently ended. Cards were strewed across the table, and a blond male with an unruly beard was gathering and shuffling.

Rat-Face sat, pulling Ryn into his lap. Beef sat, and Ryn caught the slightest jingle of coins. She eyed Beef, hoping to catch his attention, but his gaze was pinned on the shuffling cards.

"Why don't I do that? Go get yourself a drink, on me." Beef set a few silvers on the table and slid them to Beard.

"If you insist." Beard grabbed the coins and headed to the bar. By the slur to his words, he'd already had a few too many.

Beef shuffled, and Ryn suspected he cheated. She didn't gamble and didn't have the patience to learn sleight-of-hand, but why else offer to shuffle at the expense of coin? Unless he knew he would make those silvers back with interest. Beef's gaze flickered up and briefly met Ryn's, then moved over her head. To the bar.

Footsteps sounded on Ryn's left. A dark-haired male approached the table. He was tall and viciously handsome with tousled black hair and glittering blue eyes. Pointed ears marked him with strong fae blood, and he carried himself like he knew it.

Flashing a cocky grin, the dark-haired male dropped a fat coin purse onto the table. "Mind if I join?"

Beef eyed the purse like a drunk eyed a tankard. The suspicion and annoyance vanished from his features, and he smiled at the stranger. "If you're willing to lose those coins, have a seat."

The dark-haired male sat with controlled, fluid grace. His voice matched his looks, a delectable sound in her ears, velvet cultured with a noble's lilt. Posh and educated, dark and decadent. A promise wrapped in silk and gold. It made her toes curl in her heeled boots. Oh, she could listen to him talk for a while.

Beef eyed the beautiful noble with a barely masked scheme unfolding behind his eyes. Ryn recognized the look. Beef planned to cheat the noble out of every coin before the night was over, and then Ryn would steal it from Beef.

The plan was simple.

Beard returned, and another game began. Beef talked during his turn, distracting the others with jokes and lewd stories. It was a trick Ryn knew—when stealing, keep eyes off the hands. The distraction worked on Beard and Rat-Face, but after five rounds, Beef had only won two, and the dark-haired noble had won three.

Beef stared daggers at the noble and forced a chuckle as he shuffled. "Beginner's luck."

"Or just plain luck." The noble tilted his tankard toward Beef before taking a drink.

"Another round!" Beef motioned toward the bar.

A cheer resounded around the table, and Ryn joined. The ale coursed through her bloodstream, not enough to inebriate her. She didn't have to be sober to rob a drunk, she just needed to be more sober than the target. She accepted another ale and laughed at Rat-Face's stupid joke, too loud like a good ole drunk.

As Beef dealt another hand, Ryn glanced at the dark-haired noble. His brilliant sapphire gaze met hers, and then he winked. *Fucking winked.*

Her drunken smile wavered. She found herself glancing at him through the next several rounds, at his tousled hair and pale skin and handsome grin. She caught him more than a few times eyeing her cleavage, and Rat-Face's hand on her thigh.

Tonight was going to be exciting.

6

THE WRONG TARGET
Ryn

Ryn laughed too loud at the drunken jokes, none of which were funny. But they were drunk, and she was supposed to be drunk, so she laughed. A few more drinks, and she would have to stop. She needed to maintain her wit, and she did not want to be caught unaware on the lap of Rat-Face. He was the type to fuck her while unconscious.

She was the type to hunt him down and leave him in pieces.

Ryn glanced at the beautiful noble.

He had steadily drunk, and it showed in his eyes. The sharpness had ebbed into the utterly delight of drunkenness. Those sparkling blue eyes of his met hers. There was something unsettling about his gaze, as if he knew her game, as if he could see through her.

She winked.

He sniggered into his ale. He was handsome without a smile, but with one, he was devastating.

Clearly, she had picked the wrong target.

She'd picked Rat-Face because of the promise of coin, but as the night wore on, she didn't know if fucking him was worth any amount of gold. Sitting this close to him, she felt a whisper of the grim coating his soul. Nasty thing.

But the dark-haired noble with the lovely smile? She would bed him for free. For fun.

Ryn tore her gaze from the handsome noble only to find Rat-Face ogling her cleavage like he had never seen breasts before. She fought the urge to shove him away and instead flashed him a too-happy grin. Painted, like her lips.

Despite the drinking, the beautiful noble hadn't lost all his coin. He'd won enough that Beef was scowling. As the round ended, the noble let his cards fall.

He won.

Beef jumped to his feet. He grabbed the handsome noble by the shirt, hoisting him out of his chair with such speed, both his own and the noble's chair toppled over. Ryn jumped from Rat-Face's lap with horror painted on her face, while Rat-Face bolted a table away, putting several other patrons between himself and Beef. The chair smacked against the wooden floor, and it might as well have been a scream for the silence it caused.

Beard was unaffected by the scuffle. He gathered up the cards to shuffle.

A stone-faced male by the bar jumped to his feet, hand on the sword barely hidden under his cloak, eyes on Beef.

"You cheating?" Beef growled. His knuckles on the noble's shirt went white.

The beautiful noble didn't look at all worried about the mountain of a male leering over him. His lips curved into a smug grin, and he said in mock-innocence, "Cheating? Me? Of course not, good sir." In a voice that sent a shiver down Ryn's spine, he added, "But can you say the same?"

"I think he's right," said Rat-Face, from his safe distance away from Beef. "You was pulling some awful good moves."

"Yeah," said Beard. "Cough out those sleeves."

By now, the entire tavern was watching. Eager for entertainment. Eager for a brawl. A few looked ready to join. And Ryn stood awkwardly a step and a half from the source of the commotion. She took a delicate step away, then another.

The barkeeper glanced toward his hired-help near the back wall, two tough-looking males in leather armor and armed with steel.

Beef noticed and threw the noble—into Ryn. She caught him, and by some miracle, she didn't topple over with his weight. He staggered, ale strong on his breath, and latched an arm around her to keep himself from falling. Beef's gaze swept over Ryn, not even lingering on the exposed swell of her breasts. Disinterested. She would have normally felt put-off by it, but then his gaze lingered on the handsome noble she supported. That gaze lingered a heartbeat too long.

Ah. Her attempts to woo him wouldn't have worked, regardless of her dress or lip color. She could've paraded into the tavern naked, and Beef wouldn't have cared. She lacked his preferred assets.

"Apologies, miss," the noble purred in her ear. His warm breath bounced off her temple as his gaze swept over her body. "For my current lack of coordination."

His gaze sent gooseflesh across her skin and heat dancing under her belly. She flashed him a smile and straightened his shirt collar. The material was expensive, though it looked common. Who was this male? Nobles tended to dress up, to look richer than they were. The only nobles who dressed down were those with wealth to hide.

The really rich ones.

She *had* picked the wrong target.

She pressed herself against the drunken noble and slid her leg between his, nudging his groin with her thigh. He responded to her touch, a villainous grin stretching his handsome face.

The stone-faced male from the bar appeared at the noble's side, looking partly horrified. He said in a voice that matched his face, "We should go."

"Not now, Neville. The night isn't over yet." Despite the slur, the words rolled off his tongue, dark and sensuous. He slid his arm around Ryn's shoulders, pulling her chest against his. The grip wasn't rough or possessive; it was loose enough she could have ducked under it. "Do you have plans this evening, my lady?"

Neville did not hide his disgust. He was a guard then, for this noble. They'd both disguised themselves as commoners.

Ignoring the guard, Ryn whispered, "Not anymore. What do you have in mind, good sir?"

He chuckled, and the sound let loose butterflies in her chest. She hadn't felt butterflies in a long time. It felt foolish. In any other fashion, this noble would be vastly out of her league. On any other night, he wouldn't have looked once at her.

But fate had spliced their paths tonight.

And graced her with a golden opportunity.

"A room, Neville." The noble nodded toward the bar. "Or two, you know. For privacy."

"Or just one if you're feeling up to it," Ryn added, winking at Neville.

The handsome noble chuckled. Neville looked like he would rather eat horse shit, but he marched to the bar.

The noble pulled her closer. A fluttering heat surged from her toes into fingers, pooling between her legs. Her mind conjured the image of him bending her over a table in the middle of the tavern—it dissolved when Neville returned with two room keys.

Ryn and the handsome noble staggered up the rickety wooden stairs with Neville a step behind.

He stumbled more than a few times, and by the time Neville unlocked their door, they were a giggling mess of limbs. They stumbled into the room, and Neville shut the door with a disapproving scowl. Ryn ignored his disgust. The guard didn't matter; the rich noble mattered. He pulled her body flush against his, and rather than fall into the bed, they fell against the wall.

His mouth crashed against hers. She tugged his shirt free of his trousers and slid her fingers along the taut skin underneath. A shiver ran through him, all the way into his lips. He lacked the soft body of a noble; instead, lean muscle met her touch. She slid her hands over his flat stomach, his taut back, and teased her nails into his skin. He groaned into her neck, giving a quick thrust of his hips into hers.

She fingered the clasp of his belt, and nearly had it undone when he stumbled—his hitched breath was the only warning before they fell. Ryn twisted, and they landed on the bed with a loud squeak.

The noble laughed, the sound dark velvet like sin. He tried to sit up, but she pushed him back onto the bed and straddled his hips. He started to say something, but she pressed her mouth against his, swallowing his words before they formed.

His hand slid along her thigh, through the slit in the dress, and gripped her hip. She shuddered at his hand against her bare skin, and she imagined that hand between her legs. His grip was gentle, almost timid. His lips mirrored the gentle touch, but it didn't stop her from imagining those lips and his tongue elsewhere. Molten desire prodded low in her belly.

She broke their kiss to adjust her legs enough to slide her hands between them. She felt along his middle, the obvious belt with one coin purse, and the hidden coin purse. Not a total idiot, then. She undid his belt, unlaced his trousers, and palmed him—he didn't respond to the touch.

A quip formed on her tongue, but she held it; the noble's eyes were closed, and his lips were slack.

The rich, drunk fool had already passed out. His black hair flounced around his head like a dark halo, curling at the ends. Beautiful while drunk, and he would still be beautiful with a hangover.

Ryn sat back, desire waning as her frustration mounted.

Fine. She could play this game too, even if sex would have been fun. She untied the coin purse from his belt and peeked inside. Copper, a few silver, and two gold. A quick search of his person revealed a hidden coin purse. It held more gold than she could count. Twenty, at least. Ryn snorted. Anyone else, and she would have felt bad about leaving him broke and hungover, but judging by his clothes and his hired help, he could afford to lose twenty gold.

Ryn, on the other hand, couldn't afford not to take it. It was rent for a year. It was coal for the rest of the winter. It was enough food to fill their bellies for weeks. It was her not lying awake at night worrying about money.

A bit of remorse slithered through her heart, but she pushed it down. Before she could change her mind, she took the coin and slipped out the window.

7

DEBT

Ryn

Ryn rolled out of bed the next afternoon, only she wasn't alone. Lu slept on her back, arm thrown over her eyes. Ryn blinked at her sister. Lu should have been awake and working on one of her sewing projects. Instead, her cheeks were flushed, her hair damp at the temples and neck. Ryn pressed the back of her hand against Lu's cheek.

Burning hot.

Too hot, sickly hot.

Panic banished her grogginess. Ryn was no healer, but she knew a fever when she felt one. Just like the fever that had taken their father, then their mother. A fever was the harbinger of the death to come.

"Lu?" Ryn asked, panic turning slippery cold. "Lu, are you all right?".

Lu shifted her arm to peek at Ryn with one eye. She struggled to focus.

"When did this start?" Ryn asked.

"I don't know," Lu said, her voice small and meek. "This morning?"

Ryn bit her lip. "I'll go fetch medicine. I'll be back as quick as I can."

Lu didn't argue. Instead, shut her eyes.

Ryn washed her face in cool water, dressed in dirty clothes she hadn't had time to wash, and grabbed the few coins they had left. They'd spent the stolen gold on food, supplies for their home, a bolt of soft fabric for Lu. Rushing to the street, Ryn didn't dwell on how much medicine would cost and how she had spent almost all her coin on securing their winter.

No healer in the market had the medicine. With each, her gut twisted. She ended up at Leander's last. He was haggling with an older female with a scar on her left cheek and scratch leathers. Mercenary, likely. Ryn took her time eyeing the cases of medicines and herbal remedies locked tightly behind the counter.

Ryn fought not to tap her nails on the counter while Leander finished haggling, and when he finally bid goodbye to his customer, she whirled around.

"Welcome back, little dove. What can I do for you today?" Leander leaned onto the counter. His use of Nobel's nickname pricked against her unease.

"I need something to break a fever," Ryn said. "My sister is sick."

Leander didn't look the least bit sympathetic. "That's going to cost a pretty coin. Several, actually. That stuff has been hotter than diamonds since the last round of winter sickness. Most folk south of the Black River can't get their hands on it, regardless of how much coin they have."

"I know," Ryn said, biting back her bitterness and urgency. She also knew how quickly a fever could take a person if left unchecked. "But Nobel isn't most people. He can get anything if the coin is right. How much?"

Leander considered her. "This is hard to come by. I can't wiggle the price, even for you. One hundred gold."

The floor fell out from under her feet. She grabbed the edge of the counter to keep herself upright. One hundred gold? She had a few bronze pieces, two silver, and one gold in her purse. Even if she'd kept the noble's twenty gold, she wouldn't have enough.

Leander's brows came together. He knew.

She set her pitiful purse on the counter. "A down payment, and I will owe Nobel the rest. He knows I am good on my word, and he knows where I live."

"Are you sure?" Leander's brows rose.

"Yes." Her voice came out firm.

Leander blew out a disbelieving breath. "Desperate, are we?"

For Lu, she would do whatever Nobel asked of her. She would bloody her hands for years so Lu didn't work in this heartless city or find a husband who could provide. Ryn could take care of both of them. She would darken her soul so Lu didn't have to.

Leander hesitated, giving her the option to change her mind.

She didn't.

Sighing, Leander vanished behind the curtain. A few locks jingled, a loose floorboard creaked, and he returned with a small bottle of white and green dried herbs. White powder settled on the bottom—ground saint's root, the near priceless herb that everyone had sought during the previous winter. Many of the plants had been killed in a late frost that spring, and with a diminished supply and high demand, Ryn didn't want to know how much a bottle cost at the average shop.

She took the small bottle and tucked it into one of the hidden pockets of her tailcoat. "Thank you. Whatever he needs, send the contract my way."

"Oh, he will." Leander pushed her coin purse back across the counter. "He loves people being in debt to him, you know."

"I know."

She would regret it when he came calling. Nobel wasn't known for his compassion or understanding.

"Oh, well, as long as you know you've just sold your soul for a few herbs, then I don't feel so bad." Leander shrugged and offered her a small smile.

She didn't return it. She hadn't sold her soul for *a few herbs*. She'd sold it to save her sister. Bottle in hand, pitiful few coins in her purse, she headed back to the hovel before the fever could take Lu too.

Lu hadn't moved. Ryn heated clean water over the stove, and mixed in a dose of the herbs. She stirred it like she had once done for their mother, while she wasted away in bed and Lu taught herself how to sew with their mother's abandoned supplies. It smelled horrible, like sickness and death, like the sick houses in winter. She let it cool slightly then brought it to the bedside. Lu didn't fight as Ryn helped her sit up and held the cup to her lips. She drank without protest or complaint.

Was Lu thinking of their mother?

Ryn hid the medicine in the bedroom. Lorelei, goddess of healing and health, frowned on unwanted guests entering the room of a sick person. Luckily, most thieves were horribly superstitious. An old fae legend warned that if one entered the bedroom of a dying person, the ghost of that sickness would follow them home. No decent thief would come into Lu's room for anything, especially not to hunt for valuables.

Dusk settled over Calcurta, and with it came moonless cold. The prelude to the incoming winter, the endless nights and brutal cold. Ryn waited in the main room, practiced her stitches on one of Lu's abandoned swaths, and waited for word from Nobel. She lacked their mother's skill with the needle, though she could manage a few rows of stitches. They weren't perfect, nothing like what Lu could do.

She dusted. She fixed the broken hinge on the cabinet. She washed her dirty clothes and hung them to dry. The cool night air was tolerable, and she donned one of her father's old tunics. From the window, she spotted flickers of light in the hovels, shadows moving about on the street below. This side of the city never really went to bed.

Dawn brightened in the east, and still no word came. Ryn's chest tightened. Those within Nobel's debt were often conscripted for the contracts no one else wanted or could complete. Suicide missions. She hoped Nobel thought her too valuable to expend. How many other blood enchantresses did he have in his employ?

She could fetch her own blood and peddle to the alchemists, but word would reach Nobel. She couldn't cut him out of a profit. He would be furious. Most alchemists wouldn't buy from her anyway, in fear of his wrath. Not to mention, she didn't know any of his blood clients, and she couldn't wander into every shop and offer a bottle. The Hunters would be on her like flies on a corpse.

Hunters patrolled the dark street. Looking for their vampire. Their plum capes were beacons, even in the dark.

Rumors whispered of vampires hiding in the darkest corners of the city, where sunlight never touched. Ryn could sell blood to them, but at what cost? There was a chance she wouldn't make it out of the encounter alive. And she would have to find them first.

No, that wasn't a viable option.

Ryn fed Lu another dose of the medicine near midday. She seemed better, or maybe Ryn just wanted her to be better. She didn't know what she would do if Lu died. Lu was the last bit of hope she clung to, and if she didn't have her sister to worry about, nothing would stop Ryn from losing herself.

8

SILVER RABBIT

Ryn

Four days, and Ryn received no word from Nobel. The air turned cold. The herbs were running low. Another dose, and they would be gone. Lu was doing better. The glassy look in her eyes had ebbed, she could hold a simple conversation, and she wasn't burning to the touch. She ate almost an entire orange Ryn had stolen from the busy market.

But they would need more medicine. The fever dwindled but did not break.

She couldn't borrow more from Nobel. She would have to find a way to make gold. Fast. It would take too long to scam enough drunk men out of their coin. She knew another way—higher risk, but better payout. It would take all night and likely some of the day.

Midafternoon, Ryn retrieved their mother's bow from the bedroom cabinet. She had kept it in good condition—once in a while, a contract called for an arrow through the heart, when Nobel wanted people to know about it. An old quiver held five plain arrows, fletched by one of Nobel's contacts.

As the autumn set fell toward the west, Ryn added layers against the cold air that would arrive come dusk. She wore thick leggings that had once been her mother's, an extra pair of socks, and two tunics. They were all barely more than rags, but she would need the layers after dark. She fastened her father's old wool cloak over her shoulders.

Lu sat in the main room, slowly stitching one of her projects. She looked ashen in the candlelight, and the shadows pooled under her cheekbones.

"I'm sure I'll be okay," Lu said when Ryn slung the quiver over her shoulders.

"I'm not taking the chance." Ryn fingered the old clasp on the cloak. Their father had insisted he was all right, as had their mother. Both were gone within days.

Lu pursed her lips. She didn't argue, like she was thinking of their parents too.

"I'll be back by dawn," Ryn promised, like she did each time she left.

"I'll be here." Lu focused on her stitches.

People went missing in Calcurta every day, and the guard couldn't search for them all. If Ryn didn't come home, Lu would be on her own.

That wouldn't happen.

Ryn would return as a ghost if she needed to. Anything to protect Lu.

THE BLOOD ENCHANTRESS

⚜⚜⚜

Ryn tiptoed through the whispering rust-colored leaves of the Red Forest. Twilight streaked the western sky with indigo and amber. The moon draped the forest in silver, muting the jewel tones of the maples for which the forest had been named. In the height of autumn, the trees were awash in crimson.

Autumn was fading. Most trees were barren and graying, while others clung to the few rusty leaves they had left. With the night came the chill, the lingering cold that wouldn't abate until dawn. A few more weeks, and winter would grasp Calcurta with a frozen iron fist. The leaves would be buried under snow that wouldn't melt until mid spring.

Ryn didn't want to think of winter, the frigid nights and numb fingers, or how pricey firewood would be. She held the bow at the ready, arrow nocked, arm poised to pull back the string, eyes waiting for the silver-white rabbit she'd followed. Oh, the coin she could get for that fur would buy two bottles of medicine.

A flash of silver to the left sent Ryn's heart skipping. It stirred northeast, and she followed. Her feet barely made a sound on the forest floor.

As Ryn ventured deeper into the forest, the chill grew heavier. It ravaged the air, the type of chill that never saw sunlight, that lingered under canopies and within the earth. It smelled of wet stone and thawing dirt. An old memory surfaced, of Ryn's mother telling stories that the smell came from bodies buried without proper burial. They flaunted their stink to lure someone to find them, to give them proper rest. If left unattended for long, they would rise and seek revenge on the living.

Ryn shook the thought. Her mother had loved horror stories, and they often left Ryn up at night, terrified that things would crawl through her window or out from under her bed if she dared to close her eyes. As she grew older, she learned ghosts were the least of the things crawling through the dark.

The rabbit seemed far too clever for its own right. Ryn followed glimpses of silver, deeper into the forest. She needed only a sliver of a moment for it to pause, to consider itself, and then she would have it.

Just one moment. Just *one*.

She could only hope the goddess of the forest felt a stab of pity.

Likely not since the other gods hadn't.

The flash of silver-white fur darted between brick pillars, spaced about six feet apart. Each pillar was engraved with a stylized *C*.

Casiano. She had reached the edge of the royal grounds.

Shit. Ryn spotted the silver-white rabbit on the other side, investigating a pile of twigs. Its long ears twitched to the north. Black eyes searched the brush. Ryn dared not breathe as she pulled the string—the silver-white rabbit darted further into the royal grounds.

She huffed and lowered her bow. No, the gods were not looking kindly upon her today.

Biting back the unease crawling up her spine that urged her to turn around and search for a less complicated game, Ryn tiptoed through the pillars. No other pelt would fetch such a high price. She held her breath as she crossed into the Royal Grounds. Nothing happened, no dark magic or volley of arrows. She blew the breath out.

She would grab the rabbit, and the king would never know she was there. Neither would his Hunters.

King Victor wasn't known for his mercy. She doubted he would feel sorry for a scrawny female poaching in his woods. Ryn feared the king's wrath more than a vampire. A vampire she could bargain with and maybe get a steady client out of. She feared Nobel's wrath far more, but most of all, she feared losing Lu.

The silver-white rabbit paused in the snowy dirt near a babbling stream.

Ryn let her arrow fly.

The rabbit didn't even let out a squeak of surprise. It flopped onto the bank, legs twitching out the last of its life.

Relief flushed through her bones like a cool breeze in the peak of summer. She hung her bow over her shoulders and started toward the rabbit. The arrow hadn't sustained much damage; it could be used again. She washed the tip in the stream, then replaced it in the quiver. With the rabbit over her shoulder, she started back toward the pillars.

A rustle on the other side of the steam drew her attention. The hair on the back of her neck rose. A chilly breeze rustled through the leaves, shaking moonlight to the forest floor.

Something within the undulating moonlight *moved*.

A deer, she reasoned, despite the shaking in her gut.

It didn't matter. She had the rabbit. It would buy medicine for Lu. She turned—to get the hell out of the royal grounds—and took a step toward the pillars, when a scream pierced the night.

Birds took flight. Smaller game scattered. A small squeak escaped from Ryn's lips.

No animal could have made that sound; that had been a human cry.

9

DEAD IN THE SNOW

Run

Unnatural silence followed the scream's wake. Ryn's thundering heart was the only sound. Any guard within range would be charging this way, toward the scream, toward Ryn. Making sure the rabbit was secure on her shoulder, she bolted as fast as she could toward the pillars.

She spotted brick peeking through the graying ash and rusty maples. So close—

A thick figure in leather armor stepped between her and the pillars. From the shoulders hung a plum cape, held by steel pauldrons.

Ryn halted. The Hunter stood by the pillars, hand on the hilt of his sword, scanning the forest. He hadn't seen her. Ryn stepped into the shadow of an elderly oak, praying the thick branches would hide her and that the Hunter wouldn't hear the pounding of her heart or smell her fear. Rumors said the vampire hunters trained like bloodhounds and wore charmed necklaces and rings to grant them enhanced abilities like the fae of old.

Ryn remained still. The Hunter followed the pillars, just inside the royal grounds, his steps as silent as a wraith. As he moved past her, she moved toward the pillars, keeping a safe distance between herself and him. She didn't know how far she needed to be to keep outside the Hunter's heightened senses, or if that were even true, but she didn't want to test it. She crept toward the pillars, toward the other side of the forest where she wouldn't be killed for poaching.

A rustle sounded behind her—a boot on cold, damp leaves.

Ryn sidestepped deeper into the shadows. Moonlight draped the pillars. Hunters patrolled in twos, and it wouldn't matter how quiet she was if she stepped into the moonlight. She might as well shout a greeting to the Hunters.

Hunters were difficult to sneak past. Difficult, not impossible. Ryn had gotten proficient at hiding in the dark and being patient.

The clouds shifted in front of the moon, stealing away the silver light. A chill grew in its absence, as if it had lain in wait. Ryn took this chance to creep along the trees, along the thickest shadows, toward the next set of pillars, where the branches of a sickly looking elm hung barren.

As she stepped on the edge of a small clearing, the clouds parted.

What she had first assumed to be a gathering of twisted roots, the moonlight revealed as the body of a female. Her skin was sucked tight against her bones, shriveled and gray, with terror etched onto her face. Her limbs stuck out as if she had fallen. Brown hair pooled around the head. Ryn caught the faint scent of blood in the air.

A rustle sounded from the other side of the clearing, where the moonlight did not reach. Ryn's eyes snapped up just in time to see a darker shadow prowling. The figure glanced back, and from under dark hair, she spotted a pale face, half hidden under a hood. It smiled—two blooded fangs studded the rose red lips.

Ryn acted without thinking—she loosed an arrow. The monster moved, but not fast enough. She heard the unmistakable thwack of an arrow sinking into meat. A grunt, surprised and predatory, inhuman and human at once. A low, menacing growl followed.

The sound chilled her to the bone, eliciting gooseflesh along her skin.

The shadowed figure slinked closer, an arrow sticking out of its shoulder.

The chill in Ryn's bones turned vicious. What the fuck was she thinking?

It slunk closer, pale fingers folding around the shaft. Ryn reached for another arrow. She wouldn't go without a fight.

The vampire paused, then retreated into the shadows with such speed and silence that, at first, Ryn doubted it ever existed. Ryn hadn't a heartbeat to consider why before a hand folded around her upper arm and yanked her back.

"Halt!" a rough male voice commanded.

Three Hunters descended on the scene. The Hunter who had grabbed Ryn's arm disarmed her and threw her to the ground, pinning her against the frigid dirt and leaves. Her bow landed with a clank. Roots jammed into her ribs and hips, and something impossibly warm fastened around her throat. It felt like rope, but it was warm against her skin, like clothing hung by the stove.

The other two Hunters took in the bloodless body.

"Dead," said a blond Hunter with a day-old beard.

He unsheathed his dagger and retrieved a wooden stake from his satchel. In the moonlight, the wood appeared white. Silver ash, poisonous to vampires. The Hunter, using the pommel of his dagger, hammered the stake into the dead female's heart. Making sure she did not rise as a thrall.

The dagger thudded in time with Ryn's heartbeat. Deeper and deeper into the dead flesh, parched organs, and dry bones.

It was then she recognized the dead female's clothing. Leathers lined with fur. Steel plates. Her plum cape lay beneath her, wrinkled and torn. Hunter. A dagger lay tossed aside, stuck into the hard earth. The female's fingernails were broken. She had fought back against the vampire—and lost.

THE BLOOD ENCHANTRESS

The hammering ended, and with it came a stout, unpleasant silence. The Hunter kneeling beside her seemed to be studying her features, as if trying to place her in his memory. Did he know her? Had they been friends?

Ryn took in the three Hunters. They patrolled in twos, which meant the dead Hunter had been paired with one of the others.

And was now dead.

"She doesn't look like one of them," said the second Hunter. He motioned toward Ryn.

The Hunter pinning her to the ground hoisted her up like a rag doll. One strong hand twisted her wrists behind her while the other held her neck in a vise-like grip.

"The ropes aren't burning," said the Hunter.

It took her a moment to realize the ropes must have been made with silver ash fibers. Few shops sold them, mostly trinkets for the superstitious, made to be strung over doorways and windows. Supposedly, silver ash warded away vampires. Ryn had never bought into it.

The Hunter who had just hammered a stake through a dead woman's heart grabbed Ryn's chin and unceremoniously shoved his fingers into her mouth. He forced her jaw open; his fingers tasted like dirt and sweat.

"There's no blood on her teeth," he said. "Or her breath."

His grip loosened, and she yanked her chin away from him. She promptly spat the taste of his fingers into the dirt.

The Hunter chuckled.

"They can disguise themselves after feeding," said the blond hunter. He eyed Ryn without emotion. "Best take her in. I don't want to be responsible for letting one of them loose, but I don't want to kill a female for nothing."

"I'm not a vampire," Ryn said, her tone more desperate than she intended.

The Hunters shared a skeptical look. They didn't believe her. Ryn's heart tumbled into her stomach, and her skin flashed clammy and cold.

"I—I saw it," she pleaded. She nodded toward where the vampire had vanished. "It went that way. I got an arrow in its shoulder."

The Hunter holding her said, "Right. I'm sure you did. You can either walk, or we'll drag you."

Ryn looked between the two Hunters, but neither offered pity or sympathy. They assumed she was the vampire. That was why the real monster hadn't advanced. It heard the Hunters and left her to be the scapegoat. A distraction while it escaped.

Fury burned under her fear, but not enough.

The Hunters hauled her deeper into the Royal Grounds, toward Nightshade Keep. The silver rabbit hung from her shoulder, bumping into her back every few steps, laughing at her failure. Ryn knew what fate awaited poachers, but she didn't know what awaited suspected vampires.

She supposed she would find out.

As the moon fell behind the clouds, blanketing the forest again in darkness, her thoughts were of Lu, lying sick in bed. If Ryn didn't make it home in time, what would become of her? If the fever took her while she was gone…

Ryn shoved those thoughts down, deep down. First, she needed to survive this ordeal, then save Lu.

10

IN HUMAN SKIN

Ryn

Nightshade Keep was a sprawling complex of outbuildings and paved walkways. In the dark, it was a nightmare of stone, pointed dormers, and spires. An impregnable wall surrounded the keep, the battlements patrolled by Hunters at all hours. The flower for which the keep was named grew in patches by every building, seemingly everywhere Ryn looked. Its pointed petals were deep purple, like the Hunters' capes.

They hauled Ryn through a small portcullis and into a rectangular building of dark stone, down a set of stone stairs, and into a dirt-floored cellar lined with iron-barred cells. A few were occupied, Ryn didn't look to see if they were vampires or just unfortunate like her.

The Hunter threw Ryn into the cell at the end. She landed hard onto a packed dirt floor littered with dark stains. Ryn didn't have time to worry about the stains—the blond Hunter followed her into the cell and searched her person. He took the quiver from her back, her skinning knife, and even the dagger in her boot. Not that it was sharp enough to do anything. The blond hunter thumbed the edge of the dagger before handing it off.

"A dull dagger is useless," the blond Hunter said to Ryn.

"If you would like to donate a new dagger, I wouldn't say no."

The blond Hunter grunted in response. He gave her one last pat-down, then took the silver rabbit. He tossed it to the other Hunter like it was nothing, like it wasn't enough gold to buy medicine. Of course, knowing the Hunters, they had access to the best healers and herbs. Not to mention a steady and impressive income.

"She's clean." The blond Hunter pushed Ryn into the dirt floor, and slammed the door before she got back to her feet. The locking mechanism resounded with a heavy series of clunks, each driving panic deeper into her bones.

The blond Hunter stood guard outside her cell, and the other two took her things and vanished out of sight.

Ryn slumped against the far wall, taking each breath as it came. The trembling set in as the dread solidified. She'd never been arrested before. She hugged her legs to her chest and fought against hot tears pushing against her eyes. She would not let the Hunters see her cry.

Unless… Could vampires cry? If tears would prove her innocence, then she would cry loud and ugly.

38

The blond Hunter glanced at her through the bars. His eyes were pale blue. Stubble darkened his jaw, a shade or two darker than his hair.

"I'm not a vampire," she whispered, almost a plea.

"You were caught over a body." His tone was flat.

"I'm aware of how it *looked*." She silently cursed the vampire that had snuck away, leaving her to suffer its fate.

Ryn pressed her forehead against her knees. Her clothes smelled like the forest, like cold dirt and sweat, but also like Lu's medicine and the spiced tobacco of the female who lived below them.

At the thought of Lu, Ryn's heart sank. She would assume the worst when Ryn did not appear at dawn. Lu would go without medicine, and the fever would return, and…

Ryn shoved the thought down before the tears could come.

She tried to think of a silver lining, but her mind blanked. The cell was marginally warmer than the forest, she supposed. Though frostbite might be better than whatever the Hunters had in store.

Footsteps marched down the hall. Booted. Rattling with weapons. Stomping with authority.

A middle-aged man appeared on the other side of the bars. Gray threaded the dark hair at his temples and through his full beard. A scar tracked from his brow to his jaw in a nasty shade of pink, stark against his umber skin. His pitiless eyes settled on her.

At his side was a broad-shouldered female Hunter with dark brown eyes and soft brown skin. Her stare pierced through Ryn, and then the Hunter had the audacity to smirk.

Then it hit Ryn—she was the Hunter who'd grabbed Ryn at the market, whom Ryn had tricked into thinking she'd been stabbed.

Well, shit.

"She doesn't look like a threat," said the middle-aged man in a grave tone.

"I agree, commander," said the blond Hunter.

"Some of them don't." The female Hunter glared down at Ryn like she had won a bet.

"Let's get this over with." The commander unlocked the iron door and marched inside. The female Hunter followed at his heels.

The commander fixed his dark eyes on Ryn. "The patrol found you over a bloodless body, yet you claim to not be a vampire." Doubt dripped in his words. "You know how many times I've heard that?"

"Several, I'm sure," Ryn muttered.

The commander scowled. His fingers tightened into the fists, the leather of his gloves squeaking.

She bit her lip. Talking back would not do her any favors. This wasn't Nobel, who loved wordplay, but no-nonsense Hunters.

"You're right," he said, words clipped. "I am Commander Wade. Right now, I have a fresh body that's been sucked dry and a guilty little girl."

She bristled. One hundred and three was hardly a girl. However much she wanted to inform him, she held her mouth shut.

"This is the third body discovered within the grounds in the past week." Commander Wade paused to let those words sink in.

Ryn paled. Three bodies in a week?

"Since vampires only need to feed once every few weeks, that means we've got a brood on our hands. Unless those monsters aren't killing for food." Commander Wade studied her features, looking for guilt. "And those are just the ones on the king's grounds."

Three bodies on the king's ground, killed by vampires. More within the city. With or without the number of bodies she had left behind, that was a lot of bloodless bodies. Ryn swallowed against her dry throat and thought of the body discovered a few blocks from her home, and the body she'd left in that alley.

She tried her best to not let the guilt show. Especially in front of the hunter who had witnessed her *with a bottle of blood.*

Commander Wade studied her face, her reaction. "And you just happen to be in those woods."

"I was hunting," she whispered, desperately.

One of his heavy brows rose. "Hunting?"

Shame turned her skin clammy and hot. "Yes. My sister is sick, and I need coin for medicine. White fur fetches a good price."

"That would explain the rabbit. I've never met a vampire who carried game around with them." Commander Wade took a flask from his belt and unscrewed the cap. A bittersweet aroma wafted through the cell, like dry wine and lemons. He handed the flask to Ryn.

She looked between him and it.

"Take a sip."

"Mother always said never to drink after strange men," Ryn said flatly.

Commander Wade didn't laugh. "This is Blood Sherry. Poison to vampires. You want to prove your humanity? Take a drink. If you die, we'll know you're lying. If you're not a vampire, then you'll just be sick for a few hours."

Oh, that sounded wonderful. He had omitted what would happen to her if she lived. Ryn suspected he didn't expect her to.

She looked at the flask's mouth. "Is that clean?"

His frown deepened.

And…it wouldn't matter. She could drink willingly, or have it forced down her throat. She uncurled from her crouch. She stood, her balance wobbly with her bound hands. "Fine," Ryn spat.

Commander Wade poised the flask's mouth against her lips, and she took a sip. He then tilted the flask—the bitter Blood Sherry flooded her mouth. She started to cough, but the commander moved faster. He moved the flask and flattened his hand against her mouth, trapping the liquid inside. He pushed her into the wall and held her there with his own weight, at least thrice her own.

"Drink it," he ordered.

She did. It took several gulps to get down the stupid amount he'd poured into her mouth, and the stringent Blood Sherry dripped down her chin and soaked into her shirt.

When she swallowed the last of it, the commander stepped back. The Blood Sherry settled into her stomach like acid, burning her insides and twisting her blood vessels into knots. She thought she would be sick—she fell against the back wall and slid to the floor. Commander Wade stood over her, waiting for it to kill her. Ryn brought a shaky hand to her mouth and wiped her lips on her sleeve.

The initial fit settled in a sickening feeling in her stomach, like her body couldn't decide between vomiting or fainting. It might have been due to her nonexistent breakfast that morning and the pitiful dinner of stale bread she'd eaten the night before.

Commander Wade scowled at her as he screwed the cap on his flask.

"Has a vampire ever not succumbed?" asked the female Hunter.

Commander Wade considered Ryn. "A few times, often right after a feed. If she is indeed our culprit, she will start showing signs within a day's time. Sooner if the sherry does its job. Even if she's not a vampire, she might be in league with them."

"I'm not a vampire," Ryn said again, this time exasperated. She slumped back to the floor. Her stomach churned, and she felt bile threatening to claw up her throat.

"That will be known soon enough," Commander Wade spat. He and the female Hunter marched out of the cell. The blond Hunter locked the door behind them. To the blond Hunter, he said, "Watch for any signs of vampirism and report it to me immediately."

"Yes, sir."

Their footsteps retreated, and Ryn's stomach gave another upheaval. She leaned against the cool stone of the wall. The blond Hunter cast her a masked gaze from his post outside the bars. Her fate was out of her hands. If the Blood Sherry didn't tear her apart from the inside out, the Hunters would.

THE DREADFUL PRINCE
Zain

Prince Zain had stopped listening to Lady Aurora before his first glass of wine. She'd been explaining the delicacies of her favorite flowers, as if it mattered. Her voice carried a sweet lilt, cultured by education and tutors, tuned to sound like what she thought he wanted to hear. The deceptive insincerity of it grated on his nerves. Her sandy hair was piled on top of her head, pinned with pearl-tipped gold, so that it exposed her sharply pointed ears. Delicate golden rings and diamonds studded her ears. Her modest dress was spring green. His mother had likely told her green was his favorite color.

His mother wanted this match. She had done nothing but talk about Lady Aurora and her pure fae bloodline for the past three months.

How *pretty* she was. How *charming* she was. How *pleasant* she was.

Aurora could be all of those things when she wanted; she painted her exterior as the perfect female, saying the perfect words in the perfect tone, wearing the perfect dress and the perfect jewelry. Everything about her screamed *perfect*.

Everything about her made Zain want to drown himself in wine. He had glimpsed the female underneath during brief cracks in her veneer. She hid her emotions like a courtier. Like Zain, she had been taught how to speak and act and think from birth. Only Zain had taken his lessons a bit…less seriously. Being a prince helped.

Aurora lifted her wine to her red lips, took the smallest sip, then replaced the glass on the table. Every movement flowed with grace and precision. She sat with her shoulders back, neck poised, spine straight, ankles crossed to the side. She spooned small portions of the soup to her lips, like she was trying to eat as slowly as possible, to draw out this awful meal.

Zain swirled his wine. He sat slumped in his chair, long legs stretched out, waiting for this torture to end. Her annoyance at his nonchalance occasionally seeped through her painted face, and he wanted to see how far he could push before she snapped like the others.

"I suppose we should discuss the matter at hand." Her topaz eyes met his, and she fluttered her lashes. "Our engagement."

"We are not yet engaged," Zain reminded her.

Her lips quirked at the corners. "Oh, my apologies."

Her smile grated on his nerves worse than her voice. It did not reach her eyes. It barely moved her mouth.

She looked at him like she had him figured out, like she was three steps ahead. No doubt she thought conspiring with his mother solidified a union as well as any vow. Aurora had played her part—acting as though she actually wanted to marry him.

From the little time he'd spent with her, he would bet gold she already had the wedding planned.

Zain sipped his wine loudly.

No one asked his opinion. Not that his mother needed to ask. His opinion of Aurora would be the same as all the other painted females pushed in front of him. They were dull, obnoxious, and drove his thoughts to violence. They saw him as a title, a stepping stone onto a higher social rung.

He hated Aurora. He hated the way she held a wine glass with three fingers. He hated the way she cleared her throat before she spoke. He hated how she didn't really smile. He hated everything about her.

He had denied every bride, and his mother warned him that if he did not choose his own bride, she would choose for him. And she had chosen Aurora. Zain refused to spend the rest of his life with this female. If his mother forced the marriage, Aurora would meet a sudden, tragic end. Maybe a broken heel that sent her tumbling headfirst down the marble stairs, or after spending so much time with *horrible Prince Zain*, she would "throw" herself from the keep's tallest tower.

"It would be a very smart match," Aurora said simply.

Her slithering voice interrupted his violent thoughts.

She continued, undeterred. "Your bloodline is pure, as is mine. There is a tapestry in our library tracing our line back to the fae of old, before humans ventured onto our lands and muddled the bloodlines."

"Yes, I've seen it," Zain said flatly. "Your father is very proud of it."

The old windbag hadn't shut up about it.

"As he should be." Aurora lifted her chin a bit higher. "Few can boast the same. Our families haven't married, and it would be advantageous to keep the pure bloodlines."

Zain fought not to roll his eyes. He drawled, "Eventually, marrying the pure bloodlines will risk inbreeding."

Her offended expression cracked through her veneer, then quickly vanished.

He sipped his wine and tried not to look delighted by her discomfort and annoyance.

"That is ages away from being an issue," Aurora said dismissively. She took a gulp of wine. "And there are other fae kingdoms to the south. We could build relations with them to strengthen the fae blood. If we don't, we risk losing what history we have left. The humans would see us all fade from the realm."

Zain wished the wine were whiskey. Or anything strong enough to numb the irritation Aurora sparked under his skin.

Bloodlines, bloodlines, bloodlines. Zain was tired of hearing about bloodlines. As if they were the only thing in the realm with any worth.

Aurora cared only for his title and lineage. All the females of court were the same, eyeing him like a piece of meat. To marry Zain would make her a duchess. What female didn't want that? Zain's hand was second only to his brother, Esben, whose *duchess* would one day become *queen*.

Of course, Esben was engaged to a lovely foreign princess, which left the available females to prattle on about Zain, the lesser prince.

He heard the rumors—that no noble female in Calcurta would court him, and his mother had to go to the edge of the kingdom to find him a wife. The courtiers discussed him in whispers, how unpleasant, how disagreeable, how miserable of a husband he would be. One female had even accused his parents of ignoring the gods' omens, that Zain's sickly childhood should have been clue enough to throw him away.

The old familiar darkness crawled around his heart and squeezed.

He tilted his wine glass up, emptying it into his mouth. He slammed the stem back onto the table. The servant appeared like smoke to refill it.

"...think, Prince Zain?" Aurora was staring at him. Expectantly.

He sipped his newly filled glass of wine, then brought his listlessly gaze up to meet hers. He drawled, "Did you say something?"

A pale pink blush warmed her cheeks, and a vexed embarrassment twisted her features. She was not used to being ignored. She was used to garnering all the males' rapt attention. She assumed Zain would be like the other males, eager to listen to every word, desperate for a flash of admiration or affection.

The idea made him want to vomit.

Aurora cleared her throat. "I mentioned the stronger fae bloodlines. There has been talk to organize matches to keep the bloodlines strong."

He hummed his dislike. He didn't want to be forced into marriage for the sake of blood, and he didn't see the purpose of forcing others into it. Nobility or scum, he didn't like the idea of squeezing humans out of the kingdom simply for existing. "I suppose the next step would be to start eliminating the round ears?"

She blinked several times. "That's not what I meant, I only—"

"That fae blood is by nature superior to all others and therefore all others should be dealt with accordingly?" Zain raised his brows.

Her blush deepened, the anger faded into embarrassment. "I—I..."

"Is this the type of small talk your father engages in with his…connections?" Zain spoke the word with distaste. "These wouldn't be the same connections he happens to owe a considerable amount of gold, would it?"

At that, her eyes grew large. Her blubbering stopped.

She hadn't expected him to know of her father's double-dealings. He had made considerable gold with backdoor dealings, but after a few bad calls, her family needed money. Who better to seek out than a prince?

But it wasn't anger that flashed across her features. It was fear.

"My father's company is as strong as it has ever been," Aurora said. Just like that, the fear vanished from her features. Again, she was the perfect courtier.

Zain drank greedily from his wine. He no longer cared for this line of talk. Eyeing her face over the rim of his glass, he asked, "What do you think of these recent murders, Lady Aurora?"

The spoon in her hand stilled.

"I think it is a horrible thing." Her lips flattened. She added in a whisper, as if she worried vampires might slither out from under the rug, "My father is worried about a resurgence of vampires."

Zain fought to keep his face neutral. "My father is prepared for the worst."

Her lined eyes widened, though with hunger, not fear. Vampires were a hot topic for the gossip circles, and she might learn something no one had yet heard, thus making her more important than the other females. Even if it lasted for a few minutes.

Zain gulped his wine, letting her starve for information a moment longer. Then he said, "The Hunters are well prepared for the worst at any given time, so whatever the vampires are planning will be squandered before it blooms."

Her expression fell imperceptibly. "That is good to know, Your Highness."

He flashed her one of his cocky grins. "Esben will be leading them, so have no fear."

The golden prince will save the day, he almost said. Had he been drinking something stronger than wine, he might have let the words slip.

He would not sully his brother's name in front of this gossip-hungry court mouse. Setting his wine aside, he stood. His half-eaten soup made his stomach churn.

"I apologize, but I am not feeling well." Zain tucked his hands into his trouser pockets and left without Aurora's farewell.

Hopefully, he would never see her again.

12
CONSEQUENCES
Ryn

Ryn spent an unknown amount of time lying on the cell's dirt floor. No position offered comfort from the Blood Sherry twisting her insides. Her skin flashed between sweating and shivering. She didn't pass out or vomit. It was constant misery, a continuous wrenching of her gut without results, an eternal undercurrent of pain rippling through her organs.

Voices came and went outside the cell. Footsteps and shadows.

Finally, when the torment receded, Ryn pushed herself into a sitting position. Her arms strained with the motion. Her muscles ached. Her head throbbed. Her tongue felt like sand. It took too long to focus on the cell around her.

Lanterns burned in the hall. It could have been midday or midnight. She had no sunlight to go by.

The brown-eyed female Hunter stood guard in the hall. She glared down at Ryn with disgust and superiority.

"Looks like you're not dead yet," said the Hunter.

"Because I'm not a vampire." Ryn's voice reflected how horrible she felt—dry, strained, and hoarse. She swallowed against a dry throat.

The Hunter nodded to the side. To Ryn's surprise, someone had brought in a small wooden stool on which sat a washing basin. She crawled over to it, not minding how pitiful she looked, and dipped her hands into the cool water. It looked clean, but she was used to bathing in the canal water so it didn't matter if it wasn't. She brought a handful to her lips. Cool, mineral-laden water rushed down her throat, easing the distress and burn of the sherry.

Ryn took the time to wash her face and hands, mindful to not splash the water on the floor and turn the dirt into mud.

"You had blood on you that day," the Hunter said lowly.

Ryn paused her washing, staring into the murky depths of the now-dirty basin. "It was a trick," she said. "And it worked. I got away." It wasn't entirely a lie. She had tricked the Hunter into thinking she'd been stabbed.

"And you also ran. That marks a guilty soul."

"Because I refused to give that weaselly little man coin," Ryn said, not hiding the fury in her tone. "When someone tells the Hunters about you, there is no second side to the story. You would have dragged me here or killed me on the spot without a second thought."

The Hunter considered those words, her expression masked.

Ryn sat back against the wall to let her skin dry. She felt better, though marginally so.

"You also pissed off Lady Aurora," the Hunter added.

A smirk tugged at Ryn's lips. "That wasn't my intention."

"You sound remorseful."

Ryn cracked an eye open. The Hunter watched her, arms crossed loosely over her chest, one foot propped on the wall behind her. She wasn't holding onto her sword like the other Hunter.

It would seem that Ryn's survival of the Blood Sherry had loosened their desire to kill her.

"You want the truth?" Ryn leaned forward. "I'm not sorry. She's likely a spoiled little brat who's never been humiliated in her life. A dose of it is good for the soul."

The Hunter raised a brow.

"Just like rejection," Ryn added, echoing words her mother had said years ago. "It keeps us humble."

The silence stretched. Ryn leaned back against the wall.

"What will happen to me?" Ryn dared to ask.

"Since you haven't shown signs of vampirism, it will be the king's decision," said the Hunter. "Considering you were poaching in his woods."

Of course.

She was cleared of one accusation, but the Hunters had another. They would not let her go, she realized. Her heart crawled into her lungs and stayed there, because she knew the odds of getting out of this mess were slim.

Her time of judgment came sooner than she expected. Hunters arrived at her cell, led by Commander Wade. They did not bind her hands, but Hunters held her arms in iron-like grips, hauling her between them.

"You will stand before the king for your crimes," Commander Wade said, his tone grave and final.

Ryn hadn't the will to comment. Everything about the Hunters screamed finality, and it drove dread deeper into her bones.

The Hunters hauled her out of the jail the same way she'd come; only this time, the sun shone on Nightshade Keep. It glittered off the stained glass windows, yet the dark stone of the keep seemed to soak in the light. Stone and dirt paths wound between outbuildings, gray and dull save for the patches of deadly nightshade.

The Hunters hauled Ryn along narrow paths, past patrolling Hunters, and through a side door into the largest building in the keep. They took her through sunless halls too narrow and bare for royalty or guests—reserved for criminals and guards.

At last, the dim halls let them out into a well-lit antechamber full of mulling nobles and commoners alike. Their voices rose and echoed off the walls. Commander Wade ordered for them to move, and at the sight of Ryn, the crowd parted. Nobles and commoners wedged closer to catch a glimpse as she passed. Whispers surged, about the *vampire girl* and *poaching*.

Guards opened a set of heavy double doors, and Commander Wade marched through. The Hunters—and Ryn—followed. Several more Hunters fell in behind them, their boots heavy on the floor.

They entered the throne room as guards dragged another criminal out. The blond male hung limp between the guards, common clothes hugging his protruding gut. He was not a slum rat like Ryn. Just a poor sop who'd gotten caught breaking the rules. He looked up at Ryn with defeated eyes, cold acceptance.

The throne room dripped opulence, from the shining white marble, the polished rosewood paneling, to the reflective tile on the floor. Sunlight poured in from tall windows, making everything glitter and gleam. The air reeked of polish and perfume. Nobles in their finery lingered on the edges of the rectangular room, within the shadow of the arcade, while more gathered on the mezzanine, to watch commoners and criminals beseech and beg the king. Entertainment for those who wanted for nothing.

King Victor Casiano sat on his ornate throne of gleaming rosewood and golden inlay. Several windows behind the throne were angled so that their beams of light intersect over the dais, over the king. His golden crown caught the light and made him seem godly, as if he emanated light.

Despite his age, he kept trim. Silver threaded his blond beard and his hair. A thick leather sword belt hugged his middle, and the decorated scabbard was not for show. That sword had severed countless vampire heads from their shoulders. He beheld Ryn with bored disdain.

To the right of the throne stood Crown Prince Esben, a younger version of his father and every bit as broad, blond, and intimidating. He shared his father's disdain.

The procession paused before the king, and the Hunters threw Ryn to the ground. Somehow, she managed to catch herself before her face smacked into the tile. Her dirty, clumped hair tumbled forward, blocking her view of the dais.

She pushed herself onto her hands and knees—and caught her reflection in the shined tiles. Disheveled. Dirty. Grimy. She looked a few breaths away from vomiting. Her complexion was pale, her eyes were bloodshot, and dirt smudged her cheek. Her ears pointed through her dirty hair. The high polish of the title made it look like two of her existed, mirroring her other self in an equally horrible situation. Ryn let herself pretend that her other self had some brilliant escape plan, some witty plea to let the king pardon her crimes. Because the real her had nothing.

The chatter of the throne room quieted, and a hungry silence settled. Ryn's entire body clenched. What bravado she had managed to hold onto fled like shadow before the sun.

Commander Wade stepped forward. "Your Majesty. This criminal was discovered over a bloodless body on your grounds. After a dose of Blood Sherry and several days in the dungeon, we have deemed her not a vampire. However, we believe she is an accomplice to a brood."

Those words elicited feverish whispers from the courtiers gathered to observe and those waiting to speak to the king.

Ryn kept her head down. She didn't want to see how many courtiers gawked at her like a pig about to be slaughtered.

Accomplice? What happened to her poaching? What did a vampire's accomplice do? Why did they think she was one? What had she done to make them think that?

Silence settled once more, and then King Victor spoke, his voice heavy and firm, filling the space, "The punishment for associating with vampires is death."

Ryn's fury melted into panic.

That was it. These Hunters didn't care about the poaching. They didn't want to be wrong, so they were going to kill her anyway. She jerked her attention from the floor to the king, tossing her mess of hair back with the motion. The king's attention was to the commander, not to her.

He wasn't even looking at her when he ordered her death.

"I was poaching!" Ryn's voice filled the space, hoarse from her dry throat. "Poaching! I'm not a…whatever you called it."

King Casiano's fiery gaze met hers, and Commander Wade shifted with the fluid grace of a Hunter—backhanding her. Ryn hit the tile with an unladylike clatter, and then a heartbeat later, the pain set in like a fire on her cheek.

"Fucking hell," she spat, hand on her cheek. She pushed herself up and glared at Commander Wade.

"You will not speak," the commander snapped. His fist clenched like he might hit her again.

"Commander?"

Over the buzzing in her ears, Ryn became aware of the strange silence that had settled over the throne room. Commander Wade glanced toward the voice. Ryn followed his line of sight to a tall, lean, dark-haired male who now stood to the left of the throne. He hadn't been there before. The sunlight washed him into little more than a shadow wearing a fine suit of deep black and emerald.

"My prince?" Commander Wade straightened.

Ryn's heart and gut twisted in opposite directions. The dark-haired prince could only be Zain. Of all the people in the room to take notice, why did it have to be him?

Prince Zain sauntered out of the blinding sunlight of the dais and onto the throne room's floor, the light bringing out the blue-black of his hair. As he stepped into the shadow, his glittering, mischievous blue eyes met Ryn's. He tilted his head at her, and a cocky grin spread his lips.

She realized her mistake with a sickening prickle in her gut. The dark-haired male from the tavern, the noble she had robbed—it hadn't been just anyone.

It had been *fucking Prince Zain*.

And by the look on his face, he recognized her.

She had stolen from the prince, from the royal family. She might as well have stolen the king's own coin purse.

"Your Highness?" came King Victor's questioning tone, but also a warning.

Prince Zain's lips curved in a sinister smile. A male about to get revenge. A shiver traveled from the crown of Ryn's head and into her toes. The prince looked to his father, then to a female in a gold and white gown who looked utterly appalled. Ryn assumed her the queen. Zain's eyes landed once again on Ryn, and his smile stretched. The look on his face made Ryn want to melt into the floor.

"I have made my decision." Zain motioned toward Ryn, his smile vicious and cold, and then announced to the deathly silence room, "I have chosen this female as my bride."

13
TEA WITH THE QUEEN
Ryn

Ryn hit the parlor floor hard enough to bruise. Footsteps stormed around her, and she managed to right herself and sit back on her rear before Queen Portia charged through the doors with the fierceness of a lioness.

The queen stood tall and proud, nostrils flaring in fury, looking down her pointed nose at Ryn. Royal guards flanked the queen, and the blond Hunter stood by the door, hand curled around the hilt of his blade. Beside him, the broad-shouldered female Hunter glowered. Commander Wade had not accompanied them.

Ryn scrambled to her feet, feeling like a joke in her dirty and tattered clothes compared to the queen and the spotless, priceless carpet she had hopelessly mucked. She'd haggled with the shadiest shopkeepers, looked crime lords in the eye, and drained dry the worst of the city, but something about the Queen of Sovann made her bones tremble.

The *fucking Queen of Sovaan*. The mother of the male whom Ryn had stolen from.

All this over a few lousy coins. She doubted it had even made a dent in their coffers, which meant this was all about revenge.

"You." The queen barely contained her fury, all twisted into a single word. Aimed at Ryn like an arrow.

Ryn, feeling foolish and cornered, bowed. "Your Majesty."

It seemed inconsequential, but not bowing could equate disrespect, and that equated to a very bad time. Or, in Ryn's case, a worse time.

The queen seethed. Rage rolled off her person like perfume.

Ryn swallowed and glanced to her feet, at her filthy leather boots with mismatched strings, at anywhere that wasn't the queen or the pissed off Hunters behind her. Waiting for her signal to end her like they wanted to.

"My son insists on your hand in marriage," the queen said, as if the words were being forced out of her, as if they were torture.

Ryn bit her lip. Yes, she had heard that announcement. The whole damn room heard that announcement.

Prince Zain had announced Ryn as his bride in front of the entire royal family and however many courtiers and commoners and guards were in attendance. The guards hadn't allowed Ryn a moment to consider the announcement before hauling her out of the room at the behest of the queen. It hadn't been quick enough—whispers seethed between the nobles and commoners as the Hunters dragged Ryn out of sight.

Gossip would've already hit the Black Canal by now.

Queen Portia took a controlled step toward Ryn. She dared to glance up and meet the queen's icy glare.

Oh, if looks could kill, Ryn would have been dead in the throne room.

"I apologize, Your Majesty." Ryn's voice came out a wisp.

"Your tone lacks sincerity."

Ryn caught the accusation in the queen's voice, but she didn't know what to say. Did the queen believe Ryn planned this mess? That she had coaxed the prince into marriage? If only she were that conniving and charismatic.

Of course, the prince's outburst had gotten her out of a death sentence. Or at least delayed it a few days.

Queen Portia closed her eyes and took a deep breath. When she opened her eyes again, the rage lessened into something colder and calmer. Ryn didn't like it. It was the cool fury of a fae queen, with a horde of Hunters and guards at her disposal, who could kill Ryn with a word.

The queen tilted her head toward the royal guard on her left, and said, "I want her cleaned up and in the Gilded Parlor for tea. Take her to the Sturgis Suite."

Three guards closed in around Ryn, led by the brown-eyed female Hunter.

The queen motioned to the brown-eyed hunter, and said to Ryn, "This is Hunter Irene. She will be in charge of you for the duration of your stay. Should she see fit to end you, I will not question her motives. Understood?"

For the *duration of your stay*. So, the queen intended to get rid of her in one way or another.

Ryn met the fierce brown eyes of Irene. She looked back with cool indifference. "Yes," Ryn said to the queen. "I understand."

"Good," the queen snapped, the word laced with warning. "Try anything, and it will be the last thing you do."

With that, the queen swept out of the room with the grace of a storm. Her heels echoed down the corridor like hail.

Two guards grabbed Ryn by the arms and lifted her between them. They hauled her out of the parlor, through spacious corridors, and to a suite with cream walls and golden trimmings. The plush rugs, the crystal chandeliers, the polished paneling—it all screamed opulence. Old money, royal money. A small army of servants were dusting and fussing over the pillows on the sofa.

THE BLOOD ENCHANTRESS

When the guards hauled Ryn through the doors, all motion stopped. They looked to Ryn like an exotic animal, one wrong look from biting heads from shoulders.

Hunter Irene marched forward and snapped, "You're dismissed."

The servants hurried from the room, eyes downcast as they passed Ryn. Whispers surged like winter's wind once they reached the corridor.

"I've got her from here," Irene said to the other guards.

The guards released Ryn's arms at the same time. The one to her left said, "We will be in the corridor."

"You," Irene said to Ryn, "this way."

Ryn followed the Hunter through the sitting room, through a spacious bedroom dressed in the same cream and gold, and into a bathing room. A massive claw-foot tub waited, the water steaming. A servant stood at the side, sprinkling pale salts into the water, humming.

Irene cleared her throat. The servant straightened and spun, clutching the bottle of pale blue salts to her chest.

"Oh, hello. I'm Kari." She bowed quickly. "The queen asked that I tend to your needs while you are staying with us."

Ryn snorted. "I get my own servant?"

Kari paled several shades, and her eyes widened. Fear blossomed on her girlish features. "I—I meant nothing by it, miss."

"And here I thought I'd be dead by now." Ryn laughed. The steam curled against her cold skin, decadent and welcoming, making her all the more aware of how filthy she was.

"The day is still young," Irene muttered. She pushed Ryn toward the tub. "Now hurry up. The queen should not be kept waiting."

Irene posted herself just inside the bathing room door while Kari set about undressing Ryn.

"I am capable of undressing myself," Ryn protested.

"This is my given task, miss," Kari said without pause. She pulled the cloak from Ryn's shoulders and tossed it to the floor. She pulled apart each layer of dirty, threadbare clothing.

"These are men's clothes," Irene said, nudging the dirty tailcoat with her boot.

"They are the clothes I had," Ryn said defensively. "Forgive me for not coming to court prepared in my best velvet dress."

Irene's expression remained unfeeling. Did she realize they were the same clothes Ryn had worn that day at the market?

The tub was large enough for several people, and the hot water rose above her breasts. The salts made it silky and sweet-smelling. Ryn wasn't given time to enjoy it—Kari scrubbed her skin and hair with sharply sweet soaps. Ryn swore several times, sure that Kari was scrubbing off the top layer of skin.

Irene stood by the door, looking bored out of her mind.

Finally, when Kari deemed Ryn clean, she pulled the drain. The filthy water sank through the hole in the bottom of the tub. Kari towel dried Ryn's skin and hair, then combed a tonic into the gnarled strands. She spent several long minutes tugging, untangling, and yanking—Ryn winced each time, sure her scalp was bleeding.

"Just a bit…unruly," Kari said as she fought a particularly tangled knot.

"Apologies for not brushing it out for the last several days." Ryn glared at Irene, who couldn't be bothered. "I was locked in a cell."

Kari swept Ryn's hair into an elegant bun and secured it with golden pins. She then helped Ryn into a soft cotton chemise. Back in the bedroom, a dress of cream waited. Kari silently helped Ryn into a corset and tied it with deft fingers. The boned material hugged Ryn tighter than she was used to.

"It's not even that tight," Irene muttered.

"Do you have to wear one of these contraptions under that leather?" Ryn snapped back.

"No."

"Then shut up."

Irene made a small sound, and Ryn would have sworn she heard a smile. Just a small one.

It wasn't that the corset was too tight—Ryn had never worn one. All her clothes were baggy, and she didn't mind her breasts being free. It made moving easier. Besides, corsets were pricey and took two people to put on and take off. Ryn had no need for corsets, for she had no need to dress up.

Next came the shoes. They were a bit too big, and Kari found an extra pair of socks in one of the drawers. That helped. Then came the dress.

"There you are." Kari stepped back to admire her work. "You look…like a lady fit for tea with the queen."

Ryn detected uncertainty in Kari's too-happy tone.

"Looks can deceive." Irene looked Ryn up and down. Her unfeeling mask had returned.

"I agree." Ryn shifted in the dress. It felt cumbersome, but not like her cloak or layers. This dress had too much useless fabric, no pockets, and too much…everything. Ryn tugged at the tight lacy cuff.

"Stop fidgeting." Kari smacked at her hands. "Ladies don't fidget. At least not in front of the queen."

Ryn half laughed, though it felt hollow.

Kari and Irene escorted Ryn into the corridor. The two guards standing outside the room fell into step behind them.

Both gawked at Ryn like they had never seen her before.

"There *was* a female under there," one of them said.

Ryn had a quip at the ready, but Kari urged her forward. "Don't keep the queen waiting."

Guards a step behind, Kari and Irene escorted Ryn through the king's manor and to a parlor on the second floor. Queen Portia stood by the windows, draped in golden light. She wore a different gown than before, this one a deep blue and less ornate than the one she wore to court. Royal guards stood at the edges of the room.

The sun warmed the Red Forest in exhausted jewel tones.

"Sit," commanded the queen.

When Ryn didn't move immediately, Kari gave her a small shove between the shoulder blades. Ryn crossed the room to the small table set for two. It stood within the wash of sunlight, making the porcelain shine and crystal sparkle. The teapot alone looked more expensive than everything Ryn owned combined. Twice over.

Ryn adjusted her skirts and sat, ready to get this tea date over with.

The queen meandered to the table with the grace of a swan and sat. "Are you not used to wearing shoes?"

Ryn flexed her toes. "Not shoes a size too big." She quickly added, "Your Majesty."

The queen didn't look amused. Instead, she studied Ryn like a painting. That gaze traveled over her face and lingered on her ears. "You clean up well, at least. I had my doubts if there was a female underneath the dirt."

Ryn fought to keep a straight face. "I apologize for not taking your opinion into account when they threw me into your dungeon and kept me there without a proper washing."

The queen's stare bore into hers. After a long moment, the corners of the queen's red lips curved. The cold fury in her eyes had faded, like her anger had gone with the changing of a dress. "And my son demands you as his bride."

At the reminder, her heart gave a frightful lurch. "Do I not get a say in that?"

"That is what you're doing now." The queen's smile turned a shade venomous, a trained court smile. "Are you capable, or do I send you back to the Hunters for execution?"

And there they were: Ryn's options. Play the prince's game or return to the Hunters and face execution for being in the wrong place at the wrong time. Such a high price for poaching. Rejecting the prince seemed a far higher crime, given the royals' prideful disposition.

"First," the queen started, nose high and tone demanding. "I have already secured a marriage for my son to a pure fae bloodline. What of yours? Your ears boast of a strong bloodline. We will have your blood tested, but I would rather hear your lineage from you first."

"I'm not sure," Ryn said.

The queen frowned. Her tone was condescending. "You're not sure?"

"I only know of my parents. We never talked about bloodlines. They're dead, so I can't ask them."

The queen heaved a sigh, like her parents being dead was nothing more than an inconvenience. "I shall inform the alchemist to have you tested. Secondly, your name. Ryn is an odd name for a girl."

"It's short for Sabryn."

The queen hummed. "Surname?"

"Evren."

"I've not heard that name before. What did your parents do for a living?"

"My mother was a seamstress. My father worked in a warehouse."

"I'll have one of the scholars look into it." The queen nodded, and Ryn noticed the servant by the door. Taking notes, the feather quill moved at an alarming speed.

"First lesson," the queen continued, "Never sit before royalty."

Ryn frowned. "You told me to sit."

"Second, never argue with the queen."

"Are you making that up?"

"It doesn't matter." Queen Portia wore a venomous smile. "I am queen. Now, would you pour us tea?"

Another test. Ryn owned an old teapot but knew nothing of etiquette. The queen's superior grin suggested she suspected as much. Ryn reached for the teapot and poured two, just as she would have done at home. She replaced the teapot where it had been.

"Would you like to know where you went wrong?" The queen raised a brow.

"No, but I'm sure you're about to tell me."

Out of the corner of her eye, Ryn saw Kari flinch.

Queen Portia motioned to the teacups, her tone clipped. "Pour for company first. You then fix it for them. Only after you have prepared their tea do you pour your own."

Rules, rules, rules.

"My apologies," Ryn mimicked the queen's delicate venom.

"We also need to work on your sincerity," the queen said.

Plastering a courtier's grin on her face, Ryn threaded her tone with all the false niceness she could muster. "How does Her Majesty take her tea?"

"Better, but you look like you're plotting my murder."

Ryn didn't deny it.

"First, the sugar." The queen motioned to the bowl of cubes. "One lump or two, don't offer three. It is considered unladylike to take more than three."

"One lump or two?" Ryn asked in her false tone.

"One."

Ryn gripped the delicate silver tongs and gently dropped one cube into the first cup. "Milk?"

"No, thank you."

Ryn stirred the tea until the sugar dissolved, then handed it to the queen, who accepted it without brushing fingers. Given the small size of the cup, Ryn was impressed.

The queen took a sip. "Prepare your own."

Ryn bypassed the sugar and milk. They hadn't the extra money for it, so she had gotten used to living without them both. Not that the tea needed it; it tasted far better than the bitter leaves sold in low town.

The queen monitored every motion like a starving hawk.

"I have tried to talk my son out of this nonsense, but he insists." The queen released a quick breath, a dignified huff. "Given that he announced it to the entire throne room, I will entertain him until he grows tired of you. Then you will be on your way. Unless you give me cause to send you to the executioner's block where you belong. Is that clear?"

Ryn felt the threat in the air, a dagger against her throat. She swallowed a gulp of tea. "Yes. Your Majesty."

"Good." The queen sipped her tea. "You will live in the keep for now. We will do what we can to make you look presentable." She raked her eyes over Ryn. "At least from a distance."

Ryn bristled at the insult. She didn't want to die for something stupid like poaching, or something even stupider like being falsely convicted as an accomplice to a vampire brood. This pretend engagement to Prince Zain might save her in that regard, and give her time to escape the keep with her head still on her shoulders. It would be a roof over her head, a massive tub with running water, a soft bed, and servants to handle food and laundry while she plotted.

She might even snag a few things to quickly sell, like a silver hairbrush or earrings. To make sure Lu had what she needed while Ryn was in the keep.

The thought of her sister sent a wave of nausea through her bones. Suddenly, the finest tea in the kingdom tasted like sand.

She needed to get to Lu and make sure she was okay. In the meantime, Ryn could make this engagement work in her favor. The only problem would be Prince Zain himself.

14

TWO LIARS

Zain

Zain hadn't felt so elated in…years. The look on his mother's face when he announced the female as his bride! Zain had never seen his mother so flustered, or his father so speechless, or the courtiers so dumbfounded they couldn't speak.

Zain looked at his reflection in the vanity mirror in his bathing room. He wore a mad grin, and his eyes were wild.

He couldn't stop smiling. Or laughing. He'd laughed more in the last few hours than he had in years. Whenever he thought of his father's face at the announcement, he laughed.

There was a chance the female from the tavern was as much a bore as the others, but he didn't think so. She hadn't been that night, though he was drunk and she was pretending.

After Zain's announcement, the Hunters hauled the poor female out of sight. His mother rushed after, trying to calm the building storm, but little could be done. Zain demanded no harm come to her, and his mother had promised. She might be overbearing and a gossip, but his mother would hold her promise.

Of course, that had been after she called Zain reckless, foolish, and several other things in an attempt to make him rescind his proclamation.

He refused.

Esben had led Zain out of the throne room and away from where the Hunters stole his bride away—a distraction, likely. They had slipped into the servant passages to eavesdrop on the courtiers in the antechamber. Courtiers and guards sizzled with nervous energy, whispering and gossiping of the prince's sudden betrothal to a criminal. They whispered about her possible connection to the vampiric murders, how Zain pulled her from the execution line.

Sabryn, Commander Wade called her. *Sabryn Evren.*

By the time the next court session started, rumors flew about the two of them, everything from a secret romance to childhood friendship to love at first sight. Rumors flew of the mystery female just as madly, calling her everything from foreign princess to vampire to assassin.

Zain could barely contain himself! He hadn't had as much fun in years.

"This will be all over the city by sundown," Esben had muttered as they left the nobles to gossip.

"Sundown?" Zain had laughed, startling a few servants hiding in a nearby alcove, pretending to polish a suit of armor. "It won't take one hour to reach the river."

Sabryn was currently having tea with his mother. Poor thing. His father ordered Hunters to guard her at all hours. A sample of her blood was sent to the alchemist, and the scholars were digging through the archives for her family name. Zain expected his mother to find some inadequacy that would guarantee Sabryn's fate with the Hunters, and yet, Zain felt an unfamiliar swell of hope in his chest.

When word reached him that Sabryn had survived tea with his mother, that hope swelled to a crescendo.

Noble females cowered before the queen. Even Aurora shrank before her. If Sabryn could stand eye to eye with his mother, then it confirmed his suspicions. There was more to her than the scant dress and sultry glances.

It made it the idea of her being a vampire accomplice all the more probable.

It made her more exciting.

❋❋❋

That evening, Zain donned one of his finer suits to dine with his betrothed. The tailcoat was deep emerald, the double-buttoned vest dark-gold-and-emerald brocade, pressed trousers and undershirt deepest black, his leather boots polished. He slid a gold and onyx ring onto his finger, the onyx surrounded by emeralds and diamonds. He wore a heavy golden chain around his neck, the pendent an emerald the size of an infant's fist. His black hair was combed back.

Tonight, he dressed like a prince.

He would no longer court these manic females; he would court one. *Sabryn.* If, in the future, he tired of her, perhaps some tragic accident would befall her. He wouldn't worry about that just yet. Right now, she was the answer to his problem.

A shuffle came from the bedroom. "We should be leaving, Your Highness," said Neville. "Unless you want her to arrive first."

"That wouldn't be proper." Zain sauntered out of the bathing room. He turned in a circle for Neville's appraisal. "How do I look?"

Neville hesitated, a furrow between his brows. "Like you care about this dinner."

Zain raised a brow.

"You couldn't care less about the others," Neville said calmly. He knew Zain well enough to speak openly, and Zain knew Neville well enough to know he meant no offense. He was critical but plainly so. "Your manner of dress and your attitude suggests this dinner is different, and by extension, the female."

"This isn't just any female, Neville." Zain started for the door, feeling lighter than he had in a long time. "This is my *betrothed*. Miss Sabryn."

Chuckling, Zain threw open the doors to the corridor. The royal guards standing outside didn't so much as flinch.

Zain arrived at the library parlor first—a quaint space of mahogany and leather—with Neville and his small horde of royal guards his father insisted upon, with vampires leaving dead Hunters in the woods.

Servants were arranging the table, lighting the candles, and making sure no speck of dust from the library below had snuck in. When Zain entered, they all paused to bow.

"Don't mind me." Zain sauntered to the sideboard by the secretary. It was mostly for looks, as was the woven map of the kingdom hung between the arched windows. The territories were not marked, and the rivers were inaccurate.

He poured himself a whiskey and sat in one of three leather armchairs by the windows. The guards stood in the corridor outside the parlor, and Neville took up a guard's post by the windows. Within range of Zain and the table set for two.

The king's face drifted to the front of his mind, and Zain snorted a laugh. One of the younger servants cast a wary glance in his direction, then averted his eyes. Zain sipped his whiskey, daring him to look again. He did not. Zain wouldn't have ordered his death—he was feeling far too happy.

The servants finished and hurried out, as if Zain might strike them down for a wrinkle or misplaced strand of hair. Then the room was empty.

"What do you think?" Zain asked Neville.

Neville considered it. "I think it is wonderful that you've made a decision. The queen will stop hounding you, and you will stop complaining about it."

Zain chuckled, the sound dark and low.

"You will also stop upsetting the poor females of the court," Neville muttered.

Zain rolled his eyes. Unmarried females had been hounding him since he reached marrying age. The number dwindled with each rejection, as he refused each snobbish, idiotic female who cared more for dresses and gossip and titles than intelligent conversation.

"I worry for your betrothed," Neville said.

"My betrothed survived tea with my mother," Zain reminded him, swishing his whiskey.

Neville inhaled to speak—then a rhythmic tapping sounded underneath the wind at the windows and the sputtering of the candles. Footsteps.

The parlor doors opened, and a retinue swept inside. At its center stood his mysterious female, Miss Sabryn, dressed in cream, looking like a lady save for the scowl on her otherwise lovely face. Hunter Irene stalked a step behind, looking like someone had stolen her favorite sword.

Zain remained sitting. Swirling his whiskey, he took in Sabryn head to toe. She met his gaze without flinching.

Silence burned. The wind hissed through the drafts and pressed against the windows.

"Is this the same female from the throne room?" Zain raised a brow, not looking away from Sabryn as he sipped his whiskey. "It's hard to tell without the dirt and baggy clothes."

Sabryn flushed a darling shade of pink.

"The wonders of a bath and a corset," she said in a forced pleasant voice threaded with the same deadly fire as her eyes. She brazenly looked him up and down. "You also look nice. Or you do from here. Hard to tell when you're sitting down. According to your mother, it's proper to be standing when your guests arrive. She was standing."

The air in the parlor tightened. The guards tensed, eyes flashing between Zain and Sabryn. With every heartbeat of silence, the air tightened until it was nearly suffocating. Zain kept his eyes on her, and she held his. Without blinking. Any other female would have looked down or shrank inward. Sabryn cocked an eyebrow, as if waiting for his next move.

This was going to be fun.

He leaned forward, elbows on his knees.

"Or that is what your mother said." Her bravado faded. "She is clearly in charge, so I am going with her word. *Your Highness.*"

Neville's fingers curled around the hilt of his sword. The servant standing behind Sabryn went deathly white. Few dared to talk back to the royal family, especially in their own home. Especially to him. Sabryn had already escaped death that day, and she seemed unafraid of toeing the line. But seeing how she was his betrothed, he would let it pass.

Zain made a show of finishing off his whiskey, standing, setting the glass on the sideboard, and then sauntering to the table—all without taking his eyes off Sabryn. Each footfall sounded like a heartbeat against the floor. He sauntered to her side of the table and pulled out her chair.

"My lady," he said.

She sat, breaking their stare.

"Dinner, please." Zain commanded.

Servants scuttled like mice.

Zain sat on the opposite end of the table. Neville repositioned himself to Zain's right, and Hunter Irene posted herself to Sabryn's right. Nothing would escape notice between the two of them.

Zain straightened a winkle in his napkin as he said, "Is this your first three-course meal?"

"It is," Sabryn answered without shame. "I do hope you ordered something hearty. I am famished. The meals in your jail are lacking."

He couldn't stop the smirk from curving his lips. "Having an appetite is unladylike."

"Manners won't stop my stomach from growling."

A servant stepped forward to pour their wine. He poured Zain's first, then hers. She lifted the wine to her painted lips, taking a long sip and leaving an imprint of red lips on the crystal's rim.

Zain sipped his own wine, taking her in again. Despite the heavy dress, she was thin. The sort of thin that came from skipping meals. Her cheekbones sunk a bit too much, and her collarbone protruded. The bones in her hands were pronounced. Not that she was unattractive, quite the opposite. A few healthy meals, and she would be steep competition for the females of the court.

"I see you've already helped yourself to a drink." She motioned to the whiskey with her wine.

"To pass the time."

"You expected I'd be late?" She raised a brow.

He flashed her a grin. "Maybe I was nervous."

Her full lips tilted upward. He'd kissed those lips. He was drunk, but he had kissed them. Zain stole his gaze upward before she noticed, but by the glint in her eye, she had.

"Nervous about me?" She sipped her wine, cocking the glass to one side to better see him.

"You *were* caught in the woods over a dead body," Zain mused. "At night, might I add. Any male would be at least a little concerned."

"And yet you want to marry me?" Her expression shifted from playful to curious. The question burned through her eyes.

Why had he picked her out of the execution line?

Did she not already know the answer? Zain doubted she wanted to die, and he didn't want to marry Aurora. This arrangement solved both of their problems. He couldn't outright say it with servants and guards listening, especially without knowing which reported directly to his mother. Every word said in this room would be reported to her.

Thankfully, by some grace of the gods, Sabryn hadn't blurted out something incriminating. Zain needed to tilt the whispers that would reach his mother's ears in his favor.

Zain sipped his wine without looking away, then said plainly, "Tell me, do you believe in love at first sight?"

By the hesitation and doubt in her eyes, no. But she seemed to understand the underlying meaning of his words, of this dinner. They were playing, a charade, and everyone in the keep was playing. Like it or not.

She said lowly, "I think you and I remember that evening differently."

He cocked a brow. "It *is* a bit blurry. But I remember you very well."

It was not a lie.

Pink heated her cheeks once again. Had his compliment embarrassed her? Any other female would have swooned.

The doors opened, and servants ushered in the first course on gleaming silver platters. The soup was buttery squash with flecks of spice. As the lids rose, Zain found himself watching Sabryn's reaction. At first, her eyes widened and her lips parted, then her brows came together and her lips crinkled.

"Disappointed?" Zain lifted his soup spoon. "It is only the first course."

"Can't say I know what that means." She looked at the spoon in his hand, then chose the mirroring one among her silverware.

"The courses complement one another, their flavors and seasonings connecting on the tongue." He brought a spoonful of soup to his lips. The crisp flavor of fall melted on his tongue.

She studied him a heartbeat longer, then mirrored the action. She took the first bite with a moan, like she'd never had anything as delicious.

"It is improper to moan at the table," Zain whispered.

Sabryn took another spoonful of soup, glaring at him.

He smirked, letting his imagination run with what sounds he could tease out of her.

It took her a few tries to mimic his loose grip on the spoon, and her fingers were still angled wrong, but he made no move to correct her. Underneath the makeup, between glances when she didn't think he was looking, something darker flashed across her features. Too quick for him to grasp. A bit too much like a courtier and yet at the same time nothing like them at all.

Sabryn Evren was no noble, yet she learned remarkably fast. It made her far more interesting than the others.

15

A MOONLIT WALK ON A COOL NIGHT
Ryn

Ryn couldn't believe it. The drunk noble from the tavern had been Prince Zain. She'd almost fucked a prince.

It explained his confidence, the swagger, the hidden wealth. He had gone into the city in secret, with a single guard. In common clothes.

And now she sat across from him in Nightshade Keep, as his betrothed.

It had to be a joke or a scheme. He couldn't *actually* want to marry her. She was…nothing. She had no lineage, no wealth, no family connections, no anything. He was a prince, albeit an arrogant, unpleasant, and entitled one. He was handsome, no question about that, and the purr of his voice had her stomach in knots and her chest full of fluttering insects, but despite how he flashed those blue eyes at her throughout dinner, something darker lurked behind. Ruthless and calculating.

Prince Zain didn't have room in his cold heart to save her from an unwarranted fate because of his sense of chivalry.

From all she'd heard about Zain, he was neither chivalrous nor kind.

If he was, he'd be married to some golden-hearted princess by now. His mother wouldn't have had to find a bride on the far flung edges of the kingdom. Zain could have any female in the kingdom or the next, any noble daughter or courtier, yet he had pulled *her* from the execution line—it had to be because of the night at the tavern, the money she'd stolen. She had humiliated him, and he wanted revenge. Yes, that had to be the reason. She could fathom no other.

She needed the prince—his revenge was the only thing keeping her away from the Hunter's execution block.

It took all her energy to pretend like she belonged at the table with him, like she was the one with the evil plan, but between the sweet wine and the most delicious food she'd ever had, a comfortable ease slid into her awareness. She hadn't eaten her fill in…years, save for the occasion splurge after a good week.

The guards watched her like hawks, ready to pick out her eyes and rip out her throat at the slightest motion from their prince. They took in every word she said, every glance, every wrong utensil.

The whole thing felt staged. An audition.

Zain danced around the truth of their meeting—playing the story far more romantic than a bar fight and a stolen coin purse.

As if he, too, were on a stage.

Ryn didn't add anything to his story and left her answers vague. With each answer, he eyed her, his gaze a sultry warning.

Dinner ended, and the pale amber of the lingering sunset framed the Red Forest as black silhouettes stretching into the horizon.

The prince shifted in his seat. He'd caught her staring out the window. Her face warmed. She couldn't pretend that everything about the keep and the king's manor didn't dwarf her entire existence. She tore her gaze from him and focused on swallowing the remainder of her wine. And…dinner was over. A panic bubbled in her stomach at what might happen after. Would she be allowed back to her guest room?

Zain set down his empty wine glass—his fifth—and stood. He smoothed the front of his vest and his tailcoat, then set his gaze on her. "Would you like to take a walk, Lady Sabryn? The gardens are quite a sight in the moonlight."

Ryn was sure she had misheard him. A walk in the moonlight? Was that his way of killing her in the dark?

In her hesitation, a spark rose in his eyes, quickly followed by surprise. He was not a prince used to waiting, or the horrors of rejection. Especially by females. He was used to being the one doing the rejecting, making others wait—and Ryn took pleasure in turning the tides. She pretended to consider the offer, and every moment that he waited for her response, that spark grew sinister.

Not wanting to push too many buttons in one night, she dabbed her lips with the napkin as the queen had advised—gently, as to not disturb the color on her lips—and stood.

She slid her arm through the prince's offered arm, and purred, "Lead the way, Your Highness."

The glimmer of impatience faded from his face, locked away behind a calm mask of arrogance.

His title sounded like a curse on her lips.

Zain led the way through the dusty, lemon-scented library, taking each step as if he had nowhere he'd rather be. Lanterns shed a flickering light over the bookshelves. The shadows seemed thicker between them and underneath, like cobwebs in the farthest corners. If the silence or the lack of patrons bothered Zain, he didn't show it. His ease made Ryn nervous. It was the same casual charm he'd carried at the tavern, like he had an ace hidden up his sleeve. Of course, some of that came with his title—as a prince, he was among the highest society in the kingdom. He could order her death in a single breath. The law wouldn't see it as murder but justice. She would be brushed aside and forgotten, like dust swept out the door.

She was, like it or not, at his mercy.

He led her through the manor, down corridors lit with cloudy sconces, tittering with whispers. Guards stood at intervals, and servants found things to do within the halls. They snuck glances at the prince, Ryn, and the retinue flanking them.

Guards opened the garden doors. A cool wind swept in, and a shiver peppered Ryn's skin. The dress was heavy, but it left her neck exposed. Zain did not shiver. The dark grounds stretched into the edges of her sight, lit with sparse hanging lanterns.

They strolled along the paved path that wound through the gardens. Unlike the wild and untamed royal grounds, the gardens were trimmed and artfully arranged. In the late autumn, it was mostly dead, save for shaped conifers, jewel-toned mums, and bushes of deep burgundy. They passed a bed of small shrubs with purple needles that fading to black at the tips. Ryn had seen dried needles in those colors in herbalists' shops. She didn't know the name, only that they sold well despite their cost.

Just a pocket full of those needles would likely buy firewood for a month. Ryn forced her hands still at her sides.

Zain guided them along a narrower path lined with conifers. Their guards were forced to walk single file behind them. Neville stalked right behind.

"Miss Sabryn," Zain said lowly, so that only his guard might hear.

"Ryn," she whispered back.

"What?" He glanced at her. The moonlight washed his stupidly handsome face in silver and turned his blue eyes dark silver.

A particularly cool breeze whistled through the conifers. "My name is Ryn."

"Commander Wade called you Sabryn."

"Yes, Ryn is short for Sabryn. It's what everyone calls me." The handful of people she knew, anyway.

"And if I refuse?" His lips turned up in that sinister grin.

"Why would you refuse?"

His lips tilted up, that sinful grin. "Maybe I like your name."

Heat rushed to her cheeks. She looked away before he could notice.

"I wanted to bring you out here for more than the garden," Zain whispered.

Her heart thumped. She fought to keep her posture steady. "Is that so?"

"I wanted to speak without listening ears."

She glanced behind them at his guard.

"Neville doesn't count," Zain said. "I trust him, but I don't know your guard. Mother assigned her to you. Everything you say, my mother will hear. As will my father."

She swallowed. "I guessed as much."

"Good, then you're not a fool." Zain let out a quick breath. It fogged from his lips. He steered them down another narrow path.

Neville lagged a step, giving them more room to speak.

Zain inhaled to speak—

"Why are you doing this?" Ryn blurted.

He closed his lips and smiled. "I was about to explain."

She motioned him to continue.

"You have likely heard that Mother is in the process of arranging my marriage to Lady Aurora. I refuse to marry her. I refuse to be forced into a marriage for the sake of bloodlines or whatever rubbish my parents deem important at the time. She is playing the royal game, and I don't want to play. I refuse to marry simply because my mother demands it."

"And…you want to marry me?" Ryn's brows rose. Her doubt doubled.

"The only way to end my mother's nagging is to marry," Zain said simply. "And you happened to walk into my life." Surprise flashed over his face. "Oh, you aren't married, are you?"

"No."

"Seeing anyone?"

Ryn hesitated to answer. She'd kept any relations purely physical. "No one serious."

"Surely they can't compete with me." He flashed her a grin. "I am a prince, after all."

"Surely the court females *can* compete with me," Ryn said. "I have nothing to offer in terms of dowry or land."

"Then it is a good thing I require none of those things." Zain patted her arm and tilted his head toward her. Then his grin fell into a flat line. His voice dropped to a chilled whisper. "We both get what we want in this arrangement. My mother will stop fussing over my love life, and you bypass execution. However, if my mother catches wind that I am only using you to stave off her advances, then she will likely override me."

"And throw me to the gallows," Ryn added darkly.

"That too."

Of course, he would talk nonchalantly about her execution. She was a pawn to him, an object to stave off his mother's nagging. Not because he liked her or thought she was pretty enough. She was a means to an end.

"Yet you never asked me what I wanted," she whispered back. "Or if I wanted to marry you."

"You would rather die than marry me?" His brows rose, and he flattened his hand over his heart. "I'm hurt."

His words sent an icy tendril into her heart. Those were her options. "No. I would rather live."

"Exactly," he said. "This works out better for both of us. You don't die, and I don't have to marry one of my mother's conniving puppets."

She supposed he was right. Still, the idea of being tied forever to Zain made her gut twist and her lungs squeeze.

"Now that we've settled that little matter, I think we should stick to the story that we met at a tavern and fell madly in love at first sight," Zain said. "It's common knowledge that I went out that night. It will keep the gossip-mongers at bay."

Ryn nodded along to his story. If Zain hadn't passed out that night, would it have changed anything? If they would have tumbled into the bed, if she would've slept next to a stranger—would it have mattered?

If she stayed here, what would happen to Lu?

Thinking of Lu twisted her entire being.

"What is it?" Zain whispered, so low she didn't think even Neville heard. The words were rough, annoyed. His brow furrowed. His grip on her arm tightened. "Is it me? I'm aware I am the lesser of two princes. I apologize for not being the golden prince of Sovann." The last words rang with bitterness.

"It's not you," Ryn whispered. She put on her best sad face and hugged his arm to her side.

His icy gaze followed the movement, and his entire arm tensed. He looked like he would rather be anywhere else than touching her.

"My sister is sick with fever. I don't know if she's already dead or waiting for me to come home…" She swallowed and fought to produce a few tears. It didn't take long; fear and guilt over Lu churned through her emotions. The frigid night air stung at her eyelids, at her false tears. "I want my sister brought here."

Zain wore no sympathy. "It's a bit early to be demanding things."

Panic surged under her skin. "My sister could already be dead," she whispered, digging her nails into the sleeve of his coat, enough she knew he felt it. His gaze didn't change. "If she's dead because I've been locked up here, then it doesn't matter if the Hunters kill me." That got his attention. Despite having more to lose than he did, she made her counteroffer. "Bring my sister here, and I'll be your obedient little wife or whatever it is you want. Please. My sister is all the family I have left."

Zain's lips flattened. His expression went unreadable. The night turned his eyes into black pools.

With every moment that passed in silence, her heart slowed with dread.

"I don't know if I like this sincere side of you." He raked his eyes along her panicked expression and teary eyes. "I miss the mouthy criminal."

Her bones turned to wet sand. Had she overstepped? Zain could find another female to take her place in a heartbeat. There were plenty of desperate females who would kill for the chance for a steady roof and warm meals. Ryn had dared to ask for more, and by the look on his face, he did not care about Lu.

Ryn had unknowingly taken a step away from him, loosening her grip on his arm. Zain remained unreadable and silent. Hot tears, real tears, pushed against her eyes, gathering along her lids, chilling in the night breeze.

Heartless and cold. Wasn't that what everyone said about Prince Zain?

Zain tugged her arm back into his. Her unsteady feet threw her into his chest, and he grabbed her other arm, holding her there. His hot breath hit her temple.

"If it will make you happy," Zain whispered. "I'll send the royal guard there first thing tomo—"

"Tonight," she said. "Right now."

"There she is, my fierce little poacher." Zain chuckled, the darkness in his eyes glittering like nightmares. The velvet sound trickled down her spine. "I will send the Royal Guard to check on your sister. If she still lives, she will be brought to the keep. Come, darling of mine, let us inform the guard of their new task. And get you out of the cold. You're shivering."

She'd been shivering since they stepped outside.

Zain steered her around a waterless fountain and toward the manor. In the distance, the barracks glowed. Hunters patrolled the grounds and the Red Forest, looking for the wayward vampire that had escaped—the one that framed Ryn for murder.

"I can feel you thinking," Zain said.

"I was thinking about the vampire I saw," Ryn said. His arm tightened. "It's still out there."

"The Hunters are the best at what they do," Zain said.

"Clearly not, because they missed one."

They'd missed several, counting those lurking in the slums. But what did the Hunters care for the poor who lived there? What were the poor if not fodder for the monsters to protect the wealthy?

He frowned. In the lantern light, his eyes were again blue. "They were distracted by a lovely female in the forest."

"Oh yes, the armed female in dirty men's clothes with a dead rabbit over her shoulder," she mused. "That's why they tied me up and hauled me into their dungeon?"

His lips quirked. "I take it you're not into that?"

She frowned. "That's not an appropriate question."

"Considering we are to be married, I think it's important to know. I want to know what I'm getting myself into. Any kinks I should be aware of?" Zain's brows rose.

She didn't think she liked being tied up. At least, she didn't like the idea of it. None of her trysts had ever proposed such a thing; neither had she. She'd heard stories from the brothels—clients who asked for ropes or chains or masks.

Zain's prodding stare made her think about being tied up—with him—and the heat on her face turned feverish.

"I vaguely remember you being on top," Zain said as if it were a casual conversation to be held in front of his guard. "Is that your preference?"

Her blush turned fire, yet she teased, "Do you need a female on top?"

He chuckled, as did Neville behind them. "When she knows what she's doing, I don't mind. Otherwise, I prefer to do the pinning."

A warm shiver shot down her spine.

"Oh, I should have asked," Zain whispered, low so that only Neville heard. "You do enjoy men?"

"Yes," she whispered back.

"Have you ever kissed a female?"

"Have you ever kissed a male?"

"Yes, and I didn't like it. I don't know what you see in them."

A laugh found its way out of her throat. A pause, and then she realized he waited for her answer. Biting her lip, she said, "I might have."

"And?"

"It was all right."

Zain chuckled.

The path widened, their guards walked closer, and Zain turned their conversation into pleasant, useless chatter—nothing scandalous that could be taken back to the queen.

They arrived at the Royal Guard barracks as the shift changed, giving them all the chance to spy the female who, according to rumor, had stolen Zain's heart. The Captain of the Royal Guard was not happy about Zain's order to venture into the slums, but he didn't argue. Ryn stood beside Zain as five guards on horseback raced to fetch her sister.

She imagined what rumors would rage in low town when the Royal Guard showed up looking for Lu, and among the nobles when they discovered she lived in a smoke-stenched hovel by the canal. Both filled her with a different sort of shame.

As they returned to her guest chamber, the day caught up with her. Exhaustion settled into her bones. She had slipped out of the Hunter's grasp and execution. She and Lu would be all right. They would live in a manor with servants and hot water.

For Lu, Ryn would marry the arrogant prince. She would warm his bed, cater to his needs, listen to him whine about the troubles of princely life. For Lu, Ryn would endure. That she had a means to protect Lu for the rest of their lives was a comfort she hadn't felt in…ever.

Back in the keep, their retinue shrank to their two personal guards.

"Is there anything else I should know?" Zain asked.

Ryn would have to tell him about her debt to Nobel, but…later. "No, I think we've both had enough surprises for one day. I just need some sleep."

They paused outside her chamber door. Zain glanced down the corridor, unimpressed.

Ryn slid her arm from his, and the two of them hesitated outside her chamber door. She bit her lip. This felt like the part that she should say something. Do something.

Biting back her pride, she said, "Thank you for sending those guards."

The gratitude left her feeling weak in the knees. She wasn't used to thanking people. She wasn't used to anyone doing anything for her without expecting something in response.

"A successful marriage is one of understanding and compromise," Zain said, though the words came out rehearsed. "As a dutiful husband, I am willing to indulge in the occasional demand. And, once wed, your sister will be my sister."

"Dinner was also delicious, and the walk was lovely," she added. "The company was…commendable."

He chuckled, the sound velvet and decadent and husky from the cold. "Commendable?"

She didn't replace the word. Despite all she had heard about Prince Zain, he was commendable. Not a gentleman, not a chivalrous warrior, but…adequate for a prince. Not to mention she had no other males to compare him to. She had never courted anyone or been the subject of romantic affection. She wasn't sure how to respond to affection.

"I agree on all accounts, Miss Ryn." He pressed a kiss to the back of her hand. His lips were dry and soft. The sensation sent a wave of spider-walking gooseflesh over her skin. Her heart skipped a few beats. She had been kissed, but not on the hand. Not by a prince. Holding her hand between them, his fingers explored the calluses on her own. "You know, Miss Ryn, you owe me a bag of coins."

The fluttering in her stomach made it easy to smile. "You know, my prince, they're *our* coins."

Chuckling, he opened her door. Ryn took the first step over the threshold but stopped short. Sprawled over the rug was a shriveled, lifeless corpse, its limbs bent and gnarled, mouth wretched in silent scream.

16

FIRST SNOW

Ryn

The blood drained from her face, the floor wobbled, and she stumbled backward as Neville rushed into the sitting room. Ryn stumbled into Zain's chest and clutched onto his tailcoat as if the fabric could somehow save her, preventing the horror from ingraining into her mind, from freezing her bones solid. It didn't.

She had seen the shriveled bodies at the hand of her own enchanting. But the body before her… As the blood loss became irrevocable, as death settled over a body, the limbs stiffened. This female, a servant by her plain gray dress and apron, had been attacked by a vampire and drained, arms and legs frozen in a state of defense. Her fingernails were broken, and her left wrist bent in the wrong direction—broken.

She had fought back. Just like the dead Hunter in the woods.

Stones sank to the bottom of Ryn's stomach. A vampire had been in her chambers. Her chambers within Nightshade Keep, the home of the Hunters. The keep was supposed to be an impregnable fortress.

"Send for the Hunters," Zain commanded.

Footsteps thundered down the corridor.

Strong hands settled on her shoulders and pulled her closer. Enough to smell the spearmint on his skin. Clean and sharp. Ryn inhaled it, letting it ease her senses, a balm like the mint tea her mother used to drink. Ryn hadn't cared for the taste, but the smell brought her a strange sense of comfort.

"Send word to my father," Zain said, his tone softer than was a moment before. His warm breath hit her ear.

Another set of footsteps raced down the corridor.

"Across the hall," came the sober voice of Neville.

Zain draped his arm around Ryn's shoulders and tucked her into his side, into his steadiness, and ushered her into the parlor across the hall.

Unlike her chambers, it wasn't prepared for guests. The candles were unlit, the drapes drawn, and it smelled of stale coffee and dust. Ryn quickly scanned the shadowed corners for lurking figures. She found no pale faces or bloodied fangs, only darkness. Irene lit the lanterns, spilling flickering light across the blue rugs and heavy drapes.

"That makes two bodies," Zain said, the words tight. His grip tightened.

Two bodies connected to Ryn.

Zain looked more annoyed than worried, despite bodies being left at opposite ends of his home. How dare these vampires interrupt his evening.

"You think this is my doing?" Ryn whispered. She didn't have to speak loudly with him standing so close.

His brows rose. "No. You have been under constant watch since the Hunters found you in the forest, and you have been with me all evening. Not to mention the Hunters declared you are not a vampire. However, with this being the second body thrown into your path, it will raise questions."

That he didn't think she was responsible shoved an unknown burden from her chest. Then his words sank in. "Thrown into my path?"

"The first body was likely a coincidence, however this body was left in the very chambers you were to occupy. In the sitting room. On display." Zain's voice lowered to a dangerous whisper, and he added, "Whoever left that poor sop dead, they chose that location."

"But why?" The question tumbled from her lips as a plea. "What did I do?"

His arm tightened on her shoulders. His voice purred, "That is the question, isn't it?"

"It could be you pissed off the vampire in the Red Forest," Neville nodded to Ryn, "and he wants revenge."

Ryn didn't believe it. Zain and Neville thought she was innocent. They were on her side. Her instinct was to doubt them, to assume it was a trick, but…they had no reason to.

"Vampires have a history of holding grudges," Irene said.

"They're mad I took the blame for their kill?" Her fury turned a shade hotter.

"Vampires aren't known for their compassion or understanding," Neville added with a shrug. "More likely, you interrupted."

Dozens of heavy boots thundered down the corridor. Zain tucked Ryn even closer into his side, as leather armor and plum capes filed into the guest room with the force of a windstorm. Hunters surrounded the body so Ryn could only see slices between their legs and arms.

A dreadfully familiar figure filled the parlor doorway, glowering down at Ryn with more hate than she thought possible. Zain's arm tightened on her shoulders, and she shrank into his chest as he turned his body to be between her and the king.

"Father," Zain said, the greeting as pleasant as an afternoon breeze. "It would appear that someone is unhappy with our newest houseguest."

"Indeed." The king's voice rolled like thunder. He seemed so much larger than he had that morning in the throne room. "A vampire has killed a servant in my home. I will be posting Hunters in my halls tonight, until this brood is found and dealt with." His gaze settled on Ryn. "Clearly, you won't be staying in those rooms tonight, not while my Hunters investigate. Without other rooms prepared, and seeing that this body was found in your chambers, you will spend the night in the dungeon. I—"

"She will not," Zain said at once, his command battling the king's.

The air thickened, and despite Zain's calm exterior, his hand tightened painfully on her shoulder.

"No other chambers are prepared for a guest," the king argued.

"She will stay in my chambers," Zain said.

"That. Is. Indecent," said his father, each word a threat.

"So is the body currently on display across the hall," Zain countered. "I would like to keep those I cherish closer rather than farther, Father."

Ryn's skin prickled under his arm. *Cherish.* He said the words without hesitation, with genuine heart. He was a remarkable liar.

"You aren't married yet, Zain." The king's glare made Ryn's knees weak, even when aimed at Zain. "And the dungeons are highly guarded. It will be safe."

"I'm not proposing we share a bed," Zain snapped. "She will stay in the adjoining room. Nothing will happen while Neville and Irene stand guard. I refuse to allow her to be thrown back in the dungeon."

The king growled, his lips curling and his eyes blazing. Ryn's muscles clenched in fear. She had never heard a male make such a sound, like a rabid wolf baring its teeth. This was the king who had led the first Hunters into the Red Forest and decimated the vampire threat. This was the king who had painted the Red Forest in vampire blood. His gaze made her want to find somewhere to hide, and she shrank inward without realizing. Zain's arm on her shoulders remained steady; he nudged her back as if to warn her against backing down.

"We both know this is foolish," the king hissed. His gaze moved to Ryn.

The queen had been intimidating, but the king was death incarnate.

Ancient power pulsed from his being. It filled the parlor as it had the throne room, as if he could squish her with a thought, as if she were a bug, inconsequential to his existence. He glowered down his nose at Ryn like he would rather her be thrown into the cold than sleep in the same room as his son, but before he could argue further against it, the Hunters requested his attention in the other room.

King Victor huffed and turned his glower onto Zain. "Fine. Mind yourselves. Your mother will not be happy about it."

"Oh, I'm sure there will be a lecture waiting for us both," Zain muttered as the king joined the Hunters. "We should leave before he changes his mind or Mother appears."

Zain nudged Ryn between the shoulder blades. She hadn't realized how stiff she'd been standing. Another nudge, and she let him escort her out of the parlor, past the Hunters, and down the corridor. Neville and Irene marched close. Irene held the hilt of her blade with white knuckles.

Two bodies.

Two *conveniently placed* bodies. Thrown into her path. Either by vampires or by fate. Had she pissed off the vampire in the forest? That didn't explain how a vampire got into Nightshade Keep, let alone into the king's home, without being detected by the Hunters.

The royal wing was grand. A golden runner spanned the length of the corridor. Portraits depicted dead kings and queens, knights, nobles, and scholars. The doors were all twice as tall as she was, the wood highly polished and carved with intricate designs, the hardware dark scrolling brass. With the late hour, everything was quiet and dark. Even the shadows seemed too quiet.

Zain guided her into his sitting room. The walls were softened with dark green tapestries threaded with golden designs, rugs of varying styles spotted the floor, and one side held floor-to-ceiling bookshelves filled with thick tomes, delicate baubles, and a few busts. A library ladder had been pushed to the far end, near a cozy reading nook of dark leather chairs. At the far end, heavy emerald drapes were drawn over tall windows.

Zain slid his arm from her shoulders and started across the room, undoing the buttons of his tailcoat. He heaved a sigh. "Make yourself comfortable."

Ryn tiptoed into the room. Like the rest of the manor, it felt far too opulent for her presence, but Zain's chambers felt more…lived in. Homey. Her eyes snagged on the bookshelves.

She'd never seen so many books in someone's personal possession. Just one bookcase would cost more gold than she'd ever had. There weren't bookstores on her side of town. Few shops sold them. Books were a commodity most couldn't afford.

"Do you like to read?" Zain drawled, his words exhausted. He stood on the other side of the sitting room. His unbuttoned collar revealed the pale skin of his collarbone.

"I've not had a lot of opportunities," she said, feeling embarrassed. "I *can* read, if that is what you're asking."

"It was not," Zain said, the words as masked as his princely expression. "The keep has a grand library, as you saw. It is open to you." He tossed his tailcoat over one of the chairs. "Your chambers are through here."

He stepped to a set of double doors. An identical set of doors stood on the opposite side of the room. Like traditional homes, the sitting room joined two bedrooms. One on either side. It was designed for a husband and wife, since arranged marriages didn't always come with the desire to share space.

Zain opened the doors to Ryn's chambers. Ryn tiptoed closer with Irene at her heels. The bedroom was dark and musty. Most of the furniture was covered in sheets. To Ryn's surprise, Kari and three other servants hurriedly prepared it, dusting, yanking sheets off the necessary furniture, and straightening the bedclothes. Kari hastily lit candles, shedding light over the room's shrouded things.

"My lady," Kari said breathlessly, with a quick bow of her head. Dust clung to her sleeves. "These rooms will be fit for a lady in no time." To Zain, she bowed deeper. "Your Highness."

Within the candlelight, Ryn could tell the walls were dark blue. The floor was the same warm wood as the sitting room. The candlelight sparked on the ceiling, bits of metal—no, stars. Golden stars dotted the deep blue ceiling.

It looked like a bedroom from a dream.

Kari pulled the sheet from a lovely writing desk, and the others uncovered a handsome armoire with a curved top and little spires on either end. Empty bookcases lined the far corner, surrounding the dormer window. She could imagine it overflowing with books, and Lu sitting in the dormer with a book propped on her legs.

Maybe, by dawn, Lu would be here. They could laugh about the whole ordeal together.

"You have an extra bedroom attached to your sitting room?" Ryn lifted a brow. "And you don't use it for anything?"

"What use would I have for a second bedroom? I have a perfectly good bedroom of my own." Zain eyed the handsome armoire, expression tired and bored. "This room belonged to my grandmother, my father's mother. No one has used this room since she passed."

Zain tucked his hands into his trouser pockets and gazed up at the ceiling. In the dark, with his throat exposed, without the heavy tailcoat, he looked like he belonged on the street, not in the king's manor. The candlelight gave his handsome features a darkened, worldly edge. He could have been one of Nobel's suave business partners, or a bartender who knew too much about everyone, or a quick-thinking thief.

THE BLOOD ENCHANTRESS

Ryn had heard the stories. Everyone had. During the vampire war, the Abrani clan attacked the old castle that once stood on the other side of the Black Canal. Now, it was little more than ruins. Prince Victor Casiano and his Hunters stormed the vampire's keep, slaughtering them in a single night, and claimed the fortress as their own. He renamed it after the poisonous flower that bloomed from the earth after vampire blood was spilled.

It should have felt strange being in what had once been home to a vampire clan. It didn't. It felt stranger to be in Zain's dead grandmother's bedroom.

"Do you remember her?" Ryn asked. "Your grandmother, I mean."

Zain hesitated. He looked like he didn't know if he wanted to divulge the information. "Vaguely. I was young when she passed. According to my father, she wasn't the same after the war."

"What happened?"

"Her husband, daughter, son-in-law, and her first grandchild were killed in the vampire's attack on the castle," Zain said plainly. "She never overcame the grief."

Ryn wished she could take back the question.

"I inherited these rooms once I outgrew the nursery," Zain continued as if nothing dire had been discussed. He glanced about the bland space. His gaze fell onto the bed as Kari dressed it in cream and gold linens. It was twice as big as Ryn's bed back home. "My bedroom is on the other side of the sitting room. Traditionally, the bride or groom only moves into their royal suite after the wedding."

Ryn hummed as she took in the space. The bedroom itself was three times the size of her hovel, and the sitting room was twice the size of the bedroom. Did they expect her to use all this space? For what?

She felt the need to say something nice, but she also felt the need to jump out of the window and run like hell away from all of this. It was too good to be true. No one ever did anything without wanting something in return, and though Zain had laid this bargain before her, she couldn't help but feel like she was missing something. Some vital clue to shed light on this strange twist of events.

One of the servants whisked open the curtains on the far window. Muted moonlight draped inside as dust motes floated to the floor. The windows creaked open, and the servant swept dust outside. Cold air rushed inside, eliciting a chill over Ryn's bones. Kari sparked a fire in the hearth.

"What do you think?" Zain asked.

"I thought I'd be dead by sunset," Ryn mused, smirk pulling at her tired lips. As if sensing her thoughts, a few snowflakes tumbled past the window.

"First snow," muttered the servant with a scowl. "That explains it."

The first snow brought all manner of evil and bad luck, according to folklore. Vampires lurked in the dark and relished the cold of winter. Ryn had always heard vampires celebrated the first snow like the fae of old celebrated the first bloom of spring.

"First snow before the last leaf of autumn falls," Neville added, staring at the snowfall with an unreadable expression. "That is an omen of a long winter."

"That is just a wives' tale," Irene spat, crossing her arms. "It'll melt by sunrise."

Neville cocked a brow at Irene, like he hadn't anticipated someone talking back to him, but underneath it, he wore surprise.

Footsteps marched into the sitting room. Zain retreated a step to see their guests, and Ryn followed—royal guards.

Ryn's heart skipped a beat, but then she realized these guards were those sent to find Lu. A different kind of dread threaded under her skin, like ice and magma all at once.

"Prince Zain," one of them said in greeting.

"Report."

The guards bowed, then the guard in front said, "We went to the home. It was empty. There was no one inside." The guard met Ryn's eye as he added, "No dead either."

"What?" Ryn's voice came out a breath.

"We asked the neighbors, but the woman in the…home below reported nothing. She hadn't seen the female in question in days."

Of course, the old bat would say that. No one in the slums trusted the guards. The guards upheld the law most people in low town broke to survive; they were the enemy. Most days, Ryn would thank the old woman for lying to the guard, but right now, she wanted to claw the hag's eyes out and demand Lu's whereabouts.

Though, if Lu were dead, her body would have been there. It gave Ryn a cold hope.

"Thank you," Zain said pointedly, glancing at Ryn with a cool indifference, as if the report meant nothing to him.

It irked her, then she remembered his warning. Everything would be reported to the queen. Every word, every emotion. Ryn needed to be as calm and cold.

"Yes, thank you," Ryn echoed.

"You are dismissed." Zain nodded to the guards.

With a quick parting bow, the guards left.

Zain straightened his shirt and started toward his room. "Well, I'm off to bed, love. If you need anything, you have your guard and your maid. There are more guards posted in the corridor." Zain turned before reaching his bedroom door. He ran his eyes along her frame. "Both Neville and Irene are trained Hunters, and no vampire will get to you without going through them first. Sleep well."

With that, Zain and Neville went into his room. Only after his bedroom doors shut did Irene step up to her side.

"You look exhausted." Irene nodded to the bedroom. "And His Highness is correct. To bed with you."

Ryn returned to the bedroom with burning anxiety churning in her chest. Irene closed the door behind her, muttering something too low for Ryn to hear. Not that it mattered. Ryn couldn't hear anything over her own thoughts—where was Lu? Was she okay? Was she dead? Did she try to come find Ryn and die in an alley?

Kari released a breath of relief. "I always feel like I'm walking on broken glass around him. I can't believe you handled him so well, my lady."

Ryn blinked. She'd forgotten about Kari.

"I have my talents." Ryn faked a yawn.

"High time to rest, my lady. You have certainly earned it." Kari motioned for Ryn to turn, and the odious task of undressing began. Kari then helped Ryn into a long-sleeved ivory gown that looked and smelled like it had been in one of the dressers since Zain's grandmother had last worn it.

The bathing room was half the size of the bedroom, a masterpiece of gold and blue. Stars dotted the ceiling just like in the bedroom, only a different constellation. She didn't have the patience for a full bath, so she settled for washing her face in cool water. While she washed, servants brought in the few pieces of clothing that had been brought to the other room for her and stashed them in the many drawers.

"There are more Hunters in the corridor," one female whispered. "Three more than this morning."

"I wish they would stand guard by my room," said another. "Two dead by vampires, one in the keep. I don't think I'll be able to sleep tonight."

Ryn wasn't overly fond of gossip, however she had heard plenty of interesting and useful information from blabbermouths—so she listened.

"Do you know who it was? Who is dead?"

"Her name was Starla, I think. She hadn't worked here for two weeks."

"The extra Hunters are to make sure none of those monsters come lurking," whispered Kari. "Starla was bringing fresh linens up to Miss Sabryn's room."

"You think it was looking for her?"

"Why else would it risk coming into the Keep? I heard the Hunters talking," Kari said so lowly that Ryn barely heard her. "No one was in the corridor when the attack happened, and the guard who was supposed to be there is nowhere to be found."

The other two gasped.

"Missing? What do you mean missing?"

"Meaning the poor sop is likely dead somewhere," said the first girl, her tone a shade fearful. "Who's next? What if it takes one of us because we're between it and its prey?"

"Get on with it," Irene spat. "We haven't got all night."

The servants scurried to finish preparing the room. None of them uttered another word.

Ryn didn't like being referred to as prey. She was no one's prey. But what if they were right? Was the vampire trying to get to her?

Ryn sighed into the towel. If a vampire wanted her dead, she was safer in the keep than outside it.

She drifted back into the bedroom full of a dead queen's clothing and collapsed into the massive bed. The bed smelled like the nightgown, like dust and death.

Irene posted herself inside the bedroom door. Kair tiptoed around the room, extinguishing candles, as only after darkness swept over the bed did Ryn wonder if Zain's grandmother had died in this room, in this bed.

It didn't *feel* haunted.

The bed was infinitely better than her lumpy mattress, tucked into the corner of the tiny bedroom she and Lu shared.

Her heart squeezed. She couldn't sleep when she thought of Lu, alone and afraid and sick. Despite the guards' report, she doubted every word. Lu could have hidden with the old woman downstairs, or she might have gone out. In the middle of the night. In the snow. With a fever.

Soon, Irene's relief came, and the new guard posted herself in the sitting room, not the bedroom. Ryn slid from the bed. She was used to tiptoeing around the sleeping and unaware, and tonight was no different. Carefully, she sorted through the dresser until she found her boots and a heavy jacket. They hadn't saved her father's tailcoat, it seemed.

THE BLOOD ENCHANTRESS

Ryn pulled on a pair of gloves with old-fashioned metal clasps at the wrists. They likely belonged to the dead queen.

She didn't need them; Ryn did.

To find her sister, she would tempt ghosts. She didn't need the prince's help, or his guards. She would find Lu on her own.

17

AN EMPTY HOVEL

Ryn

Ryn wouldn't be able to leave her chambers by the main doors. Not with the Hunters posted outside, and not with her personal guard standing at her bedroom door. She likely wouldn't be able to get anywhere from within the royal wing.

Her bedroom overlooked the arched roof of a corridor lined with steeples and flying buttresses with complicated stonework. The snow steadily fell, blurring the air in gray-tinged darkness. It would be difficult for the guards to see anyone.

She eased the window open enough to slip through and climbed onto the stone ledge underneath. She climbed down the stone and onto the arched roof, hanging onto the steeples as she made her way across. The icy cold seeped through her gloves and cloak, and the nightdress was useless. She might as well be scaling Nightshade Keep naked.

By the time she made it to a window on the floor below, her fingers were frozen and the skin on her legs had gone numb. It took several moments to unlock the window from the outside with one of her hairpins, but Ryn finally slipped into a dark parlor.

Sneaking through Nightshade Keep had never been on Ryn's bucket list. Between the royal guards and Hunters, few shadows remained unwatched for very long. Maybe it was because she had already escaped death once that day, or the unknown fate of her sister; whatever the reason, Ryn felt a rush of recklessness urging her forward.

She tiptoed down a narrow corridor that ended in an L-shape. Pausing at the corner, she listened for footsteps, rustling of clothing, or breathing—none of which she heard. She eased around the corner, nimble as a ghost, and walked right into Neville's chest.

A gasp fell from her lips, and she stumbled backward. Neville remained unfazed, as if he had been waiting for her. His arms were crossed, his lips tilted downward, yet his eyes gleamed like he had caught her in the act. He blocked her path forward, as immobile and impassive as the stone walls.

"It's not what it looks like," Ryn whispered.

Neville took a calculated step closer. Ryn held her ground and his stare. She had stood her ground with much nastier men, beefier too.

"You mean you're not trying to sneak out of the keep?" Neville's brows rose. "Not trying to contact your vampire brood?"

"The first part of that is true, the second is bullshit." Ryn straightened her shoulders. "I don't believe what the guards reported about my sister. She's out there somewhere, and I can't sleep without knowing what happened to her. I'm going to find her myself."

"You think yourself more capable than the guard?"

"In this particular case, yes."

Neville studied her, his gaze unyielding. Footsteps sounded behind him— the patrolling guards. Ryn paled. If they caught her here, there would be no talking her way out of it. As the light of their torch brightened, Neville yanked Ryn down the passage and into a shadow nook, out of sight of the guards. Neville pressed her into the shadow as the guards came closer. The barrels made it a tight fit for the two of them.

The guards came closer, their torchlight glowing brighter with each footfall. Ryn's heart hammered in her ears; she knew what it would look like if the guards looked into the nook—Zain's betrothed having a tryst with his guard. Which was better than the truth.

The guards and their torchlight passed—and continued down the corridor. Ryn's panic subsided only slightly; Neville still pressed her against the wall. Only after he stepped back into the corridor did she breathe.

"This way," he whispered, so low she barely heard him.

He led her down the corridor, avoiding the guards like a trained thief, and to a door hidden behind a dreary tapestry. The wood was heavy but plain.

"This leads to the servants' passages," Neville whispered. "Only guards and a few servants know about it, when we need to come and go without being seen."

Ryn looked him over. "Why show me?"

"You want to get out without being seen?" He nodded to the door. "Use this one."

Shaking her head, she asked, "No, why are you helping me?"

Neville studied her, thoughts churning behind his masked Hunter expression. He took a step closer, one full of the menace of a threatened guard. "I want to trust you, Sabryn. I want to trust you like my prince does, and I am willing to give you this chance to prove yourself worthy of that trust."

Trap. Every fiber of her being screamed, *trap.* But a small, childish part of her wanted to believe he meant what he said. Hunters were supposed to be good. "What if I don't come back?"

Neville smiled. "You told the Royal Guard where you live. We will find you."

Shit. She had told them exactly where her hovel was and how to get inside. "Even if it meant I was out of your hair?"

"You think Zain would let it slide? No." Neville shook his head. "He announced your betrothal to the court. The noble houses know your name. There is no hiding in the slums. Someone will come looking for you, if only to just get you out of the way."

Ryn scowled. "Out of the way of what?"

"Out of the way of the prince," Neville whispered. "There is power in marrying a prince. Beyond money and a title, there is power."

And people killed for power.

Ryn rubbed her face. This was all too much for what little sleep she'd had.

"Consider this your chance to show us who you really are," Neville whispered, the words a dare and a threat. He nodded toward the unguarded servants' door.

Ryn hated having to prove her worth. She knew her worth, and it wasn't very much. Not that she wanted Neville to figure it out.

She tiptoed toward the door. Neville didn't stop her. She let herself into the shadow-filled passage with Neville at her heels. The passage ended at an identical door in the stables, behind the tack room. This time of night, the stables were quiet. Horses with gleaming coats and braided hair filled each stall.

Neville helped her ready a mare, then held his hand out to help her mount.

"You couldn't have grabbed pants?" He eyed the exposed flesh of her legs, barely hidden under the woolen cloak.

She blushed. Her gloved hands tightened on the reins. "I was in a hurry."

"The horses are well-bred and well-trained," Neville said, stroking the horse's neck. "This girl will find her way back to the keep if you let her loose."

"Do you want me to return or never come back?" Ryn cocked a brow. "It's hard to tell."

Neville met her gaze. His own was unreadable. "I don't know. I don't know what your intentions are, and I don't want my prince to be in danger. If you become a threat to him, I will end you."

"So…you want me to leave? That's why you're helping me sneak out?"

"No, I'm helping because you would have been caught at the gate, and that would have been a headache for everyone. I know you and Zain don't love each other. This world isn't for you, but I won't bar you from it. You want to play with the royals, Ryn? Prove you can handle it. You want to marry him? Prove you are worthy."

Neville stepped aside and held his hands behind his back, his expression stony, his stance defensive. A guard. Ryn couldn't decide his game or intentions. Not that it mattered. If Ryn had to choose between Lu and being a princess, Lu would win a thousand times over.

THE BLOOD ENCHANTRESS

She guided the horse out of the stables and onto the street. After Ryn found Lu, she would worry about Neville and Zain.

⚜⚜⚜

The ride to her hovel seemed too long and dark. By the time her hovel came into view, pearly snow gathered on roadways, windowsills, and rooftops. It muted all but her own breath and the clomping of her horse's hooves on the cobblestones and gave the night a strange, unearthly stillness.

Vampire holiday indeed. Paranoia trickled down her spine, reminding her of all her mother's stories of dark magic and lurking monsters. She kept her eyes on the alleys, where the shadows gathered deep. Normally, she found refuge in the alleys and shadows, but not tonight. Not when dark magic ran amuck.

The chill needled deep through her skin and into her bones. Why had she not grabbed a shirt or trousers? Her nightdress absorbed the cold, pressing it against her skin. Her wool cloak might as well have been silk for all the defense it offered. Snow dusted her shoulders. Flakes pecked her face.

She could enchant her blood to be warm, but she had only ever done it with small areas. She couldn't heat her entire body, so she settled for her fingers; they seemed colder than the rest of her. She focused, and glorious heat burst through her fingers.

It only reminded her how cold the rest of her was.

Ryn climbed up the side of the hovel, like she had done thousands of times. She brushed the snow from the window ledge and slid into the dark, cold inside. She took a deep breath of the familiar dust, canal musk, and smoke. Home.

Like the guards had reported, Lu wasn't there. The bed was empty. The cabinets had been gone through and the perishables were gone, but everything else was exactly as it had been. No one had moved in while she'd been gone.

A creak sounded—someone pushing the window further open.

Ryn grabbed the handle of an iron skillet as she turned. A darkly clad figure slid into the darkness of the main room, eyes glittering between a woolen cap and thick scarf. For a moment, Ryn was back in the Red Forest, staring into the eyes of a thirsty vampire. Liquid fear coursed through her veins, cold and icy and heart-stopping.

"Nobel said you'd come back eventually," came a familiar, raspy voice.

"Gil," she whispered. He worked for Nobel. "Where is Lu?"

"She's fine." He eyed her white-knuckles grip on the skillet. "There were guards here earlier, you know. Looking for her."

Fine. Lu was fine.

Alive.

Relief washed over her bones like warm water. Tension released from her shoulders, and she fought the urge to collapse.

Gil chuckled. "Nobel sent me to fetch you a few nights ago. Had a job lined up. But you weren't here. That poor sister of yours was shivering and feverish, all by herself."

Guilt tore through Ryn's resolve like a knife, wrenching through her gut and tying it in knots.

He took another step closer, leaning in as he said, "I asked Lu where you were, and she hadn't seen you in two days. You went into the Red Forest and never came back. I was feeling a pinch of remorse, you know, because Lu's one of the sweet ones, and I took her to see Nobel."

Her guilt twisted sideways. "And?"

"She's with Nobel."

Ryn knew what those words meant, but in that moment, all she could think about was Lu's health. "And is she okay? Has the fever broke?"

"Yeah. Nobel saw to that. She's being taken care of. Well-fed and warm. That sort of thing." Gil waved his hand dismissively.

Ryn couldn't stop the relief from weakening her knees. She sank to the dirty floor. Lu was okay. Lu was alive. The fever had broken. Fed and warm.

Slowly, Gil's warning settled. Nobel had taken Lu as collateral. Ryn was already in his debt, and he would keep her that way. He would use this moment of his compassion whenever he wanted something.

"He wants to see you," Gil said dryly. "Someone's been watching your place, waiting for you to come back. He knew you would."

"Of course, I would." Ryn straightened. Now she really wished she had worn something more substantial and less intimate. As if sensing that thought, Gil's gaze raked over the white material visible between the front seams of her cloak. She pulled the cloak tighter. "But I have to be back in the keep before dawn."

Unless someone had already discovered her bed empty. Unless Neville had already alerted the guard of her departure. In that case, being with Nobel was far safer than being in her empty hovel.

Gil nodded toward the window he'd left open. The winter chill slithered in and spat snow on the floor. "Come on. Nobel probably already knows you're back. Can't keep him waiting."

Ryn followed Gil into the snowy night. Snow piled into the hoofprints leading up to the hovel, and dotted the horse's mane and saddle. Ryn brushed off the snow and climbed into the saddle. Gil took the reins and guided the horse south. The snow quickly covered her shoulders and hood, seeping through the material.

Nobel had several meeting places around the city, and Gil took her to one not far from her hovel, in the back of a tavern that never closed. This time of night, the rowdy crowd paid little attention to Ryn and Gil as they skirted the edge of the room to the stairs tucked behind the bar. The barkeep nodded to Gil, but said nothing as he and Ryn started up.

In the upstairs room, Nobel sat at a handsome desk. Two mercenaries stood behind him, armed and ready to kill. Nobel himself wore dark trousers, shined boots, a dove gray tailcoat with ebony buttons, and a fur-lined overcoat. It was an odd outfit; he looked ready to attend a ball, not deal with thugs and lowlifes in a dirty tavern. He was handsome, charismatic, and brilliant; the combination of those traits had allowed him to climb the slum's social ladder to the mastermind he was, and it was why no one had been able to take him down. He was five steps ahead of all his competition.

Ryn wasn't sure how old he was. He had strong fae blood, and he proudly wore gold in each ear, studs all the way up to the points. He had soft tawny skin, sandy hair swept away from his face, and bright brown eyes streaked with green. At the sight of her, his face broke into a wholesome smile. It even met his eyes, but she knew better.

Once, Nobel's grin had sent butterflies into her toes.

"Look who decided to come home." Nobel stood and met her in front of his desk. He embraced her, then cupped her cheek with a frigid hand. This close, his cheeks and nose were pink from the cold. He took in the chemise and cloak. "Interesting choice of clothing in this weather. Especially during the first snow."

"It was a rushed decision," Ryn explained.

Nobel cocked a brow, and Ryn told him about the rabbit, the bodies, and Zain's proposition. Nobel took the whole thing in with a smile. When she finished, he laughed. It was a warm sound that filled the entire room, and likely the one below, yet it put her one edge.

"You, my little dove, are engaged to Prince Zain?" Nobel's brown eyes glittered like wet topaz. He leaned forward and purred, "I hear he's rough in the bedroom. Is that true?"

"I—I wouldn't know. We've not been engaged a day." Heat burst through her cheeks and down her neck. "My sister?" Ryn whispered to Nobel.

Some of his cockiness retreated. "Your sister is in good health. I've taken care of her. I took her out of that rathole of yours. It's no place for a nice female like her to live alone. Without you there, I worried some scoundrel would come along and make himself at home."

"Where is she?"

"Safe," Nobel said, flashing her a small smile. "At one of my private residences."

One of, meaning he wouldn't tell her which one.

Panic prickled along Ryn's spine. Swallowing her pride, she forced herself to meet his eye, and said, "Thank you. I was terrified something would happen to her while I was locked in a dungeon, and what I'd find if I made it out, and I worried…" That Lu would die alone, cold, and afraid. "Thank you, Nobel. What do you require of me in return?"

Noble's smile stretched. "I do have one task that's been sitting for a while. No one qualified has been able…or within my range. But here you are. Like…fate." He stepped around his desk and withdrew a black leather folio. Within that folio, he withdrew a folded piece of parchment. One of his many contracts. Nobel handed the parchment to her.

The handwriting was scrawled and small, not Nobel's or any of his scribes that she knew, but she was able to make out enough.

Her heart sank.

Noble chuckled. "And there goes what little color you had in your face. Don't faint on my floor, little dove."

Gil peered over Ryn's shoulder at the parchment. "Are you shitting me?"

Noble straightened his tailcoat. "No. Ryn, this is your new task, and I will consider your debt paid in full. I might even throw in a favor or two."

Paid in full?

Impossible.

Ryn fought to regain her composure. To save Lu and herself from Nobel, all she had to do was assassinate King Victor Casiano.

18

WARM CIDER, COLD HANDS

Ryn

Frozen silence drenched the ride away from Nobel's tavern. Ryn spent the cold, snowy ride brooding on the impossibility of her task.

Assassinating the king.

A fool's errand. How long had Nobel had the contract? If he hadn't been able to find a worthy assassin, that meant none of them were stupid enough to take it. Seasoned assassins declined it. They knew the risks. Yet Nobel expected her to complete it.

But Nobel was right. She had a unique opportunity that no assassin before her had—she had a bed in the keep, inside the royal wing, a few doors down from where King Victor slept. Though she doubted the task would be any more doable from the royal wing than outside the keep.

The snow chilled her to the bone. Her fingers were icy and numb. A shiver shook up and down her spine.

She didn't go back to her hovel. There wasn't anything left there.

The darkness seethed around her, and Ryn felt it watching.

She knew darkness couldn't watch or think, but the sensation tickled along her awareness as if she stood in front of a crowd. It felt like someone lurked unseen and without form, as if the darkness itself was sentient. From the bodies and what the hunters said, there were vampires lurking in Calcurta's darkest corners. On tonight, their holiday, how many had watched her?

The horse kept a steady pace toward Nightshade Keep. Too many things crowded her mind, like Lu being in Nobel's care, her own engagement to an unpleasant prince, and planning to assassinate the king. All the while, the cold sank deeper into her bones. Impossibility deep, until she doubted she would ever feel warm again, until the fires of hell sounded like a dream.

When at last the keep came into view, she felt a few heartbeats from freezing to death. A guard stood by the servants' entrance, and panic slithered along her frozen insides. However, when the guard met her gaze, he simply nodded and motioned her inside.

"Hunter Neville said you were out," the guard said. "He asked me to watch for you."

"Thank you." The words tumbled from Ryn's shivering lips.

The stables were dark, the horses resting. A male servant jumped from where he'd been leaning against the empty stall.

"Neville asked me to wait for your return," the servant said quickly. He motioned for the reins. "I will handle the horse from here, my lady. You need your rest."

"Thank you," Ryn said. Uneasiness sharpened, twisting her gut into knots. Was Neville being kind, or was he playing a game of his own?

Morning came with a vicious chill. It seethed through the drafts in the manor, through the leaded windows, through the corridors. It whistled like an army of ghosts, a remnant of the night of first snow. Ryn stirred when Kari added a log to the fire, the log clunking against the others and sending embers flying. Irene stood at the bedside, scowling down at Ryn.

Sunlight filtered around the heavy drapes and between the middle seam, giving the room an ethereal glow. The ambient light glittered against the golden stars set about the ceiling.

"Prince Zain requests your presence for breakfast, my lady."

Ryn mumbled and rolled onto her side. Her body craved rest. It felt like she had barely slept at all. The bed was so warm, and the air was so cold. Just as her thoughts began to sink back into the comfort of sleep, the blankets were yanked off. Ryn gasped and pulled her limbs inward.

"Your bath is warm and ready!" Kari's cheery voice trilled.

Ryn crawled out of bed, limbs sluggish and still feeling the biting cold from the night before, and set her bare feet on the rug. She didn't know what time she'd crawled back into bed, only that it had been late. Too late.

The bath steamed. Ryn sank into the warm water and fought to stay awake. Kari talked all the while about things that needed done, things that needed tossed, and things that needed ordered. Ryn half listened. In truth, the chatter was the only thing keeping her awake.

"I'm sorry you didn't sleep well," Kari said absently as she tallied the contents of the bathing room cabinets.

"It was the new bed," Ryn lied. The bed was heavenly. It was the first decent bed she had ever slept in, and what little sleep she had gotten was fantastic. Far better than she generally did. Back home, every groan and squeak woke her. Sounds in the night could vary between a mouse, a thief, or the stacked homes about to collapse.

"I will have the staff tidy up the space while you are out today," Kari said. "Is there anything you would like to request? A favorite perfume? Favorite sweet? Favorite wine?"

"Out? Where am I going?"

Kari grinned as she arranged glass bottles of different colored salts in the tallest cabinet. "Her Majesty wants to start planning your wedding."

Ryn blinked. Oh, right. She was getting married, and the queen hated her. Another day of icy glares and pointedly vague questions meant to upset her or find fault. She hadn't gotten enough sleep for that.

Kari scurried from the bathing room, leaving Ryn alone. She took a deep breath, filling her entire chest with the humid, bath-salt hinted air.

Assassinate the king.

The slums were supposed to be separate from the problems and tedious peddling of the nobles and their political gambles.

If she killed the king, then the crown prince would claim the throne. A thought struck—had Esben sent out the contract? He wouldn't be the first royal to knock off an immediate family member for personal gain. Ryn hadn't met Esben, but rumor painted him as a good male.

The opposite of his younger brother. Her betrothed.

Had Zain sent out the contract? He pulled a criminal from the execution line as his bride, so it wasn't a far jump to think he would have his father killed.

But what did he have to gain? Was there a contract on Esben too? Did Zain seek the throne?

Ryn climbed out of the bath, dried herself, and pulled her nightgown back on. The smoky stench of her hovel clung to the threads, as did the heady cologne of Nobel's office. She didn't mind walking around in it, but she doubted the royals would tolerate *such improper behavior*. The queen's tone ferreted through her thoughts as Ryn pulled open the heavy doors of the ornate armoire. A not-so subtle creak resounded in the room.

Well, good thing she didn't search it the night before.

Within were ancient dresses in outdated shades of blue, gold, ivory, and green. In the bottom drawers she found equally old underthings, a few corsets and stays, stockings, and chemises. Or were they nightgowns? In the dressers, she found simpler clothing. She pulled out a dress of cerulean and gold. Even as old as it was, it was likely worth more than everything she owed put together.

Ryn was holding the dress up when Kari returned.

"Oh, here. Let me help." Kari proceeded to toss the dress onto the bed, yanked the nightdress over Ryn's head and replacing it with an ivory chemise and undershorts, then a corset, then the dress. She tied up the strings with deft fingers. "There you are. The queen will be ordering new dresses for you today, I hear."

"This will do." Ryn ran her fingers over the heavier material. Good material. It would have cost several bottles of blood, if not a whole male's worth.

Kari inhaled to speak, then pulled back her words. Her gaze quickly roamed over the dress.

"You don't think so?" Ryn raised a brow.

Kari swallowed and paled. "I… No, it's not that. It's a lovely dress." Ryn narrowed her stare. Kari bit her lip. "It's…just…outdated. About four hundred years outdated."

"Well of course it is," Ryn said, motioning to herself. "It's supposed to be Zain's grandmother's. But I have no other option."

"Of course, my lady." Kari banished any emotion from her face.

Kari shooed Ryn to the vanity and fussed over her hair. She pinned it with pins forgotten in the bottom of the dead female's jewelry box. If Kari noticed the end of one slightly bent after being used as a lockpick last night, she didn't mention it. When she decided Ryn was ready, she ushered her into the sitting room.

At first, all was blinding, terrible, intrusive sunlight. Ryn's eyes slowly adjusted. Harsh morning light flooded into the sitting room from the wall of windows, where the emerald drapes were tied back with golden cords. The table in front of the window was arranged for two. Zain lounged in a tall-backed chair, the sunlight gleaming against his eyes and washing the color from his pale skin. It made him look sickly.

Neville stood against the wall, just outside of the sunlight's wash, taking in the room with indifference.

Zain wore a handsome housecoat of dark green brocade and a black sash, the shirt underneath black. He sipped tea, his blue eyes trailing along her body. The corner of his lips turned up in a sneer. She bristled.

"You look lovely this morning," Zain drawled.

His tone suggested otherwise, but she ignored it. Instead, she sat across from him, smoothing the musty skirt and crossing her ankles to the side. "Your grandmother had excellent tastes."

"A few hundred years ago," Zain quipped.

"Would you prefer I explore the keep naked?"

"I would," Zain said, hand to his chest. "But I'm sure my mother would faint. I could lend you one of my suits if you'd rather."

"Oh, I would never look as dashing in them as you, *dear*." She took the opportunity to rake her eyes over him.

His sneer turned into a vicious, knowing smile. Like his damn suits, it looked good on him. He was beautiful, with angled features and porcelain skin. The suit he wore was tailored perfectly to his tall, lean frame. He held himself with intelligence and precision, leisurely but controlled.

The sitting room door opened, and a servant hurried inside. She carried a small, covered tray. She set the tray before the prince, then lifted the lid.

On the tray sat a crystal glass of…reddish mud?

Zain lifted the glass to his lips and drained half of it in a single gulp, then the rest in a second. Disgust passed over his features, and he set the empty glass on the tray. The servant hurried away without saying a word.

"What was that?" Ryn asked.

"A tonic," Zain said, his voice mirroring the disgust on his face. He poured himself a cup from the teapot, took a swig, then another. "It's for my health. I was born with a heart condition. Don't ask me what's in it because I don't know. The alchemist created it. I drink one every few days or so, or my heart will start acting up, skipping beats and whatnot."

Ryn blinked. She'd heard rumors of Zain's fragile health, but only rumors—secrets kept by the royal family.

Whatever the tonic was, it worked. Already, the sickly pallor of his skin faded.

She reached for the painted teapot, and poured herself a cup. Zain had already made a cup for himself, so she assumed the rules of tea-making didn't matter. She'd assumed it was tea, but the amber liquid that filled her cup had a reddish tint to it, and it smelled spiced.

"Do you like cider?" He motioned toward her with his cup.

She hesitated to answer. She'd seen it advertised this time of year, but she never had the extra coin to spend on it. In her hesitation, his calm gentlemanly exterior sharpened. He tilted his head, noticing her hesitation.

Swallowing, she admitted to it. "I've never had it."

"Cider?" His dark brows rose.

"It's expensive." Her cheeks heated. She was complaining about not having enough to a prince who didn't want for anything. "When I've got three silvers to my name and food to buy, cider isn't something I think about. I realize not having enough of something isn't familiar to you."

Zain started to say something, then pursed his lips.

Ryn brought the cider to her lips. The rich aroma wafted with cinnamon and allspice and citrus and apples. It flowed down her throat, sating the memory of frozen fingers and needling cold.

Breakfast was light, apples and toast and sweet butters. Zain seemed content to ignore her entirely, as if they each sat alone. After the food was eaten and plates removed, the awkwardness set it.

And Ryn realized she sat with the male who would be her husband. Would every morning be like this? Awkward breakfast and separate rooms? She'd not thought about marriage, save for how nice it would be to have someone else in the house bringing in money and helping out, but…marriage always seemed like a fairy tale. Something from children's stories of fated romance, of love so strong a look could bring a female to her knees and drive a male crazy.

This…wasn't that. It was convenient, an act.

Lu was far more likable. Males saw her first, if they saw Ryn at all. Ryn kept hoping for Lu to meet someone who made her happy and brought in extra coin, maybe someone who knew how to cook.

Ryn hadn't met someone who made her think about marriage. She'd rarely thought past her next meal since their mother had died.

And now she sat with a prince, her betrothed. If her mother were alive, what would she think? She'd likely ask Ryn if she was ready for the wedding night, for the bonding of two souls.

Her heart skipped a beat.

Zain noticed. His eyes flickered up from his plate and met hers. His brow cocked. "Everything all right, dearest?"

"I was thinking about Lu," she lied, face heating. She had the feeling he knew exactly what she was thinking about.

He tilted his head, confused.

"My sister," she hissed.

"Ah, yes. The missing sister." Zain straightened his napkin to perfectly align with his plate. "I will inform the City Watch. If she buys an apple from the market, they'll find her. I will send someone to watch your…house."

"I know it's a shit place to live," Ryn snapped.

Zain's brows rose.

She hadn't gotten enough sleep to play word games. She reeled her bitterness and anger back in. "I had only what I needed to survive, and I didn't need a palace to do so."

"Or a door, from the report."

But the guard who had reported back to Zain and Ryn that night hadn't said anything about a door—which meant the guard spoke to Zain separately. Her gaze flickered to Neville. His face betrayed nothing. Had he spoken with Zain about her excursion the night before?

She fumed. "Doors invited people inside, so we blocked ours. A lot of people did."

"Yes, the guard had a terrible time climbing to the window." Zain said those words carefully as he sipped his cider.

She sipped her own and glared at him over the rim. His smile turned cruel. Her face burned, and she had the urge to throw the cup at him. How dare he mock her while he grew up in a warm keep with servants and running water and all the food he could eat.

"You're starting to look a bit murderous, love," Zain said.

Biting her tongue, she didn't bother denying it. If they shared only one meal together, she could live in the keep with Zain. She could trade warm baths and decent meals for enduring Prince Zain's attention for a few hours.

At least for a while. She doubted Zain would look fondly at her when she killed the king.

An idea struck. "It occurred to me that you did not give me a proper tour of your home. If it is to be my home as well, I should be able to travel within it without getting lost."

"You're worried about getting lost?" Zain cocked a brow and his lips quirked.

"Maybe I want to map it out for my grand heist." She winked.

Zain chuckled, the sound dark and velvet. "Good luck with that. The Hunters keep a tight watch. Even the best of thieves haven't made it out alive."

Neville shifted, but Ryn pretended not to have noticed. If she went through with this marriage, with the assassination, she needed to know her way around.

19
NIGHTSHADE KEEP
Ryn

The king's manor was far more complex than Ryn had thought. It had three towers, four dining rooms, two ballrooms, and a stupid number of guest rooms, parlors, and closets within its five floors. Ryn meandered alongside Zain, her arm draped through his, with Irene and Neville a step behind. He guided her through the library. This time of day it hummed with gentle activity—scholars and nobles lingered in the stacks and in reading nooks.

The layout was simple enough, though well guarded and well lit. Servants scurried about, yet Ryn rarely saw them in the main halls, which meant they entered and exited the numerous rooms with trays of food, baskets of laundry, and cleaning supplies another way. Hidden servants' passages crisscrossed between rooms and floors.

Everyone gave Zain a cautious, gossip-starved stare—and a wide berth. Zain acted as though he didn't notice. He used the tour to needle her with questions.

"What is your favorite color?" Zain asked.

She thought about it, but no color came to mind.

"Mine is green," he added.

"Clearly." She looked him up and down. He still wore his green housecoat. "You're also a fan of emeralds."

His expression remained masked, yet his index finger twitched; he wore a thick golden band set with three emeralds. "You're observant."

"You're obscenely obvious," she quipped.

One of his brows lifted. "You don't have a favorite color?"

"I..." She pulled back her words.

He tugged on her arm. "Oh, come now. I need to know these things. How else will I know what shade of roses to send you on our anniversary?"

"I like the color of the rain at sunset," she said in a single breath.

His brow furrowed.

"When the sun peeks out from under the clouds, and the rain is this...golden orange silver color. It's pretty."

Zain hummed. "I'm sure the florist will know what color that is."

His dismissive tone irked her and brought a heat to her cheeks. She shouldn't have told him. She should have picked some common color.

"Oh, I'm sure it is a lovely sight." Zain tugged on her arm. "Just because I've not seen this phenomenon doesn't mean it's not pretty."

She glared at him, and he only smiled.

"What is your favorite wine?" he asked.

"Cheap."

He chuckled. "Well, that won't do. I prefer whiskey, but as far as wine goes, I enjoy the semi-sweet blackberry blend from the Sun Vineyards."

"Never had it." Ryn hadn't even heard of it.

"They don't make bad wine," Zain continued. "My fathers prefers an imported wine from the south, made from plums. It's far too sweet for me. It's like drinking syrup."

"Sweet, I guess," Ryn whispered. The cheap wines tended to be sweet. To hide the cheap burn and aftertaste.

They entered a hall on the second floor with decorative pillars carved of dark stone, potted white flowers with a delicate scent, and a dreary feeling. Neville and Irene stalked behind.

"Here we have the history of the keep." Zain motioned to a series of paintings between the pillars, each as large as ballroom windows. The first depicted an ancient and gloomy castle. Pausing in front of the painting, he added, "This is the vampire stronghold that once stood here. The Abrani clan."

"It looks like something from a nightmare," Ryn mused. Indeed, the artist had used dark, bloody reds, gloomy plums, and steely grays. Shadows nestled in every window and doorway. Behind it, the Red Forest was a vicious gray, like death, and spotted with rusty red.

"I suppose that is what the artist believed." Zain escorted her to the second painting. It showed the same keep, only during battle. Fires raged from the courtyard, windows were broken, and bodies littered the ground. Smoke tainted the sky in grays and reds, and blood turned the ground crimson. Soldiers in leather fought vampires in black. "This is Prince Victor's vengeance on the Abrani clan after the vampires infiltrated the castle and killed his father, sister, and her husband and daughter. They also ravaged the castle, ensuring that it would be reduced to rubble."

Ryn's gut twisted. She had heard stories of that time in history. Anyone old enough to have lived during it had the same to say—it had been a nightmare.

"The hastily crowned King Victor brought the war to the vampire's doorstep with his newly formed Hunters." Zain frowned at the horrid battle painting. "He slaughtered them all and claimed their home as his own. He said once that he couldn't rebuild the castle he'd lost. He said he would rather be reminded of his victory over the vampires, than the family stolen from him."

Ryn gazed over the blood-soaked dirt, bodies strewn on the ground, over windows, in pieces, spiked on the many steeples. "So much slaughter," she muttered.

"You defend the vampires?" Zain's brows rose, though not in anger or shock. In curiosity.

"No, but…" She bit her lip. But what? "It's just a lot of killing."

Death took a toll on one's soul. Murder or otherwise. What would she feel if she reached into King Victor's blood? Did killing a vampire count? Did a death on a battlefield count the same as-murder in a dark alley?

She felt Zain's gaze, studying her reaction. Banishing any emotion on her face, she tugged him to the next painting. The battle had ended, the fires put out, the sky cleared and a brilliant blue. The fae were victorious, led by King Victor, who held his bloodied sword aloft, his hunters around him.

"The vampire stronghold sustained considerable damage," Zain said. "The first several floors had fire damage, save for the undercroft."

"Undercroft?"

Zain nodded. "That was how my father began his assault. He used the tunnels to smoke the vampires out. The heat from the fires rose up through the ground. Vampires can't take the heat, so they were weakened. It was brilliant on my father's side."

"And this undercroft is still there?" Ryn said, trying not to sound overly enthused. "Under the keep?"

"They're horrible and creepy," Zain said. "Mostly used for storage and for the guards to get across the keep quickly and without notice. The kitchens are a part of the old tunnels."

"The undercroft makes for a larger larder," Neville added.

"Why?" Zain cocked a brow at Ryn.

Her stomach twisted as she tucked that information away. "Could these vampires be sneaking in through the undercroft?"

Neither Neville nor Irene looked concerned.

"The undercroft has been checked," Neville said. "Many of the passages collapsed during the siege, and more have collapsed in the centuries since. We have sealed any way into or out of the keep through the undercroft, and we have closed most of the entrances throughout the keep. There's no way for a vampire to get in, unless they could turn themselves to vapor and shimmer through a cave-in."

"Vampires are crafty." Zain pinned a humored gaze on Neville. "Maybe they *can* turn into vapor."

Neville's straight-line mouth fell into a frown.

"*There* you are," came a pleasant male voice.

Zain and Ryn turned at the same time. A handsome male in a fine gold tailcoat and ivory trousers made his way down the corridor. He was built like a soldier—wide, tall, and muscular. He wore a curious, albeit hapless grin that brightened his entire face. His blond hair tousled to his shoulders, his hazel eyes sparkled, and he looked every bit as stupidly handsome up close as he did far away.

It took Ryn a moment, but she recognized him from the throne room.

"Esben," Zain said in greeting.

"Zain," Esben greeted in return, though he looked at Ryn. The wariness in his expression put her on edge. "You have yet to introduce me to your lovely companion."

"Sincerest apologies," Zain said, not sounding sincere at all. "Dearest brother, this is my betrothed, Sabryn Evren."

"My lady." Esben paused a respectable step away from her, and it took Ryn a heartbeat to understand the expectant expression. She held out her hand, and Esben placed a chaste kiss on the back of it. "It is an honor to meet you."

"Ryn, my love, this is my older brother," Zain said, the words lacking the ease of a few moments before. "Crown Prince Esben."

"A pleasure to meet you at last, Your Highness." Ryn bowed her head. It wasn't every day she was introduced to the future king. She thought of what Neville said about this not being her world. This world was for princes and females in puffy gowns, not females like her.

"Please, just Esben. You are to be my sister, after all." Esben glanced at Zain, the expression guarded.

Ryn had the gut feeling Esben saw Ryn like his mother did, a temporary fixture. Like he didn't believe the love story. Of course, Esben knew Zain better than she did, and he likely suspected the truth. As Lu would.

You, falling in love at first sight? With a prince? Ryn could imagine Lu laughing. *And then the gods decreed it would be summer all year.*

"Did you need something?" Zain asked Esben.

Esben shrugged, and Ryn noticed the letter tucked in his pocket. Sensing her gaze, he patted the letter. "I received word from a certain fair maiden this morning."

"His betrothed," Zain whispered to Ryn, loud enough for Esben to hear. "Princess Petronella, third daughter of King Ludwig."

Ryn nodded despite never having heard either of those names before. Knowing neighboring kings and their spawn wasn't necessary growing up. It barely felt necessary now.

"I was heading up to read it and write my response when I heard you talking," Esben said. "I thought it would be a good time to introduce myself." He flashed Ryn a handsome grin. Like Nobel, it reached his eyes.

Heels clicked on the hardwood, and Zain tensed under Ryn's touch. A heartbeat later, she realized why. A blonde female glided around the corner with two guards a step behind. The emblem on their uniforms picked Ryn's memory. The female wore a gown of cascading emerald skirts, golden brocade bodice with shimmering emerald embroidery, and slim sleeves. She walked with her nose pointed toward the ceiling, and her lips were painted blood red. Her gaze met Ryn's, and in an instant, Ryn knew she disliked the female.

And then she realized who she was.

"Lady Aurora." Esben greeted her with the same warmth he'd greeted Ryn. He glanced between Aurora and Zain, his expression cautious. "Pleasure seeing you here, but I must be going. I told the servants to meet me in my study with tea, and I don't want it to grow cold. Farewell."

"Farewell, Your Highness." Aurora purred in a voice a few pitches higher than sounded natural.

Ryn heard females do that—pretend to have a higher, softer voice to make themselves appear more feminine, more vulnerable. Because apparently males liked that. Ryn would rather vomit than talk like that.

Esben stepped away, his guard at his heels, and Aurora took the distraction to look Ryn up and down. If she recognized Ryn from that day in the streets, she didn't show it. Of course, Ryn had been hooded and dressed in a male's clothes.

"You must be Lady Sabryn." Aurora's voice strained on the title of lady, as if it physically hurt her to say it. "I have heard so much about you, and it is wonderful to meet you."

"Who are you?" Ryn asked in a fake pleasant tone.

Red bloomed across Aurora's cheeks.

Zain struggled to contain his delight. His grip on Ryn's arm tightened, his lips curved at the edges, and his eyes glittered. It seemed he delighted in tormenting Aurora as much as Ryn did.

Aurora inhaled, puffing herself up. Her skirts ruffled with the motion, and Ryn fought to hold a smile off her face at the memory of the female with her legs straight up in the air, her skirts puffing around her legs.

"I am Lady Aurora Banach," she said with the indignation of an offended noble. "I *was* betrothed to our dear Prince Zain."

"Ah." Ryn glanced at Zain with her best love-stricken expression. "Zain mentioned someone, but I didn't catch the name. My apologies. These past few days have been…wild."

Aurora eyed Ryn like a pissed-off cat. Her words came out sickeningly sweet as she said, "That is wonderful to hear. I had planned on staying at Nightshade Keep for a few weeks to get to know my…betrothed, but since our fates have changed, I supposed we will get to know each other instead." Her smile turned cruel. "I daresay we will be fast friends. Odd how fate works, isn't it?"

Oh, those were thorns in her tone. Ryn fought to keep the grin off her face.

"Fate is a tricky thing." Zain's tone mirrored Ryn's lovesickness. "I was content to believe that true love only existed in books and tall tales, but…" Zain glanced at Ryn. "But now I think I believe in mates."

Mates. The word sent a feverish panic under Ryn's skin. No one believed in mates anymore—that two souls could be fated to complete one another, *soulmates.* Children believed in mates. No one had claimed to have found their mate in…centuries. Like the fae magic of old, it had faded into history and folklore.

The word settled over Aurora like cold water. It washed away her mask and revealed the shock and bitterness underneath, but only for a moment. Then it was gone. Hidden behind her polished sneer.

"That is so romantic," Aurora said, her words sweet as rat poison.

Ryn played into Zain's game. She smiled like a love-stricken girl and flashed a bashful smile at him. She could pretend to be his mate, or she thought she could. She wasn't sure how mates were supposed to act, if they acted differently at all.

"Queen Portia is looking for you," Aurora said. "She has been waiting to take you into the city. Your chambers were empty, and your maid mentioned a tour. Lucky me that found you first."

"No, no, lucky me who got to finally meet you," Ryn said like she meant it.

"Oh, that's right," Zain said, a bit of guilt in his words. "You shouldn't keep Mother waiting, darling."

He made a show of twirling Ryn out of his arm, then placing a cool kiss to the back of her hand. He held her hand against his lips a heartbeat longer than proper, his gaze boring into hers. Mischief sparked in his eyes, like he couldn't wait to see them shred each other apart.

"Until this evening." Zain and Neville started down the corridor.

"Until this evening," Ryn repeated, trying to say the words like she meant it. She turned her attention back to Aurora, who had gone a shade of pissed-off pink. She looked at Ryn with nothing short of hatred.

"Her Majesty graciously asked me to accompany you." Aurora plastered a smile on her red lips. "I have been looking forward to seeing the royal city."

Ryn took Aurora's offered arm, and the two of them started down the corridor in the opposite direction.

Aurora's grip on her arm tightened almost painfully, and she hissed, "I don't know who you think you are, but you will not get in my way."

Ryn fought to not roll her eyes. She whispered back, "Don't waste your breath, sweet pea. I've been threatened far worse by far more dangerous people."

Irene caught up to them, and no more words were said.

The silence lasted barely a breath before Aurora's sickeningly sweet tone returned, and she talked about the stores she wanted to visit, the gifts she wanted to buy for her friends back home, and the latest fashion trends. Ryn said little. She knew little of popular stores or fashioned trends, and she didn't care to.

Not only would she have to spend the day with the queen, who hated her, she would also spend it with Zain's former betrothed, who also hated her.

Great.

20

BLOOD BETWEEN BROTHERS

Zain

Zain had been a sickly child, often confined to the nursery on warm days in fear of heatstroke or too much excitement. He was kept separate from the other children, only allowed to socialize after the alchemist concocted the tonic. By then, his reputation had formed as the sickly little brother of the wonderful Prince Esben.

Everyone *loved* Esben, and few boasted the same of Zain. The younger prince preferred books to people, silence to chatter, and had a nasty habit of pissing people off. He loved sending the painted, perfect nobles stumbling over themselves. And the nobles hated him for it.

He lounged in his bedroom, in his favorite reading chair, failing to concentrate. He usually kept the doors to the sitting room open, but now they were closed.

It was no longer *his* sitting room. It was *their* sitting room. His and his wife's. Or wife-to-be. They were not yet legally bound, though his mother was trying her best to derail the union. Gods only knew what she had planned for the females' outing. With Aurora, of all people. Zain wouldn't be surprised if Ryn was the victim of some freak accident, leaving Aurora the only available option. Zain bristled at the idea.

He had overhead Sabryn's servants tittering about her and Aurora as they cleaned Sabryn's bedroom—it was hot gossip.

His comment about being mates had only added fuel to the fire.

Poor Sabryn.

Ryn, he reminded himself. Such a short name when all the noble females preferred long names. They seem to think the longer their name took for one to say, the more important they were. Not with Ryn. She didn't bother with impressing him with her wealth or status or looks. She was…herself. Laid bare.

And it would seem she also enjoyed pissing off nobles. Or she didn't care about pleasing or placating them, which he found admirable.

It didn't escape Zain's notice that his father had placed Ryn in the farthest guest room from his, far enough they wouldn't be able to meet secretly. If Zain hadn't taken her on that moonlit walk, it would have been her bloodless body splayed.

The thought had occurred to him several times. Was it the same vampire she saw in the Red Forest? If so, it had somehow entered the keep undetected and killed without alerting the Hunters, Royal Guard, or servants.

Zain didn't doubt the vampire had come looking for Ryn. Why else pick that room? Vampires were notorious for their grudges.

Giving up on the book, Zain slumped against the velvet. He brought his fingers to his lips, thinking of Ryn's hands. She had more calluses than a noble. It suggested she knew how to use her hands.

He would be lying if he said he hadn't thought about her hands. He'd thought about those hands and her mouth, and what sound she would make in the crux of passion. Would she be loud or quiet? Would she turn submissive or dominant? With females, he could never tell until he got them in bed and they unleashed.

He wanted to see Ryn unleashed.

A knock sounded on the sitting room door. Neville marched forward from his place in the bedroom, across the sitting room, and muffled voices exchanged words. Zain waited for Neville to return, then braced himself.

"One of your mother's servants." Neville shut the bedroom door. "She wants the entire family to eat dinner tonight. Lady Ryn included."

Zain chuckled. "She wants to throw poor Ryn into the fire."

"The fire?" Neville raised a brow.

"I believe Mother aims to frighten Ryn into fleeing or giving up the engagement. If not with the outing, then with dinner," Zain explained. "I also believe Mother underestimates her. There's a hellcat under her skin."

Neville hesitated.

Zain knew that look. His guard had more he wanted to say. "Yes?"

"Your Highness," Neville started, taking a step into Zain's view.

Zain knew that tone. Neville only referred to him by his title when he had something less than ideal to say. "Speak what you will, Neville. I won't toss you out."

No, he wouldn't get rid of Neville. Of all the guards Zain had gone through, Neville was by far the most pleasant.

"I want to propose the possibility that her intentions are not what they appear," Neville added. He met Zain's eyes. "She was found over a body in the Red Forest, and another body appeared in her chambers."

"Yes, I've heard." Zain sipped from his whiskey. It was his first glass. Usually by this time of day he was on his second or third. "Quite the coincidence."

"Too much for my tastes." Neville adjusted his stance from passive guard to trained Hunter. It set Zain on edge. "And you have invited her into your chambers."

"She is heavily guarded," Zain reminded him. "By Irene. You said Irene was terrifying."

Neville nodded, a hint of fear in his eyes. "It takes a strong female to join the Hunters. I would not cross any of them."

"You trust Irene?"

"Of course," Neville said without hesitation. "She is a respectable Hunter. I would trust her with my back in a fight."

"There are Hunters and guards posted in the corridor." As annoying as they were. "And there are a dozen tasked with following her around. Besides, she's harmless."

"She is anything but harmless," Neville said quickly.

"How can you be sure?" Zain raised a brow. "Or are your senses that sharp when it comes to the fairer sex?"

Neville scowled. "She lived in the slums. Those streets kill the weak like unwanted rats. For her to have survived on those streets, she would have to be dangerous. As dangerous as everyone else down there."

That made her all the more interesting.

"And," Neville added lowly, his face grave. "She snuck out last night."

Zain paused, whiskey at his lips. "What?"

"I don't know where she went, only that she headed in the direction of the slums," Neville whispered, so the guards posted outside the door wouldn't overhear.

Sneaking into and out of the keep was next to impossible. Zain knew. He'd tried several times. Each attempt had ended in failure, or Neville's help.

Zain took a swig. "What do you think that means?"

"It could mean a lot of things. She might be meeting with this vampire brood, or other nefarious sorts. The slums are full of them."

"She could also be checking on her affairs," Zain added. "She was locked in a cell for a few days with no knowledge of her sister or her home."

Zain didn't want to believe Ryn had nefarious plots, but he couldn't deny the coincidences of the two bodies. Had she deceived him? Had she planned this entire thing? Or had she fallen into a mishap with the Hunters and saw him as a way out of that mess, as he saw her as a way out of his mess? Ryn seemed to be made of steel, something far stronger than any other female he had met.

A headache started behind his left eye. Too many thoughts, too early in the morning.

He finished his whiskey in a single gulp, then stood. "You know what sounds good? A good glass of spiced wine."

Neville scowled at the empty whiskey glass. "It's not even midday."

"All the more reason for wine." Zain strolled across his bedroom. He grabbed his tailcoat from the chair and tugged it on, quickly buttoning it.

As children, Zain and Esben often snuck into the kitchens for sweets. The habit stuck around as they grew older. It was a bit of childhood whimsy he refused to let go of, only he had broadened his tastes to include wines and liquors.

He felt Neville's presence behind him, far enough to not feel like a shadow, but close enough to strike should something happen. Not that anything would happen—or he would like to think. A vampire *had* snuck into the keep.

Halfway down the corridor to the kitchens, a familiar presence fell in step beside Zain. It took up the entire corridor, like a wet blanket.

"Brother," came Esben's voice. It boomed off the stone walls. Esben's hand landed on his shoulder. He flashed his handsome, hapless grin. "Where are you off too at this hour?"

Zain shrugged, a feat with his brother's heavy hand on his shoulder. "Oh, nothing horrible. Just setting fire to the drapes. Might let a mouse loose in the servant's quarters."

Esben laughed—the hearty sound rumbled. He patted Zain's shoulder, jostling him. "Don't worry about him, Neville. I'll watch him from here."

"Return him in one piece, Your Highness." Neville bowed his head to Esben, then started back down the corridor. "Or I will never hear the end of it."

Esben hefted his arm around Zain's shoulders—the weight nearly made his knees buckle—and guided them toward the kitchens. Esben had always been bigger and stronger, and Zain was used to shoving his self-loathing down, but the sudden weight of his brother's arm and the way he had effortlessly dismissed a Hunter stirred the old jealousy. It burned in his chest.

Where Esben had been gifted with the build of a fae god, Zain was tall and lean, a reed next to his brother's bulk. Zain had wanted to join the Hunters like Esben, but Father refused. Zain's health was too unstable, his heart too weak.

Despite that, it was hard to hate Esben. He had a heart of gold. His laughter filled every room.

"You don't have to escort me to the kitchen," Zain deadpanned.

"I was headed there anyway. I was off to see Ann. I heard she was trying a new experiment with winterberries." Esben wiggled his brows.

Ann, one of their cooks, used to sneak them pieces of sweet dough or cookies when the other cooks weren't looking.

"Then I confess, I was off for something sweet," Zain said, hand over his heart. "Of the spiced and fermented kind."

Esben laughed, then his lips flattened. "I also wanted to get you alone to ask you about your new...*friend*. Ryn, was it? I've heard the story from the servants, but I want to hear it from you. You told Aurora you believe she is your mate?"

"My, word travels faster than the plague." Zain scowled. "Why so interested, Brother? You could never stand it, when someone prefers my company. Go ahead and try to steal her from me. This one will choose me too."

Esben rolled his eyes and held up his finger. "I tried to steal one female from you. Once. I was young and stupid."

And that old wound still stung. Not as bad as it once had, but still.

"You are implying you are not those things now?"

"Enough of the games, Zain." Esben frowned. "How did you meet this girl? I've never heard of her before today. No one has. Is she really your mate?"

Zain could tell Esben the truth, or he could lie. Esben had kept Zain's secrets before, but he also had a strong sense of justice and truth. Zain didn't know if Esben would see this lie as one that needed to be exposed for his own good.

To be on the safe side, he lied.

"It is not the most daring of stories. It's a bit embarrassing." Zain stuffed his hands into his pockets. He didn't have to pretend embarrassed—it *was* embarrassing. "We met at a less than ideal tavern one night. We were both drinking. We just…collided." Not a lie. "As for the mate thing, I…think so. I'm not sure."

Esben looked doubtful. "You met at a tavern?"

"I might have started a bar fight." The night, while blurry at certain points, stained his mind. "This thug pushed me, and I stumbled like a drunk, right into Ryn. She caught me. Held me so I didn't crash onto my face like a fool." He swept his hand in front of him, letting Esben insinuate what he wanted from his lack of words. "I don't know if that is love at first sight, but it felt like it. When I saw her in the throne room, about to die, I…had to do something. I refused to let her slip through my fingers."

Esben nudged his shoulder into Zain's with a wide, knowing grin. "I don't think that sounds foolish. I wouldn't have believed you if I hadn't been in the throne room."

"Why not?"

"Because you're a good liar when you speak, but your eyes give you away." Esben winked at Zain. "You were looking at Ryn like she was a goddess descended into the room, despite being covered in dirt and ill-fitting clothes."

Zain hummed a note. He didn't remember looking at her like that, but if it furthered the story of their love, then so be it.

"Is she okay with this?" Esben asked, brow raised. "Getting married."

Zain feigned sheepishness. "We talked that night. Took a walk so there wouldn't be a dozen servants listening. I…told her how I felt. She, uh, reciprocated the feeling."

That wasn't entirely a lie either. They had talked that night, and she had reciprocated his feelings of the necessity of their union. Love could be faked as long as they needed it. He would've had to fake it with whoever his mother pushed him into marrying, especially Aurora. It came easier with Ryn, knowing she understood the game. She played along effortlessly.

"Do you know anything about her?" Esben asked as they entered the kitchen corridor. "Family? A job? Debt? Estranged cousins? Rumors have it she's connected to the vampire broods lurking in the slums. She could be—"

A scream echoed off the stone.

A clatter—like wood smacking stone. Esben instinctively reached for the blade at his waist. Another scream—Esben darted for the sound.

Zain allowed him to take the lead. Esben was allowed a sword; Zain was unarmed.

The commotion led them to the storeroom, where several servants lay dead on the floor. Two darkly clad figures remained, one held a bloodied knife, the other held one end of a wooden crate.

"Hold," Esben commanded, his voice a boom off the stone.

The figures turned—milky pale skin and red-rimmed eyes looked out from under the hood. *Vampires*. Zain's heart lurched, sending the uncomfortable wash of panic through his veins. The vampire brandished his bloodied dagger and bared his fangs.

Esben surged forward with the force of a gale.

Zain fell back a step, feeling utterly foolish. He had no weapon. Even if he did, what could he do?

Esben took out one vampire in a whirl of force and steel, and then turned toward the second. The vampire dropped its side of the crate—glass shattered and rattled. Blood seeped through the slats in the crate. The metallic scent of it stained the air as easily as it stained the floor. Bitter and heady.

Zain blinked from the blood—Esben threw the second vampire to the floor. Both monsters were dead, adding their dark blood to the bright red seeping between the stones. Zain's heart sped. "What the hell," Zain breathed, hand on his chest.

"Dead," Esben nudged the second vampire with the toe of his boot. "Brother?"

It took a moment for Zain to realize Esben had shifted his eyes to him, to the hand against his chest.

"I'm fine." Zain dropped his hand to his side. He motioned to the dead. "Vampires. How did they get in?"

"Father needs to know of this at once."

"I suppose we should have left one alive to ask questions." Zain braved a step into the room. With the vampires dead, the cold dread faded. He'd never been this close to a vampire. They looked less…monstrous, not like the illustrations in his father's books. They had the fangs, red-rimmed eyes, skin paler than death, but they also had the pointed ears of the fae. They wore dark clothes. "They're dressed for stealth, but I don't see any other weapons aside from the knife. The lack of weapons or armor suggests they weren't prepared for a fight."

"Vampires… Shit." Esben gripped his blade with white knuckles. "We've not had a problem with vampires in decades, let alone in the keep. This is a declaration of war. These monsters violated our home. "And…" Esben's gaze fell on the crate currently bleeding onto the floor. Fresh, bright blood.

"What is this?" Zain whispered. Fear of what it truly was, what it meant, struck him worse than finding two vampires in the basement.

Esben opened his mouth, but just as he did, footsteps thundered down the corridor. Three royal guards appeared, steel in hand.

A young woman in servant's clothing was with them. She looked wide-eyed at the dead vampires and their dark blood on the floor.

"This girl says there were intruders," the first guard said.

"There were," Esben confirmed, nodding to the vampires. Their pale skin and redden eyes were obvious, and there was no hiding what they were. "Father must hear of this at once. You, fetch the king."

One of the guards hurried off.

The young woman stared at the dead servants, and brutal realization settled into her features. To her credit, she didn't wobble or even ask what happened.

Esben sheathed his blade and stepped toward her. His voice softened as he asked, "I'm sorry this happened. Can you tell me what you saw?"

She brought her eyes from the body to Esben. "I heard Sophie scream," she said, her voice detached. "I…thought… I didn't…" Her gaze found the dead vampires. "She told me to run to the guard. She said… She said there were three vampires. I… I ran."

"It's going to be okay," Esben assured her, flashing his princely grin.

Zain glanced at the crate. The blood seeped from the wood, staining the grain, the stones, the grout. He lifted the lid.

Inside, green glass bottles nestled among straw and old cloth. All but two were cracked and leaking their bloody contents. The bittersweet aroma curled against his stomach.

"What?" Esben appeared at his side.

"Blood." The word came out breathless.

Zain met Esben's eye, and the question bounced silently between them. Why was there a crate of bottled blood in the keep? Did the vampires bring it in with them, or had they come in looking for it?

The servant's brow rose, and this time, she swayed.

Esben straightened. "Take her back to the servants' quarters," he said to the guards. "Make sure there is someone to look after her."

A guard led the young female away.

"She'll be scarred for life," Zain deadpanned once the servant was out of earshot.

"This isn't a joking matter." Esben stormed to the crate, not worried about the blood getting on his boots. Already, it clotted and dried at the edges. It might have been a trick of the light, but the bottled blood seemed to shimmer. It made the blood of the vampires and that of the servants' look dull.

"I wasn't joking." Zain swallowed a growing sense of unease.

"Your tone indicated otherwise." Esben frowned.

Zain shrugged. "Can't help that."

Esben picked up one of the few remaining intact bottles. Inside, the blood swished as if freshly squeezed from its source. "This could only have been done with magic."

"Why is it here?" Zain tapped his fingers on the side of the crate. He had a few ideas, but none he wanted to voice to Esben.

"How did the vampires get in?" Esben looked around the storeroom. "The only way is from the kitchens, but they would have been seen."

"That leaves the larder," Zain mused. "Neville did suggest vampires could turn into vapor. They could have squeezed in through a dark sewer grate. You know as well as I do there are far too many secrets buried under his keep, Brother."

Secrets Ryn had asked about. Had she been prying, or was this another coincidence? How many coincidences could he allow her? Esben was right—he knew little about her.

Esben's face darkened.

There were a few passages in the undercroft that one could navigate if they crawled. It was not impossible for a vampire to have slithered up from the depths of the undercroft, or for one to have crawled through the ancient tombs to get into the keep. Unlikely, but not impossible.

Mosquitoes, his father had once referred to vampires. Able to slither through the smallest hole.

"We should take these." Esben lifted the remaining bottles.

"Oh, splendid idea." Zain took the one Esben thrust into his hands. It was still warm. Like a bottle of spiced wine left by the hearth.

"So, if any more of those beasts come looking, they'll have to come to us. Maybe we can bargain," Esben added. He used the bottle in his hand to point to the one in Zain's, like a morbid toast. "They'll want these back."

Zain didn't like the idea of taking the blood or holding it or being so close to it. He was about to voice this protest when more footsteps thundered down the corridor. Several pairs of them. King Victor appeared with his armed retinue, red-faced from running. He took in the bloody mess, dead vampires and servants, and then broken crate. His gaze landed on the intact bottle in Zain's hand.

"Father," Esben started.

"This can't be," the king spat. He cursed. "Vampires in my keep. In my home. Threatening my servants. Killing my servants. This will not go unpunished."

"The servant mentioned three vampires," Esben said. "The two dead suggest the third is still alive."

The king looked murderous.

A cold panic surged through Zain's veins. Were these vampires responsible for leaving the dead servant in Ryn's chambers and the body in the grounds?

"It must have run before we arrived. It could be hiding in the keep," Esben said.

"The servant said the other servant yelled about three, she did not see them," Zain mused. His heart still beat rapidly. His voice came out breathless, and he hated how pathetic he sounded. "It could have been a mistake."

Esben scowled at his brother.

King Victor didn't seem to hear him. He took a step into the room, expression calm and furious. "Hunters will scour the keep from top to bottom until we find how they got in and where this third monster is hiding. Until then, we continue as normal." He looked to Esben, and then Zain. "They want to rattle us. Disrupt our resolve. They will not. They will not see us rattled. Esben, get your brother back to his chambers. Make sure Neville is there. Then meet with your squad."

"Yes, Father."

Zain was too rattled to argue. It wasn't until he and Esben had left the kitchen corridor behind that the demeaning order settled.

"I could have walked to my room on my own," Zain growled.

"You could have." Esben held his hand on his sword. "There are Hunters in the keep. After this, they'll be on high alert. As will the guards. You probably would have been fine."

"Probably?" Zain raised his brow.

"There's always that chance our missing vampire is lurking in a shadow, waiting for the chance to strike."

"And what benefit would they have from slaying me?"

Esben chuckled, though it lacked his usual mirth. "They wouldn't slay you. Not at first. They'd drag you back to wherever they're squatting and drain you dry first, or turn you into a thrall."

Zain had heard rumors of what thralls were forced to do. Their minds, bodies, and souls were tied to their vampire masters. One bite—that is all it took to either kill a body from toxins or turn it into a thrall. Zain held in his repulsed shiver. He would rather be dead than exist as a mindless slave.

They arrived at Zain's chambers. Neville spoke softly to another Hunter, and by the disgruntled look on Neville's face, he knew about the vampires in the kitchens. Esben nodded to Neville, then as Zain let himself into his chamber, Esben and the other Hunter strode back toward the kitchens. To rally and hunt, or whatever it was the Hunters would do.

Zain strolled into his chambers as if nothing bothered him, just like he had for most of his life. Unease squirmed underneath his polished exterior. He fought to stay composed. The vampires and bottled blood were but a fraction of it.

"Do you need anything?" Neville asked from the bedroom, from his post.

"A drink. Whiskey."

Neville marched to the sideboard in the sitting room. Zain turned the tap on the bath. His hands shook. The whiskey clinked onto the vanity.

"Thank you." Zain took a greedy gulp.

Zain shut himself in the bathing room. He needed what precious alone time he was allowed. He needed to sort through the rampaging thoughts before they swallowed him whole.

21
BLOOD AND FUR

Ryn

Sitting across from Queen Portia in a carriage with buttoned velvet seats and polished wooden walls, Ryn felt like an imposter.

Ryn had never shopped for fun. She shopped for necessities, like food and firewood, but never something as frivolous as clothes. She and Lu wore their parents' clothing. When something ripped, Lu sewed it back together. When something became too worn to wear, it became a rag. When it no longer constituted a rag, it became fire kindling. For the occasions when she needed to dress up, Nobel supplied her with whatever she needed.

At least she'd been saved from Aurora's presence. She rode in her own carriage with her own servant and guard. The queen had insisted she ride separately, and Ryn hadn't missed the look on Aurora's face—like she'd been slapped. The look vanished within a heartbeat, but Ryn had seen it.

Ryn wasn't stupid. She knew why the queen invited Aurora, or why she invited Ryn on their already planned trip—to rouse the competition. Queen Portia wanted Ryn to see the viable competition for Zain's hand. It was far too much drama for Ryn. If this were the slums, the queen would have left her dead in an alley somewhere. There wouldn't be so much parading about and whispered threats. There would be a dagger and death, and the problem would be solved.

She preferred the dagger to this nonsense.

Queen Portia wore a blue gown threaded with white and gold, and white gloves lined with golden fur. The same fur lined her cloak and framed the hood. Ryn couldn't imagine how much that fur had cost.

"Fur is in this season," Queen Portia said, her diction clear and crisp.

Ryn pulled her eyes from the golden fur and met the queen's gaze. She wore superiority, like she needed to prove herself better than Ryn, like she needed to remind her of her status. What she didn't know was that Ryn didn't need the reminder of how worthless her life was.

The queen's nostrils flared, and Ryn suspected she had missed a cue.

"Fur is in because I want it to be," she said, her words clipped.

I don't fucking care. Ryn held in what she wanted to say, and said meekly, "Okay."

She needed to be pleasant with the queen. Her future mother-in-law. She could make Ryn's life very difficult.

Queen Portia's gaze turned wicked. It reminded Ryn of Zain, of how his eyes glittered with dangerous mischief, of how he knew his own power. "What do you think of fur, Sabryn?"

"It's warm," Ryn answered.

The queen's gaze crinkled slightly. That wasn't the right answer.

Ryn cleared her throat. "It is lovely. Quite fashionable."

"That is better," said the queen. Her lips fell into a straight line. "You are catching on."

And, being queen, she was always right. Regardless of how nonsensical.

"I think red fur would look lovely on you." The queen trailed her clinical gaze along Ryn's features. "It would complement your coloring."

"I agree," Ryn said.

The queen's smile returned, though it was cold and calculated. Ryn might as well be sharing the carriage with a hungry, pissed off snake.

But for Lu, Ryn could play this game. She could appease the queen with nonsense chitchat, let her be right, let her dress her up like a doll.

"The alchemist reported that you are not with child."

The sudden shift in conversation snapped Ryn's attention. She blinked at the queen, unsure of what to even say. Queen Portia wore no humor. She looked down her nose at Ryn with that same coldness.

"I had your blood tested." The queen's lips pursed. "I thought that might be the reason Zain stole you as his bride."

The queen's gaze shuttered, and a sliver of relief slid through her masked expression. Odd, considering how hard it was for a full-bloodied fae to get pregnant and carry a babe full term. Ryn bristled as understanding dawned—the queen's relief had nothing to do with a prospective grandchild, but a prospect grandchild with Ryn's filthy common blood.

"We missed a crucial step in that process," Ryn muttered.

The queen let out a small harrumph. "You are hiding things from me, Lady Sabryn. I can see it on your face."

Nothing beyond trying to kill your husband and being an enchantress. Both of those would get her killed.

Thankfully, Queen Portia could not read thoughts. She continued to stare at Ryn with clinical evaluation, like the answer might appear on her forehead. Ryn held herself calm—like she sat through a meeting with Nobel.

"If I find you have fooled my son and tricked him into this engagement, it will not be an execution waiting for you." The queen's cold eyes burned. "It will be far worse."

Ryn tried not to let the threat needle too deep. No doubt the queen would follow through, that there would be something horrible that made her wish for the sweetness of death's oblivion.

"Unless it is he who has tricked you." The queen's plucked and perfect brow rose. Her smile turned cold.

"Some might say love is a trick," Ryn said, despite how foolish it sounded.

The queen laughed. "Not when you carry a title, girl. Love is a game, a weapon, and often deadly." Her smile flattened. "He claims you are mates. I don't believe it."

"I'm not sure I believe it," Ryn mused softly, like a secret. She felt the queen stare like a dagger at her throat. She put a hand to her chest, where in the stories the mating bond existed. She twisted her features in contemplation. Dropping her hand, she said, "I don't know what it's supposed to feel like."

Silence stretched between them. The queen stole her gaze from Ryn to glance out the carriage's small window.

Like Ryn, Queen Portia didn't know what to think about mates.

Ryn had known from a young age that true love was not for females like her. It existed for females like Lu, kind and gentle and full of love to give. Females like Ryn survived. She took the burden so Lu could believe in things like love. Darkened her soul so Lu's would remain bright.

"There was something else interesting on your blood report." The queen said the words softly, but with a bite.

"Oh?" Ryn glanced up.

The queen wore a curious smile. "Your expression suggests you don't know the purity value of your blood."

"Half dirt and half canal water, I'm sure." The comment slipped out before she caught it, yet the queen didn't reprimand her.

Instead, the queen smiled. Albeit a cold and confused smile. "Your blood is pure."

It took a moment for the word to settle. *Pure.* Ryn blinked, sure she'd misheard. Only nobles had pure fae blood.

"That can't be right," Ryn breathed.

"I was surprised, but the alchemist ran it twice," said the queen. "Your blood is pure, not a single drop of human blood. That explains your ears."

Ryn blushed, right to the tips of her pointed ears. She had the urge to tug her hood over her head.

"The scholars researched your surname, but they found nothing. It likely isn't your real surname." The queen tilted her head, studying Ryn like a painting. "However, one of the older scribes brought me an interesting piece of history.

About two hundred years ago, a daughter of the Crestin family married below her class. The family disapproved of the union and disowned her. Her name was erased from their family tree. It's like she never existed, and Lord Crestin has gone to great lengths to bury the affair."

Ryn went clammy. Her mother had never talked about her family, and Ryn had never asked. Her father had a brother who lived outside the city and worked as a farmer, but Ryn's letters to him about her father's death had gone unanswered. Either her uncle didn't want anything to do with them, or he was dead too.

"If Zain continues on this path, then we can use this long-lost bloodline to our advantage," the queen said. "It will give the nobles something to chew on, and it proves you're not some half-human tramp he scrounged up. We might be able to persuade the Crestin house to recognize you as a lost daughter. We will need to keep it quiet for now, until I have a chance to speak with Lord Crestin in private."

The queen continued to talk, but Ryn wasn't listening. Was her mother a disowned daughter of a noble house? Her mother had never hidden her ears or worried about them, and in Ryn's memory, she had a quiet grace and regality that neither of her daughters had inherited. Ryn's father had sharply pointed ears, but from what Ryn knew about his family, they were farmers. Working class. Hardly noble.

Her parents were in love, the storybook kind of love. Ryn remembered how her mother brightened when her father came home, how they kissed goodbye every morning. A daughter who married below her station—could it be true?

Cast out. Erased from their family as if she never existed. For love.

The carriage took them first to a delicate dress shop, its tall windows displaying jewel-toned dresses of emerald and topaz, the cloaks and gloves lined with white and gold fur. Knee-high leather boots with gleaming buttons up the sides. Brooches of gold. Gleaming brocade. Corsets with ribbons instead of strings.

Royal guards stood at the door and just inside.

"The Royal Guard has secured the shop," Queen Portia said, noting Ryn's gaze. "We have it to ourselves."

"Oh," was all Ryn could say.

THE BLOOD ENCHANTRESS

The queen straightened her skirts. "I want to shop without commoners clamoring for attention only to complain and ask for things. Not to mention the pickpockets."

Ryn bit her tongue to hold her words in. Of course, the queen would see commoners as an annoyance. Bothersome things.

The footman opened the carriage door. The queen stepped out, her annoyance replaced with a pleasant and sweet expression as she waved to the crowd gathered. As if she cared about them. However, as Ryn accepted the footman's gloved hand and stepped onto the street, she understood. People gathered behind the guards, gawking and pointing and shouting at *her*.

"That's her, that's the prince's girl!"

"There she is!"

"There, right there, that's her!"

"She is marrying Prince Zain!"

Irene appeared between Ryn and the crowd, blocking her view. She set one hand on Ryn's back and ushered her into the safety of the deserted shop.

Once inside, Ryn released a shaky breath. "I see why you don't want them in here."

Queen Portia flashed Ryn a knowing look. "Those vultures would eat you alive."

Ryn wanted to argue that she was tougher than the puffy dress made her look, but the quiver in her bones suggested otherwise. She'd never been a people person, and crowds made her anxious. She was comfortable with quiet and shadows, with the familiar loneliness that came with it. People were different.

"You aren't a person in their eyes," the queen said lowly. "Not anymore."

Ryn met the queen's vicious, sad gaze. Before she could say anymore, Aurora sauntered into the shop with her guards close behind. The guards closed the doors and posted themselves in front of them. More stood outside, visible through the leaded glass.

Ryn had almost forgotten about Aurora.

Almost.

The plump seamstress was far too welcoming. She ushered Ryn into a dressing room, stripped her to her underthings, and began the odious process of measuring everything inch of her body. All the while, Queen Portia, Aurora, and the seamstress chatted. They talked about colors, designs, fabric, patterns, and styles.

The queen decided what colors would go best with Ryn's dark hair and soft brown skin. Aurora parroted every decision and complimented the queen's style choices.

Ryn stood still as the seamstress measured and dressed her like a doll. No one had ever bought her clothes, let alone an entire wardrobe. The queen wanted these dresses, and she was paying for them; Ryn let her. If this would make the queen happy, Ryn would endure a fitting. For Lu, she would endure twenty.

And the queen was right. Ryn looked good in red.

More than a few times, Ryn caught Aurora's eyes in one of the many full-length mirrors. She wore a calm, unfeeling mask. Assessing.

Probably planning Ryn's accidental death.

The queen and Aurora chatted about people Ryn had never heard of, noble houses, and events. Nonsensical conversation. The words were like flies, buzzing but never landing.

Hours later, with a dozen dresses tucked into the carriage and thrice as many to be delivered upon completion, Ryn sank into the velvet seat with an exhaustion she had never felt before. Queen Portia had spent more coin in a single swoop than Ryn had in her entire life, likely twice over. They came to the next shop, and Ryn followed the queen. Again, the guards blocked the sidewalk. Again, a crowd clamored for a glimpse, shouting and gawking.

It felt as though Ryn had left her spirit behind in the carriage.

She entered the shop with Irene close, and the scent of sugar hit her hard. Blinking, the bright shop came into focus—the colorful displays of spun sweets, chocolates, truffles shaped like flowers, hard candies in every shade imaginable, soft caramels, fruit jellies, and candies she had never seen or heard of.

Had she died in the carriage? Was this the afterlife?

"This is just for fun," Queen Portia whispered. "You were looking a bit pale. A bit of sugar will give your cheeks some color, and your waist more girth. You are far too thin."

The shop, Ryn soon learned, made the queen's favorite chocolates. The queen ordered a box of them to be delivered to the keep, and insisted Ryn add her own candies. After an oddly stressful walk around the display, the queen added two boxes of assorted chocolates to the other without hesitation.

Ryn returned to the carriage feeling numb. She thought of that one piece of chocolate, the one she made last as long as possible. She would soon have two boxes of chocolates. *Two boxes.* Playing Zain's game certainly had perks.

The next shop was for hats, then next for shoes, and the next for ribbons. An entire fucking shop for *ribbons*.

Ryn couldn't fathom the coin Queen Portia spent on her. If the queen wanted to get rid of her, why spend all this coin?

Of course, it would be little more than a notch in the kingdom's coffers. Still, each transaction hurt like a knife twisting in her frugal gut.

"It isn't just about shopping, Lady Sabryn," said Queen Portia. "It is about being seen. Right now, the city craves a glimpse of the mysterious female who stole Prince Zain's heart. Word has spread that the two of you are mates. The people love it."

There—the hateful displeasure on those words. Zain had called them mates, and now everyone in the city was talking about them, about Ryn. Not Aurora. It was a crafted move, Ryn realized as she sat under the queen's glare. She couldn't easily remove Ryn without upsetting the people.

"The life of royalty is exhausting." Queen Portia let out a small, delicate sigh. "People will be watching you at all times. Looking for weaknesses to exploit, flaws to exaggerate."

Ryn tried to let the threat roll off her shoulders, but it hooked onto the edges of her heart. She had plenty of flaws and weaknesses. Leaning forward, Ryn whispered the question she'd been thinking all morning, "If you don't want me to marry Zain, why are you going through all this trouble?"

The queen studied her, nose tilted upward slightly. "Because you need to look the part, dear. You can't wear Queen Tessie's old dresses, they're horribly outdated." She rolled her eyes as if that should've been obvious. "And when this engagement falls apart, Aurora will be there to comfort Zain in his grief."

"Grief?"

"Over you, dear." The queen's lips curved in a cold, sinister smile. "Did you think you could simply back out and go home? No. Not after the people have seen your face and know your name. The entire city has heard of the mysterious Sabryn Evren. If you back out, it will be to the executioner's block. Of course, that's not what the kingdom will hear. They will hear of your tragic death, the prince's broken heart, and how Lady Aurora was there to put the pieces back together."

Ryn's blood ran cold. She had known her options from the start, yet hearing the threat from the queen's mouth somehow felt worse. Marry Zain, or lose her head.

And the queen was prepping Aurora for Ryn's untimely, tragic death.

The queen opened her mouth, however snapped it shut at the sudden sound of galloping hooves. A shout rang out, and the guard posted on their carriage shouted back; the carriage paused.

Queen Portia sat up straight, brow furrowed. Ryn reached for her magic on instinct, and felt the male right outside, relief and fear combining in his blood. Not a threat.

The sudden and extreme use of her magic sent stars across her vision, followed by swift nausea.

The male dismounted and opened the carriage door. He was a breathless royal guard, his hair windblown, the horse sweaty.

"Your Majesty," he said, bowing his head to the queen. To Ryn, he breathed, "My lady."

"What is it?" the queen snapped.

"There has been a disturbance at the keep."

22

TO GET AWAY WITH IT

Ryn

The royal carriage returned to Nightshade Keep under heavy guard and heavier silence. Ryn sat with her hands clenched in her lap. Three vampires had found their way into the keep. Two dead, one missing. Assumed to be hiding in the keep.

Queen Portia said nothing. Her leisurely demeanor was gone and the rigid queen returned. Tension radiated off her like cold from ice, dread of vampires and rage at the invasion of her home. Ryn didn't want to know what she would feel if she touched the queen's blood, how vicious and cold the emotions. Ryn had found in her bloodletting that females' emotions were complex, twisted things; males' emotions were blunt, more primal.

Ryn couldn't help but wonder if one of the vampires was the one from the Red Forest, or the one that killed the servant in her chambers. The Hunters couldn't connect her to the incident in the kitchens. Ryn hadn't been anywhere near the keep. She had been under the watchful, critical eye of the queen.

A dozen guards met the carriage, and those guards closed around Queen Portia and Ryn as they made their way from the carriage house to the keep. All held the hilt of their blades and looked like they expected a vampire to lurch from the darkness. Irene walked at Ryn's side, angled to defend. The queen's guards, two of them, both females who looked like they could fight a bear and win, stood in the same defensive position.

Guards escorted Queen Portia and Ryn into the first floor of the southern tower. Copious sunlight filled the space. A round table sat in the center of the room, surrounded by stiff-backed wooden chairs. The king sat at the head of it, with Esben on his right, and Commander Wade on his left. Hunters with decorated uniforms had gathered, as well as a middle-aged man in Royal Guard attire, the royal healer, the white-haired alchemist, and a stern-faced female Ryn had never met.

Zain stood with Commander Wade. They had been talking; however, that conversation ended as the queen entered. Zain looked first to his mother, then to Ryn.

His cerulean gaze held hers, and when no smirk pulled at his straight-line lips, she knew something more than vampires had happened.

Nervous energy filled the room. It crawled along Ryn's skin and needled into her bloodstream. It chittered and tapped against her bones like fingernails. The unwanted sensation prickled along her senses. She clamped her magic and held it close, fearing it would give her away.

Queen Portia sat beside Esben, and no one said a word as Ryn sat beside the queen. She didn't know what else to do. Zain glided to the chair on Ryn's other side, expression glum and eyes dark. He reached for her hand, his own cold but steady. Hers trembled. It was a show, she knew, for the room to witness. A display of affection for his mother to see. The touch steadied her regardless, even if it were pretend.

King Victor cleared this throat, signaling the room into silence. All eyes were on the king. Even the sunlight seemed to still in his presence. The silence settled as he surveyed those gathered. His eyes lingered on Ryn for a moment too long, and she felt the accusation there, the damning desire to throw her the executioner's block, to blame this string of vampire attacks on her. Like she was unworthy of his meeting room, unworthy to sit between Zain and Queen Portia.

Ryn agreed wholeheartedly, but the look on the king's face made her think of his murder. His blood would be a high commodity. Royal blood.

Maybe he would fall down the stairs after one too many glasses of wine, or be stabbed through the heart by one of his guards. It wouldn't be terribly hard to frame a guard. Especially if it were a guard's dagger.

It frightened her how quickly that plan formed.

Zain brought their laced fingers into his lap, against his thigh. He squeezed her hand as if he knew the dark turn of her thoughts—a ridiculous notion, but guilt stung her heart.

"Vampires were found in our cellar this morning," King Victor began, his voice grave as death. "Hunters are investigating as we speak." His gaze moved to Commander Wade, who sat arrow-straight and stone-faced. "I consider this invasion an act of war. Regardless of how many of those demons still exist within my city, my kingdom, we will eradicate them. Every single one."

The king's gaze landed on Zain, and his entire body tensed. His grip on Ryn's hand turned painful. She rubbed her thumb along his index finger, her attempt at reassurance. It seemed like something a supportive, loving wife would do. It had been so long since she had touched someone, she wasn't sure if she was doing it right. It seemed to work; Zain looked to her, gratitude in his eyes.

Or pretend gratitude. She couldn't tell.

King Victor continued to talk, but she wasn't listening. She was looking at Zain, at the despair in his blue eyes, at his disheveled hair, at the wrinkles in his shirt. Something had happened for him to have arrived at this meeting looking anything but perfect.

Esben and the king wore the same—residual panic, a fractured confidence. What happened in that cellar? Zain's air of discomfort bothered her. Something else had happened, something more he couldn't say in front of the council and his father.

Not like he would tell her, his pretend lover.

"…have heard of Miss Sabryn Evren," King Victor said, drawing her attention off Zain. The room now looked at her. "We hope to hold a royal wedding before the spring."

Her heart skipped a beat. Spring? Zain's unreadable gaze met hers. Like their imminent wedding was nothing.

Spring was barely a season away.

A murmur of joy broke through the glumness, but it wasn't sharp enough to slice through the darkness.

The king leaned forward, hands flat on the table. "Hunters will sweep every corner of the keep. Every room, closet, and cabinet. I apologize for the inconvenience it may cause, but we cannot leave any shadow overlooked. Those demons hide in slivers of darkness, and we will not leave any. I want light burning throughout the keep at all hours, at every door, in every room. I want Nightshade Keep to be a beacon to its people that we will outshine these monsters, as well as to any threat who thinks they can attack us."

The orders went on, and Ryn's hands went clammy. She couldn't help the guilt that crawled up her spine that whispered how everything was her fault—it started with her trespass into the Red Forest, with her impatience. If she would have just waited for Nobel to send her a contract, she wouldn't be in this mess, and it would be the royals' problem. She wouldn't be in the middle of it.

Of course, Nobel would've likely handed her the king's assassination anyway, and then she would be stuck outside trying to get in.

She would kill the king to save Lu, and now she had to do it before spring.

Dinner that night had been planned as a family affair, but due to the events of that afternoon the king canceled it. The king and Esben joined the Hunters on their sweep of the keep. Zain and Ryn took a private dinner in their sitting room. The glum feeling inched over the entire keep, thickening with the sunset. From the tall windows of the sitting room, Ryn watched lights spark to life in every part of the keep, every room, every turret, every tower.

"We will spend a fortune in lamp oil and candles," Zain muttered, watching the same from the other side of the table. He sipped his wine.

Zain had asked for two bottles for dinner, and he was on his fourth glass. Like Ryn could talk—she was on her third. She'd never been able to afford enough wine to be drunk, but tonight she drank freely. It wiggled in her bloodstream, loosened her thoughts, numbed the anxiety left by the hustle. She hadn't much of an appetite until halfway through her second, and then she'd nibbled on the rye bread and rosemary butter while Zain revealed what had happened in the cellar.

"Esben and I were nearly to the kitchens when we heard a scream." Zain paused for a healthy drink. "Esben rushed to help, and we encountered two vampires. Esben slaughtered them before they could mutter a threat or excuse."

"Quite the warrior," Ryn mused.

"He's just like our father." Zain stared into his wine. His expression was stony. "He went in blade first, while I stood and watched. I'm not allowed a blade."

"Why not?"

Zain scoffed. Bitterly, he said, "The same reason I wasn't allowed to join the Hunters. I am too *sickly*. Hunters need to be in pristine health and physical prowess."

Ryn digested those words and the bitterness. He didn't look sickly, not like he had the first morning. "And you can't carry a blade or learn how to use it because you might get sick?"

"It is my heart." Zain tipped his wine to her. "The excitement might stop it altogether. Not to mention, I might hurt myself."

"That is part of learning to use a blade."

He laughed. It was small, a bubble of humor. "I agree, as do Neville and Esben. Father, unfortunately, has the final say. I am forbidden from joining the ranks of the Hunters. I spent my time reading while Esben learned how to dance with steel."

"Can you dance without steel?"

He cocked a brow. "Enough to pass in court. Why?"

In truth, she had no reason why she had asked. The wine addled her thoughts, and she jumped from one to another without caring why. "What would you have done to the vampires if Esben had captured them instead?"

"Interrogation," Zain said plainly. "Who knows the vampires' plans and motives better than the vampires themselves? It seems foolish to murder them outright. Anyone else would have been given a chance to explain themselves."

She hummed as she swirled her wine. "It sounds, my dear prince, like *you* are defending the vampires."

Zain met her gaze. A beat passed, then another.

Ryn tilted the glass back and took a drink. As she straightened, the world wobbled. It took a moment for Zain to come back into focus.

"We're taught that vampires are creatures of evil, malicious, and envious of the fae," Zain said, his tone lowly and somber, barely slurred with the drink. "We are punished for questioning it, for thinking anything else. There are no vampires left to counter those beliefs, except those forced into hiding. My father brought peace to this kingdom by violence and slaughter, yet he preaches peace with our neighbors. Who's to say we can't have peace with vampires?"

Ryn chewed on those words, what her mind caught of them. Zain tiptoed close to vampire sympathizer. In the eyes of the Hunters, being sympathetic was as damnable as being a vampire. Unless she had misheard him. Unless he had said something else and her mind filled in the gaps with words he hadn't actually said.

Zain laughed, a cultured and practiced sound. "See what wine does to me?" He took a healthy drink.

Silence fell between them. Ryn didn't think she had imagined his words.

"I think…if there is a chance for peace as opposed to fighting, we should take it," she said.

His full attention snapped to hers. "I agree, Lady Ryn. But as to your other question, I doubt I could have been a warrior like Esben even with all the training Hunters endure. I used to think I could, but there is something else in Esben that makes him the way he is." He drained his wine in a single gulp. "Something chivalrous and ancient."

"And you think there's something in you that makes you the way you are?" She raised her brows.

Zain didn't answer right away. He stared into his empty wine glass, face unreadable. "I suppose there is."

"And you think whatever makes you the way you are isn't as good as what is in Esben?"

Cold silence answered her. Zain's expression hardened—brow crinkled, lips pursed, body tensed—and she knew she'd hit a nerve, one buried deep.

"I used to think that if I was more like Lu, everything would've been better," she admitted to him through the haze of wine. "If I'd have been softer, kinder, and all the things good females are, we wouldn't have struggled to survive, like everything bad that happened was my fault."

"Is that so?" Zain asked, his voice softer but distant.

"If you had the same something as Esben, then you'd be just like him," she said, because her words made perfect sense to her. "The world has an Esben. It needs a Zain too."

His blue eyes met hers, the doubt evident on his face.

Ryn slid her hand across the table and held it open. His doubtful gaze looked at her hand as if she'd set a snake between them, and she feared he would reject the notion, and as the heat of foolishness began to settle into her skin, he set his hand into hers. Before he could change his mind, she closed her fingers over his.

"You don't give yourself enough credit," she said. "Don't forget the part where you saved my life. Your brother stood by the throne in silence. Esben was content to let me die. You were not. You showed compassion."

A pink blush heated Zain cheeks, his brows shot upward, and he looked away as a laugh burst from his lips.

"I'm serious!" Ryn's voice cracked. She pulled her hand from his. Red-hot embarrassment heated her face and neck.

"I know you are, which is what makes it so adorable," Zain said, a genuine smile stretching his face.

This smile was different from ones she had seen before. It was genuine and just for her. She had teased that smile out of him.

His smile flattened as he searched her face. "What is it?"

"I knew you could smile," she said, leaning back.

That genuine smile appeared once again. Softer. "Anything is possible, or so I've been told. Maybe I needed the right person with the right words."

"And you almost didn't want to marry me." Ryn sipped her wine.

Zain chuckled. The curve of his smile faltered, and something darker passed under his expression.

"Did something else happen this morning?" She softened her voice, the same tone that had coaxed him to smile.

Zain poured himself half a glass. "The vampires were carrying a crate of blood."

"A crate of blood?" Her mind painted a wooden basin with blood sloshing around inside.

"Bottled blood."

The wine turned sour on her tongue. Her throat tightened. Her skin flashed clammy and cold. *Bottled blood.*

As far as she knew, she was the only enchantress who could bottle blood.

"Ryn?"

She drained the rest of her wine in a single gulp then set it beside the open bottle. The sitting room tilted, the floor shifted, and then it swayed the other direction. She blamed the wine. "It… I don't like it. Bottled blood. Vampires in the keep. It…makes me feel like I might throw up."

Her blood, the blood she had bottled with her magic, had somehow found its way into the keep in the hands of vampires. Could they trace the magic to her? If the king discovered her as a blood enchantress, they would use it as evidence of vampire collusion. Not even Zain would be able to protect her from the wrath of the Hunters.

She had long suspected vampires to be among Nobel's buyers. He had never volunteered the information, and she had never asked. She hadn't wanted the damning knowledge on her soul. If she didn't know, she couldn't sell the information. That's how she liked it.

If she didn't know, she could pretend it didn't exist. But to know her bottled blood supplied vampires unsettled her. Willingly or not, she *was* a vampire accomplice.

"Ryn?" Zain stared at her over his wine.

She pulled her gaze from the breadcrumbs on her plate and to Zain. "I didn't have nearly as many problems when I lived in low town."

A small smile stretched his lips. "Perhaps you should stop drinking."

"Or drink more."

His smile stretched a bit further. "Or drink more." He poured her another glass.

She accepted the wine and took a drink.

"You know what bothers me most?" Zain asked, looking over her left shoulder. A heartbeat, and then his gaze met hers. "That the blood was as fresh as yours would be if I cut your throat."

The words rattled her already unsettled nerves. Her voice came out small. *Play dumb.* "But…how?"

"Magic. It couldn't be anything else."

She swallowed against her dry throat. "But there is no more magic."

"The only magic left in the realm is vampiric," Zain whispered. "According to history, ancient fae had magic enough to command the wind and rain and even the earth. Vampires hunted fae magic and used their blood to boost their own, until fae magic faded." He let out a sigh. "Now the only magic that exists is tainted and cursed."

"Like bottling blood," she said weakly.

Zain nodded. "Like bottling blood."

"Like vampires." The words constricted against her wine-addling lungs.

"Historians suggest vampires were once fae, but they were twisted by a blood curse or disease that turned them into what they are," Zain said, eyes on his wine. "It is a strange thing to think, that vampires were once fae, like us."

"I've never heard that," Ryn whispered. The warmth seeped from her skin, and she could not keep warm. Vampires had always been vampires, cruel and bloodthirsty monsters, or so she'd been told, or so the Sun Council proclaimed. "Is that why we hate them? Because they stole our magic?"

Zain considered the question. "History books suggest the Abrani vampire clan had a good deal of magic, whether by their own or by theft is unknown. My father in particular hates them because they killed his family, but there was a long trail of animosity and bloodshed between the Casiano and Abrani houses before the war."

A strange gaze came over Zain's eyes, almost like a longing. Curious, Ryn reached out to his blood. Without touching his blood directly, his emotions were muted, but she felt enough. Longing, disgust, betrayal.

She withdrew before he noticed. Such a strange set of emotions. What could he long for with a sense of betrayal and disgust? Disgust at himself for longing for it, or disgust at what he longed for? Who had betrayed him? Was he thinking of his brother, the golden prince who joined the Hunters when Zain could not? Or was he thinking of the vampires who had invaded his home, or the Hunters who hadn't caught them? The vampire who hid somewhere within the keep?

And she realized she didn't know her betrothed well enough to know what he was thinking.

"And Sovann is among the only kingdoms with a vampire problem," Zain said a bit bitterly. "We are far enough north that our mild summers and long winters are ideal for vampires who thrive in the dark and cold, not to mention the caverns in the mountains, and the lands beyond that are too hostile for fae or human inhabitants. A vampire would shrivel and burn in the southern climates."

Ryn wondered what it might be like to live in a place where vampires weren't a threat, where darkness didn't spread fear, where winters weren't brutal and unforgiving.

A cold wind whistled against the windows, through the eaves and invisible drafts. As the king commanded, Nightshade Keep glowed like a beacon. Shadows remained between the spots of light, on the roof and on the grounds, and Ryn doubted every shadow could be eliminated. Like vampires, shadows slithered through the smallest cracks.

Under all this suspicion and fear, if the king were to be found bloodless, vampires would be blamed. Ryn would be blameless.

She could use the unease for the perfect murder, and get away with it.

Zain set his empty wine glass on the table, the clink drawing Ryn's attention. He stood without taking his eyes off hers. Panic slithered under her skin; had he glimpsed murder in her thoughts? Zain stepped around the table, paused by her chair, and after a terrifyingly few too many heartbeats, held his hand out to her.

"Have you ever danced, Lady Ryn?" His velvet voice rolled over her skin.

Panic easing, she took a gulp of her wine. "No. Dancing isn't something I've had time for, unless it's drunk dancing at the tavern."

Zain smirked. "I'm talking ballroom dancing."

She laughed. "Oh yes, I danced all the time. Ballrooms are quite popular in the slums."

Zain fought to keep his princely demeanor. "You will be expected to dance at balls and celebrations, including our wedding. Best get a start on your lessons." He glanced over his shoulder. "Neville, could you play for us?"

Neville stalked to the rosewood piano in the corner and began to play a sweet, charming melody from the keys. It was nothing like the hectic drums and strings of the taverns.

Ryn had a witty comment about Neville's ability to play on her tongue, but Zain took a step away from her and bowed forward like a gentleman. He extended his hand to her again.

"May I have this dance, my lady?" His voice rolled off his tongue like honeyed wine, dark and velvety.

It might have been the wine or the sly grin on his handsome face or how he looked at her from under his dark lashes, but she slid her hand into his. He led her into the middle of the room, set her free hand on his shoulder, placed his hand on her waist, then held their fingers to the side. Ryn had seen the position before, but seeing it from a distance and being in it herself were different. She stood close to Zain, but a respectable space remained between her chest and his.

Zain began an easy dance that matched Neville's song.

Ryn had never danced like this before. Zain looked at her like he had nowhere he would rather be. No one had ever looked at her like that. She told herself it was the face of a prince, raised to be suave and elegant, and yet… She pretended it was real. Even just for a dance.

She pretended someone could look at her like that, feel that way about her, and she wouldn't be alone for the rest of her life and die a miserable old wretch. If she lived that long. She pretended mates really existed, and the undefinable bond between her and Zain was what had caused him to pull her from the execution line and what kept her in the keep.

He twirled her around the floor while Neville plucked out a melody. Zain spun her, then as she came back to him, he held her closer than before. Close enough his warm breath puffed against her temple. He leaned closer still. His lips brushed hers. Her treacherous body responded with a surge of heat, most of which traveled down her stomach and into her core.

"I'm supposed to lead," he whispered.

"You are."

Chuckling, he added, "You are supposed to follow my steps. You are leading."

"Why do you get to lead?"

"The gentleman leads." He wiggled his brows.

"Oh, is that supposed to be you?"

"Unless you would rather be a gentleman?" His smirk stretched and he shamelessly looked her up and down. "I'm sure we could find some trousers to fit you."

"The *gentleman*," Ryn said with a scoff. "That is sexist."

"It's tradition."

"Doesn't mean it's not sexist."

His smirk turned sinister, sending a shiver down her spine. "Then by all means, lead away," he purred.

He paused, giving Ryn the chance to lead. She looked at their combined hands, her hand on his shoulder, his knowing gaze. She didn't know how to lead a dance.

Zain laughed, a low sound that twisted the pooling warmth low in her belly. He swept her back into the dance.

"When you learn to dance," Zain said against her temple, "you can lead."

They danced around the sitting room as the ambient light from the keep draped inside in warm golds and amber, as the winter hissed against the keep. Ryn lost track of how many songs Neville played, how many times Zain twirled her out and brought her back, or how many times his lips brushed against her hair. She imagined it was real, that the heartless prince felt something for her, that the warmth singing in her veins was real.

And then the music ended, and a strange silence settled over the sitting room.

Ryn found herself leaning Zain's chest, far closer than they had been. Zain blinked, then stepped away like he'd been burned—she told herself he was just as surprised at their closeness, but whereas her cheeks heated into embarrassing pink, his demeanor remained unaffected.

Because it wasn't real. This was pretend. An act.

And she felt ridiculously foolish.

"I-I'm going to retire for the evening." She stepped away from him. "That's, uh, what you royals say, isn't it? Retire?"

"It is, yes." Zain filled his wine glass, then lifted it to his lips, watching her every movement with an unreadable expression.

The warm, fuzzy feeling fluttering through her veins evaporated.

"Then I will see you tomorrow, *darling*." Ryn poured herself a fourth glass of wine. Wine in one hand, she curtsied with the other.

Irene and Kari followed her into the bedroom, one scurrying and the other marching.

23

IN THE DEEP

Ryn

Ryn headed straight for the bath. Irene posted herself in the bedroom while Kari followed without hesitation and turned the tap for hot water then twirled to gather towels. Ryn sorted through the cabinet of salts and oils. New scents had been added, florals and odd names she couldn't connect with a smell, like *moon flower* and *summer storm*.

What the fuck did summer storm smell like? "Did the queen choose these?"

"She did, my lady." Kari arranged the towels on the stool beside the tub.

Ryn dumped *summer storm* salts into the rising water. The bathwater turned a pale green and filled the room with a sweet floral laced with a sharp musk. It wasn't bad. Ryn had little experience with salts or perfumes, and few shops in low town even sold them. The upper markets reeked with scented everything, salts and candles and oils.

But Ryn reminded herself as Kari untied her corset, she was a princess. She could afford luxuries. Especially if the crown paid for it.

Ryn set her wine glass on the thick ledge of the bath, then sank into the perfumed water. Kari scurried away, and Ryn was alone. Blissfully alone.

Steam curled toward the ceiling. Two dozen candles burned within the bathing room, reflecting off the polished marble and scrubbed tiles. Light reflected over every surface, yet shadows remained.

Would Hunters be enough to stop vampires from slipping into the keep? They already had. Twice. Slipped right under the Hunters' collective nose, into the keep and into the kitchen. For what purpose?

That there might be a vampire resurgence worried her.

But they wouldn't harm her. They needed her magic to harvest blood. Of course, if they took over, then they wouldn't have to hide in the shadows and they wouldn't need bottled blood. They wouldn't need her.

Lost in her thoughts, Ryn didn't hear the bathing room door open—she heard it click shut. Panic set in, hot and fluid—Kari wouldn't have shut the door so quietly. Irene would have burst in, and she wouldn't have taken a post inside the bathroom unless something was wrong. Ryn whipped her head around, wet hair sticking to her cheek.

Her skin flushed hot as coals.

Zain stood behind the door. He had left his tailcoat behind and wore only his black shirt and trousers. His sleeves were rolled to his elbows, revealing a wash of his pale skin. One hand held his half-full wine glass, the other held the neck of the bottle. His eyes were clear, piercing blue, and settled on her like a blade at her throat.

"What are you doing here?" The sudsy water rose halfway up her breasts, though she doubted Zain innocent of what breasts looked like.

He took measured steps toward the tub, his limbs loose, his expression soft but unreadable. "I am making sure my *darling* is doing all right."

She tipped her half-full wine glass. "With more wine?"

He pressed the wine bottle to his chest in mock shock. "Of course, with wine. I would have brought chocolates, but I have none."

"You don't have chocolates?"

"I'm not my mother," he said, chuckling. "I've never had much of a taste for chocolate."

Ryn cocked a brow. "Who doesn't like chocolate?"

"I am fond of the sugar candies," he said with an easy shrug.

"And your being in here has nothing to do with me being in the bath?"

Zain flashed her a mischievous grin. "My motives certainly had nothing to do with your bath, or that I knew you were naked."

Chuckling, she asked, "What else would I be doing in there?"

He sipped his wine. "Hiding from your nanny, I suppose. They're watching you, you know. Reporting to the Hunters and my father."

"Yes, and now she'll know you were in here." She tilted her head. "She'll assume the worst."

Zain didn't seem to mind. He strolled over to the tub and sat on the marble ledge, body angled toward hers. He set the bottle on the floor, glass clinking against the tile. "Maybe I wanted to see what I missed that night at the tavern."

His husky tone sent a shiver down her body, despite the warm water. Heat pooled between her legs. Zain, as if he could see it on her face, grinned like a wolf. She bit her tongue as intrusive thoughts about what she had missed that night seeped into her mind.

"Wouldn't you agree?" Zain leaned closer. He dipped a finger in the water, swirling the suds on the surface.

Ryn trailed her gaze down his front. She hummed and hid her smirk behind her wine. "I doubt it's worth getting out of the bath for."

His dark, sensual laugh sent heat down her spine where it settled low in her stomach. Zain dipped two fingers into the bath, swirling the suds, closer and closer those two fingers swirled, until they paused before her breast. With his eyes locked on hers, those fingers grazed the skin of her upper breast, then trailed down to her peaked nipple. His grin stretched and his eyes darkened. He rolled her nipple between his fingers.

Her hips bucked of their own accord, and she bit her lip before a whimper escaped.

"Oh?" Zain whispered, the sound as velvet as the steam. "Like that, do you?"

When she didn't answer, he pinched. She gasped, the pleasure mixing with pain.

"Do you like this?" Zain whispered, the sound edged with demand.

He pinched harder.

"Yes!" The sound tore out her throat. Her wine jostled, almost spilling.

Zain laughed, a velvet sound, and in a smooth motion, he knelt on the floor behind the bath. A clink—he set his wine glass on the floor. He grazed her fingers, then slid the wine from her own. He brought his other arm around her, grazing his fingertips along her shoulder, her collarbone, then dipped below the water to take her breast in his palm.

Lightning flashed along her nerves and bones and into her sex. Had she not been in the bath, she would have been soaked.

Zain leaned in, hot breath on her ear, and whispered, "Imagine my tongue instead of my fingers."

A soft moan escaped her as he tugged on one nipple then the other, pleasure mixed with pain.

"Imagine my teeth," he whispered.

Her toes curled. Oh, she wanted those teeth. She unclenched her fists and slid a hand over her thigh, over her sex. A moan fell from her lips, then he pinched her nipples so hard it hurt.

"No," Zain whispered in her ear. "Not yet."

He pulled her arms to her sides.

Her heart thumped, and it somehow curled the tension so tight it hurt. She thought she might come just at his voice.

"I have a rule for you, sweet Ryn," he whispered. "You will not touch yourself, at least not until after our wedding night."

"And you?"

A hum was her response.

"Will you touch yourself?" Her voice was breathless, and thinking about his cock didn't help.

"Do you want me to withhold?"

"Yes. If I have to suffer, so will you."

"Oh, my sweet Ryn, who said anything about suffering? Are you suffering right now?" He paused to let her answer, and when she didn't, because she wasn't, he whispered, "If you want to keep me from touching myself, you'll have to do it for me."

His fingers teased her nipples in identical movements, one hand a heartbeat after the other, sending pleasure shooting into her toes and curling at her clit. The next had her head falling back into his shoulder. Her wet hair soaked into his shirt.

"Is that a yes?"

Breathlessly, she said, "I accept your challenge, *darling* Zain."

He slid his hand down her naked front, to where her sex throbbed. Water soaked his rolled sleeve. He circled her clit, tortuously slow, then grazed his finger over it. He circled, stroked, and circled again, each tease bringing her closer. She bucked into his hand, moaned into his shoulder, as he tortured her clit and thumbed her nipple.

The glorious abyss crashed over her, sending stars and velvet darkness across her vision, making her forget the bath and the keep. Zain's chuckle resounded through it all, sensual and full of desire. Before the ecstasy faded, his mouth was on hers.

He swallowed the sound, then stood, bottle in one hand and glass in the other, grinning like he'd won. She felt a flush of embarrassment, but before he could comment on it, he left.

Ryn heaved a breath, body tingling with lingering ecstasy.

Challenge, indeed.

24

FROSTED FOREST, FROSTED SECRETS
Ryn

Kari drew the curtains around Ryn's bed to block out the light from the hearth. Her skin reeked of *summer storm*. The hearth warmed the other side of the curtains, and the ambient light from the keep glowed through the windows. Would anyone have trouble sleeping with so much light?

A sliver of sweet pleasure remained in her bloodstream. She couldn't keep her thoughts from drifting to Zain and how he had brought her to climax with just his hands and his words. It would be a shame when this marriage fell apart after she assassinated his father.

If she played her cards right, Zain wouldn't know she'd done it. Someone else would take the fall, Esben would inherit the throne, and she and Zain could still play this game of marriage. Ryn and Lu would live cushioned lives, sipping fine wine and eating expensive chocolates in silk dresses.

But first, she needed to get rid of King Victor.

She fell asleep plotting his murder.

In her dreams, she was in the Red Forest. It was night, starless and deathly cold. Ryn hunted an elusive silver rabbit. She cornered the rabbit in a dark alcove, and then she felt a horrible presence behind her. Dark and slithering as death itself. She turned, and found only red-ringed eyes and bloodied fangs. It lunged for her, moving impossibly fast.

She woke with a start.

At the crackling of the fire against dry wood and gentle warmth against her face, her first thought was how expensive firewood was and how little coin she had. She sprang upward to douse the fire and save the wood, only to find herself in a velvet cage of deep indigo. Bed curtains. The fire crackled on the other side.

Ryn blinked; the last two days returned.

The silver rabbit, the vampires, the prince, her task of killing King Victor to save her sister from Nobel. Her betrothed and his talented fingers and husky whisper.

Sleep felt ages away. Ryn pulled her knees to her chest and let the panic of waking up in a new place subside.

She pulled the curtain aside and slid out of bed. The fire crackled from within the marble fireplace, muted by a gold folding screen. Logs stacked in the grate beside it.

The pale glow of dawn seeped through the curtains in shades of palest blue and soft gray. Ryn usually slept until midday or after, but with the vampire nightmare so fresh in her mind, she knew she wouldn't be falling back asleep. Sliding her feet into her new house slippers—leather and lined with reddish fur, because Queen Portia had insisted she needed them, and right now, Ryn agreed—and tiptoed to the window.

Ryn rarely witnessed a sunrise. For her, it represented a deadline. The sun banished the shadows of night, exposing her deeds, and it had been her goal to be on her way home, coin in hand, before the day began. She had seen plenty of sunsets, but there was something different, almost sleepy, in the way the day unfolded. She didn't know how many she would see, so she savored the soft grays and blues as they brightened over the east into yellows and golds.

By the light snoring, Kari slept in the servant's room. Ryn pulled a thick cardigan over her nightgown and let herself into the sitting room. Irene did not stand at her post. Instead, the night guard stood in her place. She was a middle-aged woman with a scar on her cheek and braided flaxen hair. She beheld Ryn with indifference, the same as all the Hunters. She said nothing as Ryn crossed to the small library and curled into one of the chairs, if nothing else but to watch the sunrise through the large windows.

Ryn was used to this—waking up alone and being alone. Only she usually woke with a stiff neck and back from sleeping on an old mattress and a growling stomach from skipping dinner. For once, her stomach was full and her body was well-rested.

When their father had died, he left a hole in both their family and their income. Ryn had stepped up so their mother wouldn't have to work twice as hard. While their mother had taught Lu to sew and introduced her to her clients, Ryn cultivated her magic. She'd met Nobel and agreed to become a monster so her mother and sister didn't have to.

Ryn hadn't saved her mother, but she would save Lu. No matter how many kings or queens stood in her way.

The sun steadily rose, brightening the east, washing the keep and the city in golden daylight. Still, the lights in the keep burned.

"They say in ages past, people rejoiced in the sunrise," came Zain's husky voice from his open bedroom door.

Ryn started; she hadn't heard the door open.

He strolled into the room, wearing an emerald robe over a black sleeping shirt, bare feet slapping against the floor. The sunlight washed over him, alighting his tousled dark hair and pale skin. He turned his back to the windows, dousing his expression in shadow. He took slow, measured steps to where she sat, then sat in the armchair beside hers.

"You don't get a night guard?" Ryn nodded toward his bedroom doors. No guard stood watch.

"I'm sure they're in the hall." Zain leaned back in the chair, sighing. He glanced at her guard. "It means they don't trust you."

She harrumphed. Her guard stared at the wall, stone-faced.

"Trouble sleeping?" Zain asked.

"No," she said. "I woke up early. I thought I'd watch the sunrise for once."

"Once?"

She shrugged. Without revealing too much, she simply said, "I haven't had a lifestyle where I could afford to just sit and watch the sunrise."

Zain rose to his feet. "Well, that won't do. Come, let's take a walk."

She frowned. "A walk? Right now?"

"Yes, an early walk to stir the mind."

While Zain changed into one of his suits, Ryn changed into a pair of leather shoes, delicate enough for a lady, but also sturdy enough to wear without breaking an ankle. They were also touched with reddish fur.

With the night guard who hadn't said a word to either of them at their heels, Zain and Ryn slipped into the keep's quiet corridors. More Hunters stood on guard. One of them fell in step behind them, with the night guard.

"Vampires return to their shadows at sunrise," Zain whispered as they tiptoed down the stairs. "That's why there aren't as many Hunters during the day as there are at night."

That made sense.

"How do you know this?" Ryn asked.

Zain guided her into the first floor, toward the back which led into the gardens. "My father has written a great number of books on vampires, their habits, their lifestyle, their eating behavior. He might be the best source of knowledge about vampires, if only he didn't bristle every time the subject came up. It's like a war horn to a soldier. I've read every one of them at least once."

"So studious," she mocked.

He quirked a brow. "Would you rather me be dull and uninformed?"

"No, I'd rather you be you."

The words had come naturally because they were true. She would not wish Zain to alter his personality for anyone, and she hadn't yet found a fault she would change.

Her words settled over Zain like he had never heard such a compliment. His brows rose, his smirking lips slackened, and his cocky expression faded into one she'd not seen before—soft surprise.

"What?" she asked.

"I don't think anyone has ever said that to me."

He said no more. They entered the garden, and as the guard opened the doors, the frigid air of early winter wafted inside. It seethed through the seams and threads of Ryn's woolen cardigan and needled her skin as if she wore nothing. The cold didn't bother Zain, and he strung his arm through hers and set off at a stroll.

The gardens were barren but beautiful. Frost covered every leaf, stone, and tree limb, dusting the gardens in powdered diamonds and silver. Zain took her on a different path this time, one better suited to admiring the frosted gardens. They passed a massive greenhouse, the green-tinted panes thick with condensation in places, the plants within green with life.

They followed the winding path through a grove of skinny trees. Their branches spread above them in a massive web. Red and yellow leaves spotted the path, each dusted in silver, sparkling like diamond dust in the sunlight.

"I keep thinking about how those vampires got in," Ryn whispered. "I think they got in through the undercroft."

"Is that so?" Zain's brow rose.

"I know Neville said the entries were sealed, but if it's anything like the city sewers, it's a maze," she argued, hoping this first step of her plan would work. "The vampires who once lived here would know how to navigate it. There might be secret passages or hidden doors. I doubt the Hunters could illuminate every shadow down there."

A long moment passed, and Ryn felt her feeble plan crack at the edges.

"I agree," Zain whispered back. "I've been in the undercroft a few times. There are countless tunnels and ancient storerooms. It has a strange feel about it, like there is a ghost standing behind you and another hiding around the corner."

He shuddered.

"How far do the tunnels go?" she asked. "Could it, say, reach the city?"

He cast a side glance at her, his gaze knowing. "If a vampire snuck into the undercroft at an unguarded location and knew the layout, they wouldn't have a problem sneaking into the keep undetected."

"Exactly."

"Even though my father supposedly sealed every exit."

"Obviously not."

His grin stretched. "Is this what you've been thinking about all morning?"

She shrugged. "I feel like they're targeting me. It bothers me."

"Well, if they are, there isn't a way into the undercroft in the royal wing," Zain said, the words meant to be reassuring. "Esben and I used to sneak down there through the kitchens. There's a trapdoor behind the larder. The staff use it as extra storage. That is where we suspect the vampires came from."

A moment of silence passed, during which a cardinal flew overhead, a streak of crimson against the silver forest beyond. It landed in one of the hundreds of bird feeders hanging throughout the garden.

"But I believe my father is keeping things from me," Zain added in a low whisper, enough his guards couldn't overhear. "He and Esben know things I don't."

"Why?"

"My father doesn't trust me," Zain whispered. He grimaced. "It has only gotten more prominent since this vampire business began."

King Victor didn't trust his younger son? Zain had that air about him, like he could be plotting murder at any given time, but for his own father to withhold information gave Ryn an odd feeling. Of course, she couldn't talk about someone plotting murder.

"Why tell me this?"

Zain cocked a brow. "First, you are to be my wife. Regardless of how this union came about, trust is the foundation of any marriage. I need you to trust me, Ryn. I need to be able to trust you."

The words were knives, each one.

"Okay," she whispered, unsure of what else to say. She didn't trust him. But she needed him to trust her, and for him to think she trusted him. "I agree. We need to be able to trust each other. It would make this marriage smoother."

He flashed her a soft smile and pulled her closer. He leaned in, and she met him. The kiss was chaste, but soft in a way that felt unlike Prince Zain and his dark edges. He lingered against her lips.

"You're shivering," he whispered. "Back to keep with you."

They started back along the path to the glowing keep. Ryn replayed his words, namely the instructions on how to get into the undercroft. If she could use the tunnels to get from one corner of the keep to the other unseen, it would make killing the king easier. It would also give her an escape if her plan went wrong.

25

THE COLOR OF RAIN AT SUNSET
Ryn

Ryn spent the next few days lounging and contemplating her assassination plan. Packages arrived, more each day. Ryn and Kari spent each morning putting her new things away. Kari suggested getting rid of the old armoire for something larger, but Zain adamantly refused; he said he remembered hiding in it as a child, when his grandmother was alive, and it would stay. Ryn had no strong feelings toward the armoire; however, it irked her that he cared about what furniture she had in her room. She held it in. It was just an armoire.

Queen Portia brought her a list of history books noble daughters would have read and studied in school, and Irene and a handful of guards escorted Ryn to the library. Guards and Hunters stood in every corridor, leaving no shadow unwatched. It would be difficult to sneak between them or make a sound in a room without someone hearing.

Ryn fell into a strange routine of assassination planning, reading, and chocolate sampling. All the while, Hunters searched every room in Nightshade Keep for evidence of vampire activity.

Then, on the fourth day, over breakfast, Zain suggested they take a carriage ride through the city. To let the people see his bride.

"To let them see me?" Ryn cocked a brow.

"To also get out of the keep," Zain added. His tone matched his frown. "I'm about to lose my mind with all these guards, and Aurora is stalking the corridors for a chance to corner me. Neville refuses to see her as a threat."

She stared into her tea. The last few days blurred together in her memory. She hadn't spent so much time doing nothing in…years. Since her parents were alive. She had spent the last decade working and sleeping and drinking to forget all the working.

"A carriage ride sounds lovely." She flashed Zain a smile.

He tilted his head. "You're looking a bit murderous, love."

She ignored the comment and sipped her tea.

After breakfast, Kari dressed Ryn in a dark green dress that flowed around her legs like water and dipped lower in the front than others. Lace decorated the bodice, hiding her cleavage behind a floral design. The long sleeves ended in matching cuffs. Zain wore a lovely green suit, and as they met in the sitting room, his eyes grazed over her.

"Your mother picked this dress." Ryn twirled.

Zain hummed. "That is concerning. She usually hates things that I like."

Guards escorted them through the manor and to the carriage house, and they set out in a gleaming cage of rosewood. Guards on horseback surrounded the carriage, the hooves clomping inharmoniously on the cobbles.

Ryn and Zain sat shoulder to shoulder with little space between their thighs. The windows were open, allowing the people glimpses of the couple inside. It also allowed the winter air to fill the carriage.

"You haven't told me where we're going," Ryn whispered.

"I have not," he said. "I want it to be a surprise. It is one of my favorite places. Cold?"

Her teeth were nearly chattering.

He slid his arm around her shoulders, tucking her against his side. She leaned into his warmth.

"Have you heard the rumors about us?" Zain asked.

"That we're mates?" She snorted. "Your mother isn't happy about it. She said it makes me harder to get rid of."

"Because the people adore a love story," Zain mused. "Look out the window. See how the people clamor for a glimpse of the mysterious Sabryn Evren, the female who stole the cold prince's heart."

She lifted her head from his shoulder and peered into the busy street. Indeed, heads turned and craned to look inside the carriage.

"They say it is a real love story," Zain said without humor. "Like mates from ancient times, like Staley and Uma."

Ryn wanted to scoff. Staley and Uma were mates from an ancient legend. They were separated and searched for one another for decades, crossing deserts and climbing mountains and enduring the hottest summers and coldest winters, until they at last found one another again.

"You would walk across a blazing desert for me?" she asked. She wouldn't for him.

His smile turned sinister. "Would you let me ravage you for a week straight if I did?"

She chuckled while heat rose in her cheeks. She hadn't forgotten that part of the legend, but her parents had left it out of the version they told. Once reunited, Staley and Uma fucked like starved animals. One line of the story depicts Staley's erection that lasted from sunrise to sunset, during which he ravished his lover near continuously, and there was no count to her pleasures.

"Do you think you could last that long?"

Zain chuckled, the sound building a fire under her skin. "You are lucky the windows are open, Sabryn. Or I would have you on your hands and knees."

"Is that your position of choice?" She tried not to be bothered with how those words heated her skin.

He pressed his lips closer to her ear and whispered, "I'll tell you mine if you tell me yours."

Her gaze dipped to his lips, and before she could fathom an answer, the carriage stopped. The sudden lurch startled them both. Zain composed himself quickly, straightening his jacket while she smoothed her skirts. The footman called out to the guard, one of the horses snorted, and the door opened. Zain climbed out first, and held his hand out for Ryn. As she followed him to the street, whispers surged like winter's wind. A crowd had gathered, staring at the two of them with wide eyes and pointed fingers.

Ryn heard her name in the whispers, as well as *mates* and *princess*.

Zain squeezed her hand. They stood before a grand building of dark stone and pale shutters. He led her inside through a set of wide double doors, into a space with low, golden lighting and plush seats. The atmosphere was posh, the seating sparse, and the guests clean and well-dressed. A delicate chatter filled the air, along with the soft melody of a cello duo. It smelled of wine and perfume. As Zain guided her to a cushioned booth, a well-dressed male appeared at the table.

"Your Highness," the server bowed his head.

"My usual, please. For her as well."

The server bowed his head again and vanished.

"What is your usual?" Ryn lifted a brow.

"You will have to find out, love." Zain leaned into the cushy seating, looking like he had nowhere else he would rather be.

The server returned with a bottle of white wine with a frosted aftertaste. Ryn sipped the wine and leaned back with Zain, admiring the cozy atmosphere.

"This is your favorite place?" she asked.

"One of them." He turned his glittering eyes onto her. "But there is more after this."

She held her expression calm. She felt the eyes of the other patrons on her like gooseflesh. "There's more to this surprise? What have I done to deserve this?"

As the server appeared with a tray of food, Zain leaned in and said in a husky voice that sent shivers down her spine, "You have graced me with your presence, love. You make me want to share things with you."

The server lingered as he shifted the plates to the table. Listening. Every word they said would be all over the city by evening.

Ryn didn't take her eyes off Zain's.

Butterflies fluttered around her stomach at his words and his velvet voice, and she had to remind herself it was pretend. He didn't mean those things. But they were supposed to be mates.

She twisted her features into girlish glee. "I look forward to it."

Zain pressed a kiss to her lips. When they parted, the server was gone. Zain's usual turned out to be assorted meats, cheeses with tiny pieces of pepper, olives, and a pot of earthy smelling tea. The flavors changed depending on the order one ate the various foods, and Zain showed her each one; they laughed as she tried the best flavor combinations and the worst, after which Zain laughed loud enough to startle the next booth over.

It was a genuine laugh, warm and soul-deep. And, Ryn realized, she was having fun too.

She rinsed her palate with the white wine. Over the rim of her glass, she watched Zain's expression change—the humor vanished from his face, his eyes fell to the table, and he put a hand over his heart.

"Zain?" Ryn asked, setting her glass aside.

He dropped his hand, and the look was gone. The arrogant prince returned. "It's nothing."

It hadn't looked like nothing, but Ryn didn't argue. As they left the restaurant arm in arm, she noticed a change in his demeanor. He talked less. His skin was paler. Even his breathing seemed shallow.

The carriage paused outside a long building made entirely of greenish glass.

"A greenhouse," Zain explained, lips a flat line.

They climbed onto the less crowded street. Guards stood outside the greenhouse doors as Zain escorted Ryn inside. The young-faced florist seemed delighted and horrified at their presence. She eyed Irene with a knowing suspicion and dislike, but left them to their own devices in the greenhouse.

The air was warm and wet. It reminded Ryn of a summer storm before the rain, when the air thickened with humidity enough to coat her skin. It smelled like wet soil and fresh flowers. They meandered through the isles of flowers and ferns. Ryn didn't know where to look first. There were so many colors and shapes and arrays of pedals. Roses and lilies and daisies and snapdragons and hundreds of flowers and colors she had never seen before.

"Ah, here we are," Zain said. Even his voice seemed lackluster.

He paused before flowers with beautiful orange petals. Ryn had never seen such a flower before.

"It is a hibiscus," Zain said. "This is what the florist showed me when I requested a flower the color of the rain at sunset."

Her heart clenched. Those had been her words. Her favorite color. Not only had he remembered, but he had actually found a flower.

"Ryn?"

She blinked and realized her eyes were wet.

"Is it that bad?" Zain whispered.

She shook her head and wiped at her eyes. "No, no. This is…great. I didn't expect you to remember."

A small smile broke his grimace. "You underestimated me."

"I did." She leaned into him and kissed his cheek. Zain had continuously surprised her.

Pretend.

He was pretending.

It didn't feel like it. Of course, that was the goal. They were supposed to be mates, and they needed everyone to believe it.

So they needed to act like they believed it too.

Zain wobbled, and again put his hand against his chest. Over his heart. His breath shuddered. His entire body trembeled. "I…"

"Zain?" Ryn turned his body full toward him.

"It's nothing."

"This is clearly not nothing," she hissed.

He stumbled. His skin looked waxy and pale, each breath hitched. He clutched at his heart. "This…air bothers me."

"Then we should leave." She tugged him toward the entrance. They started ungracefully through the aisle.

"I didn't…" Zain took a shuddering breath. "I didn't take the tonic this morning. It would seem I am…due for a dose."

She scowled. "You skipped your tonic?"

"I usually…don't need one so soon," he said between shallow breaths. He leaned more fully on her, and as they turned the corner, he collapsed.

Ryn shifted just in time to catch him, but his weight sent them both to the damp, dirty floor.

"Neville!" Ryn shouted toward the door.

Footsteps rushed from behind her. Ryn put her hand against Zain's chest. His heart skipped every other beat. He struggled to breathe. Sweat covered his face and neck. His hands shook.

The footsteps came closer.

"We need to return to the keep at once," she ordered.

Zain's distant gaze flickered to Neville—and that gaze sharpened. It was not the look one would give to a friend coming to their rescue; it was steel, defensive, and panicked. Ryn turned. The male behind her was not Neville. He did not wear the uniform of the Hunters or the Royal Guard; his mismatched leathers and the assortment of daggers marked him as a mercenary. The intent scowl on his face marked him as a threat, so did the blade he unsheathed and swung toward Ryn's neck.

26
CHIVALRY AND FOOLS
Ryn

A scream tore out of Ryn's throat as the mercenary lunged, as his blade caught the misty greenhouse light, as Zain's dead weight occupied her arms and prevented her from throwing herself out of the way. She squeezed her eyes shut and buried her face in Zain's shoulder.

No knife pierced her skin.

The mercenary grunted. A thump followed—a body landed in the loamy earth of the greenhouse tables, then thudded on the stone pavers of the ground.

Ryn peeked up.

The mercenary lay dead on the ground with a dagger hilt sticking out of his chest. Neville stood over him, slightly breathless, scowling. He bent to retrieve the dagger, but his hand paused above it. Footsteps rushed—Neville grabbed the dagger, pulled it out, and spun in time to slash the blade across another mercenary's throat.

"Ambush!" Royal Guards appeared down the greenhouse isle, Irene leading the pack. They scattered around Ryn and Zain. Ryn didn't have a spare breath to question what it meant. Footsteps thundered through the greenhouse. Mercenaries in mismatched steel plates and leathers surrounded them, blades out.

The fight started like thunder. Ryn bent closer to Zain. In her arms, his breaths had grown quicker and thinner. His skin paled to a waxy white. Ryn pressed her hand over his heart. The beat was erratic. Zain's unfocused blue gaze met hers, ripe with panic and helplessness.

He sat up with Ryn's help, and leaned onto his knees.

"I'm sorry," he said, the words barely audible over the scrapping of the fight around them.

"Don't be," she said.

Bodies slammed into the greenhouse tables of flowers and herbs, sending pots and trays crashing to the ground. Rich, dark soil and torn stems and petals scattered across the paving stones, soaking up the spilled blood. Ryn dared to look—the bodies were both mercenary and guard.

Irene parried one mercenary in front of Ryn and Zain, then cut swiftly to a second. Watching her sent a chill over Ryn's skin. Irene knew how to fight, and she used her smaller stature to her advantage. She wielded her sword like an extension of herself, dancing instead of fighting.

And in the blink of an eye, with one wrong step, the mercenary's blade caught Irene's side. Blood sprayed onto the ground, and she let out a growl of pain. A curse escaped through her gritted teeth.

The mercenaries moved in calculated grace. As the one who had attacked Irene stepped back, the other swung forward—eyes on Ryn.

A deeper instinct took over, and Ryn grabbed the legs of an upturned metal stool. She flung herself and the chair upward with as much strength as she could. The hard seat cracked onto the mercenary's temple. Blood sprayed down his face. He stumbled, but did not fall. In a panic, Ryn latched onto the bloody gash on his temple, seized the whole supply within his body, and *twisted*—his body dropped onto the paving stones. His head smacked one the stones as his own blood tore holes in his heart and lungs.

She released him, and as the blood pounding in her own ears subsided, the horrible gurgling and gasping of the dying filled her head. The dying mercenary looked at her, panic and fury focused on her. His chest shilled. His eyes dimmed.

A cold hand touched hers. Zain's. His trembling fingers squeezed hers like he knew.

"We saw them sneaking through the back garden," said a guard. His voice was distant.

The guards and Hunters closed in around Ryn and Zain.

"Feel that?" Irene spat. She clutched her bleeding side.

"Magic." Neville nudged the mercenary Ryn had killed.

The word sent tension through the guards. Ryn clutched Zain's hand. Because magic meant vampires.

"Is one of them a vampire?" one of the guards asked.

"They're dead, so it doesn't matter." Neville sheathed his sword. "We return to the keep at once. You three, search the bodies and find out if anyone saw where they came from."

While the three guards searched the bodies, Neville hoisted Zain to his feet and helped him to the waiting carriage. Tense guards surrounded it. Ryn climbed into the carriage and helped Neville lift Zain onto the bench. The door shut, and the order to move rang out. The carriage jostled forward at a quick pace, and the guards rode in tight formation around them.

Zain leaned back, and Ryn shifted so he could rest his head in her lap. She pushed his sweat-damp hair out of his face.

"I am sorry," he said again. His eyes were closed.

"Don't be," she said. "You haven't done anything."

"I ruined our outing and made a scene."

"I believe our attackers were the ones who made a scene," Ryn corrected.

Zain cracked his eyes open, trying his best to focus on her. "Now you see me at my weakest. My condition. My uselessness. This… This is why my father forbids me from…joining the Hunters. I am too weak."

"What happened?" Ryn draped her hand over his heart. It beat far too slow.

"I was…" Zain swallowed and closed his eyes, as if the effort of holding them open was too much. "I was born early. Troublesome birth. Nearly…killed my mother. I have…a weak heart. Too much stress, too much heat, and I…shake. My heart…threatens to stop. The alchemist…concocted his tonic that helps."

"That muddy tea," Ryn mused.

The barest of smiles twitched on his pale lips. "The tea."

The carriage rattled along without stopping. The guard cut through the streets and traffic with royal authority. Was Zain's condition that serious? Panic liquefied in Ryn's veins. If Zain died before they wed, what would happen to her? Her hand trembled where it rested against his chest. He lifted a hand and closed his fingers over hers. Icy cold.

"You hit him with a chair," he whispered. His eyes were closed.

"It was a stool," she corrected.

A small smile curved his lips. "A stool." His smile flattened. "No other female has…committed such…chivalrous acts for me."

"Chivalrous?" She chuckled. "No male has ever called me that."

"They are fools," he whispered. His blue eyes peeled open. It took a moment for him to focus on her. "Any male…would be a fool…to overlook you. They would…be lucky to have you."

He shut his eyes and took a shuddering breath. On that breath, she thought she heard what sounded terrifyingly like her name.

It made her heart thump and her skin heat. No one had ever said that about her. Males hadn't ignored her, but no one had wanted anything more than a night's company. She was not the marrying type. Her lifestyle didn't allow for long-term relationships or marriage or love. Those things were for others. For females like Lu who had more kindness in a single hair than most people had in their entire bodies. For males like Esben who had chivalry in his veins.

But for Ryn? She wasn't chivalrous or kind or loving.

No, Zain was delirious. That had to be it. Delirious with skipping heartbeats and a cold sweat. He couldn't know how his words landed, how they made her chest feel like she had swallowed too much air.

A series of shouts signified their arrival at Nightshade Keep. The carriage rumbled into the carriage house and halted, all the while shouts sent guards and servants skittering, for the king, for the alchemist—Prince Zain needed a tonic.

Ryn remained in the carriage with Zain, clutching his shirt. His breaths shuddered, and every few he would stop breathing and her own heart would speed—then he would take a shallow breath.

"Hold on," she whispered.

She realized then—she didn't want him to die. Because she needed him, she told herself. She needed him in order to save herself and Lu.

Footsteps thundered into the carriage house. Neville wrenched open the carriage door, and a short, white-haired male in sage robes climbed inside. He held a steaming cup of Zain's muddy tea in his fingerless gloves. The alchemist pressed the teacup against Zain's pale lips.

Whether the feel of porcelain against his lips, the smell of the tea, or the warmth, Zain stirred. His eyes fluttered open. He drank the tea one small sip at a time.

The alchemist held his unblinking stare on Zain, his expression clinical and unfriendly. By the wrinkles on his face, he didn't smile often. Everything about the old male gave Ryn an uneasy feeling. He reminded her of the males she'd been sent to drain dry.

The color slowly returned to Zain's cheeks. Under her palm, his heartbeats steadied. The alchemist tipped the teacup up until Zain drank every last drop.

The alchemist drew the cup back. He spoke in a monotone voice that mirrored his clinical gaze. "And is the prince all right?"

Zain groaned and rolled his eyes. "Yes, I'm fine. Thank you for your…timely arrival."

Relief swallowed Ryn's being at the sound of his voice, his usual annoyed tone, as if he wasn't thankful but irritated at the old male. He sat up with mild difficulty.

"Rest, Your Highness." The alchemist retreated from the carriage and repeated the order to Neville. "Make sure he gets sleep, Hunter."

"Sir." Neville eyed the alchemist with dislike. He turned that stare onto Zain. "You heard him."

"Yes, yes, to bed with me." Zain stumbled out of the carriage. Neville tried to catch him, but Zain shooed away his arms. "I can walk."

Ryn stepped out after him, and realized Zain held his arm out for hers. His face was blank, almost hateful. Exhausted. Annoyed that his episode of weakness had ended their outing and caused a stir within the keep. She strung her arm through his and they started through the keep in silence. Neville and several guards followed on their heels.

Irene went to the healer's hall to tend to her wounds.

Zain did not speak until they reached their chambers. Their guards remained in the hall, save for Neville. Zain paused halfway into the sitting room, and without looking at Ryn, said, "No one has defended me like that before, not unless it was a guard. You had no reason to, yet you rushed to catch me. You stayed with me as we rushed back to the keep." Still, he did not look at her. "Thank you, Ryn. For that kindness."

Without another word, Zain slid his arm from hers and strode toward his chambers. His posture lacked his typical pride and easiness. He walked like he hadn't slept in days, like he would be unconscious before he hit the pillow.

Neville posted himself by the main chamber door. Ryn glanced at him, Zain's closed chamber door, and the new mountain of packages sitting by the table.

A bath, she decided.

The hot water would help her disentangle whatever the hell had happened that afternoon and the mess of feelings making her chest and head hurt.

27

LOST IN A BOOK

Ryn

Ryn spent the rest of the afternoon going through her packages. There were so many of them. She didn't remember buying so many gloves or scarves or chemises or slips. Yet she had more than she would need and in more colors than she thought possible.

Kari put her new things away. In the armoire. In the chest of drawers. Ryn sat on the bed, watching as servants hauled the dead queen's things away by the armload, watching Kari replace the empty drawers with Ryn's things. The queen had even sent a new rosewood jewelry box with shiny black lacquer. It was a beautiful thing to house her beautiful new jewelry—rings and necklaces of gold and silver. How many bottles would it have taken to buy all of these things?

So many things. Gloves. Leggings. Chemises. Sleeping shirts. Socks. Underthings. Corsets. Tiaras. Hairpins. Makeup. Glittering body oil. Perfumes. Heels and boots. Stockings. A cloak to go with every color of dress, some lined with fur and others not lined at all, some velvet and others heavy wool.

It was a ridiculous number of things. Before, all of Ryn's clothing occupied a single drawer of a dresser shared with Lu.

Once all the packages had been opened and their contents admired and put away, Ryn's chambers felt strangely quiet. She glanced through her open bedroom door. Across the sitting room, Zain's door remained closed. With all the servants coming and going, Neville had repositioned himself outside Zain's bedroom door. His gaze lifted from the window and met hers, masked and calm.

Ryn didn't quite understand it.

She wanted Zain to be all right.

The healer arrived, along with a hot cup of tea, to make sure Ryn hadn't sustained any injury. Ryn asked her if Zain would be okay, and the healer didn't act concerned.

"He'll be himself again by tomorrow," the healer said. "You should rest, my lady. You have had a trying day."

Ryn's bedroom smelled different. The musk she'd gotten used to had gone with the dead queen's clothing, and instead a sharp perfume lingered. Ryn didn't remember choosing a perfume. Another thing Queen Portia had chosen for her.

Or had Aurora picked out her favorite scent so that when the queen got rid of Ryn, the bedroom would be ready for her?

Ryn didn't understand the queen's motives. She spoke of Ryn's demise, and then spent a fortune on dresses and shoes and jewelry. She sent chocolates, then dreadful history books. Ryn nibbles on those chocolates—her favorite so far was the creamy truffle filled with sweet mint. Her mother would have loved them.

The day ended with a strange silence.

Kari helped Ryn into a new cotton sleeping shirt and tucked her into freshly laundered blankets. They no longer smelled like a dead queen and dust, but like sweet floral soaps and sharp pine.

It didn't feel the same without Zain. Had she really gotten so used to this place that the idea of losing it hurt?

Absurd.

Ryn slept longer than she intended to, and when she woke, Kari had set out a blue dress for her to wear, along with ivory underthings and boots. The sunlight spilling inside was bright, too bright for early morning. It was midmorning, at least.

Ryn sat up, the shuffle of blankets calling Kari from the sitting room.

"Good morning, my lady." Kari bowed her head. "Should I call for tea?"

"Yes, please."

Kari scurried to order tea and returned before Ryn had gotten out of bed. She helped Ryn dress, and when she stepped into the sitting room, servants were arranging tea and toast and sliced fruits—for one.

Zain's door remained closed. Neville stood beside it. Her own guard—the Hunter female with the scar—stood in the corridor.

While she ate, she waited for his door to open. It didn't.

After Ryn ate her fill, and without anything else to do, Ryn took the first of the queen's reading assignments to the armchair. She read. One page at a time. The thin paper, tiny text, and archaic dialect made it hard to concentrate. She found herself reading slowly, and reading the same passages multiple times. Was the author trying to be confusing on purpose?

Did reading books like this make one smart? Or did it make the nobles feel smart?

The doors to Zain's bedroom opened, and he strolled into the sitting room. He wore a simple black jacket over plain clothes. The color had returned to his face, though he looked sleepless and haggard.

"You look like you're about to throw that book at someone," Zain mused. "I do hope it's not me because I missed breakfast."

She waved his concerns aside. "No, no. It's your mother."

Chuckling, he said, "I would be lying if I said I hadn't also contemplated throwing things at her." He paused by her chair and bent forward to read the title of the book. "Ah, she has bullied you into reading our history. That is a shame. Let me summarize the book for you: my grandfather was a good old soul with a mind for politics. He liked to keep everyone happy, despite the turmoil it sometimes caused. He opened the kingdom to trade with our neighbors, striking the treaties we still hold, and bringing the kingdom out of the despair of the war with Ginrali. He signed the treaty with Ginrali. The remainder of his reign was plagued with border disputes, bandits to the south, and vampires in the north. He didn't want a war with vampires, but his indecision caused a war with the vampires."

Ryn glanced at the thick tome. "Is that really what this is all about?"

Zain leveled a bored glare on the book. "It's a very wordy story, and it goes on and on about every little thing in the treaty, the war, and every little fistfight along the border, a few war heroes, but that is the gist. That's all I remember from it, and I was forced to read it aloud."

"Aloud?"

"Under the supervision of the royal tutors, of course. This was after my formal lessons were finished." Zain rolled his eyes. "Because I was expected to speak efficiently and clearly. Esben endured the same. I once had to stand for five hours straight and read that cursed book."

"Five hours?" She couldn't fathom reading aloud for ten minutes.

"I may or may not have called our reading tutor an ugly old hag." Zain shrugged. "It wasn't undeserved."

Ryn let the book fall back onto her knees. "So, I didn't miss much by skipping formal education?"

Zain's expression fell. "My mother has been talking, I take it. No, you didn't. It was mostly for the noble children to form their own alliances and get a taste for the backstabbing foolishness that we would have to survive as adults." He rolled his neck over his shoulders. "Have you eaten lunch?"

She blinked. Indeed, the sunlight had shifted from midmorning to just after midday.

Ryn raked her eyes over him. "Are you going somewhere?"

He glanced down at his plain shirt. "I am having lunch with Esben, and then I am heading to the barracks to train with Neville."

"Train?" She shut the book and set it aside. "Train for what?"

"Swordsmanship," Zain answered. "I am not permitted into the ranks of the Hunters, but I am allowed to know how to defend myself. Despite not being allowed to carry a weapon."

"You don't need to carry one," Neville said.

Zain rolled his eyes, then fixed his stare on Ryn. "Care to join?"

Ryn pretended to consider it, then shook her head. "Play in the dirt with sweaty boys, or read until I fall asleep? I'll read."

Zain chuckled, despite looking a bit disappointed. "Suit yourself, love. If you change your mind, we'll be on the training grounds."

Zain and Neville swept into the corridor, leaving the sitting room empty save for Ryn. Her temporary Hunter guard stood in the corridor. Irene hadn't returned from the healer's hall. Kari had left with a basketful of laundry. She would be a while—lingering to gossip with the other servants.

Which left the entire chamber to Ryn.

Who was she to pass up such a gracious gift?

Setting her history book on the foot of the chaise, she tiptoed to Zain's bedroom door. Heart pounding, she let herself in.

Structurally, it mirrored hers. He decorated it in emeralds, golds, and black. The whole space felt dark and musty, closed off. Like a room that hadn't been dusted. Like clothes that hadn't been washed. And yet everything was polished and pristine and perfectly in place. It felt like Zain, cold but warm, pristine but capable of comfort.

She didn't know what she intended to find. She just didn't want to read any more boring history.

A bookshelf stood by the window, next to a deep green sitting chair. She meandered through the space, running her fingers along the emerald bedspread, along the sculpted mantel, and tiptoed into the bathing room. It smelled like him, the crisp scents of his soaps. His clothes from the day before were piled on the tiled floor.

His armoire held jackets, tailcoats, shirts, and trousers in the same dark greens and blacks he usually wore. The chest of drawers held the same colors, save for a few brighter shades shoved to the back. She fingered lilac trousers in the back of the second drawer. She tried to imagine Zain in them, but the look on his face in her imagination mirrored her own response—it was not a fitting look for him. Not compared to his dark suits and rich emeralds. His brother seemed more the type for lilac.

Her fingers grazed something underneath, something too hard and solid to be clothing. Lifting the trousers, she discovered a book. Shoved in the back of the drawer.

Why hide a book unless it was worth hiding?

The book was old. The faded title had specs of gold where it had once been, the spine was worn, and the leather cracked in several places. She carefully opened it. A delicate script in faded black ink read *Vampires: Habits and Lifestyle Through the Ages* by Ugert Malanort.

Malanort? What kind of name was that?

Ryn flipped through the first several pages. The same delicate script filled each page. The edges were brittle and faded, but it was not the wear that came with time. Someone had read this book extensively.

But why would Zain have such a book hidden in his drawer? Why not have it on a shelf?

Voices in the corridor drew her attention and spiked her panic; she replaced the book and the lilac trousers and shut the drawer as quietly as she could. She scurried back to the chaise, picked up the history book, flipped to a random page, and hadn't a heartbeat to spare before Irene let herself into the sitting room.

Irene cast a suspicious glance at Ryn.

"Oh, thank the gods you're back." Ryn put a hand over her racing head. Willing it to slow. "That other Hunter is boring as hell."

Irene harrumphed and positioned herself inside the sitting room, putting an end to Ryn's snooping.

28

A TRUSTED GUARD

Ryn

Servants arrived with lunch—for one.

They had piled enough food on her plate for two. She wouldn't finish it. She stabbed a sausage with the fork and tried to imagine reserved Zain holding a sword.

"How is Zain with the sword?" Ryn asked.

"Decent."

"When you say decent…" Ryn motioned with her fork.

"He wouldn't be a challenge to an experienced swordsman," Irene said curtly. "However, he is capable of holding his own."

Silence settled, with only Ryn's chewing and whistling of the winter wind. She washed down the spiced sausage with the citrus-flavored tea.

"May I ask you a personal question?" Ryn glanced at Irene over the rim of her teacup.

Irene's blank expression never shifted. "You may ask."

"That female back at the greenhouse," Ryn started. There—a subtle shift within Irene's unreadable mask. "She knew you."

"She did."

Silence returned. Ryn was starting to think that was the end of it, that Irene would tell no more. So, she poked it.

"She didn't seem to like you," Ryn added.

Irene inhaled, held it, then released it slowly. "She married the male I was supposed to marry, and she resents me for it."

Ryn blinked. "You were supposed to marry?"

"Yes." Irene leaned back against the wall. "You won't let this go, will you?"

"No." Ryn shook her head. "If you don't tell me, I'll have to ask around until someone tells me the story."

Irene heaved an annoyed sigh. "I was born into a noble house. I never cared for the strutting and gossip of the ladies' circles. I preferred the sword to gossip and breeches to dresses, and it marked me as different. Not in a good way. I was not the perfect daughter my parents wanted. I didn't want to exist for the goal of seeing how many children I could have, or how much gold I could spend on a single dress. I wanted to do something that mattered, really mattered. So I joined the Hunters." Irene met Ryn's gaze with the fierceness of burning steel. "I do not regret the decision."

"Not even a little?" Ryn asked.

"Not even a little." Irene's otherwise grim mask broke into a small grin. "I might be disowned, but I have found a family here. One better suited to me. I lost a title, but I gained my freedom."

Ryn looked down into her tea. The amber gently steamed. "And I have done the opposite."

"My lady?"

She shouldn't have said anything, but she had, and she couldn't take the words back or pretend she hadn't said them. Looking up from her tea, Ryn met Irene's determined brown eyes. "I had all the freedom in the world, and now I'm here smothered under a title."

Irene studied her for a long moment. Cautiously, she asked, "You don't want to marry the prince?"

Panic bubbled in Ryn's chest like ice. She and Zain were supposed to be mates. Tied together through fate and true love. Ryn swallowed a gulp of tea. "It's not him. It's…everything else. It's being followed day and night, watched like a thief, and paraded around like a…"

"A doll," Irene finished. Understanding warmed her eyes, alongside pity.

"Like a doll," she agreed. "I…care for Zain, I do, but…he comes with restraints. Not the fun kind either."

Irene chuckled. "I wouldn't be so sure. I've heard rumors of what Zain prefers."

Ryn cocked a brow and leaned forward. "Oh? What sort of rumors have you heard, Hunter Irene?"

Irene's cheeks flushed. "I-I mean…" She cleared her throat, regaining her composure. "Only that he is rough in the bedroom."

Ryn hummed and sipped her tea. "I've heard."

"But you don't…know?" Irene tilted her head in doubt. "Even though you shared a room at the tavern?"

Shit.

Embarrassment heated Ryn's cheek.

A furrow appeared in Irene's brow. "You wear your guilt too openly, Lady Ryn."

She couldn't lie her way out of it, not entirely. So, leaning forward, eyes downcast, Ryn told a partial lie. "We didn't…do anything that night. We kissed. We…" She struggled for the word. Fondled sounded too crass for the manor's walls. "Zain passed out."

Irene blinked, and then a laugh burst from her lips. Warm, hearty, and from the whole chest, it filled the sitting room and brightened her entire face. It turned her into a beautiful creature, even as her shoulders shook and tears gathered along her eyelashes.

"He passed out?" Irene wiped at her eyes. "I wouldn't have guessed he was such a lightweight."

"He drank a lot," Ryn defended. "I didn't."

"That is why you left?"

"He fell asleep in the middle of the bed," Ryn said flatly. Not a lie. He had passed out with his limbs splayed across the narrow bed. She couldn't have curled into him had she wanted to, and she hadn't wanted to. "And I…left."

"Did you feel it that night?" Irene asked, her tone softer.

The mating bond. Ryn had no idea what it was supposed to feel like other than what the stories suggested. A chord between two souls, deeper than bone, than pain, than dreams. But what did that feel like? "I…don't know. Maybe? I don't understand it or why or how, but…we kept glancing at each other. I thought it was just the buzz from the ale, the warmth sliding through my skin, and the attention of an attractive male." She thought of the fluttering in her chest that night, the way his velvet voice had rolled over her senses like sin and honey. "I'd never felt anything like it. It was enough that when I got the chance, I went with him to the room. I wanted…more of him."

"Had you known who he was, would the night have gone differently?" Irene asked.

Ryn wasn't sure when the conversation had turned to personal questions about her, but Irene had shared a personal story.

"Honestly, I don't know." Ryn would've sat on Zain's lap, not Rat-Face's.

Of course, had she known the dreadful and horrible Prince Zain was at the tavern, she wouldn't have gone. She would've picked a different location. To avoid him. Had she known who he was, they would not have met.

"Do you wish to take up the blade, my lady?" Irene asked. "We could find you a suitable instructor. Not me. I have been told by the recruits I'm too angry."

Ryn shook her head. "No. I don't have the coordination for swordplay. I can barely dance without tripping. The queen has already mentioned a dancing instructor, though I'm certain she plans to kill me before it becomes an issue."

Irene chuckled. She didn't deny it.

Zain's training lasted into the evening. He returned covered in sweat and dirt.

The chamber door startled Ryn awake—she'd fallen asleep on the chaise with the history book on her chest. Her legs were twisted in her skirts, pins had fallen from her hair, and strands had fallen onto her face while the mess of Kari's work hung to the left. By Zain's amusement, she looked frantic.

"I told you the book was riveting." Zain chuckled as he made his way to his room.

Ryn sat up and tried to calm the rat's nest of her hair. A crick in her back made her flinch.

Zain went to wash, and Ryn set the book aside. Her mind had ingested all the heavy narration and dense prose it could in a day. Neville stood in the sitting room. Irene had left, and the night Hunter stood guard in the corridor.

Ryn stretched the kinks out of her back and neck, earning several pops. She took a step toward her room, but Neville sidestepped in front of her.

The motion startled her; she hadn't seen or heard him move.

He glared down at her with a guard's suspicion. "I'm willing to indulge in this whim of Zain's, but be warned—if anything happens to him, I will hold you responsible."

She frowned. "So, if he falls down the stairs, it's my fault?"

His scowl deepened.

"That is hardly fair."

Neville took a step closer to her, leaving little space between them. He gripped the hilt of his sword, leather of his glove squeaking. "You forget I was at the tavern too. You were there to target him. You caught the scent of money and latched on like a bloodhound."

She bristled. "If you remember, Zain pulled me out of the execution line. I didn't ask him to do that."

Neville only glared. "He will lose interest, just like all the others."

Others? That one word rattled into her thoughts.

Neville noticed. "What? You think you're the only female he's ever fawned over? Claimed to love? He's a fucking prince. You're nothing. If you so much as harm a hair on his head, I will hunt you down to whatever dark corner of the realm you're hiding in and drag you back here for the death you deserve. Understand?"

A roiling fury burned under her skin. "Why is everyone dead set that I'm the problem?"

"Because you are the one who doesn't belong," Neville said lowly.

She wanted to hit him, but she knew it would end badly for her. "Where is this coming from? I thought we were past these petty insults."

"I've had time to think about what happened yesterday," Neville said. His gaze sharpened. "Those thugs knew where to find us. They surrounded us. They were looking for Zain, not you. They struck when he was weakest."

"And you think I somehow planned that entire thing?" Ryn turned to fully face him. "First, I had no idea where Zain planned on going. Two, I had no idea he'd collapse on me. You are just looking for someone to blame, and you already hate me, so I'm the easiest target. And, that you are looking for someone to blame suggests you have no leads on who actually ratted out our location."

Neville's lips pursed.

She'd guessed right. They had no idea.

Ryn had no desire to be in the same room with Neville and his bad mood; she marched into her bedroom. She didn't feel tired, not with having napped, but she washed her face in cool water and changed into a nightdress. Thankfully, Kari had dressed her in stays rather than a full corset.

She climbed into the bed but Neville's words resounded. Would Zain get tired of her and this charade? Dark thoughts circled as the sitting room went dark—as dark as the king allowed. She pretended to be asleep when Kari came to tend to the hearth and exchange the candles. Not long after, Kari's light snores escaped underneath the servant's door.

Ryn dressed in dark clothes and once again slipped out the window. The cold seethed between her skin and clothes like needles. Lights burned all over the keep, glowing in every window, but heavy clouds hid the moon and deepened the shadows.

Ryn climbed across the keep's roof, through a parlor with a burning hearth, past clueless guards and a few Hunters—which didn't make her feel better about vampires sneaking in. If she could do it, so could a vampire.

Candles spotted the kitchens but left far too many shadows between them. The staff had gone to bed. Cleaned pots and pans hung from racks and cluttered shelves. The sharp scent of soap stung the air, along with the warm spices and hearty aromas from dinner. Several knife blocks stood in a row, their various handles of well-worn wood sticking up. She thought of grabbing one—to be prepared for anything—but how would that look if she were to ruin into a guard or a Hunter? Someone would find it missing too.

She tiptoed through the quiet corridors, past stores of sugar and flour, tins of tea and bundles of drying herbs, and paused before a healthy stock of wine casks and dusty bottles. A single candle lit the chamber. Ryn ran her fingers along an open crate of dark wine. The labels identified it as the king's favorite wine. Plum, wasn't that what Zain said? Hadn't he said it was too sweet for him?

Ryn didn't like overly sweet drinks. Sweetness masked poison.

A skittering made her jump—two eyes peeked at her from the doorway. A cat.

"Shit," Ryn breathed.

The cat flicked its tail, then continued its silent patrol of the kitchen. Likely for rodents.

It took a few corridors to find the larder and the trapdoor—an ugly thing of ancient wood and iron. Ryn heaved it upward with a squeak, then climbed into the darkness of the undercroft.

29

INTO THE UNDERCROFT

Ryn

The ladder ended at a small platform that led down to a roughly carved spiral staircase. The darkness was heavy, and each step into the dark made her heart lurch further up her throat. Each stair took her deeper into the undercroft's ancient tunnels. Knowing vampires once roamed the undercroft—and still might—made her feel like an intruder, like she was about to interrupt.

At last, the stairs ended at a dimly lit hall. Torches were spaced far too wide apart and left generous shadows between them. So much for lighting up the entire keep like a beacon, Ryn thought. It would seem the Hunters and King Victor believed the undercroft impregnable enough to leave it dark.

She tiptoed down the right passage, crafting a map in her head. The walls ate the sound of her footsteps. The undercroft was musty, dark, and spotted with features of the long-gone era—rusty torch brackets, broken hooks for lanterns, and gashes in the stone. The passage crossed another, and she tiptoed right again. She mapped each turn in her head. Each turn, hall, and chamber. Countless chambers had once lined each hall, but most had since caved in. Those remaining were filled with jars—hundreds of jars, dusty and left to rot.

Ryn paused outside a chamber where the ambient light glowed enough for her to see. Some of the jars were plain, others ornate. Through the thick and dust-heavy cobwebs, she noticed the jars were filled. Ryn tiptoed into the chamber, and realized with a jolt of horror what filled the jars.

Ashes.

Vampires, at death, were burned.

Ryn's heart thudded, and she stumbled into the hall. Why would the Hunters leave vampire ashes down here? And *so many* of them.

She thought of what Zain said about Victor's revenge on the Abrani clan, how the slaughter came with vengeance. King Victor lived on top of the graves of his enemies, both the vampires he slaughtered and those who had come before. He might as well have danced on the dead and then spit on them.

Ryn shuddered. Her mother had always warned them to respect the dead.

She shook herself. She didn't have time to gawk at vampire ashes. She had more important things to do.

She forced her legs to move forward. Darkness lingered thick in the undercroft, swallowing entire halls, lingering heavy under torches. A darkness that never saw the sun. A perfect place for a vampire to hide.

She paused when she heard footsteps. Booted, sure, and armored. Accompanied by a torch. The light spilled on the stone and dust, coming closer with every step.

Ryn slipped into the nearest ash chamber and flattened herself against the wall. The footsteps came closer, as did the torchlight. Ryn's heart lurched into her throat. There would be no excusing her presence in the undercroft. Zain would not be able to save her from the Hunters' wrath.

The Hunter passed. The torchlight faded down the hall.

Ryn eased out of the chamber just as the Hunter and his torch turned the far corner. Out of sight. Leaving her in near darkness.

The Hunter wasn't trying to be quiet. She'd had plenty of time to vanish. If a vampire were hiding down here or sulking about, it would have no trouble sneaking between patrols. The Hunters must truly believe the undercroft secure if they patrol it so nonchalantly.

Ryn headed the way the Hunter had come. It looked much like the way behind her, with collapsed passages, doorways filled with broken stones and rubble. She spotted what looked like ancient scorch marks and ash swept into the dust at the corners. Evidence of the ancient battle that had decimated the vampire clan, and the fire that ravaged the stronghold.

She couldn't imagine the horrors of such an attack. The power required to level portions of a sturdy keep to rubble and smoke.

A soft sound came from behind her, like a sigh.

Ryn froze, the hair on the back of her neck stood on end, and she turned. She saw nothing but shadows. But it felt like the shadows were looking back.

A vampire still lurked somewhere in the keep, hiding somewhere.

Ryn continued onward, paying more attention to the space behind her. Zain was right about the sensation of being followed, like a ghost trailed her and another waited just ahead. It felt like spirits lurked in every shadow. Observing. Waiting.

She didn't like the feeling.

She crept forward, dodging a few other Hunter patrols and well-lit passages. She assumed they were like barracks or offices; the voices of multiple Hunters drifted out of each.

She felt eyes on her back with every step.

It might have been the haunted nature of the undercroft. King Victor had slaughtered the vampire clan and burned the keep. How many had died in these halls? How much blood had soaked into the stone?

She crept by passages that had once been caved-in but since reopened, with fresh timber and clean stone holding up the ceiling, and other passages were sealed with stone and mortar. More charred stone.

Surprisingly few Hunters patrolled the undercroft, like they had completely dismissed the possibility that vampires could slip through the darkness. Their dismissive behavior annoyed her. Of course, she hadn't seen any other way out of the undercroft, unless they existed in the well-lit corners where the Hunters lingered. Standing guard, she supposed.

Still, if a vampire snuck into the undercroft, the chances of it getting into the keep above were slim.

Yet several had.

She entered a hall just as musty and dusty as the others, only it smelled different. It reminded her of dirt-floor basements, and old things left to gather dust. Stale. Chambers lined the hall. Instead of the open chambers of ash, these had wooden doors.

No sound came from within. She felt no pulses within, no blood supply, no heartbeat. Did vampires have heartbeats?

Why put doors on chambers unless they were hiding something important? Like a way out.

Ryn folded her fingers around the cold iron handle and tugged. The door gave. Her panic spiked, but then dimmed as the door opened on silent hinges. Crates and boxes filled the room. Storage. Ryn closed the door and moved to the next, hoping for a staircase or some pathway outside the keep.

The next held crates and barrels. The third was also being used as storage, but it was not just barrels and crates. It was…stuff. Furniture. Piles of books and scrolls. Piles of what looked like furs. Odd things for a king to keep in his basement. Curious, she stepped inside.

She fingered a few of the books, the leather faded and cracked, the pages worn and feathered with dust. In the ambient light of the hall, she could barely make out the words along the spines. A few were in a language she didn't know. She carefully tilted one book from the shelf, unleashing a wave of dust. The book was written in the same small, calligraphic characters. She closed the book and replaced it on the shelf.

One spine read *The Life of King Saydai* by Ugert Malanort. Ryn had never heard of him, but that didn't mean much.

The author's name tugged at her mind, and with a painful jolt, she realized where she had seen it before. The same author had written the book about vampires hidden in Zain's dresser. She scanned the rest of the books. *Variances of*

Blood. Decrees of King Seymour. Biography of Duchess Claudette Monroe. History of the Abrani Clan.

With each title, Ryn's heart sped.

All these books were about vampires. She would bet gold the books in the unknown language were about vampires too.

A cold panic slithered over her skin. She should not be here.

She glanced around the room, at the furniture and piles of things. Had it belonged to the vampires who once lived here? Why would King Victor allow any of this to survive? He hated vampires and everything about them, yet she stood in a small vampire treasure trove. Hidden under the keep.

She refused to believe King Victor didn't know it existed. He had to know. Zain knew—he had one of the books.

And kept it hidden.

Her curiosity got the better of her. She walked deeper into the room. Nothing had charred edges or water stains, yet the musty sooty stench of fire lingered. The lack of damage suggested it was salvaged after the fire. But it didn't make sense for the king who had vowed to hunt down every vampire in the realm to keep a trove of their things.

Ryn paused at the back of the room, where a large portrait rested against the wall. It was of a beautiful female with pale skin and blue eyes. By the diamonds around her neck and size of the portrait, she was important. But why hide the portrait in the undercroft?

The female looked unsettlingly like Zain. They shared skin and hair, but also the straight nose and bowed lips.

"You're not supposed to be in here."

Ryn whirled, panic hot and fluid—Zain stood in the doorway. She hadn't heard footsteps or clothing or even his pulse. The light from the hall blanketed his front in shadow, but she didn't need to see his face to feel his displeasure.

"Zain," she gasped.

He took a calculated step into the chamber. Once in the shadow, his grave expression turned her blood cold. He closed the space between them with ghostly silent footsteps.

"You followed me," Ryn whispered, the words barely audible.

"I did." He paused a short distance away from her, within reach. His expression was cold, unfeeling.

"Why?"

He tilted his head. "You might as well have told me your plan, *love*." The word dripped with anything but love—his icy venom chilled her to the bone. "You're not a good interrogator, though you are hard to follow. I don't even know how you got into the kitchens without being seen, and I applaud your skill. Luckily, I found you again sneaking through the shadows in the undercroft."

She felt foolish. He'd told her exactly how to get into the undercroft knowing she was going to go there. "Why would you tell me where it was only to follow?"

Zain took a step closer with the gait of a predator. "I wanted to see what you'd do with it, and if you'd do as Neville said and try to use it against me. And here you are." He motioned to the relics around them. "Snooping. What is it that you're looking for, Ryn? A way out of the keep without alerting the guard? A way for others to come in?"

The words hit like daggers, each one, each accusation. "That's not what I'm doing," she said in a single breath. "I wasn't lying. I'm not a vampire accomplice."

"Then what are you doing down here?" Zain took a small step forward, enough she scented the spearmint on his skin.

Ryn stood her ground. "I was looking for an exit," she whispered. "For *me*. Not for vampires. For when this whole sham of an engagement goes wrong, when your mother kicks me out, I'll have an exit that doesn't include me losing my head. This is just a game to you, but this is my life you're playing with. When it's over, you'll just go back to being a prince without consequences, and I have to go find a new place to live, a new job, and somehow evade the assassin your mother will send after me. So, yes, I was looking for a way out."

Zain was quiet for several moments, staring at her with an unreadable expression. "Is that what you want? You want out of this? If you didn't want to marry me, you could have just said so. You didn't have to lie."

She blinked at him. "Lie? Zain, this entire engagement was so you didn't have to marry someone else and I didn't have to die. There was nothing to lie about." In a smaller voice, she added, "You don't love me. You don't even like me. Don't pretend like you do."

She started to say that she did not love him, but the words didn't come. She wasn't sure it was true anymore. Zain spiked a feeling in her chest, but whether it was love or something else, she didn't know.

Zain remained still, and Ryn feared she'd pushed him too far.

"That might have been true," he whispered. "Once."

Her heart jumped into her throat. He couldn't mean…

"Do you know who the female in this portrait is?" Zain glanced at the dark-haired woman. Nonchalant as if he hadn't just implied that he *loved* her.

"No."

Zain inhaled, and the hard edges of him softened just a bit. "This is Moria Blanchant, according to the inscription on the back."

"I've not heard of her. Who is she? Your grandmother? Aunt?"

Zain chuckled, the sound sent gooseflesh over her skin. "No, she is not."

Ryn looked again at the dark-haired female. Her pale skin. Then she saw it, the subtle red painted within her blue eyes. A vampire.

Zain took the smallest step closer, so that his hot breath bounced off her temple. "This female is the reason why I turn away any bride, why I keep to myself." Cold hands trailed up her arms and then looped around her middle, loosely holding her against him. "This female, darling Ryn, is my *mother*."

30
DARKEST SECRETS
Ryn

Ryn shook her head, sure she misheard. Zain couldn't be the son of a vampire. He was fae, son of King Victor and Queen Portia, brother to Esben. He couldn't be…

Zain's arms tightened around her. "You're shivering," he whispered.

"You're lying." She stepped out of his hold—it broke easily.

His hands hovered in the air between them, then he tucked them into his trouser pockets. "No. I'm not."

"You can't be…" She swallowed. The words, the accusation, jumbled in her throat. "You can't be a vampire."

"Oh, that is what I thought when I found this room." Zain pressed his hand against his heart, eyes wide in innocence. "I thought the resemblance between myself and this female was coincidence, or maybe she was a dead ancestor. She is not. My father's entire family tree is mapped out in his study, along with a painted likeness. This female does not appear. There is no evidence of who she was beyond the name on the back, engraved into the wood. I thought it strange that my father kept it, along with all things." He motioned around the room. "Unless he had a reason to. Unless this was my mother, and I was some cursed vampire hybrid."

"Is such a thing possible?"

Zain shrugged. The coldness returned to his gaze. This was the prince she had met in the throne room the day he pulled her from the execution line. This was the prince with the cold, ruthless heart.

"I suspect my father had an affair with this female," Zain whispered, frigid eyes locked with Ryn's. "Whether he knew what she was or not, I can't say. Though, I have had plenty of time to think about it. I look nothing like either of my parents. The queen sequestered herself during pregnancy, claiming to have been ill. No one saw her with child. The story goes that after my early birth, I remained too ill to be seen for nearly four years. Even after, they kept me locked away due to my *heart condition*, as they called it, claiming it was the result of a difficult and premature birth. It was only after the alchemist concocted the herbal tea for my heart that I was allowed to mingle with others, even my own brother. Even then, they watched me like hawks. I thought it was because I was sick. Weak. Because that is what they told me. I was a child and had no reason to not believe them. Of course, I got older. I thought for myself." He motioned to the portrait. His voice was ice. "I made my own discoveries."

"You don't know if that's true," Ryn reasoned.

Zain rolled his eyes and pointed to the female in the portrait. "Look at her, Ryn. Then look at me. We share a *face*."

"That doesn't mean…" His words rattled in her mind, catching on her own racing thoughts. The tonic. The heart condition. The king's preference of Esben. "But you're not…"

"Do you know what happens when I don't drink the tonic?" Zain's expression darkened, but it wasn't all cold hatred. There was shame and guilt. "You saw the beginning of it in the greenhouse. At first, my appetite wanes. I can't focus. My muscles weaken. With every day I don't drink it, my symptoms worsen. Heat and light make it worse. My skin pales. I tremble." His voice dropped to a vicious whisper. "And the most damning evidence, my dear Ryn, is the red that appears in my eyes."

"No," she pleaded. Her gut twisted.

"I've seen it," he said. "Imagine my realization at what I really was." He chuckled, but it lacked heart. Zain tore his gaze from the portrait and met Ryn's. "They lied about my birth. Lied about me. I have asked myself a thousand times why—"

Footsteps sounded in the hall. The brightness of a torch glowed. Zain moved with frightening speed and silence and shut the door. Several long moments passed. With each, the Hunter patrol came closer. The light came closer.

Ryn could scream. Could bring the Hunters to them.

But what would they think? They wouldn't believe her if she told them about Zain. He was their prince; she was the outsider the queen wanted gone. It would be an excuse to get rid of her, and no one would know what happened. Like Princess Lucia. Ryn's heart skipped a beat. Had the princess discovered the truth? Did they kill her to hide the secret?

Booted footsteps passed in front of the door. The blaring light of the torch passed. Ryn held her tongue.

Despite knowing what she knew, Zain was the safer option.

The footsteps and torch vanished down the hall.

"This is a conversation to be had elsewhere," Zain whispered. "If it is to be had at all."

"Oh, it will be had," she whispered back.

Zain shot her a look, then eased the door open and peered into the hall. "They're gone. Let's go."

He motioned for her hand—Ryn hesitated. She glanced at the female. The resemblance was uncanny.

Pushing those fears aside, she set her hand into Zain's.

He led the way through the undercroft's dark passages. With the revelation he had just shared buzzing in her head, she couldn't recall the mental map—first, Zain's claim about his birth mother, and second, he hadn't trusted her and lured her into the undercroft and followed her. The rational part of her mind told her to let go of his hand and run. Another part of her understood Zain was the best way to get out of the undercroft. He knew his way around.

If Zain was a vampire, was he working with the others? Could he be the accomplice the Hunters have been looking for? Is that why Zain pulled her out of the execution line?

A glow of torchlight appeared ahead, and Zain pulled her into a partially collapsed chamber to avoid the Hunter. Between the dusty, cobwebbed rubble and the stone wall, there was barely room for the two of them.

The Hunter approached, and Zain's breath hit her temple. The Hunter passed, but neither moved.

"Are you working with the brood?" she whispered.

"No." Zain's eyes were coal in the dark. "Are you?"

"No."

With her hands pressed against his chest, she felt a glimmer of his blood underneath. She pushed her magic into him—he wasn't lying. At least about helping the brood.

Relief threaded through her unease. "But…if you're… How have the Hunters not found you?"

"I sometimes wonder if Neville knows," Zain whispered against her temple. "If my father told him when he appointed him as my guard. He's never said anything, and I have never asked. I have kept my discoveries secret. I…don't know what it means for me, or why my father lets me live. He is ashamed of me, yet he keeps me alive."

The words, the tone—this was the prince underneath his hateful exterior. This was the male who laughed like moonlight. The prince who found flowers in her favorite color. The prince who sent guards to find her sister on a cold night. She felt his heart beating under her palm, and her magic pulsed alongside it. His blood didn't feel different from any other fae, but she had never felt the blood of a vampire. If she touched this blood, what would she feel?

"How long have you known?" she whispered.

"Years." Zain rested his cheekbone against her temple. "I always suspected something was…wrong with me. The more I learned about vampires and myself, I…" He sighed, the breath slow and exhausted. "The alchemist's tonic is what keeps me looking this way, like any other fae. It subdues the vampiric symptoms."

"There's a book in your drawer," she whispered.

The space was too close for him to look down, but she felt the skin around his eyes move. "What?"

"Under a pair of lilac trousers," she added. "I went snooping when you and Neville went to train."

"You…went snooping?" He leaned away as far as he could in the space, eyes glinting, brow furrowed. He gripped her shoulders, but not painfully. His expression almost looked…surprised. "For what?"

"I don't know. I had the whole place to myself, and I was curious." The decision to snoop felt foolish now. "The book was about vampires."

He half-laughed. "We're going to have to work on your trust issues."

"You're not mad?"

"No one has ever had the audacity to go through my things. And…you continue to surprise me, Ryn." His hands shifted to her waist. "Not only did you find damning evidence against me, but I just told you I'm a vampire. You have been accused of being an accomplice, and you could use me to clear your name. You could have called for the Hunter, told them the truth, and saved yourself. But here you are. Hiding with me in the dark."

Holding onto him.

Her hands twitched against his chest. "I'm not sure if they would believe me."

"I'd rather not chance it, love."

Love.

She brought her gaze to his, to the glints of his eyes. "You won't throw me out after this?"

"Why would I do that?" His brow furrowed. "Oh, because you know my greatest secret. That would be foolish on my part. I toss you out and then you tell everyone."

"You could have me killed," she whispered, fear twisting the words. She thought again of the missing princess. "Easily. The queen would be glad to hear it."

At the mention of the female who was not his mother, his expression darkened. "I could, but that seems irrational, considering we have gone to such lengths to perpetuate our love story. They say when one mate dies, the other begins to wither." A wicked grin stretched his lips. "Though it would make me look evil, wouldn't it?" He released a low laugh, and the rumble reverberated through her hands. He tightened his hold of her waist. "But to be honest, I have grown fond of you. I would like to keep you around, unless you would rather die than marry a monster like me."

"You're not a monster." The words came quickly, easily. A plea.

He stilled. "Is that so?"

"You can be a jerk," she amended. "You can be selfish, arrogant, and rude." She gripped his tailcoat, the truth of her words twisting like warm wine in her lungs. "But…you're not a monster. You can be kind, sweet, and generous." She flattened her hand over his racing heart. "There is a warm heart in there."

He chuckled, a soft sound. "If you say so, love. But, since we are confessing, I have commentary for you." He enclosed his arms around her middle. "You think you are unworthy of all of this. Of having more food than you can eat. Of having servants tend to your washing. Of having fine clothes. You are worthy of far more than what you have been given. If I could, I would give you every box of chocolate and every rainy sunset. You…" He swallowed, as if the words pained him, as if he didn't know how to say them. "You make me feel things I never thought I could."

No one had ever said such things to her. She felt his pulse. On instinct, she reached out for his blood—he wasn't lying.

Her chest tightened. Her trembling fingers grasped hold of his tailcoat as the edges of her vision blurred. She blinked—dampness spread along her lashes.

He leaned in, and she met him; the kiss felt like natural punctuation to their conversation. It was chaste and sweet, and sent a fluttering sensation along her rib cage. Zain hesitated against her lips, and Ryn wondered if he felt the same want for more that she did, for another kiss, to just stay this close.

"We should get going," Zain whispered. "Before the next patrol."

"Yeah," she breathed.

Neither moved. Then Zain loosened his embrace, and they stepped into the dark hall. Ryn immediately missed the warmth of his body against hers. Especially in the dank cold of the undercroft. He led the way, holding her hand in his.

A vampire.

Her betrothed, the cold and unfeeling prince—a vampire.

It didn't seem possible. It didn't seem real. She finally found a male who tugged on that strange place in her chest, who she might love, who she cared for and who cared for her—and he was a vampire.

Given her nature as a blood enchantress, she supposed it was poetic.

They turned into a dark hall lit by a torch at the far end. Halfway through it, a soft step sounded behind them.

"Where do you think you're off to?" came a cold, scratchy voice.

Ryn and Zain both turned as a female stepped from the shadows of a side chamber. Her red-rimmed eyes settled on Ryn, and she grinned, exposing bloodied fangs.

31

THE THIRD VAMPIRE

Ryn

The vampire chuckled. In a scratchy voice, it said, "It's the irrelevant prince and his newest whore."

Zain stepped in front of Ryn. The vampire let out a bark of a laugh and then lunged. Ryn didn't have time to scream. She stumbled back, and between one heartbeat and the next, Zain pulled a silver dagger from his boot and met the vampire's lunge with its edge. The vampire roared and stumbled back, dark blood beading on a slash across its cheek. It pressed a pale hand to the wound. Its fingers came back bloody.

Zain brandished the dagger. "Be gone, beast. Unless you want to feel silver ash steel in your heart."

The vampire hissed, fangs bared.

Ryn blinked at the blade; she had only heard of the steel folded with silver ash. Only Hunters carried it, and it went for hundreds of thousands of gold on the black market. Impossible to steal, near impossible to smith, and too hot for the average fence. Silver ash burned a vampire's skin, and a silver ash blade injected that burn into the bloodstream.

Zain carried a silver ash dagger. In his boot.

A different sort of anger bubbled under her skin. If he accidentally nicked himself with it, it would kill him.

The vampire threw itself forward with a terrible screech. The sound grated on the inside of Ryn's skull, daggers against bone, needles in her brain. She stumbled back until her back hit the cold stone of the wall. The vampire slashed its nails through Zain's sleeve, leaving a bright red gash behind—bright red, whereas the vampire's blood was dark, almost black. The vampire swung its other hand, aiming for Zain's throat. Ryn grabbed the only thing within reach—an unlit torch from its rusty bracket—and swung the head into the vampire's side. It was enough to knock the trajectory of the arc, and its nails missed Zain's throat.

Ryn readied another swing, rage and fear fueling her actions, but the vampire lurched away from her. It didn't claw at her like it had Zain, and it didn't look at her with such murder in its eyes. No, it looked at her with a sickening, heart-lurching recognition.

It knew who Ryn was.

And it did not want to hurt *her*.

This vampire must buy its blood from Nobel, and it knew what Ryn could do. It needed Ryn alive.

Later, Ryn would worry about *how* the vampire knew. In that moment, all she cared about was protecting Zain. This vampire didn't know him, which meant Zain wasn't connected to the brood.

And it wanted to hurt him.

She threw her body between the vampire and her prince. It stumbled back. Its eyes flashed between Ryn and Zain. It didn't know what to do.

Footsteps hammered against the stone hall—running. From the corner behind the vampire, Neville bolted into the hall, skidding to a halt. His worried expression at once turned into murderous calm, and he unsheathed the blade at his side.

The vampire spun, hissing at the Hunter.

"Beast!" Neville roared.

In the moment of distraction, Zain lunged fast—instinctual, like a predator pushed into a corner—past Ryn and drove his silver ash through the vampire's back, right into its heart.

The vampire shrieked, hunching forward and clawing at the dagger in its back. Ryn felt the blood gushing from its tight veins. Ryn had never felt anything like it—whereas fae and human bodies pulsed with a rich, copious blood supply that ran through every organ and vein, the vampire's blood was thick and sludge-like. Its body did not contain enough blood to keep its organs pumping. Its heart was still. Its tissues were still and cold. It felt…like a body in the moments before Ryn drained it entirely. It felt like a corpse. Within that pitiful blood supply, the poison from the silver ash barbed and slithered.

The vampire flailed. It threw itself into one wall and then the other, crashing into a chamber of ashes, sending ancient jars crashing to the stone floor. Ash and dust and cobwebs burst. It crashed to the floor among the ashes, twitching and jerking, breaths shuttered, and then it went silent. It stilled.

Dead.

Zain heaved a breath, and his cold fury melted into something even colder. Ryn recognized it. She felt the same after each dead, shriveled body she had left in the shadows. Guilt. Shame. Disgust. Pride.

He yanked the dagger from the vampire's back. Its milky skin had gone ashy, its eyes empty. Its inky blood seeped into the dust.

"Are you all right?" Zain asked, his voice reflecting his cold expression.

It took Ryn a moment to realize he'd asked her. She met his impassive, cold stare. Words caught in her throat. Instead, she nodded. Leaning against the stone wall, she used its sturdiness to guide her trembling body to the floor. She just…needed to sit.

"You killed her." Neville eyed the vampire, then the dagger in Zain's hand. "You keep that on you?"

"Always." Zain wiped the blade clean on the dead vampire's shirt, then tucked it back into his boot. He straightened and dusted off his trousers.

"Where did you get it?" Neville's grip on his sword went white-knuckled.

"It was a gift from my brother." Zain turned his attention to Ryn. He closed the space between them and held his hand down to her. "You still okay?"

"I don't know." Ryn slid her hand into his. He hauled her to her feet but didn't let go of her hand. He pulled her closer.

Neville whispered a curse, eyes pinned on the dead vampire. "We can't overlook this, Zain."

"I'm aware," Zain said with a sigh. "Father will be furious, I'm sure."

Nothing more could be said. The patrolling Hunters ran around the corner, panting from the run. Of course, with the screeching the vampire made, Ryn was surprised they hadn't come sooner. Among them was the blond Hunter who had stood outside Ryn's prison cell. He took in the scene with authoritative fury, and by the way the others stalked behind him, he was in charge.

Neville straightened. "Captain Colby, I—"

"Now is not the time for excuses," Colby interrupted with a voice that matched his expression.

Neville looked equally parts shamed and furious—a reprimanded child. He turned his shame onto his boots instead of his captain.

"Tell me what the hell happened." Colby's gaze landed on Zain, and then Ryn. Recognition darkened his expression. "And don't leave anything out. You best have your story straight by the time word reaches the king."

Captain Colby escorted them back into the main keep. They roused the healer, who wasn't at all happy to be woken in the middle of the night. While the healer tended to the wound on Zain's arm, Ryn refused to leave his side. She held onto his other hand. No matter the dirt and dust on her clothes and in her hair. Captain Colby oversaw everything. Just as he had outside her cell.

Irene met them outside the healer's wing, winded and *pissed*. She looked ready to slap Ryn, but she withheld her anger.

The Hunters escorted Zain and Ryn back to their chambers in the royal wing. Irene stomped the entire way, Neville glowered, and Colby looked like he had a lecture planned on all they had done wrong.

Ryn held Zain's hand the entire way. She didn't want to let go. Despite his nature, he had jumped in front of her when the vampire attacked. He'd protected her. She had also jumped between him and the vampire. She hadn't paused to consider her options, she just…acted. The only other person she would have defended with her own life was Lu.

She wasn't quite sure what to make of this strange feeling to protect Zain.

Once safely inside their sitting room, Ryn dropped onto the chaise and Zain glided to the sideboard and poured himself a whiskey.

"I'm going to inform His Majesty of these events," Captain Colby said. To Neville and Irene, he ordered, "Don't let them out of your sight."

Colby marched into the hall. Ryn waited for either Irene or Neville to start in. Neither did. Neville took up a guard's post against the wall. Irene stormed into the corridor.

Such strong willpower to remain silent.

Zain drained his whiskey, then poured another and joined Ryn on the chaise. He handed her the whiskey, and she drank half in a single gulp. She barely tasted it. An exhausted smirk curved his lips.

The ambient light of the keep seeped through the window, chilled and observant. A few candles burned around the sitting room. The hearth burned behind a green and gold screen.

"I'll be surprised if my father doesn't already know. There are Hunters whose sole purpose is to keep him informed at all hours. I don't know if he'll be impressed I killed a vampire or pissed I put myself in a position where I had to defend myself." Zain sighed and leaned back, shoulder pressed against hers. He turned his head toward hers, each breath a puff of whiskey perfume against her cheek. "You weren't bad yourself, love. Your form was a bit…lacking, and your footing was off. One counterattack and you would've been on the ground."

"I never learned to fight," Ryn admitted. "I learned to avoid people and conflict. I stuck to the shadows and was quiet, so no one noticed me."

"You overestimate your sneaking ability," Zain purred. "I noticed you from across a tavern, while drunk."

"No one else is like you," she whispered.

His expression softened, curious and cautious. "Is that good or bad?"

"Good," she said. Her cheeks heated. "I've never met anyone else like you. No one else looked twice at me."

"They're fools not to," he said.

Ryn couldn't believe Zain was a vampire. In that moment, with his body against hers, with warm blood pumping through his veins, he felt as fae as she did. The vampire in the undercroft had been cold, its blood condensed and dry and dark. Zain was none of those things. He felt…alive and warm.

Zain's mouth quirked, his lips parted, but the chamber door opened, silencing whatever he'd been able to say.

Colby marched inside. "King Victor has commanded that you are to stay in your chambers until an investigation is made." He bowed his head to Zain. "He apologized for any inconvenience."

"Did he really apologize?" Zain cocked a brow.

Colby blinked, then released a short sigh. "No, he did not."

Zain hummed in amusement. "Nice try, though. We have not been introduced, Hunter. Who are you?"

Colby bowed again, deeper this time. "I am Captain Colby Glen, of His Majesty's Hunters."

Ryn looked him up and down. His uniform of hardened leathers and steel plating wasn't the same as the one he had worn before. The pauldrons were wider and boasted a different arrangement of plates. He caught her staring, and she asked, "A captain?"

Colby straightened. "Recently promoted, my lady."

"Something we have in common," Ryn said.

"If you have need of me, I will be in the corridor." Colby tapped his gloved fingers on his scabbard. "Your Highness. My lady."

His suspicious gaze lingered on Ryn, then he let himself out.

Her old anger resurfaced. Did the Hunters still think she had something to do with the vampire brood?

Zain sat up and drained the rest of his whiskey. "When Father sends someone else to scold me, it generally means the inevitable scolding from Father himself will be calmer." He stood. "Goodnight, love. I hope you sleep well tonight. If not, you are more than welcome in my bed." With a wink and a mischievous grin, he started toward his room.

Ryn hesitated on the chaise as Zain trudged across the room. His posture expressed an exhaustion not evident in his words. She stood and started toward her bedroom. She felt Neville's eyes on her back, like she might summon a vampire horde from the shadows. Like this entire mess was her fault.

Which, she supposed, it was.

Ryn washed her face in cool water, then stared at her exhausted reflection in the vanity mirror. Despite the bags under her eyes and exhaustion in her eyes, she'd looked worse. The regular meals and inactivity had added a healthy layer of weight to her body. Enough her bones weren't so pronounced. It hadn't mattered before, not in the slums where everyone was a few missed meals from starving to death.

Assassinate King Victor.

Her grip on the basin turned white-knuckled. Her stomach twisted like she might vomit. The dusty, musty, ancient stench of the undercroft filled her memory, as fresh as if she stood down there. She grabbed the first bottle of salts from the cabinet and threw a handful into the basin. She plunged her hands into the water, splashed it against her face. Bright spearmint overwhelmed her senses, banishing the moldy undercroft.

Instead, she thought of Zain. He often smelled like spearmint.

She didn't know what to do about the prince.

She had uncovered a horrible secret, and he trusted her with it. Was this another test? Like how he'd told her of the undercroft? Even if she wanted to expose him, who would she tell? The king and queen already knew. No one in the slum would care. The guard wouldn't listen to her, neither would the Hunters.

She had agreed to marry him to save herself, thinking it would stave off her execution and give her time to plan the king's death. But Zain made her wonder what life might be like if things were different, if they could simply be together. He made her wonder about a life with him. He made her wonder if love existed for her.

When had this game turned so....complicated?

Zain was supposed to be terrible and utterly despicable. Easy to hate. That was the prince she thought she knew, but he was none of those things. Underneath the mean exterior, he was kind and protective and warm.

And Ryn… Ryn was falling for him. As much as she didn't want to admit it, as much as she didn't want to believe it, she was.

That wasn't supposed to happen.

Her mother had often said love had its own plan, heedless of inconveniences or complications. This was certainly an inconvenience.

Ryn had a choice. She could lean into the warm feelings Zain strummed, or she could ignore them. She could choose the possibility of love, or she could continue without it. Her mother had warned against a loveless life. Without love, she had said, life was cold and empty. Knowing now what she hadn't known then, Ryn understood her mother's warning. Her mother had left her luxurious life and status to marry the male she loved, even if it meant living in the slums. Her mother had chosen love. Ryn remembered her mother as a happy female, always laughing and smiling, especially when her father came home.

The choice seemed easy, and Ryn refused to overthink it.

Tomorrow, she would overthink and worry.

Tonight, she chose somewhere between.

Ryn changed into a clean sleeping gown. Instead of collapsing into her bed, she pulled a thick robe over her shoulders and marched into the sitting room. Neville said nothing as she marched across the sitting room to Zain's bedroom door. She started to knock, then just let herself inside. She shut the door hard behind her.

Zain was in bed, in dark green pajamas. His clothes from that evening were strewn across the floor, and his shoes were on either side of the room as if he had kicked them off with vengeance. At her entrance, he pushed himself onto his elbows.

"Yes, love?"

"What is this?" she demanded.

He blinked, oblivious.

She stormed across the room and jumped onto the bed. Zain didn't even flinch. Granted, there was plenty of bed between them.

"Is this still a game?" Ryn asked, searching his unreadable face for answers.

"Will my answer decide what happens next?"

She crawled closer. Zain watched every motion. Ryn slid her hand along his calf, up the inside of his thigh, and shamelessly over the front of his pants. His cock responded to her touch. In the sparse candlelight, his eyes widened and his lips parted. She hooked her finger in the ties.

His words tumbled in a throaty gasp, "Are you sure? Knowing what I am?"

"I'm returning the favor." She flashed him a wicked grin. "I never back down from a challenge."

She untied his pants with one hand and pulled out his cock. He made no move to stop her.

"And if we're caught?"

"Then it's your cock exposed, not mine."

His grin stretched. "Show me what you've got, love."

She stroked him until he grew hard, the length surprising; he was big. As if reading her thoughts, his expression turned vain.

She stroked him, base to tip, then took Zain in her mouth. The sound that escaped him was small, but pleasured. There would be no hiding what they were doing from Neville. Maybe he would take the offer to join. Tongue, hand, and teeth, she took her time eliciting pleasure from her vampire prince. When he came, his entire body tensed; she drank every last drop.

Zain melted into the blankets, breathless and flushed.

He looked down at her with softened eyes, the sneer gone, the arrogance melted. She licked her lips, and his grin returned. A swift maneuver—he flipped her onto her back. His strong hands slid up her legs, pushing the material up her thighs and to her hips. His fingers teased over her clit, pulling a soft moan from her lips.

He pressed a hot kiss to the inside of her knee. "You discovered me as a vampire only this evening," he whispered, each word a dark purr. "And yet you come to my chambers? I asked if you had kinks."

"Turns out I do." Ryn gasped as his fingers traced circles on her sensitive flesh.

A sinister grin spread his lips, and his fingers slid inside, one then two. Ryn threw her head back. Zain shifted, withdrawing his fingers, and as she lifted her head, his tongue met her clit. She hadn't the breath; his fingers pumped in and out, his tongue teased tiny spasms, and far too soon stars danced across her vision.

Zain pulled her back to him, and his lips met hers in a wet kiss. They collapsed into his many pillows. Her heart sped, liquid pleasure oozed through the bloodstream, and the horrors of the night were lifetimes away. Zain collapsed beside her, wearing a sleepy, victorious grin.

"Do you think it's still a game?" Zain whispered.

"I'd like it not to be," she answered.

Zain pulled the blankets over them both and held her against his chest.

She would like to be pulled from the dirt by a handsome prince, fall in love, and live happily ever after. Of course, she knew in her heart that it wouldn't last. Fate was not kind to females like her. But here, in the dark, she could pretend it was real.

32

TRAITOR'S TEA

Ryn

Ryn woke to a hand shaking her shoulder.

"My lady, the queen is on her way," came Irene's hushed and hurried voice. "It would be best if she didn't find you here."

Ryn rolled onto her side. Irene leaned over the bed—Zain's bed. The prince stirred from his place beside her, black hair tousled and shirt wrinkled. He blinked at Irene, then rolled onto his stomach with an unintelligent groan.

Irene motioned for Ryn to get up. "It'll be both our skins if she sees you in here."

Ryn groggily followed Irene across the sitting room and into her own chambers. Kari was sprinkling sweet smelling salts into the ready bath, filling the room with citrus. Irene positioned herself inside the bedroom while Kari pulled the sleeping gown over Ryn's head.

"Into the water with you," Kari said, each word fragile and hurried.

Ryn stepped into the hot water, and her rear had barely touched the bottom of the tub before Kari began scrubbing her with a stringent and floral soap. Rigorously scrubbed.

"Why are you taking off the top layer of my skin?" Ryn frowned.

"We don't want the queen to know what you two were up to last night," Kari said softly, as if the queen or her spies were listening.

Ryn didn't bother explaining that she and Zain hadn't entirely ruined their upcoming nuptials. Not that technicalities would matter.

Kari didn't let Ryn enjoy the bath—scrubbed an unflattering shade of pink, she shooed Ryn out of the water, dried her quickly, braided and pinned her hair, then hurried her into a slim gown of wintery silver. Ryn had only just slipped into her fur-lined house shoes when Kari ushered her into the sitting room.

The queen stood by the windows. The clouded daylight spilled over her butter-yellow gown and glimmered off the silver buttons on her gloves. Her hands were folded in front of her, a forlorn look on her face. She was awfully dressed up for a simple morning visit with Ryn.

Anticipation and dread dropped into the bottom of her stomach.

"Good morning," said the queen. Her lackluster tone reflected in her eyes as she took Ryn in. "I hear you and Zain had an eventful evening."

Ryn swallowed, words failing.

The queen shook her head. "I hate the undercroft. Far too many shadows and holes for spiders." She heaved a sigh. "Come, join me for tea."

They sat at the table set for two, and Ryn busied herself with pouring the queen's tea. The queen's gaze was distant, and despite her painted face, dark circles hung under her eyes. Had she been up since the attack last night?

"Ask about the sugar," said the queen, eyes on the window.

"You always take one," Ryn said, about to set the sugar tongs aside.

The queen stole her gaze from the window and met Ryn's. The glazed look sharpened. "Always ask. Never assume."

"One sugar or two?" Ryn asked, tone sickeningly sweet, courtier-sweet.

"One."

She continued to prepare the tea, then set it in front of the queen. Then set about making her own, no sugar.

Ryn sipped her tea. She held the cup to her lips, trying to find any trace of Zain in the queen's delicate features. They looked nothing alike, not when compared to how Zain resembled the dark-haired female in the portrait. Esben looked like both king and queen, inheriting his father's broad frame and tawny skin and his mother's bright brown eyes with streaks of green. Ryn saw nothing of Zain's pale skin, blue eyes, or narrow frame in the queen. The queen's jaw was soft where Zain's was sharp, his eyes round where hers were almond, and her hair wavy where his was straight.

Zain looked nothing like the queen. Or the king.

He looked like the female in the portrait. The vampire.

It supported Zain's theory of being born of a mistress or from an illicit affair. But…was it even possible for a fae and a vampire to spawn a child? She supposed their anatomy would be no different. It would have caused a scandal if the honorable King Victor, war hero and vanquisher of vampires, had an affair with a vampire.

Why else would the king keep a portrait of a dead vampire female and a room full of relics and books about vampires? Unless he had a reason to know such things, unless he had a half-vampire son to raise. If Zain was the result of an affair with a vampire, Victor would want to keep it secret. It would ruin the king's golden reputation not only among the nobles of his kingdom, but with the realm. It would ruin his reign.

Ryn thought back to what Zain said of his supposedly troubled birth, how the queen had been sequestered during pregnancy. A convenient way to hide a queen if she hadn't actually been with child, and to hide the female who had. The story of a troublesome birth would have been the perfect excuse to hide mother and son from the court, to save them from any rumors. To give the alchemist time to concoct the blood tonic to keep Zain's vampiric nature hidden.

Because of how difficult it was for fae to carry children, Ryn understood why Victor might keep a half-vampire baby. It was a baby, nonetheless, and part of his lineage. Part of the family that had been ravaged.

Across the table, the queen sipped her tea in silence. If Ryn revealed her assumptions about Zain and his true heritage, would the queen include her into the secret, or would it be the damning evidence the queen needed to have her executed?

Curious questions spurred more questions and fewer answers. Ryn had no one she could ask, at least no one who wouldn't tattle. She doubted the royals wanted anyone asking about Zain's mysterious birth.

"You are lost in thought," said the queen, drawing Ryn's attention.

Ryn blinked. The clouded daylight had turned a muted silver. Snow fluttered by the window.

"It was an eventful evening." Ryn took a drink of tea. "Zain saved my life. He put himself between a vampire and me."

"And this action surprises you?" The queen raised a brow.

Ryn hesitated. "Yes, but…no. I'm not used to people sticking up for me, or fighting for me. It's been just me for a long time. Fighting for myself."

"I see. Zain went to breakfast with his father." The queen slid her fingers around the teacup's handle, as if unsure if she wanted to pick it up or not. Her gold-painted nails caught the muted daylight.

"Zain worried his father would be furious," Ryn said, turning her expression sheepish. Downcast. Innocent. Noncombatant.

"Oh, he was. Victor paced half the night, stewing in fury." The queen released an exhausted sigh. "What happened last night is exactly what Victor strives to avoid. A vampire lurking around the keep, and Zain not only went looking for it, he found it."

"And killed it," Ryn added. The words slipped out.

Queen Portia swept her hand to the side in a dismissive gesture.

Ryn felt the burning desire to defend Zain. She didn't like how his *parents* dismissed his courageous act.

"You don't think he should have?" Ryn held her hands under the table to keep her trembling out of sight. "Or do you disapprove because I might have been killed otherwise? I would be out of your hair without you lifting a finger."

The queen bristled. "Be that as it may, my son doesn't need a knife in his boot. And a silver ash knife at that."

"That silver ash saved our lives."

"I am sure his father will have words for him about that knife," the queen said tersely.

The queen held her emotions close, each gaze and glance curated and controlled, but the subtle reaction was there—underneath the royal mask, like she didn't want to acknowledge the danger of silver ash beyond the dagger's edge, or why Zain didn't need such a dagger anywhere near his person.

Silence fell over the table. Ryn sipped her tea, eyeing the queen's over the rim. There was more to the story, but she would have to tiptoe around it. Like a courtier.

"The Hunters couldn't find it," Ryn whispered.

The queen's gaze sharpened.

"The vampire, I mean." Ryn sipped her tea as if this were normal conversation for two ladies. "Zain and I were just wandering, and it happened across our path." Ryn feigned terror at the memory. "It makes me wonder if it was looking for us."

The queen paled. "Nonsense. It was nothing more than bad timing. You and Zain happened across the wrong place at the wrong time."

Ryn nodded, feigning relief. "That is what I'd hoped."

Because Ryn had a horrible feeling it had been looking for *her*.

The queen straightened and inhaled. In a blink, she regained her royal presence. "If you are insistent on this course, then you need to understand the place you will step into. As his wife, you will have duties. As the wife of a prince, you will have court duties. You will be a prominent figure in the court, and you will be expected to attend festivities, parties, and balls. You will be expected to look the part of princess."

The queen explained her role as if she doubted Ryn was capable. Of course, Ryn mirrored the feeling. She had barely scratched the surface of being a princess or a wife, and she hadn't stepped into court since her failed sentencing.

"I have arranged tea between you and Lady Crestin," said the queen. Her gaze sharpened to steel. "In three days. You will be on your best behavior, Sabryn. If Crestin House refuses to acknowledge you as a daughter, things will not go in your favor."

"But wouldn't it be in their favor to have a daughter married to a prince?" Ryn asked. "It would bring them closer to the throne."

Queen Portia considered her with the smallest smile on her dusty lips. "Yes, it would. See? You are learning." Her smile turned venomous. "Now, we have three days to make you presentable. We should focus on your story, your tragic upbringing, and how fate has brought you back to your rightful home."

The queen talked the entire time through the tea and toast. Ryn had little appetite. Between the queen's plan to make Ryn into a long-lost granddaughter of a noble house and Zain's true nature and the looming deed of killing King

Victor, Ryn couldn't focus. She didn't know if she wanted to meet her mother's family or not. They had thrown her out, disowned her, erased her existence, because she married the male she loved—despite that, if the queen was correct, the Crestin family was the only family she had left.

"But before you meet Lady Crestin, you must prove yourself at our family dinner." The queen set down her empty teacup and stood, signaling the end of their meeting. Her cold composure returned in a heartbeat. "My husband plans to investigate the undercroft. You and Zain are not to leave your chambers without a Hunter escort, and *you* are to have a full retinue whenever you leave these chambers. Understand?"

Ryn pretended not to feel the queen's glare or her own bones trembling. Had she been told a few months ago that she would stare down the queen of Sovann, she would have laughed. Yet here she was.

Sweetly, with her fists curled under the table, she nodded. "Of course, Your Majesty."

33

ONE SPITEFUL LADY

Ryn

Ryn spent the day lounging in her chambers under the watchful, albeit angry, stare of Hunter Irene. Zain was still with his father. Not that his absence bothered her. It gave her space to think. More packages arrived, including another box of chocolates from a bakery she hadn't heard of. According to Kari, word had gotten out about her love of chocolate.

"I suspect more bakers will be vying for your favor," Kari said as she dusted the floor-to-ceiling bookshelves.

"Would you like one?" Ryn offered the golden box to Irene, whose scowl deepened like Ryn offered her poison.

Ryn slowly brought the box back to herself. She'd meant it as a peace offering. Irene had reverted back to the cold, serious Hunter who had pursued Ryn through the streets. Any sliver of friendship between them had shattered, and it was Ryn's fault. It stung to know she'd damaged a friendship, and it was an odd sensation she hadn't felt in a long time. She hadn't had the chance to have friends, to have someone to disappoint.

After her fill of chocolates, Ryn attempted to read through the dense history books, but her eyes strayed to the many books in the sitting room. She spotted a book written by King Victor—one of his dossiers on vampires. The book was not as heavy as the history books, and the slanted handwriting was slightly bigger and easier to read.

And she had a sudden interest in learning more about vampires.

She took both books and plopped onto the chaise, where the sunlight spilled across the pages. By the wrinkled spine, Zain had read it multiple times.

Was this how he figured it out?

The book was a horrifying study of vampires in captivity, under the eye of the Hunters.

Ryn read into the late afternoon. A well-fed vampire could blend in among fae, but the longer it went without blood, the more its vampirism showed. The skin paled, red circled the eyes, and its behavior became more animalistic and rabid. Physical strength increased with each day without blood, as did murderous tendencies. Vampires in starvation entered what Victor dubbed bloodlust. It was a crazed state of desperation, panic, and hunger, where the vampire knew nothing else. Rabid, he called it. Mindless beasts.

The accounts were frighteningly detailed. The king had kept an unknown number of vampires in captivity and studied them as they starved.

The whole thing left her uneasy. When she thought of vampires, her mind conjured a pale, gaunt, bloodied nightmare with sharp teeth and beady eyes. The monsters the king described in his book were just that, creatures of darkness and hate. How could Zain be one of those? If he didn't drink his tonic, would he turn into a bloodlust-driven demon?

One account detailed how a vampire escaped in confines, and how it killed four Hunters before they took it down.

Ryn's hands shook. Not wanting to read anymore horror stories about vampires, she shut the book. She tried to focus on the history books, but her mind refused. It replayed the vampire torture over and over.

The next morning, as Ryn entered the sitting room for breakfast with Queen Portia, Zain stepped into the corridor. He glanced over his shoulder at her as the Hunters shut the door, his gaze cool and unfeeling. Ryn pretended not to notice, and she tried to shove the icy feeling it gave her down.

They hadn't spoken the day before. He hadn't returned until after she had gone to bed.

The queen didn't speak of vampires or Hunters; she was content to pretend that nothing had happened, and instead filled the silence with chatter of the nobles Ryn was expected to know, the annual balls and festivities, and other things Ryn didn't care about.

"I have found you a dancing instructor," the queen said. "Your lessons begin the morning after this dinner. You will learn to dance midmorning each day until he deems you worthy of the courts' eye."

Ryn nodded along. Learning to dance didn't sound nearly as bad as trying to read the dense history books.

"I am also pleased to say that Lady Aurora would like to make amends with you," the queen said, her tone icy and practiced. It was the same voice she used to compliment and threaten.

Ryn didn't care what Aurora thought of her. She didn't care what any of the courtiers thought of her. But, if she were to live in this royal world, she needed to pretend.

"That sounds wonderful," Ryn said.

The queen chatted on. It would seem that while Ryn was sequestered in the royal wing, Lady Aurora had been attending court and visiting other females and making friends.

Making connections, Ryn thought bitterly.

"Is she looking for a suitable husband?" Ryn asked.

The queen fixed a piercing stare on Ryn. "I gave her a few suggestions of eligible bachelors."

Ryn felt the lie like the edge of the knife. The queen still assumed Ryn wouldn't last, that Zain would tire of her, or she would find a way to discreetly get rid of her. Aurora would then be able to step conveniently into the hole left in Zain's life, with all the connections and friends a princess was expected to have.

Fury slithered through Ryn's skin. She wanted to stay and marry Zain just to spite everyone.

A knock sounded at the door, and servants hauled in another round of delivered packages.

The queen set her empty teacup on the saucer. "I see you have been reading the texts I sent you, good." Her gaze danced over the history book left open on the armchair, then the wrapped packages.

Ryn wanted to scream at her, *Do you know your son is a vampire?*

But she held her lips tightly together.

Did the queen know? Or did she think Zain was the son of some common affair?

After the meal, Ryn nestled on the bed with a new box of chocolates while Kari unwrapped the packages and found each item a home within the growing wardrobe. Ryn imagined her life if she married Zain, one where she could have all the chocolate she wanted, wear silk robes, have servants do the cooking and cleaning, and spend every night with a husband who loved her.

It sounded like a child's daydream—a rose-colored version of the truth.

The queen wanted Ryn gone. Marriage wouldn't stop the queen from devising a tragic death or grooming her replacement.

If Ryn managed to kill the king without trouble, and Esben took the throne and his wife became queen, would it diminish Queen Portia's power over her? Or would she continue to strive to get rid of Ryn until her last breath?

Because Ryn still needed to get rid of King Victor. Somehow.

Like the day before, Zain didn't return until late. Ryn was in bed and half-asleep when she heard his voice. He and Neville were talking about Esben and Captain Colby—Ryn rolled over and went back to sleep.

Zain hadn't said a word to her for the past two days. His sudden coldness felt like rejection, and Ryn didn't like it. It stung far deeper than it should, needles on her bones, rocks in her stomach, ice in her veins.

❀❀❀

"Lady Aurora requests your presence for tea."

Ryn stared at the servant as if he had lost his mind. Under her stare, he swallowed. Paled. Glanced at his boots.

Ryn had no desire to see or speak with Aurora, but she'd have to share meals and tea with people she didn't like. This was likely a test set by the queen.

"Where?" Ryn asked.

"The Rose Parlor." The servant bowed. "This afternoon."

"Yes, fine."

The servant saw himself out.

Irene eyed her from her post by the window. "You might try acting like you want to see her."

"I would rather eat worms," Ryn deadpanned.

Irene didn't react. "As would many, I'm sure. But Aurora is one of many nobles who will be clamoring for your attention. Consider this practice."

Ryn heaved a sigh. Irene was right.

Midafternoon, Hunters escorted Ryn to the Rose Parlor on the west side of the manor. True to its name, the parlor contained thousands of roses. Wooden ones. Roses were carved into the wooden paneling, the stems lined with thorns, climbing into one another like a real rose bush. The carvings accumulated around the base of the crystal chandelier. Candlelight glittered off the crystals, making each glitter and glow.

Lady Aurora stood by the window, staring out at the grounds. She wore a snug red dress and pearl-tipped pins in her blond hair. Her lips matched her dress. Three of her guards lined the back of the room, observing with blank faces.

"My lady," Aurora chimed. It dripped with falsity.

"Lady Aurora," Ryn chimed in the same tone.

"So wonderful for you to agree to see me on such short notice!" Aurora flashed her a bashful, grateful smile. "You look lovely in that shade! Plum is beautiful this time of year. It is one of my favorite colors."

Ryn forced herself to return the smile. Of course, Aurora liked plum. Ryn suspected the queen had purchased many of the dresses with Aurora in mind, so she could step into the wardrobe after Ryn's tragic demise. Instead of pointing it out, Ryn held her fake smile and spun, letting the pleating panels of her dress catch the candlelight. An iridescent thread ran through the plum, glittering in the light.

"Thank you," Ryn said, the words dripping with honey.

A table was set for two. A delicate teapot and matching cups were arranged around a platter of sliced fruit. Three fat candles burned in the center of the table on brass holders.

Ryn swept her skirts aside to sit and played the role of princess while Aurora fixed and served her tea. Irene took up a post within Ryn's sight, where she could take in every motion either female made.

"I heard what happened in the undercroft," Aurora said, the words curious.

"Oh?" Ryn raised a brow. Nobel had taught her how to dig for information, and how to spot it in others. Aurora was fishing. "I didn't realize word spread so fast. Of course, I've been resting since."

"It sounds terrifying!" Aurora pressed a hand against her chest. "Vampires, here in the keep! I never thought Zain was the chivalrous type. I am glad to be wrong."

"I was wrong about him as well," Ryn whispered. A tidbit to make Aurora think she was opening up, sharing a secret. "Before I met him, I thought he was…what everyone said about him. He isn't."

Aurora blinked at her. A hesitation, a crack in the mask. She recovered quickly, plastering a fake smile on her lips. "Really? I haven't gotten the chance to talk with him much more than a few meals. Not since you arrived, that is. I am glad to hear he isn't so nasty after all."

Ryn flashed her a smile. It came out more vicious than she intended. "I never dreamed I would find my mate, and yet here I am. Not only have I found him, but he is a prince."

She brought her tea to her lips as those words settled over Aurora. It hit a sensitive reminder underneath the satin and the paint, and her expression deflated—Ryn fought hard to keep her lips in a flat line.

"That is so romantic," Aurora said, in the same strained voice one might use to express sympathy.

Ryn released a lovesick sigh. It was frighteningly easy. "I have been doing some reading since Zain took me in. About mates. I read that when one lovebird dies, the other begins to wither away. Unable to love again."

Aurora's left eye twitched. Her lips pursed.

Ryn kept going. "I never thought I would find a male who made me think about starting my own family, or…" She blushed. "…or what I would name my children."

Aurora's fingers twitched on her teacup. Her expression shifted, more than a crack or slip. Her eyes were daggers, shocked and furious and ashamed. Her lips were flat. Her neck paled where the makeup didn't reach.

"That is wonderful," Aurora said.

Ryn blinked. "I apologize. Did I say something wrong?"

"No, no, of course not, my lady." Aurora cleared her throat, sipped her tea, and tore her gaze to the side. She blinked—her eyes were glassy.

Was she…crying?

"Someone must have told you," Aurora said. Her words were clipped. "Her Majesty, maybe? I doubt Zain knows, unless he found out from his mother."

Ryn blinked. She let her own fake face fall. "What are you talking about?"

Aurora bristled. "It is no secret that our female lineage is infertile. None of my sisters or aunts or female cousins have been able to conceive without extensive medicinal aid, and only a few have been able to carry to term."

Ryn considered those words. Aurora was infertile. She wouldn't be able to have children. She wouldn't give Zain children. If she married him, they would not produce fae-vampire children, and no one would ask why. Ryn thought of the queen's quiet relief when she'd discovered Ryn wasn't pregnant with Zain's child.

The queen and king did not want Zain to reproduce.

Aurora's infertility would be the perfect solution to hide the secret from everyone, bride included.

Heaving a sigh, Aurora sat her teacup down with enough force to rattle the saucer. Ryn jumped at the sudden sound. Aurora stood. "I apologize, my lady, but I no longer feel up to this meeting."

Relief rolled off Ryn's shoulders. She stood to make a proper farewell, and to her surprise, Aurora wrapped her arms around Ryn in a tight embrace. Panic at the touch slithered through her skin.

"I don't believe you're mates," Aurora whispered into Ryn's ear. "You're a lying piece of shit that belongs in the gutter where you came from. You won't last another month here. I will make sure of it. There are plenty of deadbeats out there willing to slice up a bitch for few coppers."

Aurora released her and leaned away; for a fraction of a heartbeat, she wore hatred on her face. Then, in a blink, it was gone. She was the painted doll with the hapless smile and glittering eyes. "Until next time, Lady Sabryn."

Ryn stood while Aurora and her guards filed out of the room. Only after, when it was just Ryn and Irene, did she let Aurora's words settle.

There are plenty of deadbeats willing to slice up a bitch for a few coppers.

Ryn's heart pounded. Her pulse thundered in her ears. Irene stepped closer, asking if she was okay. Ryn barely heard the words.

Aurora not only planned on Ryn's death, but she had sent mercenaries to do the job. She had sent the mercenaries to the greenhouse.

Few times in her life had she felt such a burning surge of revenge, and each time she had tried her best to shove it down lest it get the better of her and darken her soul. But she would make an exception for Aurora. Before Ryn left the keep, Aurora would be dead.

34

DANGEROUS DINNER GUEST

Ryn

Zain left early the next morning. The queen didn't come with breakfast, and Ryn spent most of the morning soaking until the bath grew cold, tasting her small horde of chocolates, reading until her vision crossed, and napping. The sun went down, servants scurried to light the candles and lamps all over the keep, and Zain didn't return.

Was he avoiding her?

Were they keeping them apart on purpose?

The next day passed the same—Zain left early, Ryn spent it alone. Irene posted herself in the corridor. The luxurious chamber felt too big without anyone else in it.

Zain left every morning, but they locked Ryn inside. Had they changed their minds about her? Did they suspect her plans to assassinate the king?

Ryn went to bed. She woke to the opening of the door and footsteps. She sat up, slid out of the bed, and swung her bedroom door open.

Zain jumped—he stood a few steps from his bedroom door. He blinked at her, then his gaze roamed over her nightdress.

They stared at one another.

Ryn thought of the detailed descriptions of the intense gaze of a hungry vampire. King Victor compared it to looking into the eyes of death.

Looking into Zain's eyes filled her with something far warmer and fuzzy.

She swallowed and awkwardly asked, "Late night?"

Zain looked away, but not in time for her to miss the look—ashamed. She didn't have to look into his blood to feel it.

"Yes," he said, breathlessly. He said no more before he shut himself in his room.

She thought about going to him, but something in his voice wanted to be left alone.

Was he ashamed of himself, or of her? Had he finally realized her worth?

Ryn retreated into her room with a gnawing sense of defeat and rejection. She shouldn't feel this way. She'd spent most of her adult life alone, and she'd accepted that she would be alone. She'd gotten used to loneliness. She'd stopped longing for any affection beyond physical, and she had plenty of options for that.

But…she was getting used to Zain, and the idea of having a husband. His sudden rejection annoyed her.

She gripped the bedpost, trying to convince herself not to feel so horrible, when Zain's bedroom door opened. His soft steps sounded across the floor, followed by the plush of sitting and rustle of pages. Ryn couldn't quite explain the urge to go to him. Maybe it was the days spent alone, or Aurora's death threats, or the looming precipice of the end of all of this. Whatever the reason, she grabbed her silken robe and let herself back into the sitting room.

Zain sat on the sofa with a book on his lap. His black hair was damp from a wash. He wore a clean housecoat of deep sage and soft black pants. His feet were bare and his gangly feet crossed at the ankles. At the sound of her door, his eyes flashed up from the page to her then back to his page.

Ryn perched on the opposite end of the sofa and plucked the history book she'd left face-down that afternoon. She folded her legs over his lap. He didn't say a word, but he adjusted his arms and his book over her legs. A small smile tilted his lips, though his eyes remained in his book. She cracked the history book open against her thighs.

Vampire spawn or not, if they were to continue this game, they needed to at least pretend to get along. Besides, this wasn't just about her. It was about saving Lu and getting away from Nobel. If this played out in Ryn's favor, the king's murder would be blamed on vampires or an unfaithful guard, she would marry Zain, and she and Lu would spend the rest of their lives in luxury.

That was what she told herself.

She didn't know how to process the feeling of wanting to be around him. She'd never had the desire to spend time with anyone, aside from Lu.

"They haven't found anything," Zain whispered.

"Hmm?" She lifted her eyes from the page. Zain didn't look away from his.

Turning the page, he said, "Hunters have been searching the undercroft for days. There is no trace of vampires beyond the dead one. They don't know where it could have gotten in or where it could have been hiding."

"There could be more," she whispered.

Zain lifted his eyes from his book, expression tired but unreadable. "That's what everyone is afraid of."

The idea of vampires lurking in the shadows of Nightshade Keep hit differently than knowing they lurked in the slums. In the keep, Hunters were supposed to stop them.

If Hunters couldn't stop them, what could?

sss

Four days slugged by with no evidence of vampires, and the queen refused to postpone the formal family dinner any longer. Ryn chose a slim gown of layered silk the shade of strawberry wine. Being a formal dinner and therefore stuffy, Ryn pulled on ivory gloves with golden buttons that trailed up to her elbow. Kari fixed her hair with golden pins and a ruby-studded comb.

Ryn's stomach tied itself into knots as she and Zain strolled through the castle, arm in arm, with a full retinue. Irene and Neville stalked on either side of them, and Captain Colby followed. Either the king and queen were still worried about vampire attacks, or they didn't trust Ryn or Zain. Ryn didn't allow herself to linger on which one they distrusted more.

They strolled into the grand dining hall. Only Irene, Neville, and Colby followed them in and took up guards' posts by the walls.

The waning sunset bathed the room in golden light. Thousands of candles burned on the crystal chandelier. Two hearths burned, one on either side of the room. Despite the candles, the sun, and the hearths, shadows remained. Through the window, the sunset washed the city in gold and shadow.

Long oaken tables were set with ivory linens, golden runners, and delicately folded napkins—for at least one hundred guests.

Just a formal family dinner.

Guests had already arrived, and eyes darted to the doors as Ryn and Zain strolled inside. Nobles took in Ryn with barely masked scrutiny—some intrigued, others disgusted. Ryn held herself tall and proud. A princess. Despite her projected confidence, her nerves fluttered and tugged at her heartstrings.

None of the nobles looked like her mother. Would her supposedly long-lost family recognize Ryn? Or was it all some scheme by the queen to give Ryn a noble background?

"Nervous?" Zain teased, his expression a noble's unfeeling mask.

"Nervous?" Ryn harrumphed. "What would I have to be nervous about? The nobles adore me and in no way are devising ways to slither into my good graces, and I'm sure no one at this dinner is plotting my death."

Zain half-laughed, but it did not meet his eyes. "You will do fine."

"You have far more confidence in me than your mother does," she mused. She gazed at the door as three noble females glided into the chamber. None looked like Ryn's mother.

"I should mention that dear Crestin was unable to make it tonight," Zain said. At her relief, he added, "Mother feared you would be devastated. I shall impart your remorse to her."

They strolled around the dining room, skirting the clusters of nobles but staying close enough to catch snippets of their whispers—they spoke of Ryn's mysterious background, of Aurora, of the other females Zain had rejected or run off before her. One whisper spoke of Princess Lucia, and Zain's entire body tensed.

This close, Ryn felt it in his blood. Panic. Shame. Disgust.

She did not have the mind to question his response, not when her name flew on the whispers. Questioning her presence. Questioning her bloodline. Questioning their story. Questioning how Zain could prefer her over all the fine females of the court.

The words hit deeper than they should have.

Ryn pushed aside her feelings and drifted into the role of princess. High and mighty. Arrogant. Better than everyone else in the room. She held herself like the queen, like Aurora, with her nose higher than natural, confident enough not to be bothered by their questions. She held herself like Zain, cold and unfeeling.

More guests arrived, the royal assembly as Zain called them. They were the king's collection of useful people, be it from skill or connections. Zain whispered their names in her ear. There was the old silver-haired alchemist who did his best to ignore Ryn and Zain; the Royal Healer, Royal Blacksmith, Horse Master, Archery Master for the Hunters, wealthy merchants, heads of noble houses, investors, and several scowling Hunters and Royal Guards in decorated uniforms.

Zain pointed out the king's steward, the queen's steward, advisors, and a stern-looking older woman who oversaw the kitchens and servants.

The advisors looked none too happy about Ryn's presence, and the old woman who oversaw the servants glowered like Ryn had personally pissed in her tea.

"The advisors are against the union," Zain whispered to Ryn. "Or so the rumors say."

Ryn glanced away from the unhappy advisors. "I couldn't tell. How many have daughters or nieces of marrying age?"

"Several." Zain gave her a knowing look.

More guests arrived, and it grew harder to avoid conversation. Zain fell into calm, pointless talk with a noble male from a house Ryn had heard of in passing. He looked her over, unimpressed.

Another set of heels clicked against the marble floor, but Ryn paid no mind until a spec of bright green glided into her vision. It snagged Zain's attention a heartbeat after hers.

Fuck. Ryn didn't have the patience to deal with dinner *and* a viper.

"Ah, Lady Aurora," Zain said in a mock-pleasant greeting. "How lovely of you to join us for dinner."

"Her Majesty generously invited me." Lady Aurora curtsied without bowing her head or letting her nose fall. The motion jiggled the oversized emeralds and diamonds around her throat. Straightening, she turned her painted expression to Ryn. "You look *stunning* this evening, Lady Sabryn."

"Zain chose this dress." Ryn flashed him a loving look. Zain hadn't picked her dress, but she didn't need to know that. "Her Majesty gifted me so many, I didn't know which to pick."

"And I chose well." Zain draped his gaze over the dress. "You do look marvelous this evening, love. Not quite as marvelous as myself, but you are a close second in the room."

Ryn returned the lewd up-and-down. "I suppose you're right about that."

He did look good. The cut fit his long legs and lean build, and his confidence turned his smirk into something sinister. And for a moment, he was his old self, the smarmy prince, not the secret vampire.

Lady Aurora's smile turned venomous. "You two are adorable. Please, excuse me. There are many people to meet."

Aurora drifted through the crowd to where two noble males were talking with Captain Colby.

"I will never understand the female hunt for a husband," Zain said, brow furrowing at how Aurora giggled at something Colby said.

"Neither will I," Ryn added. "Poor Colby."

"Indeed."

Zain's thumb ran along her knuckles. It struck her then how quickly she had gotten used to holding his hand. The first time his fingers laced with hers, she'd been unsettled at the contact.

"Why the need to marry and reproduce?" Zain mused. "I don't like my value being tied to how many children I have. I also don't like my union with another to be used as a means to politically tie two families together as if I have no say in my life."

"I agree," Ryn said.

An awkward breath expanded between them. Ryn thought again to any children she and Zain might have. What would they be? Would they inherit Zain's vampirism? She hadn't considered having children of her own since their mother had died. She hadn't the means to feed or clothe them, let alone the clean conscience to raise decent souls.

"I'm more concerned with why your father feels this dinner necessary," Ryn muttered under her breath as yet another stranger in formal attire sauntered into the dining hall.

"He says it's important to know those close to him, especially those who live in the keep," Zain said as they meandered past the bank of windows. Winter's chill emitted from the glass. Frost and ice lingered on the edges of the frames.

"I am inclined to agree," Ryn said.

"Inclined to agree?" Zain raised a brow.

"What? Do nobles not use excessive verbiage?" She lifted her chin slightly and drawled her words in an exaggeration of a noble's educated lilt. "If only to hear themselves speak and make people across the room think they have much to say?"

Zain chuckled. "I suppose they do. Though, you don't have to pretend to be a noble around me."

A bit of her unease melted at his purring tone. "And you don't have to pretend to be an insufferable ass around me."

A beat, then he laughed.

It was like nothing between them had changed, and yet everything had. Things had been changing since that night in the tavern.

And if all went as planned, this would be her future. Married to her vampire prince, tied to the crown, with a mother-in-law plotting her demise. After the king, Aurora would have to go. Then Ryn and Lu could talk about their happily ever after within the walls of Nightshade Keep.

35

TO KILL A KING

Ryn

As more people arrived, Zain led Ryn to their seats at the head table. The other tables were angled around it, so everyone had a view of their king and his family. It made Ryn feel like a set piece, not a person.

Did she want to spend the rest of her life as a royal prop?

She glanced at the cutlery on either side of her place setting, trying to remember the function of each. In her meals with Zain, they'd not had more than a fork and spoon.

Zain leaned into her ear and whispered, "You've got that panicked look."

Forcing a pleasant smile onto her lips, she whispered back, "Where I'm from, we have one fork."

"How do you eat soup?"

"Drink it."

Zain feigned horror, yet his eyes were glittering.

Had he missed this banter as much as she had?

Zain chuckled. "Ah, the infamous silverware. Copy what everyone else does. Most nobles forget about the dessert fork anyway."

"That's the smaller one, right?"

"It is!" Zain's grin stretched, and he looked more like the cocky prince. Chuckling, he set his hand on her knee. "See, you are learning."

Though the linens hid their legs, the motion and angle of Zain's arm gave away the touch. It did not go unnoticed by the gawking nobles.

King Victor and Queen Portia arrived fashionably late, or so Zain whispered to Ryn as they swept into the room. They sat at the head table, with the king in the middle, flanked by his sons, advisors, and commanders. Once seated, servants in white streamed into the room with carafes of table wine. Ryn accepted hers and took a small sip. The queen had warned her of drinking too much before the first course. A princess should not be drunk before dessert, she'd said.

Conversations erupted all over the room. From Ryn's seat, she could hear at least five. Several discussed the missing and now dead vampire, hiding in the undercroft doing gods only knew what, that had died at Zain's hand. Others whispered of the brood lurking in the city and the shriveled bodies left behind.

Lady Aurora kept glancing at Zain, like he might return her glances. He did not, as far as Ryn could tell. He spoke to the advisor on his other side. Only after Aurora's eyes snagged on Ryn's, to which Ryn winked, did the female stop.

During the first course, which was a hearty squash soup, Ryn spoke to the stern-faced female who oversaw the kitchens and servants. She introduced herself as Miss Willow.

"Do I have you to thank for the wonderful food?" Ryn asked.

Miss Willow nodded. She wasn't concerned with petty chitchat, and Ryn admired that about her. "The cooks and staff work around the clock to keep the linens washed and armor scrubbed. How are you finding your time in the keep?"

"It has been splendid," Ryn said. It wasn't a lie. Despite the death threats, everything had been luxurious. She'd so rarely splurged on anything, instead opting for the cheaper, plain version of everything. The food, the bedding, the clothes—the king had the best of everything.

Miss Willow fell silent. Ryn turned her ear toward the whispers.

"…these vampires," said a male voice to her left. "They think it might have been an assassination attempt."

Ryn's skin prickled, and gooseflesh seared cold across her exposed flesh. Zain laughed, and she took a drink of wine to flush the feeling. Somewhere on the king's other side, Esben chatted easily, his voice like a drumbeat.

"The beasts didn't make it past the kitchen," said another voice.

"That's the thing," said the first voice. "I heard the guards talking. What if they hadn't meant to make it out of the kitchens?"

Ryn's throat was tight, and her skin had gone clammy.

"And the blood they found?"

"No one knows. That's the weird part. Why would they be smuggling blood into the keep? It's gone, and no one knows where it went."

Ryn swallowed a spoonful of soup with difficulty.

Another voice, almost too far away to hear, "What if someone let them in?"

"Are you all right, dear?" asked Miss Willow, though her tone lacked sincerity. "You're looking pale."

Zain's hand graced her thigh, and she felt his gaze.

"I-I must have drunk too much wine too fast," she lied.

Zain chuckled; Miss Willow scowled.

The conversation turned onto more pleasant paths, and Ryn eased the knots in her stomach with more wine.

With dessert came another wine, one that paired well with the fluffy mint cake. One servant brought forth a bottle of the king's favorite wine, imported from a kingdom over, reserved just for him. Ryn watched as the dark plum wine filled his goblet, as the sweet perfume of it wafted over the table. The sweetness of the scent tightened around Ryn's throat like a vise.

Ryn selected her dessert fork, then brought a shaky forkful of cake to her mouth, while the king took a healthy gulp from his favorite wine.

"Are you all right?" Zain asked softly.

Ryn washed down the ashy sensation of the cake with a healthy gulp of wine, then a second. Zain's brow cocked to the side. The concern on his face took her off guard, and between him and the tightness of her throat, she didn't at first register the coughing.

"Father?" Esben's voice drifted above the others.

The coughing grew more intense. Conversations quieted. The king's goblet crashed against the table, spilling its plum wine across the table.

"Father!" Esben grabbed his father's shoulder.

This time, silence fell.

So did King Victor.

Esben shoved chairs out of the way and pulled his father onto his back, panic and fury on his handsome face. Zain stood, then pulled Ryn to her feet and backed them both away from where the plum wine seeped through the table's linens quicker than fire. Much of the plum wine sloshed onto the floor. Zain watched with horror. Ryn didn't have to feign panic; it seethed through her skin like cold sweat.

The king gasped for breath. The royal healer knelt at the king's side and barked orders for her medicinal bag in her chambers—one of the Hunter captains bolted to fetch it—and felt along the king's chest.

"I feel nothing blocking his airways."

"Father, breathe!" Esben commanded, his voice echoing off the walls.

Zain gripped Ryn painfully. His hand trembled.

The healer felt along the king's limbs, desperately searching for the ailment. A stream of plum wine flowed past the toe of Ryn's satin shoe. The king began to seize. Cries sounded throughout the room, servants stared wide-eyed, and no one moved.

Ryn's heart skipped several beats. She had witnessed death, the dirty and scary bits before and after, but it always sent her heart flip-flopping.

King Victor went ghastly white. Blue tinted his lips.

The alchemist dropped to the king's side and nicked his forearm. He drew a bead of blood and dropped it into a vial of pinkish dust. The instant the droplet touched the dust, it turned a nasty shade of yellow.

Ryn felt it swarming in the king's bloodstream before the alchemist announced it.

"Poisoned," the alchemist confirmed.

Zain's grip tightened. "What?"

"The king has been poisoned," the healer said with more confidence.

"It can't be," Esben breathed. He too had gone pale.

"I know poison when I see it, boy," the alchemist snapped.

"You, fetch willow bark and ginger root. At once." The healer pointed at the closest servant, who then bolted through the dining room doors. "We need to purge his stomach. You might want to clear out the room. It won't be pretty."

The alchemist nodded.

Colby ordered everyone out of the room. Guards shepherded the guests out.

The Hunter returned with the healer's bag. Ryn leaned further into Zain's chest. Despite everything, watching the king suffer at her feet twisted her gut into slippery knots.

While the alchemist worked with herbs from the healer's bag, the healer set colored stones on the king's chest. Each glowed malicious shades of brown, orange, and yellow. Ryn had seen similar stones in healers' stalls in the market. The stones were not cures, but methods of finding disease and internal injuries.

"The poison went first to his heart," the healer muttered.

Beside her, the alchemist combined mixed herbs with a milky liquid—he swirled the potion until it turned a dark red. The alchemist extracted the potion into a syringe and injected it into the king's neck.

Ryn cringed, and Zain's hands tightened on her shoulders. Did a needle to the neck feel worse than a blade?

The king stilled.

Esben dropped to his father's side. "Father? Can you hear me?"

The king took a shattering breath.

"Space, Your Highness." The healer set her hand on Esben's shoulder.

The deathly white in the king's flesh brightened into a flush, then he vomited—vehemently. The entire dinner reappeared, splattered with plum wine and stomach acid. The smell was enough to churn Ryn's dinner, and she fought to keep it down.

At last, the king stilled. His chest rose and fell.

"This will do until we are able to find the antidote to whatever poisoned him," said the healer.

The alchemist scooped vomit into a vial and tucked into his pocket.

"I will study it for poison." The alchemist took another vial of the wine. "I'll know the poison by the end of tomorrow."

Esben stepped back, horror on his face. His gaze flashed up to Zain and quickly morphed into fury. "You."

Zain blinked at his brother. "Yes?"

"You did this." Esben clenched his fists, his voice full of rage and grief.

"Oh, I did?" Zain half-laughed without mirth. "I poisoned my own father? For what? Without him, the throne goes to you."

Esben and Zain stared at one another, as if they'd forgotten the people around them, as if they'd forgotten their father's still warm body on the floor between them.

"You were headed to the storeroom the night the vampires broke in," Esben accused. "You could have poisoned the wine."

"As I recall, brother, you were also headed in that direction." Zain spoke frighteningly calm, though he glared daggers. "You could be using me as a scapegoat to finally ascend the throne."

"You weren't even surprised."

"I'm rarely surprised." The words came maliciously. "But if you are going to accuse me brother, then accuse me. You have your audience." He motioned to the room filled with watching guards and Hunters.

"You found the third vampire," Esben spat. "But it was dead before anyone else got there."

"Apologies for not chatting with it first," Zain spat.

It felt like a lie, even to Ryn. Zain's hand on her arm tightened.

"All this time, we've been looking for a vampire accomplice," Esben growled out of the words, his eyes blazing. "It's been you, hasn't it?"

"You can't be serious, brother."

"Hunters," Esben commanded.

The Hunters hesitated, then started to close in.

For a fraction of a moment, Zain looked frightened. Then his bravado reappeared. He laughed. *Laughed.*

The king coughed.

"He will live," the healer said. Scowling, she added to Esben in a dry tone, "You are not yet king. You cannot condemn your brother for murder."

A Hunter stepped to Zain's side, but Zain waved him away as if he were a fly. "I am capable of walking myself out, thank you."

"No, you won't be walking anywhere." Esben growled. "You will sit in the dungeon until this is figured out. Guards!"

The guards closed in. A strong pair of hands pulled Ryn away—Irene. She had gone pale as snow, though her hands on Ryn's shoulders were steady as steel.

The Hunters surrounded Zain. Colby grabbed Zain's arm and pulled him away from the head table, to where the Hunters waited. With a curse, Zain yanked his arm from Colby's grip.

"Is this how you want to play this, *brother*?" The venom in Zain's voice was cold and laced with heartbreak.

Ryn saw it there, the pain in his eyes. The fury and indecision.

Esben didn't back down. He motioned the Hunters closer.

Zain's glare smoothed into a wicked grin. His indecision became a cold certainty. His predatory posture melted into the arrogant prince, as if he had nowhere he'd rather be, and then with a snap, he vanished.

36

HUNTERS AND PRINCES
Ryn

Ryn stared at where Zain had just stood, where he had *vanished.*

"Fuck," Irene spat. Surprise brightened her entire face, underlined with fury. "He's gone?"

"Magic." Colby glared at the floor where Zain had just been, brow furrowed, as if a monster might lurch from the grout.

Neville stood frozen by the wall. His lips were slack, his eyes wide—he hadn't known. His eyes met Ryn's, and he shook himself back into the emotionless guardsman.

But he'd seen. They all had. Zain had magic, which could only mean he was a vampire. He might as well have flashed bloodied fangs at the court.

All they could do was stare. The silence settling felt worse than whispers. It settled like a damp cloth, oppressive and heavy, and no one had the strength to push it off. Aurora looked close to fainting. A Hunter stood at her side with one hand on the female's shoulder, but she only stared at where Zain no longer stood.

Ryn glanced at Queen Portia. She stood safely away from the table, protected by a circle of guards and Hunters. Her eyes were on her husband; her face was an emotionless mask. No surprise, no wonder, no panic. Only a cold realization.

She wasn't surprised at her youngest son's display. She knew.

"Search the keep!" Esben commanded, voice filling the room. He stood over his father's prone form like a lion protecting a kill.

The command shattered the silence. Hunters charged. Guards began to shepherd the remaining dinner guests out. Footsteps thundered and clanked. Ryn felt the floor tremble beneath her heels. Ryn remained with Irene and Neville as the dining room emptied, as the alert rang throughout the keep, calling all Hunters to action.

Her heart hammered. Her pulse roared in her ears. Darkness edged on her vision. Her clammy skin tightened around her bones and lungs, squeezing each breath and making it difficult to take another. Ryn tried to reason herself out of it, but her body would have none of her logic. Panic rooted deep, around each vein and tendon.

The panicked chatter faded to an indecipherable murmur.

"Take her back to her chambers," Esben growled from her left. "Make sure she stays there until this is sorted out."

"Let's go, my lady." Irene's voice was close to her ear. Hands squeezed her shoulders and gave her a gentle push forward.

Esben growled out another command, but Ryn's scrambled thoughts made no sense of it.

Neville's calm voice replied, "Yes, Your Highness. I will keep my eye on her."

A stronger hand settled against her back. Irene and Neville guided her out of the dining room. Worried servants and guards lingered in the corridors, word spreading like a cold wind.

Someone poisoned the king.

Attempted assassination.

Zain was missing.

The younger prince, a vampire.

Guards were shouting orders, Hunters were marching down every hall and into every room, and servants scurried out of the way with wide, fearful eyes. It didn't feel real, like Ryn had passed out at the table and this was a nightmare brought on by drinking too much before dessert. Maybe she'd been poisoned.

It took several corridors and two staircases before Ryn's heart slowed to a less frantic pace. Gloom had settled over the entire keep. It seethed through the drafts and windows like the coldest night.

Once in the safety of her sitting room, Ryn collapsed onto the chaise.

Guards followed her into the sitting room, including two unfamiliar Hunters. They marched into Zain's bedroom and emerged several long minutes later, empty-handed and scowling. Without her permission or even a wayward glance at her, the Hunters searched her bedroom. Neville and Irene stood on either side of her, still as stone. Each gripped their sword.

The Hunters returned from her room empty-handed. They left without a word, leaving the room colder than before.

Neville poured a drink from the sidebar and held it out for Ryn. "Drink up," he said kindly. "It'll take the edge off."

She closed her fingers around the glass. Her fingers didn't feel like her own. None of her body did. She took a sip. The warm liquid washed down her throat with a woody, smokiness.

To Neville, she asked, "Do you think he did it?"

Neville didn't answer at once. His unfeeling gaze met hers, and he asked, "Do you?"

Ryn took another sip to help her thoughts connect. Zain had little to gain from killing his father. Esben had more to gain. Like Zain had pointed out, Esben would inherit the kingdom. By revealing himself as a vampire, Zain had tossed aside his chance at the throne. The kingdom would never allow a half-breed son of a vampire mistress to live, let alone inherit a throne.

Unless Zain was motivated not by power but by revenge or some other secret shrouding his birth mother.

It made sense, but would the Hunters believe it? The way they had so assuredly accepted Esben's order and began their search told her yes, they would.

But could she believe it?

Could she live with it?

"I don't know," Ryn whispered to the whiskey. "I should know him better, shouldn't I?"

Neville stared down at Ryn with the same distrusting, unhappy face he'd worn since Zain had pulled her from the execution line. Then, as if sensing her line of thinking, his gaze softened. "You haven't had time to get to know him. Neither have I, it seems."

"How did you not see it?" Irene asked, though her voice rang with surprise, not accusation.

Neville sat opposite Ryn and rubbed his face. He leaned forward, elbows on his knees. "I don't know. I should have. All the little things… It makes sense. I guess I wasn't looking for the signs in him. He's always been sickly." Realization dawned on Neville's features. He looked at Irene, then Ryn. "He's always been sickly."

"He drinks that nasty tonic," Ryn added.

Irene spat a curse. "That would suggest the king knows."

Neville shook his head. "What the hell is going on?" He growled in annoyance and stood. "It doesn't matter. I'm sure we will have answers come morning. The king can't hide Zain's true nature any longer. Every noble in the city will know by midnight, and everyone else in the city will know by midday. He might as well have announced it to the city."

"Then you should rest, my lady." Irene nodded to Ryn. "The night is still young, and gods only know what that monster is planning."

"We will remain on duty," Neville added.

Tilting the glass up, Ryn finished the whiskey in a single gulp. The heady smokiness scoured down her throat and into her fingertips. She retreated into her bedroom and shut the door before either Neville or Irene could follow her inside. She wanted to be alone. Needed to be alone.

The guards had ruffled through the armoire and looked under the bed, and the bathroom door was open. Sighing, she tiptoed over to the armoire doors. They'd riffled through the dresses like he might be hiding within one.

"Fucking ludicrous," Ryn spat to no one.

A rustle sounded, one that did not sound like the silken dress she was straightening. She paused, and silence pushed in.

"Are you alone?"

The voice came so quietly she thought she might have imagined it.

But she knew that velvet, sensual voice. It made her heart race and her skin heat. It did not fill her fear or unease. Instead, she felt a rush of the opposite.

"I am," she whispered back.

A click sounded from within the ancient wardrobe, then a second. The back panel moved inward, then moved. There, standing in a narrow compartment, was Zain.

"You…" Her heart skipped. Too many questions raged. "What are you doing?"

"Hiding, clearly," he whispered.

"In here?"

He motioned to the dark corner of the compartment she couldn't see. A cool breeze brushed against her face, one laden with dank and minerals. Underground.

It wasn't a secret compartment, but a passage.

He flashed her a grin, a shadow of the wicked one he'd given his brother at dinner. "This leads down and out. I used to hide here when I was a kid. That's when I found it."

And that was why he had ordered the servants to leave it. Because they would have found his secret passage. Clever on his part.

"You didn't do it, right?" Ryn whispered. Asking him twisted the guilt in her gut like a hot knife, but she had a role to play.

His grin vanished, and his blue eyes went cold. "No. I have little to gain from my father's death. Why does everyone assume it was me?"

"Well, that look you gave him didn't suggest innocence." She shook off her feeling of surprise and crossed her arms, attempting to project calm. "Or the part where you *fucking vanished*."

He turned sheepish and dusted the front of his tailcoat.

"You have magic," she whispered.

"Most of us creatures do, I'm told."

"Now everyone knows what you are," she said.

Guilt overshadowed his handsome features. "Yes, I know. I acted out of rage and spite," he said, his words mirroring the guilt he wore. "But there is nothing we can do about it now. I did not attempt to kill my father, but as you witnessed, everyone was ready to pin it on me with no more evidence than Esben's accusation."

A headache started behind her eyes. He was right. The nobles had looked to him as a murderer, a monster, even before he revealed himself.

"I believe you," Ryn whispered.

Zain's brow furrowed. "You do?"

"Yes." She didn't need to reach into his bloodstream to feel the truth. She saw it on his face, in the guilt and panic lingering in his eyes.

Zain's guilt-ridden expression softened. "Thank you. I…" He swallowed. "I'm leaving for a while, until this mess calms and Esben isn't calling for my head. He will see reason, but he has our father's long-lasting temper. He'll make rash decisions and reckless orders, and I would rather not be caught in the storm." He hesitated, unsure and timid, then extended his hand. "Come with me, Ryn."

He purred those words, soft and sensual. Something in her thorny heart melted. It didn't take her long to decide what to do. Despite everything, she would rather be with Zain in the dark and in the castle without him.

"Give me a few moments."

Ryn started the bath—the sound of the rushing water against marble covered up any other. She packed a few things into a satchel, easy to sell, easily unnoticed by cleaning staff. She pulled a heavy fur-lined cloak over the strawberry silk dress. She turned off the water. As silently as possible, she laced up a pair of warm leather boots. All the while, Zain waited by the wardrobe. He still wore the suit from dinner, impeccable save for a few splotches of dust on his back and his knees.

Ryn slid into the secret passage with Zain. Maybe it was the whiskey in her veins, but a tingle worked itself over her skin, crawling underneath it, slithering with heat and thrill. The passage was narrow and dim, winding between walls and floors, so narrow they had to turn sideways in some places and duck in others. Sounds drifted through the stone and wood, from above and below and beside them. Guards hunted the missing prince. Hunters whispered about vampire threats. Servants gossiped about the poisoned king.

Guards interrogated servants about the wine. It hadn't been uncorked. Where had it come from? Who had served him? Who had been in the wine cellar? How it was impossible, how the only answer was vampiric magic. Guards whispered of how the poison was not as easy to extract from the king's bloodstream as the healer had thought. It was cursed.

Zain heard the same whispers, yet Ryn could not see his face in the dark. Thankfully, he could not see hers.

While they snuck through the dark, the king struggled for his life.

The sounds dampened as they descended an ancient ladder carved into the stone. Underground. The faint light seeping through minute gaps in the walls faded into an almost complete darkness. As Ryn climbed, her limbs began to shake.

"I can't see," she whispered.

"I can." His cool hand wrapped around hers. "Just follow me, love."

They started forward. Ryn could barely see the outline of Zain in the dark, his shoulders and his legs. The swish of his tailcoat. The plod of his shoes on the dirt-strewn floor.

"I can't believe Esben thinks I poisoned Father," Zain said after a long bout of silence.

"Who could have done it?"

"A number of people," Zain said with a sigh. "A servant, a guard, a Hunter. There are those willing to pay a hefty price to get a monarch out of the way. Plenty of nobles who see their own game."

"There were plenty of people at dinner." Zain hesitated, then she felt his hand on the crown of her head. "There's a spiderweb. Duck under it."

He guided her under the spiderweb she couldn't see. She didn't dare ask if there was a spider watching them. Fear slithered through her gut. Not at spiderwebs or what lurked, but at her own lack of sight. Zain had no trouble maneuvering in the dark. She searched her memory of knowledge of vampires. Could they see in the dark?

Apparently.

"Not to mention the king's favorite wine isn't a secret," Ryn added. "Any staff could have altered it, even before knowing which bottle would be the one he drank from tonight. The real killer could have been biding their time."

Her words came out weak and unsure.

"But how did it get into the sealed bottle?"

A beat of silence. The question hung heavy between them.

"I-I don't know," Ryn whispered. "If the bottle was sealed…it would have been added before it was sealed."

Zain hummed. "It could have been a long term goal of some crafty assassin. Stranger things are hiding within history's pages. Esben will have a full investigation set in motion by now, and answers will be found. If he doesn't think of that, then one of the council members will."

Zain reached into the satchel he'd packed while she'd been getting ready, pulled out one of the bottles he'd snatched from her growing collection of liquors, and took a swig.

"Do you think Esben's accusation will hold?" Ryn asked.

"Father yet lives." Zain helped her step over a stone. "He was not murdered tonight, so there is no murderer. Just an attempt. I don't like that my brother was so quick to point at me. It's almost like he…"

"He what?"

"It's almost like he knows I'm not his brother." Pain laced his words, and he took a long drink. He tightened the cap and replaced it in the satchel.

How much did Esben know? He would have been a child when Zain was born, but did he remember his mother during those months? Did he remember someone else carrying the child? Or had he figured it out on his own, like Zain?

"You have to admit," Ryn whispered after a while, "magic makes you look suspicious."

"It does, doesn't it?" Zain sighed.

"It also made one hell of an exit."

A soft, listless chuckle. "It did, didn't it?"

"Stunned the poor nobles into silence," she said.

Damn the dark. Emotion lined his words, and she wished she could see his face.

"I don't know who tried to kill my father tonight. But my brother was quick to point his finger at me. Everyone adores him and loathes me, so of course they'll believe every word he says. That's how my entire life has been. There's nothing I can do. If Father dies, Esben will inherit the throne, and I'll rot in the dungeons. I need to flee while I can and observe the situation from a safe distance."

"Don't you want to find the real assassin?"

"I don't have time to hunt through the keep for the killer, especially when they're looking high and low for me. My best course is to lie low while Esben cools off, or finds the real killer instead. Not to mention that the real assassin is likely a vampire and used magic to infuse the unopened wine with poison."

A beat of heavy silence, and Ryn changed the subject, "Where are we going?"

She struggled on *we*. She wasn't used to being a *we*. She was used to being just her.

"It's a secret." She imagined that insufferable smirk on his face, mirrored in those words.

"A good secret or a bad one?"

He chuckled. "You will just have to trust me."

"I'm following you through a dark hole in the wall," she deadpanned. "I think I have crossed that bridge."

He let out a soft chuckle.

The passage led to a wooden panel much like the one in the wardrobe, and with a few clicks, it slid out of the way. Zain pushed open cabinet doors that opened into a stone-walled room filled with hundreds of dead vampires in jars. Zain closed the cabinet—it looked like it belonged, like it held the same ash-filled jars. It was far less ornate than the one in her room.

Through the doorway on the other side of the chamber, torchlight faintly glowed. By the rough-hewn stone walls, it was the undercroft. Zain led the way into the hall, glanced both ways, and then turned left. Ryn followed at his heels.

"You know your way through all this so well?" She couldn't keep the unease out of her voice.

He flashed her a wolfish grin. "That too, is a secret."

They walked for a while through the winding tunnels, dodging patrols of Hunters. Zain paused at every sound, the shuffle of feet, stomping of boots, or skittering of critters. Ryn held tight onto Zain's hand. She didn't need him to see anymore, but if she let go, she feared she would be lost in these endless tunnels. Hunters would not be as kind the second time.

"Shit," Zain spat.

Ryn glanced around him—ahead was a wall. No, an archway—filled with fresh stones and clean mortar, a different shade than the stone around it.

"This used to be open," Zain whispered. He pressed his hand against the stones. They didn't budge.

Footsteps—Ryn squeezed his hand.

"Halt!"

Zain spun the same time Ryn did. Three Hunters bolted down the corridor, their torch spitting angry light onto the walls.

"Stay where you—"

"Hold on." Zain pulled Ryn to his chest, and before she could think, the world shifted into swirling nothing.

Her heart lurched into her throat, she clenched her groin in reflex, and her stomach liquified—as quickly as the swirling sensation began, it ended. They stood in an alley, outside the keep. Above them, silver clouds swirled thick with snow. Ryn pulled away, and his arm fell from her shoulders.

"How…" She took a steadying breath. "Why didn't you do that from the start?"

"I can't go far." Zain leaned against the alley wall. Strain tightened each word. "I've never done it twice in an evening." He pressed his hand against his lower chest, the same place where her magic twisted when she used too much at once. "It hurts."

"You've over-extended yourself," she said, frowning. And it felt like his stomach was twisting around itself, like his ribs were closing in on his lungs, like there were knots deep inside him. She knew the feeling. It was a bone-deep exhaustion related to no physical muscle or bone. No stretch could ease it. "There's nothing you can do about it. Only time and rest will help."

Only after she said it did she wonder if knowing about magical exhaustion was suspicious.

Zain didn't question how she knew, only nodded. "We need to get moving. The Hunters will comb the streets when they don't find me in the keep. We need to be hidden before then." He flashed her a cocky grin. "Luckily, I know the perfect place."

"Lead the way, darling," she said, though she lacked confidence.

Zain led her along a winding route through the shadowed alleys. Winter's bitter cold seethed through the city, icy fingers wiggling through her woolen clothes. Sleet spit against the rooftops and cobblestones, clanked against the gutters and windows. The chill turned sinister. The air darkened; the sound dampened.

Wet cold was worse than just cold. It needled in, soaked through clothes and skin, and made a body think it would never be warm again.

Something tugged on the edge of her awareness. Something in the alley ahead.

She reached for Zain to stop him, but a sudden bolt of white struck his side. His hand ripped from hers.

"Zain!" She stumbled back, his name a gasp.

From a narrow alley, a pale figure stood.

Smoke slithered around his extended fingers. His red-rimmed eyes flashed from Zain to Ryn. He readied another bolt, this one aimed at her. Before she could curse or plead, the bolt struck her in the chest. It seized every muscle, bone, and thought. After that, all was darkness.

37

BROOD

Ryn

Ryn came to on a hard, cold floor. Dank, musty air filled her lungs. The stifled, dampened air and far-off dripping suggested they were underground. Bruises ached on her shoulders and legs, more so on her left side. Her head throbbed in time with her sluggish pulse.

How long had she been lying here?

It came back—the escape from the keep, the bolt to the chest, the pale-faced stranger with red-rimmed eyes.

She and Zain had been ambushed by a vampire.

She sucked in a deeper breath, expanding her achy chest and back.

"Ah, she wakes," came a voice to her left. Familiar, yet laced with contempt.

Ryn rolled onto her side. They were indeed in an underground chamber. Ancient stone bricks formed the walls and arched ceiling, and rusted iron lanterns hung from the ceiling. Candles shed a pitiful, flickering glow over the chamber. She started to push herself up—hands grabbed her arms and hoisted her upward. The chamber wobbled dangerously sideways, and her stomach wobbled along with it. When everything righted, the male before her sharpened.

Neville stood proudly in front of her. His Hunter uniform was pristine, and his expression was just as stony as the first time they'd met.

Shit. Shit. *Shit.*

They'd been caught by Hunters. She didn't know if Hunters were better or worse than vampires. But…what happened to the vampire who'd attacked?

A shifting shadow drew her attention to the far wall. The vampire from the alley stood half in shadow. His red-rimmed eyes took in the scene with delight. On the other side of the chamber stood a female with pale brown skin and red-rimmed eyes. *Two* vampires?

Ryn's stomach fell into her groin. She looked again to Neville, panic searing through her veins, but before she could voice her concern or plead for help, he smiled.

Her panic froze over. She had never seen him smile before.

"Put it together yet?" Neville's grin turned feral. He flashed his teeth; his canines jutted further than the rest, further than they should. *Fangs.*

He leaned closer, so that the candlelight glinted off his eyes. That was when she saw it—the glimmer of red around irises. So faint, if he hadn't been standing so close, she would have missed it.

Three vampires.

She shook her head, trying to shake this nightmare. Surely that was what it was. Neville did not dissolve, nor did the chamber and its vampires.

"You…?" Ryn breathed the word, unable to form a solid thought.

"He's one of them," came Zain's strained voice from behind her.

She tried to twist to see him, and only after Neville motioned to whoever held her arms did they allow her to turn around.

Zain was tied onto a table with leather straps. Green glass bottles sat on a barrel beside him, just as many as she would to drain a grown male. Ryn's heart shriveled and squeezed, and it felt as though she might vomit. The hands on her arms tightened.

No. No. No.

She *couldn't*.

"You made yourself hard to get to." Neville meandered into Ryn's view. He nodded toward the empty bottles. "You were a lifesaver, you know? You kept us well-fed. We never had to go hunting or fall into bloodlust."

Ryn trembled. She suspected her bottled blood fed vampires, but she had pushed the suspicion aside. She could pretend she hadn't done anything wrong. To hear her crimes announced made it real. It hurt deep in her soul, blackening the edges like ink. It confirmed the horrors she had committed, the murderers, the bodies. They had been slain to feed vampires.

"I must extend my gratitude to you for sustaining my kind," Neville said with a vile grin, and she knew why he hadn't smiled before. It would have given away his real self, hidden under his guard's mask. "We had plans to get you out of the keep. The Hunters stupidly assumed you were part of the brood, so they guarded you better than the king's treasure vault. We had plans to interrupt your execution. We kept our own in the keep waiting to get you alone, to save you." Neville's cold gaze slid to Zain. "But Zain got in the way, claiming what wasn't his. And he kept getting in the way."

"You imply she was yours to begin with," Zain said, his voice small, but still smarmy. "She belongs to no one."

"Oh, that is where you are wrong." Neville pointed at Ryn, then tapped his finger on her nose. "You belong to Nobel."

Just his name sent a chill down Ryn's spine. The blood drained from her face. Neville not only knew Nobel, but he knew of Ryn's debt to him.

Nobel had sent vampires to get her out of the keep.

"Oh, I know all about you, little dove." Neville's grin grew wicked. He looked her up and down with desire in his eyes.

Ryn repressed a shiver. Hunter Neville had a certain charm, the burly and surly guardsman, but Vampire Neville grinned with menace that belonged to the darkest alleys and blackest souls.

"Yet you play a Hunter in the king's employ," she whispered.

Neville rolled his eyes, and a few of the vampires laughed. The low rumbles echoed off the chamber walls, making it sound as if a dozen vampires laughed with them.

"A perfect place to hide," Neville said, grinning proudly. "Victor could search the keep from top to bottom and never find a single vampire, yet we've been right under his nose. Standing in plain sight, for centuries." Neville glanced at Zain, and his gleeful grin melted into a grimace. "I was lucky enough to be promoted to his brat's personal guard. Do you know how many times I wanted to just let the bar brawls beat you up into a pulp just to be done with you? All the whining and prattling about poor, pitiful *you*."

Zain held his face impassive until the last words, then it cracked. The vulnerable prince showed through, undone by the spiteful words of one he used to trust.

Neville fixed a curious glare on Zain. "And after all this time, you were one of us. I could have recruited you. You could have helped us. Been on our side." He sighed. "It's too late for that now. The entire city will be looking for you come dawn, and everyone in the keep knows what you are. It won't matter. I will return to Esben with your corpse, explaining how I followed you, only to find you colluding with a vampire brood, conspiring to take the throne." He slid his gaze back to Ryn. "Trying to sell your bride's blood to them."

The vampire holding onto Ryn's left arm let out a dark chuckle that sent warning bells flaring in her head. As if sensing her distress, he leaned closer. He sniffed her neck.

"Not yet," Neville snapped. His glare focused on Ryn's left. "She is to be left alive. Nobel's orders. Tonight, we dine on princeling blood."

A cheer went around the chamber, enough Ryn couldn't count how many vampires stood between her and freedom. Too many.

Neville motioned toward the table, toward Zain, who had gone several shades paler than usual. To Ryn, Neville said, "You have all the supplies you need."

The vampires released her. The one on her left slid his hands down her arm, grazing her breast with his fingers.

"And if I say no?" Her words were weak.

THE BLOOD ENCHANTRESS

Neville's smile flattened. "Then Nobel won't have a reason to keep that lovely little sister of yours alive. Lu, was it? She is a lovely creature. Beautiful, polite, sweet. Hard to believe you're related."

Her heart clutched. Kill Zain or Nobel would kill Lu.

A few weeks ago, the decision would have been effortless. She would have plunged a dagger into Zain's heart without a second thought. To save Lu, she would have done anything. But Ryn had changed. Her feelings toward Zain had changed. She…didn't want to kill him. She didn't want to lose Lu either.

She hated both options, but surrounded by red-eyed vampires, what else could she do? As if sensing his distress, Neville offered her an encouraging nod toward the table.

"We'll find you another male to play with," Neville said. "There are plenty of handsome ones out there, and who knows, maybe there's a vampire who could catch your eye." He winked, and a few vampires chuckled.

She approached Zain. He was ghostly pale, his fists were clenched, and fear shone bright in his eyes. Ryn wanted to apologize, wanted to tell him several things, like how she didn't think he was a waste of space, and how he made her heart flutter when he laughed, and how she liked his odd collection of books. But those were private confessions, and these vampires did not deserve to hear them. They didn't deserve to witness what she felt, even if it were just in words.

And Zain didn't deserve to die as a scapegoat for a vampire plot. Regardless of who or what he was.

She set her hand on Zain's, then reached for the dagger beside the bottles. It was a narrow little blade, perfect for delicate cuts on the skin. Near useless in a fight.

She pressed the blade to the side of Zain's wrist and sliced the skin. Dark red blood beaded along the incision, and within a fraction of a heartbeat, her magic pulsed through his veins, his organs, his bones. A gasp escaped his lips; could he feel her as she felt him? Anyone who had ever felt her magic in their blood was dead, and she had never asked what it felt like.

By the surprise on Zain's face, he felt something.

And he knew she had magic too.

Ryn's magic traveled through the blood and felt what he felt—remorse, grief, panic, and fear. A tremendous degree of self-loathing. A darkness crowded his soul, but not the kind that came with doing evil; it came from within, from that self-loathing, from isolation. She knew the feeling of loneliness like a second skin.

She met Zain's wide eyes. A tug on his bloodstream, and that fearful gaze sharpened. He seemed to understand her quickly forming plan as it unfolded.

With her magic unleashed, she focused on everyone else in the room. Nine bodies with various amounts of blood. Neville had the most, the female on the far side had the least.

"You don't have to take all of them," Zain whispered. "Just the ones closest."

"What are you doing?" Neville spat.

Ryn spun—the little dagger sank into the vampire closest to her. Dark, sticky blood oozed from the wound.

It was enough.

Her magic sank into the vampire's blood, deeper and faster than she had ever dared. In less time than it took for its heart to pump, her magic seized every drop of blood, every organ, every fiber, and *yanked*. Each drop became a thorn, tearing holes in the lungs, in the heart, in the liver.

The vampire let out a short-lived cry that echoed off the stone. Dead before he hit the floor.

The cost of magic sent stars across her vision, and in the moment of dizzy shock that followed, Ryn grabbed for Zain's bloodied hand. As her skin met his cold flesh, a swirling sensation stole her senses. The chamber twisted and blurred and vanished—the world righted itself with a stark halt. Zain and Ryn stood at the other end of the corridor.

"There!" Neville roared. "Don't let them escape!"

"Run," Zain gasped. He grabbed her hand and pulled her after him. They bolted through the darkness.

Ryn glimpsed the bloodied scene through the spots in her vision. Neville knelt on the ground by the bloodied vampire, dark red seeping across the stones. Cold, visceral fury pained his features. Zain pulled her around a corner and into a steep darkness as Neville let out a vicious, feral growl.

Tunnel after tunnel, Zain didn't slow or loosened his grip on her hand. Ryn forced her legs to keep up, to run despite the dizziness, to follow Zain's lead despite how she wanted to vomit.

It didn't seem to matter how far they ran—Ryn felt rage behind them, boiling and spitting embers. Footsteps thundered on the stone. Neville's voice echoed obscenities, threats, and torture. Right, left, left, right—the tunnels seemed to go on forever. No end, all darkness.

Her heartbeat drummed against her bones in protest. She had never used her magic to such an extent, or so quickly. By Zain's gasping breaths, he felt the same.

Then, when the stitch in her side threatened to rip her in half and the footsteps behind them had faded, Zain slowed and paused.

No vampires rushed them from the dark. They'd lost them. Or Neville waited for the perfect ambush.

Ryn slouched against the wall. Her chest heaved with each gasping breath. Her legs shook. Sweat coated her neck and stuck her shirt to her back.

"Well," Zain said between pants. He glanced to where his wrist had already started to clot. "There goes my trusted guard. I hope yours isn't also a monster in fae skin."

She hadn't the extra breath to laugh.

Zain glanced both ways down the dark corridor. Both led into pure darkness. He straightened, dusted off his tailcoat, then held his hand out for hers. "This way."

She hadn't the mind to ask him how he knew. She set her hands into his, and he led the way through the darkness.

She felt so utterly unprepared. She wished she was still in the keep, lounging in the steaming bath with her growing collections of chocolates. A pain struck at the thought of all of that chocolate, likely gone forever.

She had no supplies. Nothing but the clothes she wore. The vampires had taken their satchels and her cloak. Right now, she needed the whiskery more than the fur. They took something else too, something she hadn't packed, something from within. Neville had cracked the growing sense of safety Ryn hadn't realized existed. The safety of guards, stone walls, and steady arms. Of familiar faces. Of friends.

"This…Nobel," Zain started. "Is he…"

"Later," Ryn pleaded, her voice strained. "I'll explain later. Okay?"

Zain didn't push her. His fingers twitched against hers. "Okay."

Ryn didn't know what they would do. They had nowhere to go, no allies to turn too. Esben labeled them as traitors. The Hunters, Royal Guard, and City Watch saw them as enemies. The vampire brood wanted them dead. And, if that wasn't enough, Nobel had sent vampires to fetch her. He would be furious. He would see it as a strike against him.

No, she would explain it to him.

He wouldn't be happy, but she would show him she was compliant. He would have no reason to harm Lu or Zain.

To protect the two people she cared about, she would return to Nobel. Without the protection of the crown, she needed Nobel's.

Ryn tightened her grip on Zain's hand as he led them through the dark. She still had Zain, pretend or not. Right now, she was all he had too.

38

LEAP OF FAITH

Ryn

They trekked through the dark until the unfamiliar passages led into the dingy, musty tunnels running alongside the canals. The guard used them to transport criminals, the smugglers used them to transport goods, and those who wished not to be seen used them to slip into the shadows. Ryn had never been fond of the tunnels. They were a maze and spotted with guards and thugs. She preferred the shadows above ground, where she could dart in any direction at any time, where the moon would eventually give way to the sun.

The tunnels were narrow and spotted with shadows. Whispers and hisses and curses bounced off each wall and down every hall. Thugs or guards, Ryn didn't want to find out. Zain navigated the halls with ease, avoiding each pocket of activity and voice and footstep. Gradually, the populace of the tunnels faded behind them.

They must have crossed through the main tunnels.

"Why'd you do it?" Zain asked after a while of silence.

"Do what?"

"Save me."

She blinked. "You thought I wouldn't?"

"I considered the possibility." Zain started to say something else, then took the words back.

"You…" She didn't know how to explain why she'd saved him. "I like you better than those…vampires."

He chuckled though it lacked mirth.

"You don't think I should have?" She bristled, remembering the self-loathing she felt in his blood. "You didn't poison your father, so you don't deserve to die for it. Neville is working with the brood responsible for killing that Hunter in the woods, and the servant in my chambers." Which she realized had likely been part of Neville's rescue plan. "You heard what Neville said. They've been plotting against your father for centuries."

"Who says they're not in the wrong?" Zain's voice was low. Defeated.

"They're killing innocent people," Ryn said at once, her voice stronger than before. His fingers twitched against hers. "They're killing people to scare your father and his Hunters. They're…not going about it the right way. If they wanted to live peacefully, they could have asked first. No. They chose violence first."

"You think vampires and fae could live in peace even if we require the blood of others to live?"

"You can take blood from someone without killing them," Ryn said pointedly.

A pause thickened the space between them.

"You did something back there," Zain said, the words as heavy as the silence.

Ryn heaved a sigh—she couldn't hide it any longer, not after Zain witnessed her magic, not after he spilled his secret and opened his heart to her.

"I can enchant blood," she confessed. "That's how I made a living before I met you. I bottled it. Enchanted it to remain fresh until uncorked. I worked for Nobel. I…know exactly how much blood a body can lose before it becomes irrevocable."

Zain kept his gaze ahead of him, and his tone level. "This Nobel had you draining people?"

"It was the best coin I could make without selling my body," she said. "It was enough that my sister didn't have to find more work. A few nights a month, and we could eat."

"Those bottles we found in the keep, those were yours," Zain said lowly.

"Yes. I doubt Nobel has another blood enchantress employed." She sighed the cold, dank air. "I never asked what happened to the bottles after I gave them to Nobel. I didn't want to know. I had my coin, and that meant I had food on my table. I…didn't care."

"You killed people?" He didn't sound troubled by the revelation. He sounded, if anything, curious.

"They weren't good people."

"How do you know that?"

"Because when I…" She paused, because no one knew that she could feel a person's soul. Not Nobel, not Lu.

Zain's fingers gripped hers. Not painfully, but enough to let her know he was listening and that he understood secrets.

"When I come into contact with blood, I can feel a person," she whispered. "Their emotions, their desires, their soul. I can feel the darkness within someone. The people Nobel sent me to drain were never good people. Not just murderers and rapists and cheats, but…bad people. The type that didn't care who they hurt. Their souls were always dark as ink. Sludgy. I told myself it was better for them to die, that it was them or me, and I chose myself every time."

"You feel souls," Zain repeated, and she knew what would come next. Braced herself for it. "You felt mine."

"I did." She swallowed the fear that rose as she added, "And I knew you weren't horrible. You aren't a monster. Not deep down."

"Deep down?"

"Deep, deep down."

He chuckled, a light sound that warmed her insides.

"Blackened souls know they deserve what they get. They know there's no way out of punishment. When it comes, they…accept it." It felt good to talk about it, to get it out there, to have someone listen. "Horrible people have…tainted blood. The darkness within their soul clots their blood and clouds their hearts. Each damnable act darkens a soul a little at a time, filling it with bitterness, spite, and cold rage, and harms a person in far deeper ways than we can see. You… I didn't feel any of that from you."

"What did you feel?"

"Remorse. Grief. Panic. Fear."

A beat of silence, and then he whispered, "What am I feeling now?"

"I don't know," she whispered. "It works best when I'm in contact with their blood. When I'm not, it's fuzzy."

"Humor me, love."

She focused on what little magic she had left. "It feels the same, only…you're happy?"

"I am, a bit." He glanced over his shoulder at her. "I've never had someone choose me."

She blushed.

"I also have a burning question," Zain added.

"Yes?"

"If only vampires have magic, and you have magic, are you a vampire?"

"No."

"That is interesting," Zain said, brow cocked at her as they rounded a corner. "Fae magic is said to have died out centuries ago, and it was rare before then, and here you are."

"I don't know where it comes from. My sister doesn't have magic, and I don't think either of my parents did." Ryn thought of Crestin House, their proud roots to the ancient fae. She whispered as much to Zain.

"It might be a repressed trait or something," Zain said. "Like how the Monroe House are all dark-haired save for a few redheads that spot their family tree."

Maybe. For all she knew, the answer was as simple. She had no idea if either of her parents came from a family with repressed magic.

They walked in silence for a while. She wished she could feel his soul now, feel what he really thought of her magic. She'd never told anyone about it, and to have Zain in on the secret felt…comforting. It was a relief to not carry the burden by herself. She had always worried someone would discover her secret and immediately run to the Hunters. She feared admitting her secrets to anyone would lead to execution.

Exhaustion crept along her bones, tugging her on awareness. She stumbled, and Zain clasped her arm. He spoke, but he sounded like he was underwater. The tunnel righted itself, and the rushing in her ears faded.

"Are you all right?" Zain urged.

"Yes," she said, swallowing. She was terribly thirsty. "I just…used a lot of magic at once. More than I've used before."

"And I am grateful, but we need to keep moving. I'm not sure how far our friends are behind us."

Adjusting her grip on his hand, she motioned him ahead.

The tunnel continued for a while, sloped, and then evened out. A subtle roar sounded from the stone, bouncing off every wall. It sounded like breathing, like some ancient and massive beast deep in slumber.

"Oh, the gods must hate us." Zain didn't elaborate. He continued forward.

The roaring grew in volume until they couldn't hear one another over it. The air grew moist and frigid, speckled with tiny icy daggers.

The tunnel opened to a natural cavern. A waterfall cascaded from high on the rock and tumbled into a quickly moving underground river that vanished through a passageway. Moonlight reflected off the water on the other side.

Zain approached the ledge. It was a good twenty feet down to the river. Groaning, he glanced upward. "Fine. I will jump into the freezing waters." Glancing back at her, he motioned toward the ledge. "Ladies first?"

She scowled at him. "Can't you magic us down there?"

"I can't magic anywhere I've not already been." He leaned over the edge. "It's useful most of the time. Even though I can see the water from here, I haven't been in that exact spot, so I can't vanish and reappear there."

"Why not magic us somewhere above ground? A tavern?"

He shrugged. "I can't go very far, and despite what you believe, I haven't been in a lot of places within the city, and I don't remember them all exactly."

"It's a memory thing?"

"I have to remember the place well, like a marker."

She frowned at him.

"Yes, I know," he said with a sigh. He brushed dust off his tailcoat. "I'm aware of how useless it is."

"You saved us twice today," Ryn said, shaking her head. "That's far from useless."

His lips quivered into a smile. He started to say something, but voices sounded behind them. It was impossible to tell how many or how far over the sound of the falls. Ryn met Zain's gaze; it might have been guards, smugglers, or their vampire brood. Either way, Ryn did not feel up to meeting anyone.

"It's now or never." Zain squeezed Ryn's hand, kissed her temple, then jumped off the edge. He splashed into the river below.

A terrifying moment passed, then his dark head popped through the surface. He waved as the river carried him downstream. He said something, but Ryn couldn't make it out over the falls.

"Oh, fuck me." Ryn huffed. With a glance behind her at the dark passage, she took a deep breath, and jumped.

39

SAFEHOUSE

Ryn

For a terrifying moment, all Ryn knew was open air.

Water engulfed her, rushing, freezing, consuming. It soaked through her clothes and sank into her skin. The current swept her along after Zain, through the cavern, and into the swollen river. The moon washed the river in silver, and the surface undulated like a shattered mirror. It was all she could do to keep her head above water and air in her lungs.

The water moved too fast and feverish, and her sodden limbs were useless. The current yanked her this way and that, and her body collided with the hard surface of a riverbank. The river threatened to steal her away, but hands latched onto the collar of her tunic and pulled her ashore with surprising strength. Something dry and hard met her back.

Beside her, Zain gasped for breath. Water drenched his black tailcoat, his silken shirt, and flattened his dark hair around his pale face. Ryn pulled and pushed herself farther onto the bank, a feat in her sodden clothes and trembling limbs. She sent a pulse of warmth through her own blood, just enough to stem the frostbite threatening her fingertips.

Magical exhaustion twisted her insides. The muscles along her midsection spasmed. Darkness crowded her vision.

It felt like her wet clothes were suffocating her, like she still wore a corset and it had shrunk in the river with her still in it. It took a panicked breath for her to remember she didn't wear one.

"Easy, easy." Zain reached for her but paused, hand a few inches above her. "Breathe."

She rolled onto her hands and knees, gasping for breath, like she was drowning on dry land. Her stomach churned, and she thought she might empty it on the frozen mud of the bank.

"Can you walk?" Zain asked.

"Yes," she gasped.

"Good, because we need to move. We can't stay here. It's too cold and open. I thought I heard growling back there."

He stood easy as silk in the wind, and when she struggled to follow, he looped his arms under hers and hoisted her to her feet. The world shifted.

"I've got you," he said.

Each step took tremendous effort. Her limbs yearned for stillness, her body for warmth, her mind for rest. She forced herself to follow Zain along the riverbank, toward the overgrown outskirts of a winter-dead, barren forest.

They hadn't made it far from the bank when he pulled her to a halt. He bent down and motioned to his back. She normally would have protested, but with her legs about to give out and her mind spinning, she climbed onto Zain's shoulders. He lifted her like she weighed nothing, and started into the forest.

Within the comfort and relief of weightlessness, her body collapsed and her limbs liquified. Darkness claimed her.

Ryn came to on something soft. Warmth danced over her skin. Her body ached. Peeling her eyes open, she saw the inside of a small cabin. Plain wooden walls, thick mortar, washing basin, drying rack, and old cooking station. There was only one door, and by the wind whistling and the wintery light flickering underneath, it led outside. A fire burned in the stone hearth, greedy flames licking up three logs sitting on a bed of glowing embers. It filled the cabin with pleasant, glorious heat and whisked the chill from her skin.

Her skin—the blanket touched every part of her, as naked as a newborn. She turned her gaze back to the drying rack, to the clothes, to *her* clothes. And another's. She recognized the black tailcoat, silk shirt, and black trousers. Two pairs of boots sat beneath it.

Something stirred at her back, something very close. Something breathing. She glanced over her shoulder to see Zain sleeping.

A single blanket covered them both. By the pale skin visible above where the blanket rose to his chest, he wore as little as she did. His black hair was mussed and dried in odd directions. A bit of dirt smudged on his nose, and what looked like soot. From the fire.

She stirred, and so did he. His eyes peeled open, glazed and tired, then sharpened on her.

"Where are we?" she demanded

"A hunter's cabin, I'm assuming," he said, his voice groggy.

"A…hunter's cabin?"

"A hunter of deer and rabbit and the like, not a vampire Hunter," he clarified.

The panic fled as quickly as it arose.

"We're not far from the river. It would seem the gods gave us a fighting chance." He shut his eyes and leaned back into the pillow. "No need to thank me for carrying your limp carcass to this fine bed, braving the storm for kindling and dry logs, or peeling the frozen clothes from your unhelping limbs."

Ryn's panic subsided into embarrassment. "Thank you," she added, not sounding thankful at all. "My apologies for passing out."

The wind picked up, hissing at the door and down the chimney in a haunting howl.

"It's not the hunting season, so we'll be fine until someone notices the smoke. It's also snowing, so we have a while before someone comes to investigate."

She shifted under the woolen blanket, brushed her skin against the thick, rough texture. Should she feel shame for him having seen her naked? She didn't, not really. He'd already touched her, and she'd held his cock. Still, he hadn't yet seen her entirely naked, and she'd been out of it.

"Dusk is a few hours off," he said, looking at the wintery light under the door. "I'd rather not be caught outside with vampires hunting us down, and you know they will. They're vengeful monsters."

"Better to be caught in the daylight by Hunters?"

His brow lifted. "Esben will at least listen. Vampires will sooner cut out your heart." Sighing, he sat up, exposing the pale expanse of his bare back. He was well toned, the muscles shifted as he stretched his arms. Black hair dusted his chest and down his stomach.

Briefly, too fast for her to stomp on the thought, she imagined her nails digging into his skin. She bit her lip, then banished the thought. Not the time.

"If we are to outmaneuver the Hunters and the vampires, we should get a head start," Zain said. "We might be able to use the window between when the Hunters retreat and the Vampires emerge."

He shoved off the blanket and set his bare feet on the floor. He stalked to the drying rack with the grace of a cat. As she'd suspected, he wasn't wearing a stitch. Ryn didn't bother to hide her stare.

He sorted through the clothes, mumbled something about them being good enough, and tossed hers over his shoulder without looking. Her undershirt landed on her head, blocking her sight of him. By the time she untangled it from her hair, he wore trousers.

She slid out from under the blanket and pulled the shirt over her head. She kept one eye on him, but he didn't try to peek. Of course, he'd gotten an eyeful without her knowing it. It would seem that had been enough.

Dressed in dry clothes, Ryn finger-combed her nasty hair and braided it over her shoulder. It smelled like river water, sewer, and woodsmoke.

"Where are we going from here?" Ryn asked as Zain laced his boots. "Or is it a secret?"

"Hensgate District."

Hensgate District was upper middle class and average in every way. Her confusion must have shown, for he shrugged and said, "I have a plan."

"I didn't question it."

He frowned. "The look on your face said otherwise. But I won't tell you. I want it to be a surprise."

She wasn't in the mood for banter or games. Besides, his mysterious plan was better than her nonexistent plan. Motioning to the door, she said, "Led the way, my prince."

40

ANOTHER SECRET

Ryn

The cabin sat on the southern edge of the Red Forest, where the canals dumped into the river and the maples gave way to ageless oaks, birch, and spruce. It was a decent walk into Calcurta. They didn't make it far before the snow turned into a whiteout. It blurred the outskirts, the farms and paddocks, orchards and log homes, and muted the dusky sunlight into a vicious shade of frozen silver.

Ryn focused on the dark of Zain's back. She shivered as the snow soaked through her woolen layers and undid the warmth of the cabin.

Zain remained unbothered by the cold and snow, and it irked her. Mostly because the top layer of her skin was numb. A perk of being a vampire, she supposed. Sleep had done wonders for her magic; her muscles no longer squeezed and threatened to seize, and she no longer felt like lying down in the snow and dying. Her magic wasn't back at full, but it was enough to keep the frostbite away.

They meandered through the streets of Calcurta without trouble. No one noticed them in the snowstorm. Everyone they passed had their collars and scarves tucked up to protect their faces and necks from the cold, hurrying and hunched to get wherever they were headed.

City Watch patrolled on horseback in twos and threes, lanterns held aloft in the storm, glowing like the dawn. When a patrol of watchmen turned down their street, Zain steered them down an alley. Another patrol glowed at the far end. Zain spat a curse as the patrol headed toward them and pulled Ryn down an alley. Another patrol glowed a street over, the lantern glowing bright, and another lantern glowed further still.

There were far more patrols than usual. Looking for the missing prince and princess.

The lanterns were bright and obvious enough for Zain and Ryn to evade the guard. After zigzagging through alleys and side streets and even one backyard, Zain led her through an alley between two nondescript buildings and to the canal on the other side. The heavy snow muted even the gargling of the water, and ice gathered on the surface in dirty chunks. Zain led her down a narrow set of snow-covered stairs and to a gated entrance to the city's spillway.

The gate was unlocked. Muffled voices echoed off the stone walls, and the air lacked the frigid sting of the snowstorm. It wasn't warm, but it stole the bitter edge from the cold. Torches scattered the space. The voices came from side chambers, and the bulky individuals within looked like mercenaries. A few bulky guards stood at the base of ladders and narrow stairs. They paid no mind to Zain and Ryn.

It looked unnervingly like the keep's undercroft. The spillway lined each canal, offering a place for spring flooding, and they all connected. Slimy discoloration stained the walls and the floor, nearly knee-height.

Ryn never ventured into the spillway near her house. The people who liked to hang out there were the ones she went to drain. The darkest souls. The worst of the worst.

But unlike the spillways near her house, there was a stark lack of squatters and garbage, and she spotted guards standing at the ladders that led to the houses above.

Zain didn't say a word as he led her through the dim spillway. He paused at an unguarded ladder tucked into a stony alcove that led to a hatch. By the time Zain climbed the ladder and unlocked the hatch, she was too cold and tired to question him. Ryn followed him up the ladder and through the hatch.

They entered a dark cellar. She flopped onto the stone floor, the snow-soaked material of her clothes squishing and crackling around her. Zain locked the hatch—the clank-clink was heavier than a regular set of tumblers. Ryn sat up in time to see Zain tuck a fancy silver key under his shirt, where it hung on a leather string.

The lock on the hatch was heavier than most, sturdy and without a visible craftsman's insignia.

"We're safe here," Zain said without looking up at her.

"Safe?" Ryn whispered.

"Yes." Zain stood with grace that defied the rugged past few hours. He brushed his trousers off, though the water stains and dirt from the undercroft and the river remained. "This is my house."

"Your house? You have a house?"

Zain considered her, expression unreadable, then held his hand down to her. "Yes."

Her gut reaction was to smack it aside. A few weeks ago, she would have. But after their ragged escape and exposing her secrets to him and accepting his, she set her hands into his. He helped her to her feet.

"Are you hurt?" Zain glanced up and down her person. "I should have some first-aid upstairs and water for baths."

"Wine?" Ryn raised a brow.

A small smile perked the corner of his lips. "Yes, I should have a few bottles."

"Led the way, Your Highness." She motioned forward.

He stepped forward, and as she started after him, he whirled to face her. She nearly walked into his chest. His steely gaze bore into hers.

"When I'm here, I'm not a prince. There is no 'Your Highness.' No titles. No bowing. I'm just Zain here," he said, his words low. "My family knows nothing about this place. It belongs to me, just me. A place where I can just…exist. Without all the shit being a prince comes with." He searched her face with a piercing intensity that sparked up her spine. "You are the only other person who knows about it."

Another secret. Another glimpse into the male underneath the princely title and scowling exterior. Another plank for this strange bridge between them, built on fragile and necessary trust. He had trusted her with his secret vampirism, his secret hiding spot, and now this place—a refuge outside the keep. He had brought her here, a safe place, his safe place.

"Now it's ours," she whispered. She set her hand against his chest. The crust from the river and snowfall crackled under her fingers. "Seems fitting."

He glanced at her hand, then to her. "Fitting?"

"Marriage *is* about sharing everything." And they were sharing quite a few secrets tonight.

He frowned, but it lacked the hard edges of the prince she had met. With the sharing of his house, he had taken down another wall around his heart and let her inside. She stood where no one else had, where none of those prissy court females could ever be. Pride bloomed in her chest.

He remained in front of her, cautious as a waiting spider. For her answer. Confirmation.

"I won't tell a soul about it," she whispered. She put pressure on her hand against his chest. His heart thumped underneath. "I promise."

Zain looked torn, like he didn't believe her.

Or he didn't know how to. That she understood. She had spent so much of her life distrusting others and doing everything herself. She had built up a wall around her heart without knowing it. Letting someone in was a foreign feeling and went against her instincts.

"Why would I tell? I'm as good as dead in the queen's eye, and when they discover I'm missing, that'll be the end of me playing princess." She set her hand on her hips, putting a space between them. "And you could easily sell me out for being an enchantress. I will keep your secrets if you keep mine."

He considered it, and after a few heartbeats his edges softened. He shrugged off the stiff prince and settled into the easy male underneath. "Good. I'm glad we understand each other." He took a step through the dark cellar. "I'm sorry I dragged you into this. I should have just fled, but I…didn't want to leave without saying goodbye to you."

"I'm glad you did," Ryn said. "Otherwise, you would be a vampire's dinner. Gods only know what would have happened to me."

He paused before a set of narrow wooden stairs, brow cocked. "You are? Even the parts where we trudged through the dark and jumped into a frozen river?"

She flashed him a saccharine grin. "I'll find a way for you to make it up to me."

He chuckled, and the rumble of it traveled along her bones.

She already had a few things in mind, starting with her nails leaving tracks on his back.

Zain started up the stairs to the heavy wooden door at the top. He unlocked it with the same silver key he'd used on the hatch.

"Same key?" She clicked her tongue. "That's inviting a thief."

He scoffed. "I spared no coin when it came to security." He started to say something else, then hesitated. He fingered the key. "The locks are enchanted."

Ryn gawked. Enchanted items were strictly controlled by the Sun Council, and owning one illegally had dire consequences. Namely death and maiming. Ryn doubted Zain would receive the worst punishment, but he wouldn't escape. The Hunters were unbiased like that. Especially given the past day's events. He eyed her like he thought the same.

It was another secret shared.

"We had this talk," Ryn reminded him. "I won't tattle on you. My future depends on yours. If they throw you in jail, I'll probably be thrown in there too. I won't get out twice. Besides, this makes me feel better about the lack of a guard by the cellar entrance and the overall security of this place."

He fingered the leather cord around his neck. "Only this key can open any of the locks here. If a thief tries to pick one, the lockpick will break."

Clever. That way the thief would assume the lock masterwork and not enchanted. It wouldn't raise suspicions.

"What about a copy?" she asked.

"I have four."

"Four?"

"This one." He slipped the key into the heavy wooden door. "One in case I lose this one, another one in case I somehow manage to lose both of those or can't get to either of them, and one in the house."

Zain unlocked the door, and this time Ryn caught the click-clank of the key striking the tumblers, hitting all the right notes. She imagined a lockpick snapping, the sound hiding in the clinking of a lock's unmovable tumblers. The door swung toward the stairs, and Zain stepped out of the way—a silver-haired female stood at the top of the stairs, broom held over her shoulder like a club, ready to swing at Zain's head.

Ryn let out a sharp shriek at the same time the old female barked, "Zain?"

Zain grabbed Ryn's shoulder and gave her a quick squeeze. "It's fine." To the old female, he said, "There's been a development."

"Is that why you're sneaking around at this hour?" the female spat, her voice aged and stern. She lowered the broom and stepped out of the doorway. "I heard voices and assumed you were intruders. Coming up from the cellar like thieves."

"Apologies." Zain pulled Ryn up the last few stairs and into a kitchen. "Ryn, this is Bertha, my housekeeper. Bertha, this is my bride-to-be, Ryn."

Bertha grunted as she shut and locked the cellar door. She looked Ryn up and down with cynical disinterest. "My pleasure, Miss Ryn." Bertha's voice was anything but friendly.

"Housekeeper?" Ryn glanced at the older female.

"I can't live here full time, and I can't leave it empty. The guard might think it odd that the house is always empty, and I don't want anyone snooping," Zain said. "This way, it looks like the house is lived in, and Miss Bertha keeps the place tidy for me."

"If I knew you were coming, I could've prepared dinner. The bed sheets are clean, at least." Bertha crossed her arms. The motion pulled at her shirtsleeves, revealing numerous tattoos decorating her tanned, aged skin. "Now, what's this development?"

"I've been accused of poisoning my father," Zain explained, too calm to be explaining such a thing. "The Hunters are searching for me and Ryn. During our escape, we ran into a vampire brood that is also looking for us."

"You do have a talent for pissing people off," Bertha said to Zain. "Go clean up. I'll see what I can scrounge up for dinner."

"Thank you, Bertha, you are invaluable."

She harrumphed, then shooed them out of the kitchen.

It was a townhouse, tall and narrow with windows only on the front and the back and an identical house on either side. Zain's house was elegant yet simple with dark wainscotting and green wallpaper, brass sconces, and deep emerald rugs softening the long halls. A fire burned in the first floor parlor, where Bertha's knitting lay interrupted on the armchair. Zain guided Ryn past the parlor, up narrow stairs to the second floor. It smelled faintly like linseed oil and dust, and the second floor lacked the homey air of the first.

A narrow staircase led to the third floor, likely an attic space if it were like the other middle-class townhomes.

"Housekeeper?" Ryn whispered.

"Bertha is retired City Watch," Zain explained. "She dabbled in smuggling, got caught, and lost her pension with the Watch. I offered her work here. I pay her for the work and her silence."

"Does she know?"

"She knows I am a prince who doesn't always wish to be a prince," Zain said, motioning with his eyes toward the stairs.

That was all Bertha knew, and he wanted to keep it that way.

Zain led her into the bathing room. Compared to the vast bathing room in the keep, the room was tiny. Compared to her old hovel, it was a mansion. The white tiles were old and the grout was stained gray with time. The copper feet of the claw-foot tub had spots of green.

Ryn caught their reflection in the vanity's mirror. "Oh, shit."

Zain's reflection appeared beside hers, scowling. "Oh, dear. We look terrible. Considering the past few hours, we don't look that bad."

Ryn plucked a bent pin from the ragged and hopelessly tangled ruins of the bun Kari had redone three times to get perfect. Her clothes were torn and stained with gods only knew what. Zain looked worse. His fine suit was tattered, torn, and snagged. Dried snow and river water and whatever they'd trekked in through the undercroft added unfashionable stains on his tailcoat and knees. His hair fell limply against his forehead. Bags hung under his eyes. A bruise slowly formed on his collarbone.

"I disagree," she whispered. "I look normal. You look like you barely escaped death."

He released a small laugh and searched the vanity. He set bandages and ointment on the counter, then caught her eyes in the mirror.

His brow furrowed. "What?"

"I think your hair looks good like that." She cocked her head, eyeing his dirty, disarrayed locks.

He blinked at her, and the barest of blushes came over his cheeks. Clearing his throat, he returned his attention to the supplies. His voice contained an awkward note of the timid prince hiding inside. "I will make note of your hair preferences. Hopefully, you won't need me to run through the tunnels every time."

They cleaned their wounds in silence. All things considered, they made it out relatively unscathed. She had a few bruises and scrapes, as did Zain, but nothing that would need a healer's skilled attention.

"It'll take a while to heat water for a bath," Zain said.

Ryn glanced longingly at the tub. "So, how about that wine while we wait?"

While the water heated, they retreated into the second floor parlor. A fresh fire burned in the small corner hearth to ward off the wintery light outside the heavy plum curtains. Zain had a decent collection of liquors and wines on his sideboard, one to rival the one in his chambers in the keep. He poured her a glass of white wine, and himself a whiskey.

"Bertha keeps to the first floor, and I keep to the second," Zain explained between sips.

"Quite the downgrade from royal chambers," she mused. The wine was sweet and reminded her of apples.

"I don't need more space than this," Zain said to his whiskey. "She keeps the dust and rodents out, and builds fires when I happen to stop by." He tipped his whiskey to the fire. "She can go to the market easier than I can as well. Especially right now."

"I didn't need more than my little hovel," Ryn said. "It was just enough for me and Lu."

Thinking of Lu punctured her heart, smashing what little safety and relief she had found.

Ryn sank into one of the armchairs before the fire.

"What will you do about your sister?" Zain asked tentatively.

"I don't know. I want to think Nobel wouldn't hurt her just to get back at me for not helping those vampires. Without Lu, he has no leverage over me. I…need to speak with him before I make decisions."

Zain set his whiskey on the small table between the two chairs, then retrieved an old tea tin from the shelf. He set it beside his whiskey with a tired resignation.

"It is a powdered version of my tonic," he said listlessly. "I keep this here just in case I need it."

The tonic used to keep his vampiric nature a secret, to disguise the signs as symptoms of a heart condition.

Hot-cold panic rushed under her skin. "Are you feeling all right?"

He glanced up from the tin. He wore nothing but calm, his nonchalant and princely self. "Yes, but I would rather not turn into a red-eyed monster, so I take it." He worked the lid from the tin, reached inside, then paused. He blanched.

"Zain?"

He swallowed, then turned the tin so she could see. It was empty. Red dust lingered around the edges, barely enough to fill a spoon.

"What will happen if you don't take it?" she whispered, though she had a sinking suspicion. She thought of his pale skin, shallow breaths, and trembling hands. The panic in his eyes. She thought of the red-eyed vampires, their hungry stares and vengeful threats.

"I…" He replaced the tin on the shelf. "It will take a while for me to get to the deprived state. I have only ever skipped it once."

His tone tugged on her heart. It was a sliver of the vulnerable male within the heartless prince's skin. His troubled gaze met hers.

"Once?" she repeated, the single word a plea.

Zain took shamefully steps to the armchairs, took a large gulp of his whiskey, then said lowly, "You have heard of Princess Lucia, I'm sure."

Her heart clenched. "I have."

"Esben and I competed for her attention," Zain confessed, eyes on his drink. "I assumed I would lose. Esben is everything a king and good husband should be. Loyal. Brave. Handsome. Charming. And yet, she…" Zain inhaled deeply. "I…loved her, I think. She was one of the only females I felt something more than disdain for. And I hated myself. I hated everything about this body. My weak heart, my disposition, my introverted nature, and I…wanted to die. I didn't drink my tonic. I dumped it down the sink instead. I felt what I thought was my body giving out, my heart beating through my final moments."

Ryn dared not breathe too deeply or even move. This—this was a part of Zain that no one else had seen. A fragile young prince taught to keep to himself, to the shadows, to hide behind his perfect brother and demanding mother.

Zain considered his whiskey, then his expression fell. Shame. Misery. Regret. "She came to me. I was unwell. I assumed I would not make it through the night. She…confessed. She chose me, and I killed her."

He drained the rest of his whiskey.

Everyone suspected Zain had killed her, but the rumors painted it as hateful murder driven by betrayal and jealousy. The look on Zain's face was anything but. It was heartbreak, disgust, and grief.

"When I realized what I had done, I…" Zain squeezed his eyes shut. "I knew if anyone knew what had happened, I would burn like the monster I was. I knew then the truth. I deserved to burn, but I…I didn't want to die. I…" He swallowed. "I carried her body into the undercroft and left her. Hunters found her the next morning. Vampires were blamed. I don't know if my father suspected my involvement. Everyone else did, even without knowing what I was. I was obviously the evil, terrible brother, and thus to blame." He heaved a sigh laced with regret. "After Lucia's death, Father appointed Neville as my personal guard on the assumption that vampires had emerged. They had, I suppose. I had.

I knew then what I was. But after that, I took my tonic. I feared someone would discover me, that Neville would scent it on me. I feared accidentally hurting someone again. Any female I married would be close enough to know the truth, so I decided that no one would ever be that close."

And yet, Ryn sat here with him. Listening to his secrets. Sharing a drink with him in his private house.

"That was also when I saw the truth of my heart condition," he added lowly. He lifted his whiskey to his lips, then frowned at the empty glass. "The healer, the alchemist, my father—they told me I was broken. I am, just not the way they said."

"You're not broken," Ryn said firmly. It banished the pout from Zain's expression. His brows rose, his lips slackened, his edges softened. "You're not perfect, but you're not broken."

"Even as a monster?" His eyes were soft in a way they'd never been, like she had torn him wide open.

"You're not a monster," she whispered. How many times had she whispered those words to herself?

"And you know this?"

"I felt the blood moving through your body," she said. "I felt you, your soul, your being. I have felt monsters, Zain, and you are not one."

"Could you feel it, the truth of what I am?"

She shook her head without breaking eye contact. "Your blood felt no different than any other male."

He drank in her words with youthful desperation as he absently pressed a hand to his heart. Because Zain needed the tonic or blood. They had no tonic and no access to it, but she had access and means to blood.

"If I could procure blood, would that suffice?"

His expression hardened. "I don't want you to kill someone for me."

"I wouldn't need to kill them."

"Then they would know what you can do, and they would run to the Hunters. I don't want you to put yourself or your soul in danger for me."

She slumped into the chair's buttoned velvet. "Do you know how the alchemist crafts the tonic?"

Zain shook his head. "They never allowed me to know. He kept his recipes secret so no one else could replicate them. I assume there is blood of some sort within it, but I haven't allowed myself to think too hard about it." He stood and refilled his whiskey. He sipped it. "Should I consider that brood family? Distant cousins?"

She shrugged. "I don't have an answer for you."

He raked one hand through his dirty hair, then leaned forward, eyes on the fire. "If you are a blood magician with a decent job, why were you in the woods that day?"

"I needed coin for medicine," she said. "Lu was sick, and medicine to break a fever is expensive. I borrowed a bottle from Nobel, but Lu needed more. I couldn't risk putting myself in deeper debt with Nobel, so I thought I'd buy it myself. I can't sell blood on his turf, so I opted for a pelt. I followed a silver rabbit into the woods. I stumbled across a bloodless body, which is where the Hunters found me."

"All of this over a rabbit hide?" He looked doubtful.

"*Silver* rabbit hide," she corrected. "Thanks to your mother, it is in high demand. That hide would have bought two bottles of medicine."

His lips curved in a pitiful, exhausted attempt at a smile. The look didn't last long. He turned his stare into the fire, lips slack, brow gently furrowed, whiskey glass against his chin.

"What are you thinking about?" Ryn asked.

He glanced at her. "Hmm?"

"That is your thinking face," she said.

He sighed, then finished his whiskey in a single gulp. "The water should be ready."

41

BITE

Ryn

Zain opted to be the gentleman, albeit a brooding one, and let Ryn bathe first. She had never relished a wash more, and she now sat at the vanity in Zain's bedroom, combing out the tangles in her hair.

The dark wood furniture, the heavy emerald curtains, the green and gold of the bedclothes—the bedroom felt more like Zain than the rest of the house. Three tapestries of interwoven green, plum, and black hung on the back wall. A single candle burned on the vanity. It was not as luxurious as Nightshade Keep, but it was cozy. It had everything they needed, nothing more.

Having left her dirty clothes on the bathing room floor, she wore a plain off-white shirt she'd found in the armoire. It was made for a male and hung down to her thighs.

Exhaustion sagged against her bones. Night hung heavy with snow and spitting ice—it spat against the windows and walls. It felt like a week since they'd fled the keep, yet it felt like no time had passed at all.

To think, she had considered staying at the keep and letting Zain go.

Neville and his vampires would have killed Zain. Drained him dry. Then Ryn would have been at the mercy of the queen without a prince to hide behind.

That wouldn't have made her a very good wife.

She did not regret her choices. She did not regret Zain. With every secret shared between them, with every nightmare exposed, darkness revealed—she did not regret him. He feared the darkness within himself, just as she feared it in herself.

A door in the hall opened, bare feet padded down the carpeted hall, and then paused in front of the cracked bedroom door.

"Whoever could be calling at this hour?" Ryn said in a soft, feminine tone. The innocent voice of an unassuming housewife, where nothing had gone wrong, and no Hunters or vampires were hunting them down.

Zain let himself in. His damp hair glistened. He wore the trousers and shirt he'd found for himself before going to bathe. At once, his gaze traveled the length of her bare legs.

"What?" she asked innocently. "None of your pants fit me."

"But my shirts do?" He cocked a brow.

"Well, I can't just walk around naked." She could, but it wasn't as much fun. Not to mention the cold. The fires only did so much. "What would poor Bertha think?"

Zain paused by the tray of hard cheese and bread his housekeeper had brought up, but by the look on his face, he had no appetite. He moved the tray to the dresser. His movements were not as fluid as normal, but rigid, almost jittery.

"Zain?"

His attention snapped to hers, the motion agitated, predatory.

She set the hairbrush down, then stood without taking her eyes off him. "You okay?"

He hesitated to answer. "I'm fine."

She stalked over to him, and as she got closer, he averted his gaze. She touched his chin and brought his eyes up to meet hers, and as she suspected, as she feared, red rimmed his blue eyes. Faint, but there. He swallowed, his hands clenched and then released. Against her own, his skin had gone milk pale.

"Using my magic exaggerates it," he whispered, shame darkening his face.

The only supply of his tonic was at the keep, and they could not go to the keep. He would not allow her to fetch him blood.

"I'll be fine," he whispered.

"For how long?" When he didn't answer, she continued, "If you drink now, you can control it. If you wait, you won't."

He shut his eyes, indecision tightening his throat.

"I-I can't," he pleaded. "I've never… I've only drank from a person once, and it killed her."

"You were also in a bloodlust," Ryn reasoned. "You are in control right now. Think of it like drinking a cup of your tonic."

Her heart thudded with what she proposed, but she saw no other option. She released his chin and pulled her hair to one side, leaving the side of her throat exposed.

Zain took a shuddering breath. "Ryn, are you…are you sure?"

"Yes," she said. "I know how much I can lose. I won't let you take that much."

His lips quivered. His eyes trailed along her throat, to where her pulse thumped. His pupils dilated. His canines extended. According to the books, the anticipation of blood elicited a feral response. Zain clutched her shoulders with trembling hands, and lowered his lips to her throat. Her heart hammered at the touch of his lips on her pulse, her knees nearly buckled at the touch of his tongue, and a small gasp escaped at the graze of dagger-sharp fangs.

His grip on her shoulders turned painful. His fangs punctured her skin with a stinging *pop*, and as her blood began to flow, he drew her closer. With each gentle tug on her bloodstream, a piece of her flowed into him, willingly given, willingly taken. More than nourishment, it was a pierce of her healing a piece of him. Connecting in impossible ways. It was an intimacy she had never imagined could exist.

And it was *hers*.

She gripped the back of his shirt with white knuckles as the feeling enveloped her.

And then Zain pulled away.

The euphoric sensation ebbed, and she realized it for what it was—the lull. The daze that came over the victim. It came from the venom within a vampire's bite; it eased pain and helped the wound heal. Already, the punctures on her throat tingled. The venom wiggled through her bloodstream, lighting the lingering fire in her bones.

Zain licked the blood from his lips, eyes dark as he took her in. Color returned to his cheeks. The red was gone from his eyes. He shifted, loosening his grip on her middle, and his stance—his desire pressed against her thigh. Her own flooded her body, heating her blood and pooling deep in her belly.

"I know what you can do to make it up to me," Ryn whispered.

His velvet voice was a bloodied purr. "Oh? What would you like?"

She set her hand against his chest and pushed him backward onto the bed. She climbed up after, straddling his hips. Zain's gaze followed each movement, trailing her bare legs as the shirt rode higher.

"Oh, you don't have to do anything." She flashed him a devious grin. She'd been thinking about it since she'd climbed into the bath.

He started to rise, but she pressed her hand against his chest, over his beating heart, and pushed him back onto the bed. Zain's hand fell to her knees, the touch light as a breeze, soft as moonlight. She had no idea she would love the touch so much; she'd never been touched like that, and it heated the space between her skin and her bones.

His hands slid up her thighs and rested against her bare hips. "You're not wearing anything under it?"

"I'm not putting my dirty underwear back on, and yours are made for a man. They're made for different assets." She trailed her fingers along his erect asset.

She undid the ties slowly, a tease. His fingers twitched on her hips, his thumbs making small circles on her skin. Her former lovers had never been this patient. This…she didn't know. Something about Zain set a different flame under her skin. They were quick and rough, all thrusts and grabby hands. Zain made her want to take her time, feel every motion, wring out every ounce of pleasure. He made no move to rush her.

It wasn't what she anticipated from the cold, unfeeling prince.

She wrapped her hands around him, and the sound that fell from his lips sizzled against her skin. She adjusted her legs on either side of him, scooted closer, then eased herself onto him—eliciting the familiar feeling of incoming pleasure, only this time it felt…more. Something different, but better in ways she could not have imagined.

His hands tightened on her hips, and he paused; in her hesitation, he grabbed the hem of her shirt and pulled it up and over her head. His gaze raked over her exposed body, and his hands followed, cupping her breasts and teasing pleasure from peaked nipples.

She worked her hips into his, slowly at first, adjusting to the feel of him. A low growl rolled out of his throat. This, being in control, set her skin on fire. Riding the cold, impassive prince who turned up his nose at the painted court girls but who picked the street rat brought her a sense of pride. The bite on her neck tingled with its own strange pleasure. Everything seemed…more.

A few thrusts, and they found their rhythm. He thrust his hips up into hers, reaching parts of her that no one else had, parts she didn't know existed.

Ecstasy coursed through her bloodstream and burst across her vision as stars. Her body shuddered, and in that abyss of stars and heat, Zain flipped her onto her back. He kissed her, tasting of bitter metallic blood and smoky whiskey. She wrapped her rubbery legs around his waist. Each of his thrust pushed against her pulsing pleasure, again and again, until it burst once more into white stars. Zain gasped, his entire body shuddered, and he collapsed onto the bed beside her.

After the ecstasy faded, they climbed under the blankets. This was where her trysts left, or she left, to sleep alone. But Zain stayed. He did not ask her to leave. He folded himself around her. She curled into his side. She had never been so content to sleep beside someone, or so close to someone.

There, in his arms, she let herself feel a tendril of safety. At least for the moment, it didn't feel like the sky might fall.

42

BONDS NOT EASILY BROKEN

Ryn

Ryn woke to an empty bed. Cold morning light seeped between the curtains. The shirt she'd briefly worn the night before was laying across the foot of the bed, along with a dark red robe and thick socks. Winter's chill permeated the house. The fire burned low, embers glowing among the feathery ashes.

She pressed her hand against her neck. Her skin was smooth where Zain had bitten her. The only trace was a tingle of new, sensitive skin.

Ryn felt better than she had in a long time. Waking up had always come with a sense of regret for the night before, for the lives she had ended, for the blood that never hit the ground. She didn't regret a single part of last night.

For once, she didn't feel like staying in bed until she stopped breathing or drinking herself dizzy.

Such a strange sensation to wake up with a reason to get out of bed.

The chill pebbled over her skin. She slid out of bed and pulled on the clothes. Tying the robe snug, she tiptoed into the hall. The house was quiet and dark, soft in the way only mornings were. She followed the din of voices down to the kitchen.

Bertha sat at the kitchen table while Zain concocted something on the stove. He wore a white shirt rolled up to his elbows, and plain trousers. His damp hair had dried into a tousled disarray. He looked so unlike a prince and more like a suave businessman or a clever thief. But his expression was what caused Ryn's heart to skip a beat. There was warmth in his features, both a healthy glow to his skin and a glimmer in his eyes. He looked well-rested and well-fed.

"She wakes," Bertha said in the same unimpressed tone. She stood, gazed into the pot Zain stirred, nodded her approval, then left. "I've got a few errands to run. Don't burn the place down while I'm gone, please."

"Your doubt wounds me," Zain said, faking hurt. "Ryn, love, come join me for breakfast."

Bertha retreated down the main hall and through the front door.

"You cook?" Ryn tiptoed into the kitchen and glimpsed into grayish brown porridge he stirred.

"Well, no. Bertha instructed me, but she sat over there the whole time, so I technically did the cooking." His proud gaze turned a shade sheepish.

"It looks amazing," she said, nudging his back. She slid her hand over his heart—it thumped steadily under her palm. "And I am hungry."

He smiled, like the stupid porridge meant more than just food. He retrieved two bowls from the cabinet and ladled a scoop into each one. He arranged them on a tray not unlike those the servants used at the keep, then carried it into the dining room. Containers of honey, salt, and cream were already arranged. A fire burned in the hearth, and the room was gloriously warm.

"We're out of tea. It's on Bertha's shopping list. We'll have to settle for wine with breakfast." Zain motioned to the bottle sitting on the ledge of the hearth. "It's a spiced wine."

Ryn sat, accepted her porridge from Zain, and he stood still for an awkward moment, waiting for her to take a bite. She stirred honey and salt into the goop, then took a bite. It was a bit sticky, so she added a glop of cream. It helped.

Zain's wide eyes followed the motion of the spoon. She paused her next bite halfway to her lips.

"Are you going to eat?" She motioned to his untouched bowl with her spoon.

He blinked, the expression faded from his face, and he sat with liquid grace. He began preparing his porridge with quick, almost anxious movements.

"Is everything okay?" she asked. "You didn't poison the food, right?"

He swallowed a bit of porridge. "Yes, everything's fine." He added a spoon of honey.

"I don't believe you."

He swallowed a second spoonful, then met her gaze. His usual confidence was gone, replaced by something unsure.

"Zain?" She said his name as a command.

He sat straight and cleared his throat. "Traditionally, the husband makes a meal for his wife after the consummation. The…partaking of the meal is like a vow. You are…" He fought for the right words. "Accepting the marriage."

"Wouldn't the sex be accepting the marriage? Or the part where I agreed to the marriage?"

He shrugged. "I didn't make up the rules."

Ryn didn't know if she believed that old tradition. They hadn't followed any other tradition, like courting or meeting each other's families or reciting vows before the gods before they fucked.

"You would have made breakfast at the keep?" she asked.

He nodded. "I would have gone down to the kitchens. The cooks would not have been allowed to help, only instruct from afar like Bertha did. Traditionally, the groom's mother assumed the role of instruction, or some mother figure. Bertha is close enough. Though the meal would have been better with the keep's stock. I was…uh, working with limited resources."

"This is perfect," Ryn said.

"It's…porridge."

"It is porridge that you made in your house," Ryn corrected. "This feels more meaningful. More *you*."

She vaguely knew the old traditions. It, like much else, had faded with the ancient fae. Traditions didn't hold up in the slums, and Ryn had pushed out the knowledge in favor of more practical knowledge. Yet as she glanced at the warm porridge in her hands, then at Zain's boyish expression, something melted in her heart. Zain had been raised to hold traditions high, and to him, this meal was important. This was his attempt at marriage, the sharing of food after the sharing of a bed.

Did this mean they were married?

They hadn't recited vows, but they'd consummated it and now they have shared a meal prepared by the husband.

A pop—Zain uncorked the spiced wine. He poured it into two ceramic mugs and handed the first to her.

The wine was warm against her tongue, spiced with cinnamon and allspice. It burned a little, but the sweetness overshadowed the burn.

"So, we are married?" Ryn lifted her gaze from the wine to Zain. "Without the whole ceremony and parade and ball? Don't the gods have to ordain it first?"

"Each step has its own meaning. We have just gone about it in a less traditional way." He shrugged and sipped the wine. "The ceremony and vows are for the gods, the parade is for the kingdom, and the ball is for the nobles. This part, the consummation and the first meal, is for us."

"You picked us first," she said, grinning.

His smile turned a shade wicked and set her blood ablaze. "I always have."

Ryn started to say something when a knock sounded at the front door. All gentleness and heat vanished from between them, and her panic reared on its hind legs. Zain jumped to his feet, and Ryn followed. Never mind that she wore a robe and had no weapon. She followed Zain into the main hall. At the far end, the front door was in shadow. Daylight seeped through the heavy curtains on the small windows on either side.

The knock sounded again, slower and louder. No voice accompanied it.

"It's locked, right?" Ryn whispered.

"Yes." Zain clenched his fists.

A key slid into the lock. Zain tensed, but the familiar click-clank of tumblers sliding into perfect position sounded. Ryn cursed Zain's decision to have four identical keys, two of which were hidden in the keep. The door began to open, and Ryn grabbed the first thing she saw—an empty vase on a buffet, likely worth her weight in gold, and readied to throw it. All she needed was a nick or a scrape, and then their invader was hers.

The door swung open, and a female in plain clothes and a hooded cloak marched inside. She shut the door behind her, then spat, "Put that down."

That voice.

Ryn lowered the vase as the female tossed back her hood.

"Irene?" Ryn gasped, nearly dropping the vase. She had considered Irene a friend, but she had considered Neville a friend too. "How are you here?"

"Your letter." Irene motioned to Zain. "Your clues could have been less obvious."

"Clues?" Ryn frowned at Zain.

"When you were washing, I wrote a letter to Esben," Zain confessed, the words low and careful. A confession, but not as heartfelt as those the night before.

"You what?" She clutched the vase's thin neck, resisting the urge to throw it at him.

"I wanted to explain myself," Zain said. "I couldn't say everything in a letter, but I told him I would explain everything, including how I accidentally uncovered a vampire plot while fleeing the keep. I thought he would listen better to a letter than to me in person."

"And did you consider that he might send Hunters to kill us both?" Ryn hissed, and he motioned to Irene.

Zain hesitated. "That is something I considered." His eyes glanced at the vase she clutched. "I added subtle clues to the letter in hopes Esben might find this place, so I didn't have to risk returning to the keep and losing my head."

"The first letter of every sentence literally spelled out your address and where the spare key was." Irene scowled at him. "A child could have figured it out."

"I was trying to be obvious for Esben's sake. He was never good at riddles." Zain cocked a brow. "Did Esben figure it out?"

Irene shook her head. "No, I did."

"Are you here as friend or foe?" Zain glanced at Ryn then back to Irene. "Because I'm not sure how good her aim is."

"Depends," Irene said. She looked to Ryn and the vase she clutched. "Are you a part of this vampire threat?"

"No, not intentionally," Zain said carefully. He tucked his hands into his pockets, calm as he could be while facing down a Hunter. "We were just sitting down to eat. Would you care to join us?"

"There's spiced wine," Ryn added.

"It might make the story go down a bit easier," Zain said with that charmed smile of his, though it lacked the sinister edge it once had.

"Wine would be great," came a deep male voice behind Irene. A heartbeat passed, then a cloak parted and shimmered into existence, as did the broad male wearing it—Esben. He looked more haggard than the last time she had seen him, like he hadn't slept since. It gave the fierce prince a dangerous edge.

"You shouldn't have insulted his intelligence," Ryn whispered loudly.

Zain's brows rose. "Indeed."

No one moved.

Esben took the first step forward, sleepless eyes pinned on Zain. "Well, what's this story of yours, Brother? It must be good."

"Well, for starters, did you know Neville is a vampire?"

43

OVER SPICED WINE

Ryn

The four of them retreated into the dining room and its hearth fire. Ryn returned to her porridge as Zain told Esben everything, starting with how Neville and his brood had interrupted their escape.

"I couldn't say his name in the letter in case the vampires intercepted it," Zain explained. "Neville said there were more vampires hiding in the keep as Hunters. He conveniently didn't slip any names, and I didn't recognize any of them."

"Is he dead?" Esben asked.

"We barely escaped," Zain said. "They had me strapped to a table like a holiday feast, and Ryn…"

The hesitation stirred Esben's suspicion. His piercing expression met hers, and she had the horrible feeling of being exposed.

Should she confess her own magic to Irene and Esben? The words bubbled but caught in her throat. That old visceral fear crawled along her bones.

"They wanted me to kill him," Ryn whispered. Her voice wobbled. She hoped it made her seem fearful, not ashamed. "I managed to stab the closest vampire, the distraction allowed Zain to magic us out. We ran and didn't look back."

She met Zain's eye. He gave her a subtle nod. To the others, it looked like acknowledgment of the story, of the trauma, but she understood it to be his acceptance of her lie of omission. He wouldn't push her to tell the truth about her magic.

"I aimed for the heart, but I missed," Ryn said to Esben. "I was more concerned with getting out alive."

"Vampires heal differently than fae," Zain added, loosening the collar of his shirt. "I think we should operate on the assumption that none of them are dead."

"And they know you know about them." Esben stared into his spiced wine. Thinking. He looked remarkably like his father. "Few know I left the keep. These next few hours will be crucial."

Zain sipped his wine.

Irene stood by the door, glaring down the main hall toward the front door. Guarding it. Zain hadn't confessed to the enchanted locks.

Esben lifted his stare to Zain. His hard expression softened, and guilt slipped between the cracks. "So, it's true? You are…one of them?" He swallowed, as if the word pained him. "A vampire."

Zain didn't flinch. "Yes."

Esben held his stare on Zain, waiting for the next words, for the information to piece his fractured world back together—Ryn recognized the feeling. He studied his brother as if looking for the vital clue he had missed.

"But…how?" Esben asked, pleading.

"I don't know the specifics," Zain said, letting his vulnerability show. "I think Father had an affair and I was the result. I have no heart condition, never have. That was the lie they told everyone. Me included."

"Gods," Esben breathed. He slumped in the chair and rubbed his face. He looked exhausted. "It makes sense, doesn't it?"

"You're taking it far better than I did," Zain mused. "Better than Ryn too. I thought she was going to faint."

Esben looked at Ryn. "You knew, and didn't tell anyone?"

"If I had told you that your brother was a vampire, would you have believed me?" She met his stare. "Even if you would have believed me, without Zain, your mother would have thrown me to the gallows. If my options were to live with a vampire husband or die, I chose my vampire husband."

Husband.

Such a foreign word, and yet…it felt good to say.

"I just… I don't…" Esben heaved a sigh. "How did you discover this?"

"I…skipped my tonics until I saw the signs," Zain said lowly.

The exhaustion fell from Esben's features. Fear widened his eyes, slackened his mouth, and then, he breathed, "Lucia."

Zain nodded, unable to look Esben in the eye. "Lucia." He drank a gulp of wine. "I also found a room in the undercroft full of vampire relics and books and a painting of a female who looks strikingly like me."

"Relics? A painting?" Esben cocked a brow. "Father kept such things?"

"I doubted it at first. But why else keep all of it unless it wasn't important? Unless he needed to understand how to raise a half-vampire bastard son?"

"An affair with a vampire," Esben repeated, the words disbelieving. He ran a hand through his hair. "Anything is possible, I suppose. That was…centuries ago. Mother has commented on how Father has mellowed with age, and how reckless he used to be."

"Now you know," Zain said, the words quiet. "Is Father…"

"Alive," Esben said quickly. "The healer has high hopes of a full recovery. It will take time to expunge the poison, but he will pull through."

Zain visibly relaxed.

A strange silence settled over the room. Ryn watched the consideration on Esben's features, the thoughts connecting behind his Hunter's mask, the indecision. Zain kept his own emotions hidden—waiting for his brother's approval or a death sentence.

"I am sorry I accused you." Esben looked up from his spiced wine, eyes hard. "You were acting suspicious, and then the poison, and I acted irrationally. I let my anger get the better of me. I made us both look like fools before the court, and I forced you to protect yourself. I apologize."

Esben's words melted Zain's cold expression. It melted into an emotion Ryn had never seen on him. It was not the softness toward her, but the softness toward his brother. He hadn't expected acceptance and forgiveness, yet he had received it.

"I apologize for being an insufferable ass most of the time." Zain's tone lacked his usual grace and charisma. Each came out awkward; they were not easy for him to say.

A smile turned Esben's lips upward, and he clapped his hand on Zain's shoulder. The force of it rattled Zain's entire body.

"Even if we're not truly brothers?" Zain looked doubtful.

"That doesn't matter. We were raised together. We played together. Learned together. We are still brothers." Esben's hand never wavered.

Zain swallowed, uncomfortable and unable to hide behind his cold countenance and arrogance. Another moment passed, then Zain set his hand on top of Esben's.

Something passed between them, something almost tangible enough for Ryn to grasp it. It made her long for Lu, for that sisterly bond she cherished. It reminded her that Lu was still out there, at the mercy of Nobel, who might have seen her flight from the keep as a forfeit of her contract.

"What is your plan from here?" Esben asked.

"To be honest, I haven't made one." Zain shrugged. "I didn't know if you would be willing to hear me or come with a legion of Hunters."

"I needed to speak with you without an audience." Esben sipped his wine, thinking. "We should continue on the assumption that Neville and his brood are alive. They'll seek revenge on the two of you, so we continue as if this didn't happen. Let the kingdom see that I have taken my brother and his wife back, and that the real assassin tried to frame you. Let the kingdom hear how we captured and dealt with the real assassin. The vampires won't be able to stand it. It will mock them."

His wife. Ryn flushed. Did Esben know they had already made that step? She supposed they had walked in on breakfast, and both she and Zain were washed and dressed leisurely.

"We continue with the wedding ceremony and the ball as if nothing has happened." Esben stood. "It will be a target for the vampires. It will lure them out."

"What do you think?" Zain asked Ryn.

Something had changed in Zain. He no longer wore the hopelessness that had plagued him since they fled the keep. Esben had fixed what was bruised between them, and by welcoming Zain back into the home he feared hated him.

"I think it's worth a shot," she said. They had no other plan, and she liked the plan where the Hunters were on their side.

The front door opened, and Irene pulled the sword from her side. "Halt!"

"Oh, calm down," came Bertha's unamused voice. "You still in here, boy?"

"Yes," Zain called. "Irene, that is my housekeeper. Please don't kill her. It will be a nightmare to replace her."

Bertha marched into the dining room, a bag of groceries on her hip. She glared at Irene, then Esben.

"Good news, Bertha," Zain said casually. "I'm getting married. Likely very soon."

Bertha harrumphed, then continued into the kitchen. "Congratulations."

Esben raised his brows at his brother. "Housekeeper?"

"What? I hate cleaning, you know that."

Esben shrugged it off, then stood. "We should return to the keep. Mother will be ecstatic to resume wedding plans."

❧❧❧

Esben and Irene returned to the keep. They would return to Zain's townhouse the next afternoon, after delivering their plan to the queen. With the king bedridden, Queen Portia acted as ruler of Sovann.

Bertha tended to the groceries and started the preparations for dinner. Irene arrived a few hours later with a letter from Esben, inviting Zain to meet with him and Commander Wade to discuss the plan.

"I think I should go alone," Zain told Ryn. He didn't look happy about it. "The vampires will be looking for the both of us. Together."

He was right, as much as she didn't want to let him go.

Nodding, she crossed her arms. "Okay. I'll be here."

Zain wrapped his arms around her. His warm breath met her ear. "I'll be back before dark, love."

He pressed a tender kiss to her lips, then departed with Irene. Ryn watched them from the window. She watched them until they turned the corner, and then let the curtain fall back in place. With winter seething through the drafts, the crackling of the hearth, and Bertha's humming while she cooked—it reminded Ryn of home. Her hovel with Lu, of years gone when her parents were alive and loving.

Nostalgia turned to cold longing, and Ryn retreated upstairs, to the bedroom.

She needed to find out if Lu was okay. Nobel would know his vampire rescue failed. He would know she'd escaped the castle. He would expect correspondence from her.

She couldn't avoid him forever.

But if she left Zain's townhouse, she would need to get back in. To do that, she needed a key. Zain said there was a key in the house. She gazed over the room. Where would Zain hide a spare key? The bookshelves? She ran her fingers along the spines. She picked a book near the top shelf, a book of lockpicking.

Indeed, a small hollow had been carved out in the front, and a silver key slept within. In the firelight, it seemed to glimmer.

Ryn sighed. She would talk to Zain about his hiding places later.

She sorted through the dresser and armoire until she put together an outfit. Slim trousers, undershirt, tunic, overshirt of dark green wool, and a heavy tailcoat of deep black. The clothes were made for a thin male like Zain, but it worked well enough. She pulled a hooded-cloak over it all. Tucking the enchanted key into her tailcoat pocket, she tiptoed downstairs.

Bertha walked into the parlor, muttering about the fire. Ryn tiptoed to the hatch. As she slid the key into the lock, a subtle tingle flashed through her fingers and up to her elbow. In time with the *thunk* of a log, Ryn opened the hatch and slipped into the dark. As another log *thunked* into the hearth, she shut the hatch behind her.

The snowstorm had left the city a splatter of white and gray. Flurries glittered from the sky. People hurried by in furs and wools, hoods tucked tight against their faces. Ryn kept her head down and her hands in her pockets. She didn't know where Nobel was—he had places all over the city. She didn't have the time to search all the ones she knew. She needed to get back to the house before Zain returned, and she didn't know how long his meeting would take.

After three of Nobel's haunts ended unsuccessful, Ryn couldn't feel her face. Her feet hurt from the cold, despite the two pairs of socks.

Could she send him a letter via courier? She would have to be sneaky about it.

She started back toward Zain's townhouse when a shadow stepped into her path. Her entire body clenched in frozen panic, a gut response, and she readied her magic—then recognized the male as one of Nobel's guards.

"This way," he said, voice deep and heavy.

He started down a side street, and Ryn hesitated only a heartbeat before she hurried after him. He led her to a plain building near the canal. Ryn had never been here before, but it fit Nobel's style. Discreet. Humble. Plain. The guard led her up a staircase in the narrow alley that led to the second floor.

The room beyond was small but cozy and a little dusty. Nobel leaned against the curtained windows, arms loosely crossed, looking at her like he'd expected her to show up despite how quickly he had arrived. The lack of office supplies and sunlight suggested they had procured this place on short notice. Someone definitely lived in the space, by the hastily made bed, tea fixings, and messy shelves.

"Interesting place," Ryn mused. "Is it new?"

"It was graciously offered for our use by the fence downstairs," Nobel said.

Meaning he had demanded it, and the fence—likely one of his own—had bowed.

"I don't know how much time I have," Ryn started, feeling the urgency tighten in her chest. Behind her, the guard shut the door. A reminder that she was on Nobel's time. "I don't want them to notice I'm gone."

Nobel tilted his head at her, his expression curious.

Unease wrapped around her bones and tightened around her lungs. She tried to hide it behind a steely mask, a rigid posture.

"Ryn," Nobel started, casually. He cocked a brow. "You have certainly found yourself in a situation. Everyone knows your name because of the engagement. Tough to hide in the shadows when you are so well known, little dove."

"I poisoned the king," she breathed.

"Is that so?" His brows rose. "Last I heard, the king was pulling through his assassination attempt."

"The vampires you sent to rescue me nearly killed me," she said, her voice a little stronger. "And tried to make me kill Zain."

"My apologies," Nobel said, brow furrowed. Sincerity drifted over his features. "I didn't realize they would be so…aggressive about it. I—"

"Where is Lu?"

Nobel's lips pursed. She had cut him off. She had never been so bold, but she had never felt such urgency for answers. Desperation. Determination.

Uncertainty. Like he knew that, he straightened. His sincerity smoothed into his calm, calculating mask. "Luella is perfectly fine. Alive, safe, warm, well-fed, well-rested. Taken care of. But, Sabryn, the contract I gave you has not been abandoned. There is still time unless you give up. As long as King Victor dies, you and your sister will be free. Your debt to me will be paid in full."

Ryn swallowed. The answer felt horrible, yet it seemed the only way. "We're going back to the keep tonight. We're still getting married."

Nobel straightened, signaling the end of the meeting. "All I need is a dead king, and you win. Time isn't as…urgent for me. Now, I think, as long as you leave within the next minute, you should arrive before your husband."

The guard motioned Ryn back into the alley. Her heart trembled and thudded and she barely felt the cold. Ryn didn't know what outcome she had expected. Unless King Victor died, she would never see Lu again.

44

A MONSTER IN SILK

Ryn

Ryn returned to the townhouse and to a delicious aroma coming from the kitchen. Slipping through the cellar door and up to the second floor, slick as a shadow, she returned the key to its hiding place, washed the city from her face, and no sooner had she stepped out of the bathroom did Zain return.

"Ryn?" Zain's voice carried from the first floor.

"She's upstairs," came Bertha's deadpan at the same time Ryn called, "I'm up here."

She met him at the top of the stairs. His gaze ran over her clothes.

"What? I couldn't wear just a robe," she said.

"Oh, I don't mind." Zain leaned on the banister. "I think they look rather dashing on you."

"What happened at the meeting?" Ryn asked.

"I'll tell you the plan over tea, come." He headed back down the stairs, to the kitchen, where Bertha set a steaming teapot and two cups.

Ryn sipped hot tea while Zain recounted his meeting with Esben and Commander Wade. Esben had taken their plan to the queen, who by some grace of the gods, approved. Ryn's surprise must have shown because Zain chuckled and said, "She is eager for revenge for the vampires who tried to kill her husband."

An uncomfortable lump swelled in her throat. "I understand that mentality."

"Oh?" Zain leaned forward. "Is that so?"

"I would want revenge on anyone who attempted to hurt you," Ryn said. "And it just so happens that the same brood who threatened you threatened your father, so we have a common enemy. After this, I'm sure the queen will return to her hatred of me."

"Oh, come now. She is actively planning our wedding." Zain sipped his tea, letting those words sink in.

"Do you really think she'll let us go through with it?"

"It will be a grand affair," Zain said. "A parade, a ball. So many nobles and commoners coming and going. So many chances for an assassin to slip through the crowd." He wiggled his brows. "They won't be able to resist. It is the best trap we can lay. Mother will agree."

His dark tone fell like a hammer against her lungs. They planned to lure the vampires out, thinking the assassin was among them.

Her panic must have shown, for Zain closed his hand around hers. "Don't worry," he said. "We will catch them and put an end to this madness."

An end to the madness.

She didn't see how he could, when the assassin sat across from him.

How would she kill the king at her own wedding? She would be under guard. Everyone would be looking at her. It would have to be after. A knife through the heart, since her poison technique hadn't worked.

A knife through the heart, and then the knife would be found in the kitchens.

Zain held her shaking hands firmly. She let his confidence soak into her skin and pretended there was still a happy ending waiting for them.

sss

Zain and Ryn returned to the keep with their fingers laced. Irene stalked behind them, scowling and gripping the hilt of her sword like she expected vampires to lurch from the shadows. Given that there was an unknown number of them hiding among the Hunters and staff, it was a possibility. Esben met them at the gates, along with Captain Colby.

Ryn saw the looks she and Zain received from passing servants and guards alike, a mixture of shock, disgust, and curiosity. Servants paused in their tasks, dropping baskets of linens and laundry and trays of tea and empty plates. More than one teacup shattered. Guards gawked with white knuckles around their swords.

This was worse than the first time Ryn had walked these halls as the female saved by the cold prince for unknown reasons. Then, she had cowered and feared for her life. Then, she had worn dirt and grime on her clothes and skin, tangles in her hair. Now, she held her head high. She wasn't that cowardly female any longer. She was their princess, Sabryn Evren Casiano.

Zain squeezed her hand like he knew what she was thinking, like he could feel the tickling pleasure her full name sent down her spine.

Esben escorted them all the way to their shared chambers in the royal wing. The guards on either side pulled open the doors, and at first Ryn saw only packages—towering, teetering stacks of brown packages, piles and piles of them. Then she noticed the queen standing at the table, eyes wide and skin flushed.

The doors closed, and Colby and Irene took up posts just inside the room.

Esben started through the sitting room. Zain lagged a step behind. Ryn gripped his hand. She could almost feel the surge of panic, shame, and inadequacy. This female was not his mother, and now she knew Zain knew.

The queen looked to Esben, then her watery eyes fell on Zain. "My boys," she said.

Those two words loosened the shame curling around Zain's heart. He followed Esben's path through the packages, still holding tight onto Ryn's hand.

"Safe and sound," Esben said, the words feeling like a report.

As Zain approached the table, Queen Portia rushed forward, graceful as a cat, and threw her arms around him. He tensed, eyes wide, and then awkwardly returned her embrace. She held him for a long moment, then held him at arm's length. Silver lined her eyes and clotted her lashes, and by the flush of her cheeks, she had been crying.

By the shock on Zain's face, he had envisioned this meeting going very differently.

"I told her I was going after you," Esben said.

"I feared I'd never see either of you again." The queen blinked, smearing silver across her lashes.

"But…" Zain struggled to say it.

"But you're not my son," the queen said flatly, finishing his thought for him. "No, I did not grow you in my womb, but that doesn't make you any less my own." She steeled her features, once again a lioness. "I raised you. Changed you. Fed you. Helped you take your first steps. Endured your temper tantrums. You are my son. Understand?"

Zain blinked at the scolding, his shoulders relaxed, then he nodded.

"Mother, Zain agreed to the plan," Esben added. "Zain, you told Ryn?"

"She knows." Zain looked to her for confirmation, and she nodded. She couldn't quite find her voice. She had the feeling of having intruded upon something private between Zain and his mother.

Of course, if this plan ended with them together, his mother would be her mother.

"Good, good," the queen motioned to the empty chairs. "The tea is still warm. Sit. We have much to discuss."

The planning began amid the fort of brown paper packages and silken ribbons, their presence seeming to soak in the sound. The only witnesses were Irene and Colby who stood sentinel by the main door, and Claudette, the queen's personal guard, who stood by the windows. The plan—to hurry the wedding between Zain and Ryn, had far too many moving parts for her liking. Too many names Ryn didn't know. Not to mention details of the wedding itself, from flowers to guests to the dinner menu and wine selection—it made Ryn's head spin.

The conversation lulled, and Zain finally asked, "What of Father?"

"He is recovering and under heavy guard," the queen answered. "Including Commander Wade and select Hunters."

"But there are vampires in the Hunters," Zain argued.

"You think Commander Wade is a vampire?" The queen raised a brow. "He fought alongside your father at that battle that won this keep."

"I didn't think Neville was one." In a darker tone, low enough no one but those at the table could hear, Zain added, "I didn't know I was one."

The queen pursed her lips at Zain. She looked like she had more to say, but she held her words. Zain caught the hesitation. He leaned forward without breaking eye contact with her.

"Where did I come from?" he asked, the words almost a plea.

The queen swallowed. Her fingers tightened around her teacup. "That is a conversation best had with your father. I don't feel right explaining it without him."

Zain nodded, though he looked unsettled.

Under the table, Ryn reached for his hand. His cold gaze softened.

By the time the sun sank behind the horizon and doused the keep in darkness, Queen Portia had the wedding planned, from flowers to table runners, the menu and the guest list—things that left Ryn overwhelmed.

Ryn had never learned about wedding planning; she never thought she would get married or need the information.

It would seem the truth about Zain had changed the queen's feelings toward Ryn.

"The seamstress will be here first thing tomorrow," the queen told Ryn, the previous animosity gone from her gaze. "I'll have the staff ready the carriage for the parade, and have the kitchens start preparing for the ball. Oh, there is so much to do!"

Ryn didn't know what to think about the queen's kindness, or if she trusted it.

45
MATED
Ryn

Ryn spent the next several days guarded by either Esben, Zain, Colby, or Irene. Neville was nowhere to be found. According to the Hunters, he had vanished. He was the only one to vanish, which meant his vampire friends were still hiding among the ranks. Ryn had barely more than a few moments alone, not even when she bathed. Kari or Irene would stand in the room, the first talking nonstop and the second brooding. Hunters stood in the corridor at all hours.

The king remained on bed rest, tended to by the healer, the alchemist, and a poison expert. Rumor said the king was improving, that he looked forward to the wedding of his youngest son, but Ryn had not seen him. For all the positive talk about his health, the air in the keep—and the constant care from the healer—suggested otherwise.

Under the rumors, Ryn heard the truth. The poison was in the king's blood, circulating through every organ and vein.

The seamstress took her role seriously, and within a week she crafted Ryn an elegant traditional gown for the wedding ceremony and a ballgown of white and gold for the ball.

After her final dress fitting, the queen escorted Ryn back to her chambers.

"Such lovely things," the queen said. "For my wedding ball, I wore a skirt nearly as wide as I was tall. My wedding was to a king, and thus my dress had to be the biggest of them all. I had bruises on my hips from the weight of it. Bruises were a rite of passage. If the dress didn't leave bruises, it wasn't big enough." She scoffed. "I am glad that trend passed."

"That sounds dreadful," Ryn said.

"Oh, it was." The queen said with a tired smile.

Ryn didn't know how to handle this strange comradery with the queen. She hadn't threatened Ryn's life once since she and Zain returned.

Back in Ryn's sitting room, the queen motioned toward the bedroom and said, "Come in here for a moment. I want to talk."

Ryn's heart dropped. The queen had never *wanted to talk* before, and Ryn knew it couldn't be anything good. She'd been looking forward to the few moments of privacy when she readied for bed, but she held herself steady and followed the queen into her bedroom.

The queen shut the door, then without warning pulled Ryn's hair aside. She clicked her tongue. "You did, didn't you?"

Ryn's heart skipped. She pulled her hair from the queen's loose grasp and stumbled several steps toward the vanity. "What are you talking about?"

The queen beheld her with a strange mixture of motherly concern and stern disapproval. She lowered her voice, and said, "He bit you."

Oh. *Oh.*

Ryn absently pressed her hand against the side of her neck where a ghost of Zain's fangs tingled against her skin. The queen searched her features, waiting for the answer, the denial, but Ryn could not give either.

The queen sighed. "That was a horrible idea."

"He had no tonic," Ryn whispered. "It was better than seeing what would happen if he didn't take it. He was in control."

"You don't understand." The queen shook her head. "I remember when those monsters ruled this land. Hunting us fae for sport. Stealing friends and lovers for their thralls. Murdering our children."

"Zain isn't like that," Ryn said firmly.

The queen blinked, then her surprise melted into her usual coldness.

"You are not a thrall, at least." Her words softened. "Zain was not raised by those monsters, and I had hoped he would…lose those tendencies for violence and bloodshed if we raised him. He is nothing like they were, but…" Her eyes fell onto Ryn's throat, and fear twisted her features.

"It was just a bite," Ryn defended. "He took only what he needed."

"It is never just a bite." The queen shook her head. "You felt the effects it had, I assume?"

The way she said it… Ryn blushed at the memory of that night, of the burning desire radiating in her bones, singing in her bloodstream.

The queen's lips thinned. "Those monsters used their bite to have their way with whomever they wished, willing or not. That is…" Her voice wobbled, and water glistened in her eyes. "That is what happened to Victor's sister. She was taken, bitten, raped, and bled dry."

"Is she…" Ryn hesitated to say *Zain's mother.*

"No." The queen glanced toward the bedroom door. She stepped closer, eyes on the healed marks Ryn covered.

"There is something else you need to know about a vampire's bite. When two vampires mate, they bite one another. Whether Zain meant to or not, he claimed you as his mate. That sort of bond doesn't dissolve. Your scent changes. Other vampires will smell it on you, as will some fae."

"Can you smell it?" Ryn asked.

"It is faint." Her nostrils flared. "A thousand years ago, I could have smelled the difference the moment you entered the sitting room."

Mated. It sounded permanent, more than marriage, more than a vow before a god—the floor shifted under Ryn's feet. All the lies they'd told about being mates…they were supposed to be stories. Just stories. Not real. Yet the strange understanding she now possessed of his feelings, his thoughts… It connected her to him. It had started the morning after he'd bitten her.

"Goodnight, Ryn." The queen started for the door.

Ryn grasped for the bedpost to keep herself upright. As the queen stepped through the door, she found her voice to ask, "Does this mean you've stopped plotting my death?"

The queen laughed, though she didn't sound remorseful. "It would be impossible to find another now that you are mated to him. I chose Aurora because she came from a long line of infertile females, and I had hoped to avoid any grandchildren. Of course, now Zain understands why we fear any offspring."

"That was why you were angry," Ryn whispered, thoughts connected.

The queen blinked at her.

"When Zain pulled me from the execution line, you thought I was pregnant," Ryn said. "That's why you were upset."

"That is correct. Raising Zain was difficult enough, and I did not want anyone else to go through what we did, not to mention it would expose Zain for what he truly is." The queen heaved a sigh. "Aurora's father also owes a considerable debt, and she had everything to gain and little to lose. I thought she would be able to stomach being married to Zain. I hadn't planned on anyone discovering the truth, but I needed a female who couldn't say no." Her eyes brightened, and she looked more like the devious queen. "I should have known you would make a better wife than anyone else."

Ryn's heart swelled. "Why?"

"Because, like Aurora, you have everything to gain and nothing to lose," the queen said simply. "And you fought for him, and he for you. It's romantic, in a way."

The queen left, and Ryn felt a hollow sinking in her stomach. The queen was wrong. Ryn had a great deal to lose—Lu.

And if she fucked up this plan, she might never see Lu again.

46

HEARTFELT VOWS AND WEDDING BELLS

Ryn

Bells tolled at sunrise on their wedding day. Ryn was already awake, nerves and dread and a thousand thoughts churning too fast for her to process even one.

Kari and a small force of servants helped Ryn wash and dress in the ceremonial gown—a plain white gown that started at her throat and fell to her ankles. The material was thick and stitched with tiny white roses. Her hair was swept back and left down. She wore a chain of silver with an emerald pendant, a gift from the queen's personal collection, as per tradition.

"You look lovely," said the queen from where she sat on the edge of the bed.

Traditionally, the mother of the bride would have helped. The queen had said nothing of the small, broken tradition, as she stepped into the role. More than once, Ryn wondered what her own mother would have thought of her daughter marrying a vampire prince. She wished Lu could have been there, but she had no means to contact Nobel and didn't know what would happen if she did.

The queen draped a snow-white fur cloak around Ryn's shoulders and fastened the silver clasp, stamped with the royal seal.

"I know we had an uncouth beginning, but I am glad Zain met you," said the queen. Dampness clumped in her lashes. She regained herself, and it vanished. "The gods knew what they were doing when they sent you into the Red Forest."

Ryn couldn't help the uncomfortable warmth from bubbling up her stomach and into her throat. No one had ever considered her presence a blessing. For a long time, she felt like the opposite, a curse of death.

She *was* the opposite. The queen just didn't know it.

The queen kissed Ryn's forehead. "Now, let's see if Zain looks half as good as you do."

They swept into the sitting room. Zain stood beside Esben. No one had said it, but the absence of the king suggested he was still too ill.

Zain looked every bit like the charming prince in a black suit, emerald brocade tailcoat with shined gold buttons, and a black silk shirt. According to Kari, Esben had tried to get him to wear white, but he refused. Ryn agreed with his decision; the black suited him.

His sapphire eyes roamed over her, as if sensing her thoughts, but whereas his grin had once been arrogant and sinister, today it was soft and full of longing. Like he was trying to memorize her, to fix this moment in his memory.

Maybe, like her, he was surprised they had made it this far.

"You look lovely," Zain said, his voice a purr.

"As do you, my darling."

He kissed the back of her hand, then they started the loathsome trek to the keep's temple. A horde of guards and Hunters formed a protective circle around them. Down through the keep, across the snowy grounds, to the ancient temple surrounded by winter-dead roses and barren maples. The stone was cold and gray, and the windowless monolith ended in an iron spire shaped like a sun. The path to the temple was lined with tealights protected in milk glass.

Hand in hand, Zain and Ryn entered the temple's shadowed interior. A thousand candles burned, hanging from the ceiling and perched along the stone wall's narrow ledges. The firelight flickered off the dark stone and empty wooden benches.

Ryn and Zain walked side by side down the center aisle, to the sunken heart of the temple where a hooded priestess waited. Above them, the mosaic tiles of the spire's interior mimicked the rays of the sun. In the candlelight, each tile glimmered as if sunlight were trapped inside. Ryn repressed a shiver and brought her gaze back down. An illusion, she told herself. An illusion crafted by stonemasons.

The wedding ceremony by tradition was small and private. Only the queen, Esben, and their select guards were present. Ryn couldn't stop thinking about Lu. Her sister, her best friend, her only family—she should have been there. She should have helped Ryn get ready. She would have loved the regality and romance of it all.

Despite the ache in her heart, Ryn held herself steady as the priestess tied a sacred rope over their clasped hands. Ryn recited the ancient vows of loyalty, love, and fidelity, and Zain recited the same. She comforted herself by knowing she would save Lu from Nobel, and they would have a hundred balls to make up for Lu missing Ryn's wedding.

"The vows have been spoken, love has been promised." The priestess's somber voice filled the temple's dark space, a voice that disbanded sin lurking in the shadows. She lifted her hands toward the spire, the stone sun. "I present these two souls in holy matrimony, to be bound in love and honor, obedience and loyalty, compromise and friendship."

The thousand candles flashed bright white then faded back to orange and yellow. Ryn had never witnessed an ordained marriage, and gooseflesh rippled over her skin as the air within the temple shifted, charged, before the strange sensation dissipated.

The priestess cupped Ryn and Zain's tied hands with her own. "The gods have given their blessing."

A single bell tolled high in the temple. Within a heartbeat, another bell mirrored its gong, this one distant. Then another sounded even farther away. One by one, every bell in the city would ring, signaling the royal marriage.

Ryn and Zain left the temple with their fingers intertwined. The wintery air brushed against her skin, and before they returned to the keep, a light snow began to fall. In the strange silence of snowfall, bells rang. Some near, others far. It all had a strange, stomach-twisting finality that made Ryn want to vomit.

"You're shaking," Zain whispered.

"It's cold."

"You were shaking in there too."

"I just bonded my soul to another."

"Those are just words."

"Words don't make candles do…whatever that was." She had never visited the temples or even learned the gods' names or purposes.

Zain's lips quirked. "Don't tell me you've got cold feet now."

She scoffed. "It's a bit late for that."

They had already given themselves to one another. He had claimed her as his mate, whether he knew it or not. Vows before the gods should not have made her so nervous.

In truth, it was not the wedding making her nervous. It was everything that would follow, and all the ways it could go wrong.

Brunch had been arranged in the first-floor parlor, tea and egg dishes, different kinds of toasts and fruit preserves, and artfully cut fruit. A light meal for the stupid busy day to follow. The royal family ate together, their first meal as a large family.

"Vivian would have been here for the ceremony," Esben said to Ryn. "But their carriage was delayed by a snowstorm to the west. She will be here for the ball, or so the courier promised."

Ryn forgot that Esben was also betrothed to a foreign princess.

After brunch, the guard readied for the parade through the streets. The snowfall remained light. Queen Portia set a diamond-studded silver circlet atop Ryn's head, the final touch, her own crown. Princess Sabryn Evren Casiano.

The parade was simple yet well-guarded. Royal Guard and Hunters rode on armored horses on either side of the open carriage while Ryn and Zain waved to those gathered on the sidewalks. Despite the snow, hundreds lined the streets.

Bells tolled along the parade route. The sight of the prince and princess sent a wave of excitement through the crowd. Shouts for attention rose, mostly children clamoring for a glimpse of royalty. The snow continued to fall, gracing Ryn's circlet and loose hair, speckling her with ice. She sat close to Zain, her husband.

It didn't seem real.

With the snowfall, he looked regal. Like he belonged. The crown of silver atop his head shimmered in the snowy light, as if made of ice.

The snow began to fall a bit heavier. Ryn sat a little closer to Zain.

Her husband. For the rest of her life.

"You are thinking too hard, love," Zain said as he waved.

"I never thought I'd marry," Ryn said.

"Why not?"

"I…" His question was simple enough, yet the answer fumbled in her throat. "I never thought I would find someone who would want to marry me, who would think of me like that."

"You don't give yourself enough credit, dear wife of mine." He leaned over to kiss her temple, his lips cold. "I thought I would be forced to marry whomever my mother coaxed into it."

"Like poor Aurora?"

"Like poor Aurora," Zain said with a chuckle. "I doubt she would have taken a bite as well as you."

The memory brought a flush to her face. "Your mother and I had a talk about that."

"About the whole mating thing?" Zain flashed her a knowing smile. "I've read about it briefly, but none of the books written by *acceptable* scholars talk about it. I learned about it in those kept hidden in the undercroft. It's quite a big deal to the vampires. Unlike the legends of fae mates, vampires choose theirs rather than relying on fate."

"And now you have claimed one." Ryn blushed like fire. Claimed.

"I would like to think it was a mutual claim."

"I don't have fangs."

"But you were willing and proposed the idea," Zain argued. He flashed her a warm smile. "You have claimed me, like it or not. Before I realized it. That night at the tavern, you set your sights on me."

Something odd happened then, a strange connection, like a taut string between them. Tying them together. One that had been developing since that first meeting, that first touch. Strengthening with each conversation, each glance, each understanding.

Zain brought their intertwined hands to his lips and placed a kiss on her knuckles. Desire darkened his eyes and sent a hot sizzle across her skin and pooling in her stomach. The chill in the winter air didn't bother her, the snow melting on her skin didn't matter, her missing sister hanging in the balance didn't hurt so much.

He held her knuckles against his lips.

"Just the ball, and we end this vampire rebellion," Zain whispered against her skin, his breath cool and his eyes burning. "Then we save your sister and live happily ever after."

If only.

"You have yourself a deal, dear husband," Ryn said, smiling like a fool. "Now if only the carriage had walls."

His grin turned mischievous. "If only. Mother would have our skins otherwise."

"It's far too cold." She nodded toward his lap, unable to stop the smile stretching her lips.

"You underestimate me, dear wife."

"If the cold bothers you like a few tankards of ale, then I don't think so."

He laughed, deep and husky. "That ale was stronger than I thought, and I drank on an empty stomach. Bad choice. Or a great choice, depending on how you look at things. Look where those tankards of ale got me."

The parade returned to the keep as the sun tilted below the thick clouds, alighting the snow in brilliant dusky gold. It looked as though gold flakes fell from the sky, glittering and reflecting. Ryn gawked as golden snow kissed her face.

"A fitting sight," Zain whispered. He wasn't looking at the golden snow. He was looking at her.

As the horses pulled into the carriage house and out of the snow, Ryn felt something…shift. She had expected disaster to interrupt the parade, as had the Hunters. As she and Zain were escorted back to their chambers to prepare for the ball, Irene fell in step beside her.

"No sign of Neville," Irene whispered. "No trouble with vampires. It would seem the parade wasn't enough of a target for the brood."

"Hope is not lost," Zain assured Ryn as they returned to their sitting room.

Ryn's servants helped her out of the simple, traditional dress, and into the ballgown.

It was a riot of ivory and gold. The sleeves were long and lacy. The collar was high. Layers of silk formed a full skirt. Her hair was brushed and braided back, the top half up and other half down. The diamonds resting on her head and hugging her throat made her feel like a princess, but also like an imposter.

The female in the mirror was a stranger. She was someone important, someone important enough to marry a prince. The daughter of a noble house, not a monster wrapped in fae skin. The dress cost more than some in the city would see in their entire lives, and she would wear it just once, until one of her grandchildren donned it for their own wedding. The circlet and necklace had been worn by Zain's grandmother, or was it great grandmother? Ryn didn't remember.

Someone far more important than her.

Unless his grandmother had come from nothing, just like her. Ryn imagined the female in a situation like herself, born and raised poor as dirt and granted the chance to become a princess.

Of course, Ryn doubted the original owner of the circlet had enchanted poison into her father-in-law's favorite wine in a failed attempt at murder.

Ryn shoved that thought aside. *Later.* She would deal with that later. Never, if it worked out.

47

UNINVITED GUESTS

Ryn

Ryn and Zain met once again in their sitting room. He hadn't changed; he still wore his emerald brocade tailcoat, black silk, and black overcoat. A silver crown perched on his hair, gleaming in the candlelight. Again, his eyes swept along her frame, and she twirled in her ballgown, delighting in the feeling as the fabric swished outward and back again. He extended his arm, and she draped hers through it.

They made their way not to the ballroom, where the soft din of reception guests awaited, but to a parlor where the queen paced. King Victor sat at the table. He was a thin, pale version of himself, but alive. He no longer boasted the luster of a war-hardened king. He was a ghost of the male Ryn had met. His pale hands rested on the head of a cane. Commander Wade and Captain Colby stood on either side of him, along with two Hunters Ryn had seen but never met. They were older Hunters who had fought alongside the king in the Battle of Nightshade Keep. Trusted.

Hope and fear swelled that the poison still might take him; the duplicitous feelings made her nauseous.

King Victor met Ryn's gaze, and a weak smile stretched his face. "Yes, I am not yet dead, despite what those monsters intended." A cough wracked his body.

"Easy, dear." The queen's stern gaze fell on her husband. "Are you sure about this? You don't have to do this."

"But I must." King Victor accepted a glass of water from Commander Wade, and drank greedily. "If my presence draws those beasts into the light, it is a risk we must take."

The doors opened, and Esben entered with a wisp of a female on his arm. Her dark gold hair fell over her shoulder in a complicated braid, golden powder shimmered on her warm brown skin, and golden studs lined her sharply pointed ears. Her dark eyes grew wide at the sight of Ryn. She let out a delighted squeal, and rushed over and grabbed Ryn's hands in a delicate yet firm grip. She stood a fingertip taller than Ryn, and this close, Ryn saw a faint tattoo along her collarbone that vanished underneath her sky blue gown.

Esben appeared at the female's side. "Ryn, this is Vivian, my betrothed. "Viv, this is Ryn, who I can now introduce as my sister."

His lack of titles did not go unnoticed by Ryn, though she supposed she and Viv would be sisters one day. There would be no titles between them.

"Oh, it is wonderful to finally meet you!" Vivian spoke with a slight accent, her words curved in feminine charm. She had a delicate nature, yet something lingered below the act, the capacity for a queen, something stern and commanding. "Esben has told me little about you. I have always wanted a sister. I have five brothers, and it is *dreadful*."

"It is an honor to meet you at last," Ryn said, already exhausted from Viv's vigor. The younger girl and Lu would get along.

"Now, tonight might be perilous," the king said, his usual commanding tone falling lackluster. He took a deep breath, then stood, leaving heavily on his cane. Commander Wade stepped closer to the king's weak side. "But we must remain strong. United against this vampire threat. Now, let us enjoy the night."

The herald announced Crown Prince Esben and Her Highness, Princess Vivian of Dahleria first, then His Majesty King Victor and Her Majesty Queen Portia, and then His Highness, Prince Zain and his wife, Her Highness, Princess Sabryn—the only time they would enter after the king and queen.

Hearing her title and name resound through the ballroom sent gooseflesh rushing over her skin.

A hushed applause greeted them. Underneath it, whispers surged.

Ryn had heard the proclamations claiming Zain innocent, that he had been framed by vampire assassins, but by the heavy air in the ballroom, she wondered how well the news of his magic had settled with the nobles. How many knew or guessed his true nature as a vampire? Hunters lined the ballroom. Royal Guards stood between them. The uneasiness of the room settled into Ryn's skin like teeth—like distrust and suspicion. By how Zain's hand tightened on hers, he felt it too.

Ryn and Zain descended into the ballroom to a smattering of whispers. They retreated to the high table where Esben, Vivian, the queen, and the king waited. Zain and Ryn sat in the center. The king lifted his goblet for the toast, and a reverent silence settled over the ballroom.

"Good people," King Victor started, his voice weak. Before the poison, his voice would have filled the ballroom. His cane rested against the table, but he did not touch it. "These vampires will not get away with these devious attacks on my life, or on my family. They will not undermine the world we have built for ourselves within the light. They will not defeat the sun. The night must always end. We will eradicate every last one of them from this world!"

A spattering of applause followed his words. A few nobles cheered.

Zain tensed. Ryn took hold of his hand under the table.

"We haven't spoken," Zain whispered to her. "I haven't had the chance to ask him about me or my mother. I didn't know he would be here tonight."

"Do you think it's safe?"

Zain didn't answer.

"But for tonight," the king resumed, his voice wobbling. "We celebrate the marriage of my son, Zain, to our wonderful Lady Sabryn."

Another round of applause sounded, this one a bit louder. The king sat, the meal commenced, servants wound through the ballroom with bottles of wine, and Vivian engaged Ryn in pleasant chatter.

Servants carried around platters of finger foods, miniature tarts, and refills of wine. Musicians played a charmed melody of strings and woodwinds. The grand wall of windows gave a beautiful scene of the snowy gardens, the glittering snow tumbling from the silver clouds, the sun sinking behind the Red Forest.

As the meal came to an end, the music eased into a pleasant melody. Zain stood, held his hand out for Ryn, and led her onto the dance floor. Nobles and guards watched every move. Ryn twirled so that the fading sunlight and candlelight shimmered across her silken skirts, and she tried not to think of all the eyes on her, on Zain, or how many of them despised them both for being what they were.

Princess, she reminded herself. She couldn't back out now. She would forever hold the eye of the nobles, the city, the kingdom, and their scrutiny. She would drink fine wine and eat delicate spun-sugar snowflakes and all the chocolates she wanted. As she and Zain danced around the ballroom, she let herself pretend nothing at all was wrong. She indulged herself in the dream that she would live as a princess for the rest of her life, that nothing could disrupt it.

She pretended her sister's life didn't hang in the balance, she hadn't poisoned a king, and vampires weren't hunting her down.

After the first dance, Esben and Vivian joined them. King Victor remained seated, though Queen Portia danced with Commander Wade in his stead. With the next few plucks of lute strings, nobles joined them on the dance floor. In the moments before the sun fell behind the Red Forest, the ballroom was aglow with skirts and glittering crystal glasses and sparkling jewelry. Then the sun fell, and the ballroom's glow dimmed. The only light came from the hundreds of candles scattered around the room. The music seemed to dim, and even the shadows seemed to thicken.

Zain spun her out and brought her back closer than before, so close she could feel his breath against her face. Her heart skipped a beat, then another.

It all felt like a daydream, like she had died in the Red Forest in pursuit of that damn silver rabbit, or maybe the Hunters had executed her. A female like her couldn't be dancing with a prince in a ball. She was a monster, a murderer, an enchantress. She agreed to marry the horrible prince in order to save herself, to save her sister. She wasn't supposed to fall in love with him. He wasn't supposed to fall in love with her.

After their first dance, the greetings began—noble after noble queued up to meet Ryn, most curious at the female who had tamed the cruel, unpleasant prince. Some were old and some were near Ryn's age and thrilled to welcome her into their circles. The ladies of the court extended invitations for garden walks in the spring, tea parties in the summer, and wine tastings. Ryn thanked them for each, and promised to stay in touch.

Empty words, empty promises.

If her plan worked out like she wanted, like she hoped, she would have to pretend her way through those parties, endure the attention of the court.

A kind-faced female approached Ryn, her dress subtle but beautiful. She had pale brown skin and tawny hair twisted into a complicated braid. Pale eyes quickly took in Ryn head to toe.

"Your Highness," said the female with a practiced smile. She bowed her head. "It is wonderful to meet you at last. We have heard much about you, but only rumors. Congratulations on your union. I am Lady Sasha Crestin."

Ryn stumbled over her practiced words—Crestin, the house that might have disowned her mother. Zain squeezed her hand, grounding her.

"It is a pleasure to meet you, Lady Sasha," Ryn recited.

Sasha's lips curved. Her smile looked genuine, but it could have been pretend. She leaned in and said low enough that the male waiting behind her couldn't easily hear, "If what Her Majesty says is true, we will be spending more time together. Hmm?"

Ryn swallowed. Was Sasha old enough to remember her mother? Had she heard family stories of the forgotten daughter? Ryn pushed those bitter thoughts aside. *Princess.* "I would like that, my lady."

Sasha bowed her head again, then allowed the next person to steal Ryn's attention.

If her mother had belonged to the Crestin House, then Sasha was family. By blood. The very idea that she had an entire family out there she hadn't heard of made her stomach flip-flop.

Ryn met countless other nobles, ladies and gentlemen, businessmen and heiresses, old money and new.

At last, Zain guided her to the high table where Irene guarded their wine glasses. Breathless from all the greeting and gratitude, Ryn took a healthy drink of her wine. With so many people in the room, with so many nobles wanting to meet their new princess, she didn't notice the shadow of a man approaching until a familiar velvet voice sounded to her ear.

"Congratulations are in order, Lady Sabryn."

She would know his voice anywhere. Her skin flushed clammy. Her entire body tensed. Beside her, Zain's soft, bored expression sharpened into the vicious prince. Turning to the handsome male behind her, she thought her heart might burst.

Nobel wore a fine suit of crimson brocade and black silk. He was clean shaven, and his hair was slicked back. His eyes glittered as he took in Ryn's surprise.

"Nobel?" His name fell from her lips in a gasp.

But it wasn't just Nobel's appearance at her wedding ball; it was the female on his arm.

Ryn almost didn't recognize her sister in the fitted dress and jeweled necklace, deep ruby lips, and eyes lined with kohl.

"Lu?" Ryn breathed her sister's name.

Lu didn't respond. Not a blink, not even a flinch.

Ryn's heart hammered, panic seethed under her skin in a cold sweat. "Lu?"

"Now, now, little dove," Nobel purred. "Your sister is perfectly fine. Unharmed, as I promised you she would be."

Zain pressed to Ryn's side, his words a snarl, "What do you want?"

The venom in Zain's voice could have killed a lesser male, but Nobel was no ordinary male. Nobel took in Zain from head to toe, that clinical gaze lingering on his face. Few had the nerve to speak to Nobel without the utmost respect, and he knew it. Zain's outburst, if anything, humored him. A cautious smile tilted Nobel's lips.

"You must be Prince Zain," Nobel said. "How…honored I am to meet you at last."

Zain snarled a curse under his breath.

Out of the corner of Ryn's eye, Irene clenched her sword. She tiptoed closer to Ryn. The rest of the ballroom swung and drank and laughed like nothing was wrong.

"What is wrong with Lu?" Ryn demanded. Her words broke the stalemate stare between Nobel and Zain.

"Lu is in what some call a trance," Nobel whispered, grin stretching like he had already won.

"Bastard," Irene spat, pulling her sword an inch out of the sheath.

"Easy, Hunter." Nobel traced a finger along Lu's exposed throat. "Unless you want this poor female dead on your floor."

Ryn set her hand on top of Irene's. "Stop."

Begrudgingly, Irene pushed her sword back in. Fury boiled in her eyes.

"Lu?" Ryn whispered to her sister, trying to break whatever hold Nobel had on her. Lu only stared back, eyes glassy and unfocused. "Can she even hear me?"

"Of course, she can." Nobel trailed a finger down Lu's cheek. Lu turned her gaze to him, looking at him as if he were the only male in the world. "She can hear you, but she obeys me."

"I don't remember your name on the guest list," Zain said to Nobel, his tone malicious and cold.

Nobel eyed Zain for a long moment, and his grin widened. "It was, my little prince, only it wasn't the name you likely have heard. I have several, just for occasions like this."

Ryn's heart plummeted. She gripped Zain to keep upright. They had unknowingly invited Nobel into the keep, the very male who held Lu at knife's edge, who consorted with Neville and the vampire brood. And he stood before them. In a ballroom full of Hunters, unafraid.

Which meant other vampires had invaded their ball under the same nefarious means. Ryn gaze at the nobles and Hunters, any of whom could be vampires in waiting.

"Careful, little dove," Nobel said to Ryn. "How this evening ends depends on you."

"What have you done?" Ryn whispered.

"I gave you one task." Nobel's grin flattened, and he looked truly disappointed.

It had been years since she'd felt the burn of Nobel's disappointment. Her knees threatened to give, and panic darkened the edges of her vision. Her dinner soured in her stomach. Zain's grip tightened.

Nobel looked to where the king sat, guarded by Hunters. "You gave it your best shot, I suppose. Considering your skill set and experience, it could have been worse. It doesn't matter now. I have moved all the pieces into place, and despite the wrench you threw into my plans, I have managed to come out on top."

Each word hit her chest like a drum. A knife to her heart. Ryn had the horrible sensation of having forgotten something, something vital.

Zain stepped slightly in front of Ryn, eyes burning like the vicious prince he was supposed to be. He glared at Nobel as if he would tear him apart with his bare hands if the coward wasn't using Lu as a shield. "What do you mean?"

Nobel blinked, like he'd forgotten Zain was there. "Oh, she didn't tell you? Ryn works for me. I took care of her ill sister while she played games with the Hunters. In return, I asked one thing of her, giving her recent relocation to the keep."

Ryn felt the floor fall away from under her feet, felt Zain's grip on her hand turn painful, and felt the terror and heartbreak before Nobel even said the damning words.

"I asked her to kill the king," Nobel said casually, as if speaking of fashion or the weather. He plucked a flute of sparkling wine from a passing servant. He examined it before sipping. "She isn't an assassin, and she doesn't know her way around poison, which I suspect to be the reason why His Majesty is still alive." Nobel gave Ryn a knowing look. "You enchanted the wine, but not well enough, little dove."

"What?" Zain had gone ghostly white. The fury within his eyes turned cold, and as those eyes met Ryn's, as he waited for her defense, for her to tell him Nobel was lying, disbelief cut through his expression with every beat of silence. His grip on her loosened.

"Zain—" Ryn couldn't form an excuse fast enough, couldn't concoct a lie under the glare of Zain's hurt.

The betrayal and heartbreak sliced between them. Zain unstrung his arm from his, looking at her as though he had never seen her before.

"You tried to kill him?" Zain whispered.

Darkness edged on Ryn's vision. She had no lie to give, no cover story. Nobel had tossed her plan to blame vampires out the window.

Ryn was looking at Zain and didn't notice the flicker of a candle snuffing out, or another, or the shadows growing on the far side of the ballroom. She barely heard the confusion over the pounding of her own heart. Someone screamed, panic sharpened, and then wedding guests fell to the floor. Blood splattered across the marble.

Vampires had entered their ball dressed like guests in silken dresses and tailcoats, right under the Hunters' noses.

"It's all right, little dove," Nobel crooned.

Ryn felt an invisible hand touch her chin and tilt her face toward Nobel. His gaze pierced hers—the roaring in her ears faded, her panic eased, everything seemed to slow down. Nobel's calm became her own, oozing into her like a warm night breeze.

"Stop it!" Zain shouted from far away.

Hands grabbed her arms and yanked her back. As she fell, she saw red rimming Nobel's eyes. How had she never noticed it before?

She fell into the table, knocking over several glasses of wine. A glass of red seeped into the material of her gown, hopelessly staining the white and gold.

Zain stood between her and Nobel.

Nobel cocked his head at Zain. "You're defending the female who tried to kill your father?"

Zain did not answer. His fingers curled into fists. He spoke, but his words muddled in her ears, like he had gone underwater. Ryn slid to the floor, trying to shake the feeling of Nobel's stare. Her side throbbed where she'd hit the table. Wine made her hands sticky. Screamed echoed throughout the ballroom.

From under the table, she saw nobles fleeing in terror. The grunts of battle and screams and panic filled the air—yet it all seemed far away, as if Ryn was dreaming. Zain let out a vicious howl, either in pain or rage, Ryn didn't know.

She fought to regain her footing. Her entire body felt light, like it wasn't entirely hers. The ball had gone to shambles, blood splattered the floor, as did bodies.

"Ryn, get out of here!" Zain shouted from somewhere far away.

She needed to help him. She couldn't leave him to face Nobel alone, she needed—the ballroom wobbled, and she stumbled to her knees. Vomit crawled up her throat.

A blinding pain seared through her upper arm, and bright red blood soaked into her dress sleeve. Someone appeared at her side. Irene. Blood splattered on her face, and her sword glittered with it.

She danced toward Ryn's attacker, and with a few quick maneuvers, the body crashed to the floor in a heap of blooded cinnamon silk. Irene grabbed Ryn's uninjured arm and hoisted her to her feet. She was speaking, but Ryn heard little of it.

They clamored out of the ballroom and into the dark, snowy gardens. The cold seethed through her dress and down her lungs. The biting air helped to clear her foggy senses, and she took deep, gulping breaths of it, as if she had been deprived.

"…the fuck out of here," Irene was saying.

Ryn slipped on the snow or her hem, she didn't know, and landed in a drift. The snow came down harder, turning her view of the Red Forest into misty, silver shadows illuminated only by the glow of Nightshade Keep. Ryn staggered to her feet as Irene engaged a pale-faced male with murderous intent in his bloodshot eyes. Two more surrounded Irene, yet she showed no signs of backing down. None wore the uniform of the Hunters or the Guard or refinery; they dressed like commoners.

More vampires had entered the keep.

Ryn felt her blood on her arm, sticky and warm, seeping into her wedding dress, dripping into the unblemished snow. Her magic reached into it on instinct—she felt her soul.

She had done her best not to feel her own, terrified of what she would find, the darkness lurking within.

But she didn't find a soul grimed with viscous darkness or oily evil. It wasn't clean, but it wasn't the soul of a bad person.

She wasn't the monster she feared she was.

She enchanted her own blood, for her racing heart to calm, for her panic to ease. Her vision sharpened. The roar of her blood dimmed, and the screams of the ruined ball and the battle raging filled her ears.

Ryn sought the blood of those around her and Irene. Three of them. Stumbling to her feet, Ryn latched onto their blood. The three of them froze. Their chests halted mid-breath, their eyes mid-blink. Irene hesitated only a moment before separating their heads from their shoulders. The last head hadn't yet hit the ground when the garden shook.

Ryn struggled to stay on her feet, but the rumbling did not stop. Irene dropped to one knee, her words lost over the rumbling, creaking of stone, and hissing of the trembling ice. The snowy ground cracked open, and pieces of the frozen earth fell into the yawning darkness below.

"Ryn!" Irene screamed.

It was too late. The ground under Ryn gave way, and she fell into the frozen bowels of the garden.

48

LOST PRINCE, FOUND SISTER

Zain

Screams, shrill and bloodied, painful and terrified. It all faded from Zain's consciousness as the reality settled—Ryn had poisoned his father.

His wife.

His lover.

His mate.

And she had poisoned his father.

By the horrified look on her face, Nobel spoke the truth. It wasn't rage that seared along his bones or cut through his chest. It was heartbreak. Betrayal. Worse than any sword, any wound he had ever endured, any illness, any backlash from the nobles or his family. He had given everything to this female, shared his deepest secrets, his bed, his title, and she had betrayed him. She had tried to rip his family apart.

But Nobel had made her do it, had forced her hand, had blackmailed her with Lu's life. Had it been Esben on the line, Zain might have done the same.

And Zain had felt her—her panic and fear and regret. Was that the mating bond the old books talked about? The ability to sense his mate wherever she was, her thoughts and feelings, like a sixth sense.

And then Nobel drew Ryn's attention to him, and the same dreamy expression came over her face as on her sister's. A trance.

Rage, bitter and fierce and sharper than steel, coursed from deep within Zain's core. It was unlike any rage he had felt before. This was primal, visceral.

A growl fell from his lips, and his right fist collided with Nobel's smug grin. Nobel stumbled back, and Zain felt a feral satisfaction at the power in his own limbs, at the domination extended over this pompous asshole. It felt *good*.

Nobel regained his composure. Beside Zain, Ryn snapped out of it. Irene appeared at her side, pulling her away.

Zain readied another fist—

"Fuck you!" Lu screamed at Nobel, kicking him in the shin with all the strength her slight frame could muster.

Nobel hissed in pain. He reached for Lu with hate and revenge in his eye. Zain threw himself between Nobel and Lu, taking the punch to the chest. Nobel maneuvered around him, throwing Zain to the ground. Steel flashed—Esben putting himself between Nobel and Zain.

Esben let out a vicious growl and charged Nobel.

Lu appeared at Zain's side, offering him a hand. He accepted it, though he pushed himself onto his own feet.

"I'm Lu," she said breathlessly.

"Zain," he said. "I supposed we're related now."

Lu offered a small, haunted smile. Without the trance, she no longer wore the placid expression and forced sweetness. Instead, she looked at Zain with a dampened spirit. It burned Zain's rage toward Nobel hotter still, stirring his need for revenge.

A vampire appeared behind Lu, and Zain acted without thought—he magicked them out of harm's way. Lu wobbled on the landing, and mumbled a curse under her breath.

Zain glanced to the high table—his father and mother were already gone. Protected, as per their plan.

"This way!" Captain Colby appeared at Zain's side, his sword bloodied, his uniform splattered with it. "Get out of here!"

Colby blocked an attack from a vampiric Hunter, and Zain didn't need to be told twice. He magicked himself and Lu out of the ballroom, in the servant's passage that ran along the ballroom. Zain let the rush of dizziness pass, then he led Lu out of the passage, down an empty corridor, then another. He magicked them around guards and Hunters and vampires.

They landed in front of the closed garden doors, the battle on either side of them. Zain clutched at his heart—he'd used too much.

Lu grabbed his arm and hauled him through the garden doors and into the yard. She kept going, between two outbuildings, and into a courtyard of statues.

"This way," Zain pulled Lu toward the thick bushes behind a weathered bronze statue of his father. Age had cracked the bronze and weathered his father's face. Zain had always thought it gaudy, but tonight he sought refuge in the shrubbery behind it. Lu followed.

"Are you all right?" Lu asked.

"I just…need a moment to catch my breath," Zain lied. Quietly, he added, "This isn't how I thought we'd meet."

"Same," Lu whispered back. "But…are you okay?"

He nodded. He would be. "I'll be fine. What about you? Are you okay?"

Lu hesitated, and Zain took her lack of an answer to mean she was not.

"He won't bother you again," Zain said. "I promise."

Lu glanced at him, her eyes glinting in the dark. Desperation looked back at him.

"As your brother, I promise."

Lu released a soft, exhausted sigh. "I wasn't entranced the whole time. Just…only when he needed me to be."

"Like tonight," Zain added.

"Like tonight. I had no idea what he'd told Ryn. And then I wasn't, and I…kicked him. It was a gut reaction."

Zain chuckled. "It was fantastic."

Voices sounded, and Zain and Lu fell silent and still.

"I saw him run this way!" said a female voice. "He had Nobel's bitch with him."

"I didn't see him," said a male.

Zain peaked around the wide statue. Two figures stood in the courtyard. As Zain watched, a third joined them.

"Find the prince?"

"No," said the male.

"But he came this way."

They were looking for him? Why? To use him against Ryn again? Zain wished he could wield a sword or a bow or…anything. He had no means of offense. Some vampire he was. Half-vampire, he reminded himself. A half-breed, and useless as both. Useless. Worthless. A pitiful excuse for a prince.

A creak of metal—Zain glanced at Lu, but she was no longer beside him in the dirt. Panic hammered through his heart until he spotted her ten feet in the air, back against the manor's wall and her feet pressing against the shoulders of the statue. Pushing it. Her face twisted in strain, and the statue groaned and creaked and then began to tumble forward. The vampires didn't notice the statue in time. It crashed into the courtyard with a vicious crash, crushing the vampires underneath it.

Lu landed in the shrubs with a short gasp, then tumbled back to her feet. She threw a lock of hair out of her face. "Think your dad will be mad about that?"

Zain laughed. "You killed three vampires with it, so I'm sure he'll be thrilled."

Lu, neither vampire nor Hunter, had killed three vampires. Without steel or magic. Like her sister, she was something else.

That crash would signal others, and he didn't want to wait for them to arrive. He motioned Lu deeper into the keep. He wasn't sure where to go. The entire keep was compromised, with vampires in Hunter uniforms running amuck. He didn't know how many more times he could magic them to safety before he collapsed. He already felt the tightening in his chest.

They ducked in and out of sight as they traced their way toward the carriage house. He could hide Lu in his townhouse. She would be safe there.

Vampires spilled from an outbuilding, and Zain quickly magicked himself and Lu to the other side. They hit the ground running, nearly tripping, and Zain nearly toppled on the other side—Lu grabbed his collar and hoisted him upright. His fingers had gone cold.

"Don't keel over on me now, prince," Lu said, breathless.

Darkness edged on his vision, but he kept going. He couldn't stop. He had to get Lu out of here. He had to find Ryn.

His heart squeezed and skipped too many beats. The carriage house came into view. Lu rushed toward the door—a shadow stepped in front of her.

Lu skidded to a halt, and if not for her pulling him to a stop, he would have crashed into the vampire standing before them.

"You're needed elsewhere, Your Highness," Neville said with a sneer. In the ambient candlelight, the red in his eyes gleamed.

"You've really let yourself go, Hunter." Zain stepped in front of Lu.

"I don't care about her, Zain."

A second set of footsteps sounded behind them. Lu's breath hitched. Another vampire appeared behind Neville. Zain's heart gave an unpleasant lurch. He didn't think he could magic them out of here, at least not far enough to matter.

"If you don't care about her, let her go," Zain said.

Neville blinked.

"If it's me you want, I'm right here." Zain adjusted his stance and lifted his hands into the air. "But you will let her go free. Unharmed."

Neville looked between them, cautious. "Okay. You, leave."

"What?" Lu breathed. "Zain, no."

"They will kill you," Zain whispered. Neville could hear him, but it didn't matter. "Go. Find Esben."

The way Lu eyed the vampires with fear, she would be as useless in a fight as he was.

"Why can't you just…" Lu motioned them forward with her hand.

"I've used it too much already," Zain whispered.

Lu paled.

Neville scoffed. "You can barely use your own gifts. You shame your own kind with your ignorance."

"Lu, go," Zain said, not hiding the desperation in his voice. If he could save Ryn's sister, he would.

Gripping her skirt, Lu stepped past Neville. He didn't move. Lu glanced back at Zain, sympathy and regret in her eyes, then she bolted.

"Smart move," Neville said. "It would have been a shame to kill such a pretty face."

Zain didn't move as the vampire behind him approached and grabbed his arms in a painful grip. Neville sauntered closer, smug like he'd won. He reached into his jacket and pulled out a leather pouch. From within it, he retrieved a cloth.

"No hard feelings," Neville said, then thrust the cloth over Zain's nose and mouth.

Zain's breath burned and his lungs tightened. The vampire behind him held him tight, and Neville held the vile cloth against his face—the ground fell away, and darkness engulfed him.

49
UNDERNEATH
Ryn

Ryn landed on crumbled stone. The impact knocked the breath from her chest, and made the next one painful. The sound of creaking stone and cracking earth sounded above and around. Panic for survival took over, and she rolled off the mound of broken earth just as another cluster of snowy rock came crashing down.

She coughed—her chest burned. Each inhale stung.

She staggered to her feet, clutching at her side. Oh, she fucking *hurt*. Reaching into her blood, she felt it pulsing through each vein and organ. Too fast and flooded with adrenaline, but it didn't go anywhere it shouldn't. She wasn't bleeding internally. It was likely a fractured rib.

Relief cooled over her senses. She knew how quickly internal bleeding took a life, especially in the lungs or the heart.

A cut on her forehead clotted at her command, as did the gash on her thigh, but bits of stone lodged in the wound in her upper arm. She couldn't clot it before cleaning it of debris.

She took several, stinging breaths. The hole where she'd fallen was too high to climb out of. The snowy moonlight draped inside, along with the ambient candlelight glow from the keep. The clamor of the battle echoed distantly. Irene's call echoed down. Too far.

"I'm all right!" Ryn tried to shout back. She had no idea if Irene heard her.

She had fallen into an old tunnel. In the dim light, she recognized the structure as part of the undercroft. The ceiling had crumbled over an old junction of four tunnels, the weakest point, where the ancient supports had crumbled with time. The fighting must have been enough to finally bring it down.

She couldn't go back up. She could only move forward.

Ryn knelt—carefully—and snatched her silver crown from the edge of the debris. It didn't even look scratched.

If she followed the undercroft, she would find a way into the keep, and stop Nobel. She could…

Then she remembered Nobel's final blow. He had told Zain of her intentions, exposing her as the attempted assassin.

If she returned to the keep, what or who would be waiting for her?

No, she had to. Nobel still had Lu, and Ryn would break every one of his fucking fingers for touching her. She would gouge out his eyes for using his trance on Lu, for trying to use it on Ryn.

It might damn her soul to the grimy darkness, but she would do it a thousand times to save Lu.

Ryn brushed her hair out of her face and set the crown atop her head. She forced her legs to move, one step after another, into the darkness of the undercroft. Bruises flared along her body from the fall, pulsing with each step, aching with movement. Dwindling torches and lanterns shed just enough light to see by. Many of the halls and doorways had collapsed, leaving crevasses far too small for her to crawl through.

Ghostly silence slowly replaced the commotion of the fight. Winter's silence. The kind that came with snowfall. The kind that dampened the ugly sounds of the slums on cold nights, burying bodies and muffling cries, so they could pretend they didn't live in squalor and she didn't kill people for a living.

Something slid across the stone behind her. She scrambled through the dark to get away from whatever it was—like a coward—trailing her fingers along the stone wall to keep from running face-first into one.

She'd always run when things got sketchy. She dipped her toes into Nobel's dark market only when she had to, and then pretended she hadn't. She pretended she did nothing wrong, that the people she killed needed to die, that she was doing good by getting rid of them.

She ran from the fight, from the consequences. Every time.

She was a coward. She had never learned to hold a dagger to fight, only to scratch. Just enough to slither her magic within.

So she wouldn't have to get her hands dirty.

Zain had put himself between her and that vampire, and then again between her and Nobel. And she had conspired to kill his father.

She didn't deserve him.

She kept going forward. That, she could do. She could keep going. Keep pretending everything would be all right. Despite her faults, she prided herself on her persistence. She would walk through the dark until her legs quit working, then she would crawl. If she kept going, she would find a way into the keep. There were several, and she just needed one.

Something slammed into her back, sending her sprawling forward. She scrambled in her heels to move, and spun with her nails ready to claw out eyes or grab hair or anything, but she felt nothing but air. Dank, empty air and darkness. She pressed her back into the stone and stilled—silence pressed against her ears, until her pounding heart was the only sound.

She started along the passage again.

Something changed. Something in the air, like how the air shifted before the rain. She couldn't put her finger on what exactly, but before she could figure it out, a torch sparked to life.

Spinning, she stumbled back a step.

Nobel stood in the middle of the stone hall, torch in hand. The golden light illuminated his handsome face and gilded his dark tailcoat.

"Interesting meeting you here, of all the places in the city." Nobel's face twisted into a victorious smirk, like he was three steps ahead. He likely was.

He was also alone.

"Where's Lu?" Ryn demanded.

He looked to the ceiling. "Up there somewhere. Your husband broke my trance with you, and then with your sister. He has a mean right hook for scrawny male." Nobel rubbed his jaw. "Luella kicked my shin and ran off, spitting curses I didn't know she knew. Quite the spitfire when she's pissed off. Nimble too. Definitely your sister."

A burden fell from her shoulders, and Ryn released a breath that stung her chest. Lu had gotten away from Nobel. She might not be completely safe, but she was safer than she had been a few hours ago.

"Your trance?" Ryn asked, the words strained. Each word burned in her chest. "I didn't realize vampires could do that."

Nobel's eyes turned to hungry glints. Crimson ringed his eyes, and it might have been the flame, but his skin looked sallow. He grinned, and fangs poked from his lips. And…Ryn was alone in the undercroft with a vampire. A vampire with a grudge against her. A vampire to whom she owed gold. A vampire who had lost his hold over her.

But with Lu safe, she had less to lose.

"Those of royal blood can," Nobel said.

"Oh, you're a royal vampire now?" Ryn's brows rose.

"King Seymour was my uncle. He and my mother were twins." The smile vanished from Nobel's face.

The cold vengeance on Nobel's words chilled Ryn to the bone. She'd never heard him speak like that. He'd always been a savvy businessman, collected and cunning.

She had no weapons, only her weight in stained silk. He had vampire strength and several daggers she could see under his coat, and likely more she could not.

Nobel blinked, and his expression softened. "And here you are, playing princess like your sister's life wasn't depending on you." He took another step closer, and she took one back in reflex. Not that he couldn't close the space between them in a heartbeat. "I gave you one task, Ryn."

"I poisoned him," she whispered.

"And yet he lives." Nobel's lips flattened. "Did you forget about your sister while you were fucking a prince? You're not a princess, little dove. You are a killer. You are worth nothing to those fools up there. To that murderer king, you are just a pretty face. But to me, Sabryn, you are worth a thousand ships of gold."

He stole another step, she took another back—her back hit the stone wall. No where else to go. She didn't care if it made her look weak. She pressed herself against the solid stone.

"You have made yourself hard to get to, little dove," Nobel hesitated, during which her heart skipped a beat. "Not even my own could get you out of the keep."

"You sent Neville?"

Nobel heaved an annoyed sigh. "That upstart nearly ruined my plan to get you out of the castle. He has been punished, don't you worry."

Her heart dropped. "Is he…"

"He's not dead," Nobel corrected. "He is young, reckless, and bullheaded. He thought he was doing the best for our kind. He is too young to remember a time before the tyrant fae king, and he acted out of ignorance."

"He tried to kill Zain," Ryn whispered.

Nobel half-laughed. "Come with me, Sabryn. There are things you need to know about your king and your husband."

She held in what she knew, just in case. In her experience, playing dumb had worked out in her favor. Nobel loved to be right, to know things others didn't.

"Like what?" she asked.

His grin turned villainous. "Allow me to show you."

Nobel grabbed her wounded arm and tossed her through an archway. Ryn stumbled, pain searing through her arm and her side and her left leg. Gritting her teeth, she turned to spit at him, but he stood much closer than she thought—her nose brushed the brocade of his tailcoat. She gasped and stumbled back a step— her heel met open air. Nobel grabbed hold of her flailing hand and halted her fall.

For a moment, she hovered over the darkness, her feet braced against the edge, her hand squeezing Nobel's.

Then he let her go.

She fell. Dark, dank air whooshed around her. Dark walls rose around her. Nobel stood on the ledge above, torch in hand, watching her fall with that thin-lipped expression.

She did not fall far, not even far enough to scream, and landed on a heap of hard sticks. With the addition of her weight, the sticks clattered and skittered down the sides of the heap. They jabbed her back and legs and each movement she made sent more of them scattering. Nobel laughed from his perch, and hot humiliation slithered under her skin.

She pushed herself up, retort on her tongue, but the words dried up as she took in where she had fallen. She sat on a pile of bones.

Thousands of bones, gray and dry. She didn't know much about bones, but she knew fae parts—rib cages, spines, and skulls everywhere she looked. Scrambling backward, her left hand punched through a large cage of ribs. She yanked it free with a series of snaps as panic flooded her veins. Nobel's torchlight flickered off them, off the massive chamber beyond, the old stone black with shadows.

"What the hell is this?" Ryn's voice cracked.

"This is the bone pit," Nobel said as if it were normal to have such a thing under every home. "Any good vampire stronghold had one. The trick was keeping it secret from the nosy Hunters."

Ryn scrambled down the pile of bones, only to stumble into a layer of bones scattered on the chamber's floor.

How many people died here?

Nobel landed on the pile of bones, graceful as a bird, and slid down without so much as a hair out of place. His torch revealed more of the room. Doorways guarded with rusted iron bars led off the chamber, all dark.

"Where are we?" Ryn asked.

"The undercroft. Vampires need to feed at least once a week to maintain a clear head." Nobel looked at the bones with fondness. "Twice to stave off any obvious effects when under the scrutiny of observant Hunters. When the keep was full of vampires, we needed a steady supply of fresh blood."

"You just…threw the bodies down here?" Her words were breathless.

"We had to put them somewhere." Nobel shrugged. "And this was the perfect hiding place for the more…recent disposals. Don't give me that look. Not all my vampires can live off what you bottle, though you have saved many from discovery." He studied the bones, chuckling. His gaze softened, as did his voice. "To think, you were hiding in the keep all this time."

Ryn glanced to the bones, fearing an apparition within, but there was no one. What was he talking about?

"Have you lost it?" Ryn asked.

"You haven't figured it out yet?" He raised a brow at her. "It's understandable if you haven't. Even I didn't see this twist coming."

Ryn stared at him, genuinely confused. "What are you talking about?"

Nobel's eyes caught on something behind her. His brow furrowed and his head cocked to the side, listening. He stalked past her to an ancient, rusty gate. Ryn didn't hear anything, and she didn't see anything within the dark. Nobel pulled the gate open, and it let out a terrible shriek of metal on stone. It stopped halfway open. Then, with his bare hand, Nobel broke the iron gate off his hinges.

Silence followed, and for a moment, Ryn feared the skeletons might stir.

"Our answers are this way, little dove." Nobel whispered as he walked through the gate.

She didn't want to go with him, but he carried the only source of light. She didn't want to remain in the bone pit in solid darkness. Skeletons *would* start to rise. She hurried through the bones to catch up with Nobel.

Nobel wound through the undercroft's maze-like tunnels with ease and eventually guided her into what looked like an ancient dungeon. A single lantern flickered dull light into three barred cells. As Nobel and Ryn approached, something within scuffled.

To Ryn's horror, a male was chained within the first cell. He looked nearly dead, skin shallow and pale, eyes sunken and hair listless. He took in the two of them with defeat, a male who knew death would soon come for him. Punctures in varying states of healing lined his arms and bare chest. Some were a thin white scar, others scabbed over.

"What happened to you?" Ryn asked.

A shuffle came from the next cell, and then a panicked male voice said, "Hello?"

Ryn stepped to see into the next cell. Another male was chained against the wall. His wide eyes took in Ryn.

Her body nearly retched. She knew this male.

He had been the criminal tried before her that day, sentenced to death. His scraggly blond hair was matted and dirty. He had lost his belly, and his sallow skin hugged his bones tight. Like the other man, punctures marred his skin. Hundreds of them.

"Help!" His voice cracked. "You have to help me! Don't leave me here! These people are mad. They will kill me, just like they've killed the others."

"Whatever do you mean?" Noble asked casually. "What's happened to you?"

The first male with dead eyes chuckled. Ryn stepped back. Noble held the torch aloft, enough to illuminate the whole cell. The dead-eyed male's pale lips were twisted in a smile.

"There is no getting out," he rasped, his voice like sand. "Only death."

"They take blood," said the second male, his voice trembling. "Not every day, but some days. He hasn't been here in a while. I-I thought they'd forgotten about us. I-I don't want this. I don't want to be here anymore! Just kill me, please! Kill me! I would rather die than…" He sobbed.

"Blood?" Ryn repeated. Nobel didn't look surprised at all. Only intrigued. To the male, she asked, "Who comes for blood?"

"I-I don't know his name," he said. "White hair. Short and thin. He brings vials and powders. Mumbles about mixtures and temperature like we're not here."

One face floated to the front of her mind.

"Sounds familiar?" Nobel asked her.

"The alchemist," she whispered.

Nobel hummed. "It would seem King Victor has been harvesting blood to sustain his stolen son."

"But…why?" Ryn's words fell flat as his words sank in. "Stolen?"

Nobel flashed his fangs. The prisoner stumbled back against the far wall of his cell. His mad mutterings resembled a prayer.

Chuckling, Nobel started down the corridor. He took the light with him, and despite her desire to flee the other way, she followed. She needed answers, and her gut told her Nobel had them.

Her mind reeled with the word, *stolen*. The king had stolen Zain? She thought of her husband, whose mother was not the queen, who resembled a female in a portrait hidden under the keep. For the king to have stolen him, it implied he did not belong to the king, was not his son. That made no sense.

"I didn't realize it until tonight." Nobel glanced down two corridors. "When I saw your prince, I knew exactly who he was."

"Who is he?" Ryn demanded.

"We thought he was dead," Nobel said, his words a damp cloth. "Dead with the rest of the clan."

"Who is he?" Ryn asked again, desperation working into the words.

Nobel paused at a cross between two corridors, studied each path, then chose left. "This way."

They walked for a while with only his torch to guide them. The undercroft all looked the same to Ryn, but Nobel seemed to know where he was going.

"I had planned on claiming you as mine." Nobel's voice echoed off the stone. His words carried a note of longing. "But your husband got there first."

She shivered at the thought. Her wicked imagination painted it anyway, of Nobel sinking his fangs into her neck instead of Zain, of pulling her under his physical spell, of fucking her afterward. She put a hand against her neck, glad Nobel was facing away from her.

"We would have made a powerful team," Nobel continued. "My wife, the blood enchantress, queen of the Abrani clan."

"You would have made me queen?" Ryn asked. "Not your concubine? Not your mindless thrall?"

He scoffed. "That would take away your fire, little dove." He paused at a four-way and glanced over his shoulder at her. "And I do love that about you." His nostrils flared; he grimaced. He turned down the left hall, torch licking up the shadows. "But when one vampire claims another, it gives off a scent to the others. It marks you as off-limits."

"That's never stopped you before," she said.

"This is different," Nobel explained. "Your scent is not as alluring as it was before. There were times I thought about claiming you, but the claim only works if the other party is willing."

Ryn's heart skipped. All those times she suspected Nobel to be flirting. All those mornings he invited her into his bed. How many times had he almost sunk his fangs into her neck? He was right—if he had, she would have panicked. Screamed. When Zain had bitten her, she had offered her neck and blood and sex to him. She had been willing.

Nobel led Ryn through the Undercroft, each tunnel looking more and more like those before. Then, finally, he said, "Ah, here we are."

They arrived at a familiar hall with ancient wooden doors. Nobel led her into the storeroom of vampire relics. He stalked deeper within, until his torchlight graced the portrait of the dark-haired vampire female.

"There she is," Nobel said with awe and sorrow. He approached the portrait as if seeing a ghost. He spoke in a language Ryn had never heard, the words gentle but harsh. He bowed his head to the female. Straightening, he turned to Ryn and said in the common tongue, "Your husband is not who you think he is."

"I know. He's a vampire." The healed bite marks on Ryn's neck prickled.

Nobel chuckled. "Oh, he isn't *just a vampire*, little dove. He looks just like his mother."

"Did you know her?"

"Did I *know* her?" Nobel scoffed. He turned, his expression sullen and offended. "This is our dead queen, Moira. She and King Seymour were slain in their bed by Victor Casiano, while they slept, because he could not face them awake. We thought Victor had slain their infant son in the cradle." His eyes glistened with ancient grief. "All this time, we assumed our prince was dead in cold blood, all the while Victor kept him hidden. Our prince has been hiding in the enemy's house all these years."

Ryn stumbled backward into the bookshelf, ratting the ancient tomes and loosening the centuries-old dust. Her mind struggled to take it all in, to understand who Zain truly was. She stared into the dead vampire queen's painted gaze, the sapphire eyes her son inherited.

Caught in her own spiraling thoughts, she didn't hear the footsteps behind her. A hand closed over her mouth. Something foul seared through her nose and mouth, and a strong chest pressed into her back—stealing her ability to think. Her panic exploded into white fire, and then everything went black.

50

RUINED

Ryn

Ryn came to in a room with rough-hewn stone walls. She was on a pallet slightly softer than the stone beneath it. Her head hurt, her limbs were sluggish, and everything ached. She tried to sit up—the world spun, and her stomach churned. Ryn squeezed her eyes shut and took several long, steadying breaths to calm the heaving tilt in her body.

Slowly, the world leveled. Her stomach calmed.

Swallowing bile, she took another look at her surroundings.

By the stone and the silence, she was underground. Her crown lay on the ground beside the pallet. A single lantern sat on the floor just outside the iron bars of her cell. A corridor stretched into the darkness, lined with iron barred cells just like hers. Beyond the lantern's light, the darkness was complete. By the silence, the other cells were either empty or the occupants were dead.

Ryn sat up. The pain in her chest had eased, and someone had cleaned and wrapped the wound on her arm. Her sleeve had been cut away, leaving her arm bare. The other sleeve was spotted with dried blood and dirt and wine. Her ballgown was a dirty, wine-stained ruin. Or was it blood? Both? The hem was torn, the skirt hopelessly ripped, and it looked like her bandage had been torn from the skirt.

The dress was ruined, just like everything else in her life.

Ryn brought trembling hands to her face then wiggled her fingers through her hair. She found a bone fragment within a tangle. A quick shuffle sent a few more rattling to the ground.

Grime, sweat, dust, dirt, blood, and sticky wine coated her skin and hair. What a fucking mess.

She swallowed against her dry throat. She'd used Nobel's knock-out powder only once, at his behest, and she hated it. It felt like cheating. It made her grim task much more…evil. Poisons were the tool for assassins, and she had done her best not to be one of them.

Nobel was a vampire. Had always been a vampire. He had lived in the era before Victor Casiano decimated their kind. Nobel had sent Ryn to hunt down people no one would miss and drain them of blood. She had no doubt that bottled blood helped sustain his clan, those hiding in the slums, and those hiding in the keep. But her bottles couldn't have been enough for all the vampires. She thought of the bone pit, the fresh bones. They had killed regardless.

How many of Nobel's people were vampires? It didn't seem possible, but Ryn hadn't suspected Neville either.

Nobel convinced her the City Watch would suspect vampires of her murders, not an enchantress, and he had stirred the nightmarish fear of vampires by framing them. He had used her to do it, keeping his hands clean. With a steady supply of blood, Nobel and his vampires had hidden in plain sight, in the daylight, and fooled everyone. While rumors of vampires lurking in the shadows persisted worse than winter's sickness.

Just like King Victor had done with Zain. The alchemist harvested blood from condemned prisoners and formulated it into a tonic that allowed Zain to hide his vampiric nature. Was it that much different?

And Zain wasn't just a vampire, but a prince. The heir to the fallen Abrani clan. But…why would Victor steal the son of his sworn enemy and raise him as his own?

Footsteps sounded, boots on stone, sure and calm. From the darkness, Nobel strolled toward her cell. His pressed cranberry trousers were spotless, his black boots shined, the golden buttons on his ivory tailcoat gleamed. His hair was clean and combed back. He looked like himself, like the businessman Ryn knew.

"Look who is awake at last." Nobel flashed her a grin and snapped his fingers.

A young female with flaxen hair braided down her back and red rings around her irises hurried past him, silent as a ghost, and slid a tray of food and drink through the gap under bars of Ryn's cell. It was a chunk of seedy bread, grapes, almonds, and hard cheese.

"Of course, you're wearing red," Ryn said, looking Nobel up and down.

"I need to look my best for what happens next," Nobel said with a shrug.

"Which is?" Ryn raised a brow.

"You won't have to worry about it, little dove."

Her skin prickled. "You don't plan on letting me leave."

"That depends on you," he purred.

"What about Lu?"

"I haven't heard a word of her whereabouts since the ball." Nobel watched her expressions, studying her reactions. "She either escaped the keep and fled into the city, or she is hiding in the keep with the rest of them."

Ryn let her relief show—she didn't have any fucks left to care about hiding.

"Hopefully," Nobel added with a sinister grin, "she went into the city. Otherwise, Luella will die along with everyone else in the keep."

Her blood ran cold. "What? Why?"

"Change of plans. Our missing prince, my own cousin I thought murdered in his cradle, yet lives. Once Victor is out of the way, we will take back our ancestral home from those monsters." Each word contorted with a long-seeded hatred. "No longer will vampires cower in the dark while the murderer king and his ilk get fat and sleep on silk."

Silence stretched, and Nobel reeled his anger and hatred back in. He schooled his features into the handsome, calculating man Ryn knew.

She managed to say, "The king didn't die at the ball?"

"No." Nobel grinned.

Ryn had never seen him smile like that. It sent a chill down her spine. Nobel had always been calm and measured, but this Nobel was…mad. This was the real Nobel. Not the male she thought she knew. That male had been an act. The fae he pretended to be.

"You planned this all along?" Ryn asked, her words wavering.

"The general plan has remained the same, though I had to work around your arrest and subsequent engagement, the multiple failed rescue attempts, and then the realization that my cousin lives," Nobel said. "I have switched the details and hurried others, but yes. I have been planning this for a long time. Longer than you have been alive. We are so close. Nothing will get in our way."

"What of Zain?" Ryn's voice broke on his name, on the memory of betrayal in his eyes.

Nobel's grin stretched. "Once we reveal his true heritage and offer him his rightful place as king, he will either join us or die with the rest of his ilk."

"But if he is your king, doesn't he outrank you?" Ryn asked.

Nobel considered her. "Technically, yes. But he has been raised among cowards and taught to hide his nature. He is in no state to lead a clan. Not on his own, not yet. One day, he might be the king his father was, the king we thought he would become, the king he was destined to be." Nobel's arrogance melted into a righteous fury. "I will stand beside my cousin when that time comes."

"You'll just let him take control of the clan?" That did not sound like Nobel at all. "That's generous of you."

Nobel rolled his eyes. "You have no idea how a vampire clan works. Yes, there is a king, but there is also a council. I will act as king until our dear Zain is fit for the role, if he chooses to join us. I will then assume my role as head advisor, as I was born to be. This, Sabryn, is how our lives were supposed to be until your murdering king decided we were the scourge of the earth and slaughtered us because of what we are." Nobel schooled himself and pulled his anger back in. "Depending on how the next few days go, you might get to see it happen."

Her heart lurched. "I thought you said I was worth gold? Or do you have another blood enchantress to fill my role?" Her voice came out weak. Between the ache in her bones, the hunger growing in her belly, and the defeat, Ryn didn't care. Survival mattered.

"Your death would be a loss, but whether you live or die will be up to your husband," Nobel said with a sly smile. "If he accepts my offer and joins us, he will want his mate at his side."

"Zain said if one mate dies, the others withers," she argued, desperately.

"It would be…difficult but not impossible for him to find another. Few mates have actually died from grief." Nobel glanced at his silver timepiece, then snapped it shut and dropped it back into his pocket. "I have used all the time I have. Take care, little dove. I will be back soon."

Nobel vanished again into the darkness, leaving Ryn to think over his words.

As soon as his footsteps vanished, she turned her attention to the tray. The bread was fresh, the grapes plump, the cheese free of mold. It was not a prisoner's meal. Nobel wanted her to eat. Wanted her alive.

"It's not poisoned."

Ryn jumped at the voice. The flaxen-haired vampire stood just within the shadows. At Ryn's attention, she stepped closer. She wore plain clothes on her slender frame, and a short summer cloak. As a vampire, she didn't need to dress against the winter cold. It took Ryn a moment to place the young face—she was among those who had ambushed Ryn and Zain with Neville.

"I thought vampires didn't eat?" Ryn tore off a piece of bread.

"We don't need but a fraction of the calories you do," said the vampire.

Ryn took a bite of the bread. It tasted like normal bread. She ate the entire chunk, and then started on the grapes. The vampire watched her, red-rimmed eyes watching her every move, like Ryn was the threat.

"Never seen someone eat before?" Ryn asked.

"This is as close as I've ever been to someone not like us," she whispered.

"That's bullshit." Ryn sipped the weak ale from the canteen. The vampire didn't say anything. "You were with Neville that night."

"I didn't want to go with them," the vampire confessed. Guilt shadowed her features. "My brother was there, and he said I had to go."

Ryn chewed a few grapes. "How can you live in Calcurta and not have been this close to someone who's not a vampire?"

"We remain out of sight." She twisted her fingers together over her stomach. "We're not allowed to go above ground until we are of age. Until then, we remained down here."

Meaning this female was too young to remember the era before Victor forced them underground. What would that life have been like? Growing up underground, never to feel the sunlight or walk through the market, or see the clouds or stars?

"That sounds awful." Ryn plopped an almond into her mouth. Roasted and salted. Maybe Nobel did care after all.

"It's for our own good."

Ryn snorted. "Did Nobel tell you that?"

"He did." The vampire female's voice shrank. "Young vampires need more blood to stave off their hunger. The need wanes with age. It's better for…everyone."

Ryn paused her chewing to take another look at the female. She stared at Ryn like a caged predator, but there was something underneath her weariness making Ryn nervous. Lu got the same longing in her eyes when they passed a chocolate shop. The almonds on Ryn's tongue turned to sawdust, and a primal fear scorched through the veins.

"Don't worry," the vampire whispered. "Nobel has the only key to your cell. He asked me to keep you company."

Ryn banished the fear from her features and focused on the food. She was a prisoner to vampires on the verge of a coup against the king who had driven them from their keep and slaughtered hundreds of their kind. Ryn was in their den, their home, and at their mercy. Prey among the bloodthirsty.

And with her treachery revealed to the Hunters, she doubted they would come save her. Even if they could.

She was on her own.

51
CAGED
Ryn

Ryn kept as far away from the iron bars as possible. The cold stone pressed into her back, into the ripped and picked silk of her dress. The flaxen-haired vampire remained in the shadow, just out of sight. Ryn could feel her stare, the hunger within it. A fox eyeing a rabbit, just as Ryn had stalked the silver rabbit into the Red Forest.

That fucking rabbit. It had started this—as if it had known what would come, who else was lurking in those woods.

If she had waited for Nobel's contract, what would have happened? Would she be in the city with Lu, away from this mess? Or would Nobel have dragged them both into it anyway?

Her injuries had faded, and it made her question how long she'd been unconscious between meeting Nobel in the bone pit and waking up here.

Whoever had bandaged her arm had removed the debris first. Odd treatment for a prisoner. It made her believe Nobel's words about keeping her alive.

Exhaustion crawled along her consciousness, and Ryn curled into a ball as far from the bars as she could.

Her dreams were scattered and vague. Sounds of creaking and snapping and hissing woke her, and she couldn't tell if the sounds were real or within her dreams. Each sound jerked her attention to the corridor, where shadows lingered thick as oil.

Then, at last, the definite sound of footsteps stirred her. She rolled over to see Nobel sauntering down the corridor. Two males in common clothes followed. At the sight, Ryn jumped to her feet. Her dirty wedding dress swished around her legs. The male on Nobel's left looked at her with pity, which felt worse than if he'd leered at her.

Nobel paused before her cell. "I wanted to make sure none of mine had broken into your cage, and to make sure you hadn't broken out." Smirking, he eyed the bars. "Some of the younger vampires have never seen a fae up close, and a few older vampires have…unsavory appetites for more than just blood."

"What do you want?" Ryn asked.

"The time has come." Nobel unlocked her cell door, and as the iron bars swung outward, her panic rose.

"Time for what?" She stumbled backward, into the rough wall.

Nobel wore no humor. "You will see. Come."

Ryn froze—fear coursed through her veins.

Nobel nodded to the vampire on his left, who then entered the cell. He grabbed Ryn by the arms and hauled her into the hall. While the world wobbled, the other vampire thrust a bag over her head. It didn't contain the knock-out drugs like the rag, but it didn't matter—panic flared her hot through her skin.

She struggled, her breaths coming shallow. Something told her she would rather be knocked-out for whatever happened next.

"Easy," came Nobel's smooth voice close to her right. A calm hand pressed against the middle of her back. "This will only be as bad as you make it, little dove."

Her panic thumped wilder, pulsing through her ears.

"Come on, Nobel, just a taste," whispered a raspy male voice. "Just *one*."

"No," Nobel snapped. "This one is a gift for our prince. Unless you would like to find out what happens when you sip from the king's wine."

Ryn tried to ask questions, to demand answers, but the bag seemed to cut off her air supply. Her words jumbled together in her throat. The vampires hauled her forward, toward her unknown destiny. Her gut trembled. She had a stout feeling she wouldn't make it out of the vampire den. Not as herself, at least.

Stories of vampire thralls threaded through folklore and nightmares. Thralls were used like cattle, to be fed upon by their vampire master. Others still were used like whores, chained to beds or walls, for their vampire lords to use them however they wanted. Ryn always wanted those stories to be just that: stories. She did not want to become a part of those stories, a shell of herself, unable to deny her master.

The vampires hauled her along. Voices began as soft murmurs, then grew. By the sound, the chamber widened. The sound of a hundred voices traveled upward, off stone. A cavern. A large one. The floor leveled and softened into packed dirt.

"And here we are," Nobel said.

He ripped the bag from her head, tossing her tangled hair around her face. She took a deep breath of the mineral-laden, musky air. Her eyes adjusted to the light. Ancient lanterns and hundreds of candles lit the massive cavern. Something frighteningly like blood stained the cavern floor.

The vampire shoved Ryn to the ground. She landed in an ungraceful heap of wine-stained white and gold. Laughter and cheers echoed off the cavern walls. To Ryn's horror, hundreds of vampires gathered at the cavern's edge and within shadowed balconies that scalloped up the cavern's walls. Hundreds of red-rimmed eyes gawked down at her.

Ryn and her ruined dress stood out in the shadows, as if the silk soaked the light to make it glow. A beacon among hungry vampires.

She swallowed. Fear trickled up her spine like frozen fingers.

"Bring him in," Nobel commanded.

From the far shadows, iron creaked and wood whined. Several vampires wheeled in a canvas-covered cage, not unlike those that carried livestock into the market. From within the cage, something hissed and growled, inhuman and furious. Her heart sped with each creak of the wheels.

Nobel stepped into her peripheral. He carried himself like a king, hands folded behind his back, shoulders back, chin high. The cart came to a stop. Nobel held up his hand, and silence fell around the chamber.

"Are you ready?" Nobel whispered in Ryn's ear.

"What?" she breathed. *For what?* Was this how she died? A show for these monsters? No, it couldn't be. Nobel wanted her alive!

Before she could voice these worries, Nobel signaled the vampires. They ripped the canvas from the cage.

Ryn felt her own heart stop, her lungs halt, and the floor shift from under her feet.

It was Zain.

Her husband.

Her very vampiric husband.

He still wore his dark green suit from the ball. His skin had paled to a deathly white. He looked thinner, shallow and gaunt. His eyes were wide and wild—bloodthirsty. Bright crimson circled his irises, almost swallowing the blue completely. Four pearly white fangs pierced his smile, ripe for sinking into flesh. He winced at the candlelight, at the sudden presence of hundreds of vampires staring down at him.

Then Zain paused. His nostrils flared. His head turned in her direction. Those crimson-rimmed eyes settled on her with a sharpness that settled in her gut like a hook.

"And our prince has found his target." Nobel grinned at Zain like a proud father. He leaned in close to Ryn's ear, and whispered, "Did you know, little dove, that when a vampire chooses a mate, they are able to pull their scent out of a crowded room?"

Ryn absently touched her neck.

"I smelled him on you at the ball," he whispered. "And he can smell it right now. He knows you are his. You also happen to be carrying around fresh blood, blood he craves with vigor. Your blood is a siren's call." He straightened and stepped away. "Did you know, little dove, that when a vampire goes without feeling long enough, they go into a frenzied state? Your kind have named it bloodlust. Fitting, I suppose. Right now, your husband can think of nothing else but his next meal. That concoction they fed him was barely food. It doused his hunger, concealed it. Without it, his cravings returned twice as fast as it would anyone else."

Zain's bloodshot sapphire eyes bore into hers. His jaw flexed and his lips twitched, like he was gnawing on something invisible.

"Mature vampires are able to go a week or two between feeds," said Nobel. "Children can't go more than a few days. Blood sustains us, but it also gives us a glimpse of mortality. If we drink more than we need, we can blend in with fae, like Zain was forced to, like we all were forced to." His words rose through the cavern. A few vampires let out whoops of agreement. "Every day without blood depletes humanity, until hunger is all they know."

While Ryn had been healing in a cell, Zain had been starving.

Nobel sauntered to the cage, careful not to cross Zain's gaze. He paused beside the cage and closed his fingers around the release bar—the only thing keeping it closed.

Ryn realized Nobel's plan with a sickening twist in her gut. "No, no! You can't—"

Noble's grin widened. "Oh, but I need to. He can't gallivant into the keep and seize control looking like this. No. Our prince must partake in our ancient rite of first blood, before his court, to claim his rightful place as king. You wouldn't understand." His grin turned mad. "And if you are truly mates, then he won't kill you. At least, I don't think he will."

Before she could take another breath, Nobel pulled the latch. The door swung out with a vicious squeal of old iron.

At first, nothing happened.

Then Zain realized no bars separated him from her. He took a wobbled albeit graceful and predatory step forward, then another, and then he stood on the solid ground of the cavern. He wobbled like a drunk, yet his razor-sharp gaze and sneering lips made him into a nightmare; poised like a prince yet hunched like a predator. Nobel took quiet steps away, one hand on the blade at his side as he put space between himself and Zain. The other vampires on the cavern floor did the same.

Not that it mattered. Zain hadn't looked away from Ryn.

"Zain," she whispered, scrambling to her feet.

He gave no indication he'd heard or registered his own name. Before she could say another word, with unnatural speed, he charged.

52

BLOOD

Ryn

Zain slammed into Ryn, and they both hit the ground hard. His vise-like grip fastened around her arms. His legs pinned hers to the ground. He bared his fangs at her, pearly white and poised to strike. The madness in his eyes did not recognize her. Bloodlust twisted him into the nightmare she'd always thought vampires were.

"Zain!" Her voice cracked.

He paused. Was he hesitating with compassion? Or sizing up the best way to kill her?

Then, with his impossible speed, he lunged. She didn't have time to scream. His fangs sank into her neck with a sickening pop that rattled all the way down to her toes. He pulled the blood from her pulse, a little more with every suck and swallow. His first few swallows had been desperate, starving, but each after slowed. He was savoring each. Lavishing each.

Ryn felt it leaving her veins and organs, felt the strain on her heart and mind. She knew exactly how much blood was within the body and how much one could lose before death became unavoidable. Zain was taking too much.

If they were mates…he couldn't…

Darkness and weakness seeped into the emptiness left behind, pulling her soul farther away from her body.

She supposed this was some divine justice for all the death she had dealt. This was…what she deserved.

Thoughts…became difficult. Foggy.

Death had been lurking since Ryn wandered into the Red Forest, since she had taken her first contract from Nobel. She had avoided death's clutches for years. Her luck had run out. Along with her blood supply. Death's cold hands lingered at the edges of her consciousness, as tight as Zain's hand wrapped in her hair.

No—blood, she knew blood. She had made a career of bloodletting. She reached into her fleeting bloodstream, and she pulled it back. Away from her throat, away from the punctures.

Zain hesitated. A small thrill of hope bloomed within her panic. She could still survive, she could—

Light burst across her vision.

She peeled her gummy eyes open. Sunlight—bright, unrelenting, winter sunlight—poured into the cavern from a hole far above. Figures fell through the sunlight, darkly clad and furious. Cries of panic and fear and fury erupted all around her, echoing off the walls. Rock creaked and groaned as debris crashed to the cavern floor. Somehow, it missed Ryn and Zain.

Pain flared as Zain withdrew from her pulse. He hovered over her, mouth and fangs bloodied. The bright crimson in his eyes had faded to a line circle of rust. Was it her dying imagination, or did he look terrified?

She tried to say his name. She felt her lips move, form his name, but no sound came out.

Zain howled—his pain and grief surged through the cavern like a frigid wind. The shrillness seemed to shatter the very air, undulating the light streaming from above, fracturing the balance of vampires. Ryn felt it, felt the moments that followed, a strange and unearthly confusion. A male voice called from somewhere, and this time Ryn recognized the leathers of the Hunters charging toward the dazed vampires.

Tears lined Zain's blue eyes. His lips moved, pleaded, but she heard only a ringing. A rush. Death pulling her onto the other side.

She blinked, and Zain was gone. Shadows and light danced. Steel glinted. Blood splattered stone. Fire raged above.

Ryn rolled onto her side. Her body felt like sand. She'd stopped Zain, but…not in time. She had always wondered what death felt like, what those she drained felt in the moments after she took too much, when death came for them.

Hands hauled her to her feet. Someone carried her away from the light and fire and commotion.

Voices spoke—barely audible over the roar in her ears.

"…out of here," came the somber and commanding voice of Nobel. It was his voice in her ear. "Take her. I will deal with the prince."

Nobel made to hand her off, but something within Ryn snapped. All of this was Nobel's fault. He'd orchestrated the vampires, rallied them, kidnapped her and Zain, forced her husband into bloodlust, used her as bait—a desperate, vengeful rage stole over her senses.

Ryn dug her nails into Nobel's wrist, between his sleeve and his gloves—the nails Kari had painted three times and filed into fashionable points. Her nails sank into Nobel's skin, harder and harder, until she felt the first drop of blood.

Nobel spat a curse, but one drop was all she needed.

Blood. That is what she needed. Her body needed it. Warm, life-saving blood pumped through Nobel's body, fueling his organs, pretending to be what he was not. Her magic threaded through his veins, desperate not to die, fueled with visceral fear of death and burning need for vengeance. He stilled—as she enchanted his stolen blood. She threaded it out of his wrist, around her nails, and into the puncture marks on her neck.

It wasn't graceful; it was desperate. Her magic trembled. Most of the blood followed her instruction and entered her bloodstream, but some dripped onto her gown, soaking into the white silk, dripping down Nobel's fingers.

She refused to give up, to let Nobel use her, to let him hurt Zain anymore than he already had. She refused to let him get away with what he had done to Lu.

With every heartbeat, her vision and thoughts cleared. Death retreated. Nobel glared at her, frozen by her enchantment, furious and fearful. The other vampire watched with wide, confused eyes. Nobel fought back, but no one had ever managed to break her enchantment. The rings around his eyes grew bright and bloodied as she stole the blood from his veins. His heart skipped and shuddered, his lungs paused, his muscles seized—but he didn't begin to die like a fae would. His emotions didn't cease with the beating of his heart.

Instead, Nobel grew wild, feral with bloodlust.

Even without a drop of blood in his body, he would not die.

And she knew that when she released him, he would be pissed. At her. With all the unnatural speed and perchance of violence of a bloodless vampire.

So she didn't take every drop. She left a small bottle's worth and enchanted it into shards that tore through the walls of his heart, his lungs, his liver, his brain. His eyes widened, and as she released her enchantment, he crumbled to the ground in an ungraceful heap of pale skin and bulging, lightless eyes.

"What did you…" The other vampire stumbled back, eyes on Nobel. He held steel in his hands, but his grip trembled.

Ryn chuckled, the sound deep and throaty. The vampire looked up at her. He adjusted his grip to defend, not to attack.

From the cavern, the fight raged. Fire flickered.

"Your leader is dead," Ryn said, her voice uneven. A fierce wave of nausea sent her doubling over. Swallowing the bile, she forced herself to stand straight. Nobel's enchanted vampire blood mingled with her own, tingling in a way that blood should not. Like her bloodstream burned.

Ryn closed her hand around the bite mark on her throat. She tugged on the enchanted blood fighting her own. She needed the blood to mingle with hers, to connect, to blend. Nobel fought her even in death.

Death laughed at her.

The vampire stepped back, away from her. Sword readied to defend.

Ryn didn't know how to fight. She had no weapon. She had a bloodied wedding dress and spent magic. In a voice stronger than she felt and ragged with pain, she hissed, "Get out of here, unless you want to end up like Nobel."

The vampire didn't hesitate. He sheathed his blade and bolted down the passage into the darkness.

Ryn stumbled into the wall and vomited the pitiful contents of her stomach.

53

RIGHTFUL VAMPIRE KING

Zain

He had never tasted anything as sweet, as addictive, as life-giving. He had never felt such heart-wrenching grief. The maddening daze wore off with every beat of his heart. Clarity pulsed in its place, with each drop of sweet, sweet, blood that filled his veins.

He stumbled backward, the sight of Ryn's bloodless face staining his vision. No. No. No.

Anyone but her.

Anyone.

His grief tightened around his heart and lungs, squeezing his insides painfully.

Within his bleary vision, light burst from the ceiling and figures descended like crows, steel and leather and shouts. The sounds clattered together in his ears, churning his confusion. The figures blurred together as they danced. Zain stumbled backward, into the bars of the cage.

His cage.

Nobel had locked him away. Starved him into this…monster. Tried to make him kill his wife, his mate.

"You don't know who you are," Nobel had told him, standing on the safe side of the bars.

Then Nobel had told him who he was. The only son of King Seymour and Queen Moira. The rightful king of the vampires. The painted dark-haired female swam through Zain's vision in those dark hours locked in the cage. His mother. Queen Moira. King Victor had kept it secret all these years.

His mother, the dead vampire queen.

His father, the dead vampire king.

Both murdered by the male he called Father.

Zain was not the half-vampire bastard he'd thought, but a prince of a different kind.

"Once you gain control of your powers, you will be as strong as your father," Nobel had said, staring at Zain like a prized carnival animal. "Maybe stronger yet. Those murderers in the keep have kept you weak, doused your true nature with poison. Victor knows who you are, and he keeps you as a pet." Nobel had bared his fangs in anger. "We will dismantle this false fae empire, destroy our oppressors, and the man who slaughtered our family. And you, my prince, will become the king you were destined to be."

As the bloodlust had set in, Nobel's speech resounded. King. King. King.

Zain blinked, and the cavern returned. Vampires and Hunters fought, and Ryn—Ryn was gone. Rage tore through his grief, for he would rip apart anyone who dared touch her. He started toward where she had been, but a hand fastened around his arm.

"Brother!"

Zain knew that voice. He turned to face the male that was not his brother, not even half.

Esben took in Zain's ragged suit, his bloodied lips. Zain saw the disbelief in Esben's hazel eyes, saw it dissolve into morbid realization. Esben pulled his hand back, and his other tightened around the hilt of his Hunter's sword.

"Zain?" Esben hissed the name like a plea.

The blood pulsed deeper into Zain's heart, into his fingers and toes. The shouts were not as maddening, his vision not as blurred.

"I…killed her," Zain gasped. Hot tears pushed against his eyes.

His wife. His mate. The first female to see the real him, to stir his cold heart to feel love again, and Zain had killed her.

Again.

The panic and grief spiraled deeper, shaking his breaths and bones, pushing against his eyes and thoughts until he knew little else. Shame brought him to his knees.

He deserved to die by Hunter steel. Like the monster he was.

"Now you see him for what he is," came a familiar male voice. Footsteps approached, and then stopped at Zain's side. "What we are."

"Neville," Esben spat. "What have you done?"

"I've done nothing," Neville said innocently. "I am defending our prince from your murderous ways."

"I am here for my brother," Esben growled.

Neville took a step in front of Zain. "You have no brother."

Esben lunged forward and Neville met his blade. Zain couldn't move; he could only watch as his former brother and former guard fought with death in their eyes. Over him, like he meant something. Esben had brought Hunters to the cavern to find him. In that moment, Zain didn't care if Esben's intentions had been to kill him or not. He had come for him.

"Where is she?" Esben spat.

"You needn't worry over your princess," Neville said, his words a taunt. "She belongs to our prince, if she survives."

If she survives? Ryn was still alive?

Zain forced himself to stand. In that moment, Esben's attention flickered from Neville and to Zain; Neville saw the chance, and angled his next blow— Zain moved on instinct, faster than he could before, and used his momentum to shove Esben out of the way. Neville's blade instead sliced through Zain's side, and Ryn's warm blood spilled onto his ruined suit.

Neville stumbled back a step. "What are you doing?"

Zain held his ground. He planted his feet firmly, just as Neville had long ago taught him. He met the eyes of his former guard. In a ragged voice, Zain spat, "I am defending my brother."

"You're one of us," Neville spat.

"No, I'm not," Zain growled, the inhuman sound rolling off this throat.

"You were meant to be our *king*." Neville spat the words with desperate venom.

Zain laughed, the sound grating even on his own ears. Vile, just like the monster he was. Shaking his head, he grinned. "No, Neville. I wasn't. I was destined to die, just like my parents, just like all the others. Fate played a cruel joke to allow me to live."

Esben offered his blade to Zain, and he closed his hand around the hilt. Zain focused on Neville, who had betrayed him, nearly killed him and Ryn, who had tried to kill Esben.

Zain felt a vigor he had longed for without knowing what it was, a vigor his tonic had suppressed. He surged toward Neville with all the vampire strength and vitality he never knew he was capable of. Neville met his blows, defending; Zain saw the reluctance in Neville's eyes, in his stance. He didn't want to fight Zain, his damned prince, but Zain wanted to hurt Neville.

Before that reluctance ran out, Zain feinted, then drove his sword into Neville's middle. Neville dodged, but not fast enough. The blade sliced through his left side, and before he recovered, Zain yanked the blade free and drove it into Neville's heart.

He yanked the blade free and kicked Neville's body to the ground.

Each breath came a little easier, and with each beat of his heart, the roaring in his ears subsided. The cavern was deathly quiet. Zain glanced up from Neville's body. Hunters lingered at the edges of the cavern, watching Zain and Esben in its center. Vampires lay dead at their feet. The balconies were empty.

Esben approached with caution. Zain adjusted his grip on the hilt, then offered the blade back to his brother. It left Zain defenseless, but he felt far from it. The motion did not go unnoticed by the Hunters. Zain saw the uncertainty in their faces, the way most still held their blades, the way they gave Zain distance, the way they monitored his proximity to Esben.

Esben wiped the blade clean on Neville's clothes then sheathed it. He set his hand on Zain's shoulder. "Well done, Brother."

His words resounded through the cavern, and every Hunter heard. His words reassured them that Zain was still their prince, despite his fangs and bloodied teeth. Irene was the first to sheath her blade. Captain Colby followed. Slowly, each Hunter sheathed his or her blade. It signaled that the threat had been dealt with, that the battle was over.

That Zain was not a threat.

Relief sagged on Zain's shoulder. It was the acceptance that Zain feared he would never have, that he did not deserve.

Esben's lips curved in a knowing smile. "See?"

Raggedly, Zain said, "Let's hope Father shares the same sentiment."

"Before that, we have a princess to find."

<h1 style="text-align:center">54</h1>

ENCHANTED

Ryn

Ryn slumped against the stone wall of the tunnel. Nobel's body was cold at her feet. From his blood in her veins and his blood spilled on the ground, she felt the void where his soul had been. It had departed, and he was dead.

But she had glimpsed it. His soul had been dark at the edges, but it lacked oily evil or corruption. He had fully believed in the good of his cause. He had believed that he was doing justice for his kind, avenging his king and queen. His deeds had not blackened his soul.

Did that make him right?

No. Believing in something did not justify murder. Murder in the name of justice was still murder.

She had never felt a soul like his, one capable of such horrible things, yet untainted.

Ryn closed her eyes and focused on the vengeful vampire blood thumping against her magic, against her own. Fighting. It did not want to be inside of her. It knew it did not belong. Her enchantment only did so much, but every time she untwisted a thread of angry blood, another replaced it. It took every bit of control she had, every beat of magic she hadn't already spent to keep it from shredding her from the inside out.

"Here, she's here!" came a voice she vaguely knew.

Peeling her eyes open, Irene knelt in front of her. Blood congealed in the Hunter's hair, and more spotted her face. Several deep cuts marred her leather armor. One of them on her lower left side bled. Irene grinned, the small action brightening up her entire face. Panic thumped through Ryn's entire being. Irene *never* smiled.

"There you are," Irene said. "Good to see you're not dead."

"Not yet," Ryn whispered, her voice threaded with the effect to keep her blood from forcing itself through her skin. Her eyes drifted closed.

Footsteps, and a strong hand settled on her shoulder. She forced her eyes open. Esben knelt at her side. He too sported several spots of blood and battle.

"Ryn," Esben said, his voice urgent. "Ryn, can you hear me?"

She swallowed and tried to speak, but words jumbled in her throat. Nothing in her body wanted to work on its own accord. She just needed…rest for a while.

"Your Highness," came a consoling male voice. "She might be too far gone. She was bitten by a frenzied vampire. It might be best to end her suffering."

It took Ryn a moment to focus on the blond Hunter behind Esben. Captain Colby.

"No," Esben ordered. He bent closer. "Ryn, please, can you hear me?"

She put all her effort into nodding. Her lips formed his name, but barely a whisper came out. She swallowed and tried again. This time, his name tumbled as a gasp. "Zain?"

Esben started to speak, when the familiar unfeeling tone drifted over his shoulder, "I'm all right, all things considered."

Zain appeared at Colby's elbow. His suit was ruffled and torn, and blood speckled the collar and front of his shirt. Her blood. His sapphire eyes met hers—nearly all the red was gone, save for a sliver around his irises. His expression tore through her. Rather than the cold, unfeeling prince, he wore shame and guilt and grief. Tears gathered in his dark lashes.

He started forward with an exaggerated gait, like he wasn't sure how to move in his own skin. He sported a wound on his side, but it had already started to clot. Strange vampire magic, she was sure. Zain knelt at her side, and his shame melted into cold fear and wrenching grief.

Ryn sucked in her breath—she felt his emotions so sharply, so viscerally. Was it her blood in his veins, or was it Nobel's blood in her own? Was this what it was to be a thrall?

Zain cupped her cheek, his touch warm against her frigid skin. She hadn't realized how cold she was.

To Esben, Zain asked, "Will she be all right?"

Esben shared a look with Irene. Colby didn't look hopeful. He watched Ryn like a cat might watch a hawk.

They didn't think she would live. Ryn shuddered. Panic and dread threaded through the rebellious blood. Tears pushed against her eyes, too warm for her cold skin.

"I don't know," Esben said at last. "I don't know what will happen within the next few hours. But we need to get her out of here. She needs a healer."

Esben stood, and Zain easily lifted Ryn into his arms. Colby and Irene closed in on their flanks.

"Watch her for signs," Esben said softly. "I…don't think I will be able to do it."

"I will, Your Highness," said Colby.

It took several heartbeats before Ryn understood what Esben meant. Signs of being a thrall. If Zain had accidentally turned her. Once a body became a thrall, there was no reversing it. The only cure was death.

Zain held her close, like he knew.

She felt his emotions pulse in time with her heart. Rage at those who hurt her. Shame for what he had done to her. If she became his thrall, it would be his fault. He would not allow her to live as his mindless captive.

Zain had bitten her in a frenzied bloodlust, and everything she knew about vampires said she should have died or become his thrall. She didn't feel like a thrall, but what would it feel like?

She tried to reach into his emotions to tell him it would be okay, but her body refused. Her mind refused. Too much of her concentration went to calming the barbed blood within her. One drop at a time, she enchanted it to stay. To calm. To be hers. To keep her heart pumping. It might have been her imagination, but the burning had lessened.

She had never ingested enchanted blood, let alone enchanted vampire blood. Nobel would've had to get it from someone else, so whose blood currently flowed through her? Had it come from one of her bottles? As her concentration wavered, she decided she didn't want to know.

Somewhere along the trek through the undercroft, Ryn fell into a strange sleep. She felt everything happening around her, yet dreamy shadows slithered between her and consciousness. She finally came to surrounded by blankets, pillows, the cool scent of spearmint. She was in her bedroom in Nightshade Keep, the familiar bed with its drapes tied at the posts. A fire burned in the hearth. The air was warm. Pale sunlight drifted in from between the curtains, the drowsy light of a clear and cold dawn.

The din of voices rang from the sitting room, muted by the fire and the walls.

Someone stirred, and then calm footsteps sounded across her floor. Irene paused at the bedside, Captain Colby at her side.

"How are you feeling?" Irene asked.

"Thirsty." Ryn's voice croaked.

Irene poured a glass of water from the pitcher and handed it to Ryn. Sitting up, Ryn took a long drink. The cool water washed down her scratchy throat and into her dust-filled chest. She took another sip, then another.

Ryn no longer wore her ballgown. Instead, she wore a plain nightdress. Her dirty hair was braided back. She took another drink of water. Both Hunters wore caution, like prey watching an uneasy predator.

Colby sat on the bedside. "Your Highness, I have a few questions for you."

She snagged on the title. Yes, she and Zain had married. They had paraded about the city. She was, legally, his wife, his princess.

The strange feeling of being a princess subsided. She nodded at Colby. "Okay."

"How do you feel?"

"Like shit."

"Can you elaborate?"

She blinked at him. Would it be rude to throw the rest of her water at him? "Like I was drugged, beat up, and spit out."

Irene and Colby shared an unreadable glance.

"Okay," Colby said, nodding. "I am going to ask you a few more questions. Easy ones. Answer honestly. What was your mother's name?"

"Edith."

"What color was her hair?"

"Brown, but lighter than mine." Ryn absently tucked a stray hair behind her ear. "My father's name was Ted, though I think it was short for something. His hair was dark brown, like mine. His eyes were also brown."

"Do you think they're worried?"

"They're dead, so probably not."

"How did they die?"

Unease slithered into the comfort she had found while asleep. "My father died of infection. My mother died of the winter fever."

"Do you have any living family?"

"Lu, my sister." Ryn frowned. The Hunters knew this. But thinking of her sister sprang forward the familiar panic. "She escaped Nobel during the ball. Is she okay? Is she here? He had her in some kind of trance. Zain broke it when he pushed me. He…"

Neither Irene nor Colby looked worried. Rather, they looked curious.

"What?" Ryn demanded.

"She appears normal," Irene said.

Ryn blinked, then she realized. They were making sure she wasn't a thrall. Annoyance slipped through her panic, along with a stout fear. "Would I know if I were a thrall?"

"I've never had this detailed of a conversation with a thrall," Colby said, standing. "They are unable to think, unable to ask questions of their own or give complex answers. So, you pass."

Yet neither Hunter looked enthused.

"What's wrong?" Ryn asked, looking at Irene.

"Ryn, you were bitten by a frenzied vampire," Irene said. "It doesn't make sense. You shouldn't be alive."

"What happened?" Colby asked. His calm gaze grew intense.

"I…" Ryn swallowed. "I took blood from a vampire."

"I'm sorry, what?" Irene blinked at Ryn, as if she had misheard.

She wouldn't be able to hide it from them, not after what she had done. Looking into her water, she said lowly, "I can enchant blood."

"You…have magic?" Colby whispered, his eyes wide and his lips slack. "But you're not a vampire."

Ryn shook her head. "I've always been able to do it. I worked for Nobel, bottling it. It was…the best work I could get without whoring myself."

Colby looked at her like he had never seen her before. "You enchanted blood from a vampire to be your own?" He paced to the window and back to the bed, aghast. "We've never had a situation like this before."

Ryn's panic stirred anew. "Please, I didn't do anything I didn't have to. I'm not—"

"You're not in trouble," Colby cut her off. "Ryn, you are a pure blood fae with magic. Don't you know what this means?"

She paled. "Do I want to know?"

Irene laughed. "You're special, is what he means."

"We haven't seen magic in fae blood in generations," Colby said. "The king and queen will need to hear about this."

"What will they do?" Ryn asked, fearing the answer.

Irene harrumphed. "Likely ask you to have as many kids as possible to ensure your bloodline continues."

Ryn groaned.

"There's also the matter of what might happen to you," Colby said, excitement waning. "If you enchanted the blood, I have no idea what might happen next. The scholars are looking into records of thralls, but this…this changes things."

"For the better, hopefully," Irene added pointedly at Colby.

"Yes, I agree. Fae magic has been thought to be gone forever," Colby said. To Ryn, he smiled. "This proves that magic still exists."

Ryn fell back into the pillows. "Is there anything else I should know? Is Zain okay?"

Silence greeted her answer. Ryn pushed herself back into a sitting position and met Irene's guarded expression.

"Where is he?" Ryn demanded. Her heart clenched. She vaguely remembered halting his feeding. "Is he okay?"

"Zain is speaking with the king," Irene said. "In his chambers. The king thought it best to confine the two of you until the dust settles."

"Word of Zain's true nature has spread," Colby added. "His Majesty fears the repercussions. The Hunters who were there saw Zain defend Esben, but there were others who were not there."

"Rumors have also spread how Zain rushed to save his wife from the vampires that kidnapped her," Irene added with a slight frown.

Lies, but those lies might save Zain's reputation.

"It's quite the tale," Colby said. "The servants have eaten it up, especially the kitchen staff."

"Would you care for something to eat?" Irene asked. "Tea? Wine?"

"Wine, please," Ryn said, not hiding the desperation in her words. "And something with cheese. Maybe one of my boxes of chocolate?"

Irene went to pass on the order for food. Kari skirted into the bedroom holding three boxes of chocolates, and Colby stepped into the sitting room so Ryn could wash and change. Kari recounted all the gossip she'd heard—how Zain was a vampire but on the Hunters' side, how he saved Esben from the vampires—while scrubbing the grim and dirt from Ryn's hair. Ryn nibbled on chocolate.

It gave her a spike of pride to know she could halt a vampire's attack. It stole a fear that had long lived inside her, of what vampires could do—she could push them back. They were not invulnerable to her magic.

Considering she was married to one, it was a comfort she didn't know she needed.

Dried and feeling much better, Kari helped Ryn dress in a plain dress meant for lounging and a woolen cardigan.

Ryn was sore and stiff, like she hadn't moved in days. With Kari on one side and Colby on the other, she made her way into the sitting room where her wine and cheese awaited. Irene and Colby posted themselves in the sitting room. Ryn helped herself first to the wine, draining half a glass, then refilling it.

"Easy," came Esben's somber voice. He leaned against the window.

Ryn blinked. She hadn't noticed him, though she hadn't looked past the wine.

Esben had washed off the blood of battle and changed into casual clothes. Bags hung under his eyes, and a bone-deep worry underlined his expression. He pushed off the wall and meandered to the table.

"Ryn," Esben said in greeting. "How are you feeling?"

"She's not a thrall as far as we can tell," Colby answered.

Esben blew out a breath of relief. "Good."

"She has magic," Irene said quickly. "Fae magic."

Esben's brows rose, but he looked too exhausted to show much more surprise. "What?"

Ryn quickly explained her ability to enchant blood, and how she had used it to steal blood from Nobel.

Esben heaved a sigh and sat down in the chair across from her. "No more surprises for a while, please." He rubbed his face. "This is wonderful news, though. Fae magic hasn't been seen in generations."

"Yes, yes, children and whatnot." Ryn rolled her eyes and bit into a tangy slice of cheese. "How is Zain?"

Esben glanced at Zain's closed bedroom doors, and the king's guards just outside it. "He is talking with Father."

"How is the king?"

"He is…" Esben hesitated. Uncertainty came over his features.

Ryn plopped a piece of tangy cheese on her tongue and followed it with wine. "There is still poison in his blood."

Esben nodded.

"I can pull it out," Ryn said casually, refilling her wine glass.

Esben gawked at her. "You…?"

Pointing to herself, she said, "Blood enchantress."

"Okay." Esben said, nodding. "But eat first. Give them time. Then we'll talk about poison and blood."

Ryn drained the rest of her wine, then poured herself another glass. To Irene, she said, "I'm going to need another bottle."

55

THE SECOND SON OF THE WARRIOR KING

Zain

Zain had washed his mouth out with soap and whiskey, yet he could still taste her sweet blood on his tongue and in his teeth.

The Hunters had escorted him straight to his chambers. They hadn't locked the door, but Zain refused to leave. He had paced all night, unable to sleep or read or do anything but replay the night before.

He was a vampire, a known vampire, surrounded by Hunters who hated his kind. Son of the dead king. Son of the king who had slaughtered fae for sport. Who had let his own run rampant and without restraint.

Yet no one had barged into his chambers to kill Zain. No one had come for his head.

He expected it. The night had been doused in terrifying silence. Zain had spent it waiting for marching footsteps, the horns to signal an execution, for a mob to gather at the keep's gate.

He hadn't opened his curtains to see if a mob gathered. The hearth was cold. A stark darkness settled in his bedroom, a darkness he had always found cozy. He realized now it was his vampire nature that longed for the dark and cold, and why he fatigued easily in the warm, sunny days.

Then, after dawn began to glow, footsteps sounded in the sitting room. Zain paused his pacing, heart racing, skin clammy and cold. The footsteps marched across the floor, to Zain's bedroom door. A swift fist struck the wood.

"Yes?" Zain answered, the single word quivering.

The door opened, and King Victor lumbered inside. He still leaned on his cane. His retinue began to follow, but the king held up his hand. "Leave us."

None looked happy about leaving him alone. His personal guard opened his mouth to argue.

"Leave us," King Victor said again, this time as a command.

Victor shut the door, leaving the two of them in darkness. Without a word, he knelt by the hearth and took the time to light a fire. The spark spread into the dry wood, spreading its amber light over the shadows. Victor took the time to open the curtains, allowing the cold dawn light to filter inside. Then, once the light filled the space, he sat in the armchair by the hearth. His exhausted, sickly gaze settled on Zain.

The king was still ill from the poison. He looked like a ghost of himself, pale and weak.

Ryn's enchanted poison.

"You have questions," King Victor said. "Ask them. I will hold nothing from you."

"Aren't you afraid to be in here with me?"

"No." The king shook his head. "We have been alone in this room before. You were a vampire then, just as you are now. The only difference is you are aware."

A dozen questions rushed to the front of Zain's mind, but the most prominent was, "Why?" The word fell as a plea from Zain's lips.

Victor held Zain's gaze without flinching. "When I led the invasion against the Abrani clan, I had only revenge on my mind. They murdered my father, my brother, and turned my brother's wife into one of their thralls." Pain flickered over his face. "They killed hundreds of us, turned children into slaves, wives and sisters into their whores, friends into thralls. I wanted bloodshed and violence. I realize now I acted no better than those I called enemies." Victor took a deep breath. He looked older then. A king worn by war and loss. "I led the Hunters into the stronghold. We had the upper hand, because they assumed we would be mourning, that we would be in shambles without our king and crown prince. Seymore and Moira were asleep, poisoned by a spy who had slipped belladonna into the wine supply. After I had slain them, I heard a baby cry from the next room. I…I didn't know they had a child. Esben wasn't yet a year old, and I knew the sound of a babe's cry well. I found you in a bassinet, a few weeks old."

Zain couldn't move. Every word Victor said drove a strange needling sensation deeper into his bones.

"I could not bring myself to kill an infant," Victor said. "Had I been the male I was before Esben was born, I would not have hesitated. But hearing a babe's wail struck a chord in my heart I did not have before becoming a father." He leaned back in the chair, eyes on his hands. His eyes misted. "I brought you home where my wife was sick in bed, having recently suffered a miscarriage," Victor continued. "I…thought if we raised you as our own, you would be like us, rather than the vile king who would have raised you to be like him, like this Nobel monster. I am glad to see that I was right in that regard." A small smile came over Victor's face. "We had no means of feeding you the blood you needed, and we used prisoners slated for execution at first. It took years for the alchemist to perfect the tonic for you, to curb the red in your eyes, the pallor of your skin." Chuckling, Victor added, "You bit one of the servants who was tending to the nursery. We could not let her leave after that, knowing what you were."

Zain felt a chill. "You killed her?"

"Oh no, no. We promoted her. She now oversees the kitchens."

Zain rolled his eyes. Of course. "That's why that old bat hates me."

Victor laughed, though it lacked his usual mirth. A cough followed it, then a pained expression. "She is one of the few who knew."

"Why did you keep so many vampire books and relics? Why the painting of the dead queen?" Zain couldn't quite bring himself to call the strange female *mother*. In his mind, when he thought of his mother, he thought of Queen Portia.

"To learn," Victor said. "I had no idea how to raise a vampire, and after we took the keep, I wanted to avoid such bloodshed in the future. I wanted to learn about vampires and see if there was any way we could live together, as one people rather than two."

"But you hate vampires," Zain said.

"I did, once." King Victor wore grief. "I was so overwhelmed with rage and a desire for revenge that I listened to no logic. I wanted bloodshed, and I got it. I have often wondered if I could have avoided it, but it is too late to change things. What is done is done, and we cannot change it. Sometimes, I can still smell the blood and fire of that night."

The wind whistled through the eaves. Zain gazed out the window. Hunters patrolled the wall as they always had. No mob gathered beyond the gates.

"That night, when I took you from your bassinet…" Victor looked down at his hands, as if he could still feel the ghost of blood on them.

Zain felt the hesitation, and demanded, "What?"

Victor swallowed. "Moira was not dead. She heard the cry of her child. She… She struggled to get to you. She saw me, holding her child, and such fear came over her, that I could not help but think of Portia and Esben. Moira begged me to spare you with her last breath, and I promised her that no harm would come to you."

Zain thought of the dark-haired female in the portrait, Moira. His mother. Bleeding and dying, begging for his life from her greatest enemy. His stomach twisted painfully.

"I kept her portrait to remind myself of that promise," Victor confessed. "And in case one day I told you the truth, I could show you. But as fate would have it, you found her yourself." Victor lifted his gaze to meet Zain's. "Forgive me, Zain. I was a bullheaded youth with a thirst for vengeance. If you wish to be rid of me, I will not hold it against you. You have every right to be furious with me. But know this: you will always have a home here. You are my son, regardless of bloodlines."

"Even as I am?" Zain whispered.

"Even as you are." The king nodded. "I treated you differently than Esben because I feared someone discovering the truth. I feared the Hunters discovering the secret, though now I see how easily vampires vanished into their ranks. I also feared you discovering the truth, and what you would think of me. I didn't know how to explain what I had done without making myself into the villain."

Zain had gone over what he would say to his father, but he hadn't been able to garner hatred for him. Victor had raised him, and knowing now what he hadn't known then, Zain couldn't blame Victor. Zain felt no longing for the life he never had, for the parents he had never known, for the vampire reign that no longer existed. If Seymore's reign was anything like the world Nobel promised and Neville craved, Zain wanted nothing to do with it. He would rather be the second-born prince in this world than a king in Nobel's.

"I understand what you did," Zain said. His next words fizzled as they formed, eliciting an uncomfortable vulnerability. "This will always be home, and you will always be my father."

King Victor beamed, and in a few long-legged strides, crossed the space between them and enveloped Zain in an embrace. Zain couldn't remember the last time his father hugged him, not since he was a child. He awkwardly returned the embrace. King Victor broke away and held Zain at arm's length.

"I was worried this meeting would have a different outcome," the king said. "I'm proud of the male you've become."

Zain felt an unwelcome dampness in his eyes. He wiped at his eyes, shrugging off the king's arms. "What happens now?"

"The Hunters are singing your praises," Victor said. "They are telling everyone how you saved Esben and fought alongside the Hunters, despite being a vampire yourself. Esben told me what happened in the cavern, and I have informed the Hunters that you are still my son."

"And the Hunters are fine with it? The council?"

"Your brother has sworn to fight any Hunter who thinks otherwise," Victor said proudly.

A door opened within the sitting room. Footsteps and voices followed.

"It seems your wife has arrived in the sitting room," Victor said.

Zain's heart skipped. "Ryn? She's all right?"

Her voice chimed from the sitting room, muted by the door. Her voice.

Zain, still feeling like a stranger in his own skin, hurried to the bedroom door. He paused before it, regained himself, then entered the sitting room. Ryn's hazel gaze met his across the room, well-rested and warm. She sat at the table with Esben, sipping wine and nibbling cheese. Irene and Colby stood on guard.

Every pair of eyes was looking at Zain, but he saw only hers. He started toward her. Esben stood, and Zain took his place at the table.

Ryn poured him a glass of wine.

Zain sipped the wine and helped himself to a piece of cheese. Ryn sipped her wine, eyes pinned on him.

"How are you feeling?" Ryn asked, her voice softened by sleep. Her gaze wandered over his plain black shirt and trousers.

"A bit like death warmed over." Zain hadn't bothered to prepare himself. His hair was clean but ruffled. His skin was pale, though not the ghostly pale it had been, according to Esben. His eyes were free of red. He had checked every so often in the bathroom mirror.

"You looked a bit like it too." Ryn's lips curved in a tentative smile.

Zain chuckled.

Ryn's eyes flashed over his shoulder, and she stood. "Your Majesty," she started. She fumbled with her next words.

Esben stepped to his father's side and spoke lowly, so that only the king could hear. Zain watched the expression shift from surprise to horror and then into his kingly mask of impassive authority. He eyed Ryn with a masked emotion, but the intensity of it trickled down Zain's spine.

"Is that so?" Victor held his stare on Ryn. "That is good to hear. Very good. We shall meet in the healer's ward after breakfast."

The king as his retinue departed, leaving the chamber feeling strangely empty. Esben remained, as did Colby and Irene. Ryn stood until the doors closed, then she plopped back into her chair with an exasperated sigh.

"What did I miss?" Zain asked.

"I can remove the poison from your father's blood," Ryn confessed. "After breakfast, apparently."

Zain blinked at Ryn, then Esben and Irene and Colby, who had heard her.

"They already know," Ryn said. In a single breath, she added, "I told them when I woke up. They said I should've died, but I didn't, and then I had to tell them how I stole Nobel's blood and enchanted it to be mine." She finished with a gulp of wine.

"We are losing all our secrets, love." Zain tipped his wineglass toward hers.

"It's not that bad."

A servant arrived with a familiar covered tray. He set it in front of Zain without a word and lifted the lid.

His tonic.

He stared into the muddy red drink.

Silence fell around the room. Everyone watched. He would need to drink the blasted tonic, he supposed, to stem the vampire within. He lifted the warm cup to his lips.

It tasted like blood, only…stale and laden with grass and dirt. His chest tightened at the thought of how Ryn had tasted, how sweet and precious her blood had been, how invigorating—

"Zain?" came Esben's voice, cautious. He took a step closer.

Ryn's lips had fallen to a flat line. Colby and Irene were watching Zain intently.

"I'm fine." Zain forced himself to take another sip.

"Are you sure?" Esben stepped into Zain's view.

"After…" Zain glanced at Ryn, at her throat. "This tastes like someone pissed in it."

"Ah, there he is." Ryn relaxed into a slump. "That's my Zain."

Warmth surged along that strange chord between them, that mating bond. His eyes hooked on hers, on the mirrored warmth within. For him. Despite what had happened, what he had done, she still looked at him like that.

He…didn't deserve the forgiveness.

Esben set his hand on Zain's shoulder. "We will get through this, Brother."

Pride surged through Zain's chest at his brother's words and his father's support and his wife's love. Yet doubt slithered within. As if sensing it, Ryn extended her hand across the table. Zain slid his hand into hers. Their fingers laced, and she gave his hand a gentle squeeze. A reassurance. They would get through this, together.

"You made a vow, darling," Ryn said with a mischievous grin. "Don't think you're getting out of it so easily. Until death, remember?"

Zain chuckled and sipped his tonic with a grimace. "Yes, I remember, love."

He could never forget Ryn, not in a thousand years.

56

A NEW DAWN

Ryn

The afternoon sunlight glittered on the ice hanging from the windowsills, buttresses, and stonework of Nightshade Keep. Snow lingered in the Red Forest and on the rooftops. Ryn watched the crew working to fix the damage done to the ballroom and gardens. The hole she'd fallen through remained, though the rubble had been cleared.

Her magic strained from healing King Victor. Pulling the poison from the blood had been strenuous and time-consuming; it had taken most of the morning. The blood loss made him weak and tired, but without the poison, he would recover quickly. He would be the commanding king he was before.

The head scholars, alchemist, and healer had watched in awe as she worked. The scholar took notes, jotting every detail. Her magic had caused quite the stir among the scholars and researchers. She would be spending more time with them, unfortunately.

She didn't know if that was better than having tea with the ladies of court or not.

Footsteps approached, and Ryn's heart jumped into her throat. A female Hunter escorted Lu into the solarium. Her sister wore a plum gown from Ryn's wardrobe—she'd told the servants that Lu could have anything she wanted from her clothes—and the dress hung on her shoulders. Lu's eyes widened at the wall of windows and the view of the sparkling ice-covered gardens and forest beyond. Her eyes then fell on Ryn, and a squeal escaped her throat as she dashed forward. Ryn met her halfway. They collided in a fierce embrace.

"I thought we'd never see each other again," Lu cried.

"I tried to get to you, but Nobel got there first." Ryn released her. Tears lined Lu's lashes, and Ryn felt heat pushing against her eyes.

"And you're here." Lu swallowed. She looked Ryn up and down, then at Irene. "A princess. You married the prince."

"I would have invited you to the wedding," Ryn said.

"I was there for the ball, or, you know, some of it," Lu said, her voice small. Her smile fell. Darkness smothered her expression. "It was beautiful. You were beautiful."

"You would have loved the ceremony." Ryn threaded her arm through Lu's and led her to the table set for two with delicate porcelain teacups and lemon-filled cakes, and a box of chocolates. Lu, of course, went for the chocolates first.

Ryn told Lu about the wedding ceremony, the vows, the flash of the candles, and the eeriness. As Ryn suspected, Lu's eyes went wide, just as they had when their mother used to tell them stories of the dead rising and ghosts and monsters. Ryn poured tea for them both, and while Lu enjoyed the teacakes and chocolate, Ryn told her everything that had happened since Ryn left for the Red Forest on that fateful day.

When Ryn's story came to its end at Nobel's death, she asked, "Are you okay?"

Lu didn't answer at once. She toyed with the lace of her sleeve, eyes on the half-eaten teacake on her plate. "I think so. I mean, I don't remember much past waking up at Nobel's house. He helped me get better, we went to dinner, and then…it's blurry." Lu took a gulp of tea. "I feel like I've been asleep for a long time."

Ryn suspected Lu was lying, but she didn't push her.

"It'll be okay," Ryn promised. She gripped Lu's hand. "No more going to bed hungry, or wearing dirty clothes, or bathing in cold water. We live in the keep now. With all the warm water and all the chocolate you want."

Lu's pink-painted lips curved upward, though it lacked her usual mirth. "It will be different."

"You can still sew," Ryn said. "I'm sure there are plenty of materials and space. Or, if you want to do nothing for a few weeks, that's fine. We're nobility now."

Lu was staying in a suite close to the royal wing. The king had assigned her a personal guard. Servants tended to her needs. Despite it all, Lu looked like she hadn't slept. Ghosts lingered behind her eyes. Restless panic hovered under her words. Guilt twisted Ryn's gut.

"And he's dead?" Lu whispered. Her hazel eyes were pinned on her teacup. "Nobel. He's dead?"

"Dead as he can be," Ryn promised. "I felt his soul leave his body."

A dark vengeance came over Lu's face.

The world shifted under Ryn's feet. She had become Nobel's leech to protect her little sister from the dirty horrors of living in the slums, but it hadn't been enough. She had fallen into Nobel's clutches anyway.

"Lu?" Ryn whispered.

It took a moment for Lu to answer. She lifted her eyes from her tea, and when she spoke, her words were sullen. "I woke this morning to a servant bringing me tea. A steaming bath was waiting for me. I didn't dress myself or comb my own hair." She sighed, and a bit of that darkness dissolved. Though not all of it. She plopped another chocolate on her tongue. "I can get used to this. I'm going to get fat. Like in that book Dad had, the fat queen."

Ryn laughed. Their father had read to them from an old history book, and there had been a full-page drawing of a long-dead noble female. She was large and had a mountain of hair, but she wore a smug little smile. Lu had called her the happy fat lady, and as children they had made up stories about her and adventures she'd had in childhood. Adventures two poor girls could never have.

"I think that is a worthy aspiration." Ryn tipped her tea to Lu. "Make up for all those nights we went to bed hungry. I'll make it up to you for leaving you alone that day."

Lu hummed. "Chocolate, diamonds, and parties will do."

Ryn grinned. "I've heard Lord Coshal throws a spring ball on the equinox where all the females weave flowers into their hair."

Lu's smile returned. "Do you think I'll find a chivalrous young lord to dance with?"

"You'll have a line of males waiting to dance with you," Ryn said, because she knew Lu would be the loveliest female at any ball, and any male with half a brain would be stumbling over himself for a flicker of her attention.

Lu laughed, a ghost of what it once was. "Let's go to the chocolate shop tomorrow. Or maybe the day after. I'm too tired today."

"It's a date."

They clinked their teacups together.

Later, Ryn would tell her about the Crestin House and their possible relatives. Later, she would propose a tour of the keep and the grounds. Later, because right now, all Ryn could think about was how she and Lu had all the time in the world, and she planned on using every moment of it.

sss

Ryn spent the hours after lunch answering the alchemist's prodding questions about her magic and the scholar's questions about her parents. All of their questions only proved how little she knew about herself, and how little they knew about magic. She sipped her spiced wine between their questions, and half a glass in, the annoyance on the edges of her mind had dulled somewhat.

When the parlor door opened and Zain strolled inside, Ryn felt a stout relief. Colby, recently promoted to Zain's personal guard, followed.

"You are dismissed," Zain said to the scholars and alchemist.

They gathered their papers and books and quills, bowed to them both, then hurried into the library, chattering about all that they had learned. Zain's sapphire eyes pinned Ryn in place. As the parlor doors closed, he let his perfect composure slip and exposed the ruffled and sleepless prince underneath. While scholars had been prodding Ryn about her magic, they'd been just as prodding about Zain's.

"I lied," Zain said.

Ryn set her wine on the table with a soft clink. "About what?"

"When I told Esben that I didn't remember anything from that night." Zain ran his hand through his dark hair, ruffling it further. He inhaled deeply, then collapsed into an armchair angled around the burning hearth. "I keep remembering more. Bits and pieces. Sounds."

This was her Zain, the uncertain male underneath the gloomy smarm. Ryn crossed the space and sat in the chair beside his, on the edge so that their knees touched. He might not have a clear memory of that night, but she did. She'd spent the better part of the day thinking about it. His eyes trailed to her neck, where twin punctures had already healed to barely-there marks.

"Did it hurt?" Zain whispered.

"Of course it did." She furrowed her brow and offered him a cheeky grin. "You bit me. With vengeance. I imagine you packed your hatred for me into that bite."

His tongue moved over his top teeth. The marks on her neck prickled. "I couldn't hate you."

"Even after I poisoned your father?"

"Even after that," he whispered. "Do you feel…more when you are near me?"

She blinked. "Like what you are feeling and thinking?"

"I mentioned it to one of the scholars, and they said it's an indication of a mating bond," he said, blushing. "That either we are true mates, or that when I…bit you the first time, we…created one."

Mates.

Real mates, like in the stories. Soulmates.

The very idea tingled from her toes to her scalp, and sent gooseflesh over her skin. "I don't mind," she said. "This way, you can't hide anything from me."

He smirked. "You won't be able to hide anything from me either, love."

She nudged his knee with her own. "You said you remembered more of that night."

"I woke up in the cage," Zain started, his voice low. "None of the vampires would tell me anything. Then Nobel showed up and gloated about finding me. He threw the truth in my face, told me I was supposed to be this great vampire king, and he would help me. I… I thought about it. Being a king. But I knew I wouldn't be a real king. I would be a puppet. He left me in that cage. In the dark. Alone. To think about what I was." Zain trembled. "I got cold. My heart slowed, and then stopped. I was…terrified. I kept waiting to die, but I didn't. My eyes adjusted to the dark. I could smell the dank on the stone, the vampires guarding the cage just out of sight. I could hear muttering and dripping. That is where my memory blurs. The next thing I knew, I could smell you. I could hear your pulse. I saw you, and I…" Zain swallowed, fear leaking into his eyes. "All I could think about was blood. Yours. I needed it more than I needed anything, and I lost control. I am sorry."

His words sent a feverish chill down her spine and into her bloodstream. She vividly remembered his fangs piercing her flesh, feeling her blood flow freely out of her and into him. It was a feverish and mad need, entirely different from that night when she gave her blood willingly.

"Esben said you enchanted Nobel's blood and took it for your own," Zain said.

"I did." A wave of nausea rolled in her stomach at the memory. She swallowed against the bile. "I was dying. I decided I wanted to live. Nobel was holding me, and the nail design that your mother insisted upon sliced into his skin."

She squeezed her fingers together, just as her nails had punctured his skin. She still felt the stickiness of his blood under her nails, despite having scrubbed them. She had kept the pointed design—just in case she needed to poke someone else.

Zain made a face. "And…you're all right? After enchanting a vampire's blood into your own?"

Ryn half-laughed. "I haven't felt good since. I think his ghost is tormenting me from beyond the veil. I've thrown up several times, and the healer brought me this herbal bone broth shit that looked a lot like your tonic. Irene made me drink all of it."

She cast a side-long glance at where her guard stood by the door. Irene pretended not to have heard.

"But I survived," Ryn added. "As will you."

Zain's arrogance sharpened, and he grinned—pearly white fangs extended at his command. Ryn's blood pulsed, and a dangerous thrill trailed along her bones and under her skin. Heat pooled in the bottom of her stomach. She tore her eyes from his fangs to his eyes. No red lingered.

"Apparently, being vampire royalty is different." Zain leaned forward on his knees. "No one knows much about it. Few wrote about it. The scholars are utterly fascinated with my ability to magic myself from location to location. We are going to be spending a great deal of time in the library, I fear."

She groaned.

"Yes, we're special, love."

Zain vanished before her eyes, then reappeared a heartbeat later holding her glass of spiced wine. He took a sip. "And I hear my father is feeling remarkably better this afternoon. Thanks to a certain enchantress."

Ryn's heart squeezed. "That is good to hear. I… I'm sorry for what I did. I was in a tight spot, between you and Nobel, and I…"

"Picked your sister."

She nodded, remembering the darkness behind Lu's eyes. "I promise I won't poison anyone in your family again."

Zain cocked a brow. "But everyone else is open?"

"Aurora is on my list," Ryn said humorlessly. If only the female hadn't fled the kingdom the day before the wedding. Ryn had told the king how Aurora had confessed to hiring mercenaries to kill her. He hadn't promised punishment. Her shame would be punishment enough, he'd said. Bullshit, in Ryn's opinion.

Zain chuckled. "Gods have mercy if Aurora ever shows her face in Calcurta again."

"She will need it." Ryn watched Zain take another drink of the spiced wine, then she slipped the glass from his fingers. "Will you need blood? Real Blood? Eventually, I mean."

He shrugged. "Who knows. Maybe. Now that I've tasted the real thing, the tonic is a bit…disgusting."

She felt the skin on her throat tingle.

"Esben is worried about me," Zain said. "What I might do without realizing. Which is why I have a captain as a guard, not just any Hunter." He nodded toward Colby, who watched the two with a guarded expression. "But I also fear what I might do, so I don't mind. I also fear what others might do once the truth circulates."

"The Hunters have sworn to protect you," Ryn whispered. She covered his hand with hers. "Even from yourself. We'll be okay."

"How can you be sure?"

"Because I said so," she said firmly. "I'm royalty now, so what I say goes."

He chuckled. "Of course, my love. Say the word, and I will bring you the world on a silver platter." He brought her knuckles to his lips.

"The world is a bit much. We should start small, like jewels, chocolate, and sex."

"Anything for you, my love," he said, grinning.

He pulled her to her feet and pressed a heated kiss to her lips. His next kiss was more tender, stroking desire deep in her core, but she pressed her hand against his chest. He leaned away, brow furrowed.

"Not right now," she said breathlessly. She cleared her throat and regained her composure. "I promised Lu we'd have dinner together."

He sighed dramatically. "Fine. I will allow it this time, but only because you haven't seen each other in a few days." He tucked his hands into his trouser pockets. "Then you are all mine."

"And you are mine," she purred.

Zain turned to leave, and Ryn smacked his ass as he did so. Colby frowned, clearly unaware of what he had signed up for being Zain's guard.

57

UNTIL DEATH

Ryn

The next six days passed in a wintery haze. Ryn divided her time between tea with the queen, Lady Crestin, and Lu, and then she met with the scholars to go over her magic. Each evening, she returned to her chambers exhausted. Invitations arrived daily for parties and tea. She ignored most of them. She didn't feel ready for the role of princess or wife. She had not yet attended court. Neither had Zain. Lu kept to her chambers.

The odious task of vetting each Hunter for vampirism went by slowly and secretly. A list of defectors had been made and distributed to the guard and every city in the kingdom. So had a list of the dead. Ryn had yet to see either. She didn't want to.

One morning, Ryn woke up in Zain's arms. They had slept in her bed, and the curtains hid them from the looming day. They'd spent the night before wrapped around each other. She had slept better than she had in days, and she didn't want to move.

But the servants had other ideas.

A summons came for them to join the king in the throne room.

"A vampire had requested an audience with the king," the servant said quickly. "His Majesty requests your presence."

"What?" Zain sat up, not minding his naked chest.

Panic banished Ryn's sluggish thoughts. She sat up, hugging the blankets to her chest. "A vampire?"

Zain groaned. "We'll be there shortly."

The servant hurried into the sitting room, and Zain and Ryn quickly dressed. Zain had just pulled his nightshirt over himself when Kari rushed in to help Ryn get ready—a quick wash in the basin and hasty brush of her wild hair, and then she stepped into a gown of deep copper. Ryn and Zain reconvened in the sitting room. He looked refreshed and marvelous in a suit, with his hair brushed back and tousled.

"Ready?" Zain asked.

"No, but let's go." Ryn took his hand and they followed the servant to the throne room. Colby and Irene flanked them.

The throne room was filled with curious nobles, servants, and guards.

"Unusual crowd for this early," Zain muttered as he and Ryn entered.

Before the dais, five Hunters stood around a bound male with red-rimmed eyes. It was the same position Ryn had once been forced into. The vampire looked far more determined than she had felt. King Victor sat on his throne. Esben stood to the right of it. Queen Portia stood to the left. Hunters gathered on either side of the dais, ready to remove the threat from existence.

The vampire caught sight of Zain and Ryn, and he sat up a little straighter. Hope brightened his expression.

A hush fell over the throne room, and King Victor stood. Zain, in his due diligence, approached the throne to stand beside his father. Ryn followed and took a position at Zain's side.

"All right, my son is present, as requested," said King Victor. His voice boomed over the quiet room, healthy, strong and commanding. "You have the audience you requested. What is it you ask?"

"Peace, Your Majesty." The vampire bowed his head.

Murmurs rang throughout the throne room. Ryn glanced at Zain. He looked as confused as she felt.

King Victor considered the vampire's claim. "Peace, you say. Were you among those who planned to rid the kingdom of fae? Who plotted my death and tried to turn my son against me?"

The vampire swallowed. Terror slithered through his determination. "I-I was, but Nobel told us we had no other choice. We had no other option. If we were caught, we'd be killed."

"You now have another way," King Victor said, then looked at Zain.

"That is why I have come." He cast a fearful glance around the nobles and guards. "There are more of us, those who didn't want to fight. We want to live without hiding."

King Victor motioned to Zain. Ryn saw the eyes of the court shift from Victor to Zain, and she felt the collective breath as he stepped forward.

"You are in luck," Zain said casually. "We happen to be working toward a similar goal."

Ryn held her expression blank, impassive, just as the queen had taught her. She hadn't had much time to talk to Zain. Is this what he had been planning during the late dinners with Esben and their father? By the nervous whispers surging through the nobles, not everyone was keen on peace. The vampire, however, looked torn between hope and terror that Zain's statement was a joke.

"Our goal is to strive for nonviolent coexistence," Zain told the vampire, though he spoke loud enough for the entire court to hear. "Do you agree?"

"Yes," the vampire said. "We all would, if given the chance."

Zain nodded to the Hunters, who cut the vampire's bindings. He stood cautiously, eyeing the Hunters on either side of him, the courtiers watching in silence. Hunters escorted the vampire elsewhere, out of the view of the court.

The rest of the talk would happen without so many eyes and ears. But the gist of it, that Zain was spearheading peace between fae and vampires, had landed.

"Is this really happening?" Ryn whispered to the queen.

"It is." Queen Portia kept her emotions masked. "I didn't think it would work, yet we already have a volunteer returning the call for peace."

Peace with vampires. Ryn hadn't thought it possible. Yet here they were. Zain flashed her a cocky grin, and she restrained herself before the eyes of the court.

That evening, Zain confessed his plans at dinner. No one knew how to reach the vampires, so scouts had gone into the city's dark corners with open invitations for vampires that led to a secret meeting, where Hunters waited.

"You might have gotten more responses without Hunters," Ryn pointed out.

"Yes, but we had no one else capable of protecting themselves if the vampires came with hostility," Zain explained. "All we needed was one vampire to extend a hand, and we finally found one."

"Why was I not included in these talks?" Ryn cocked a brow.

Zain poured himself a whiskey from the restocked sideboard. "Until today, they weren't going anywhere. Now, the planning really begins."

The hearth burned warm and bright. A fresh stack of books greeted them, sent from the scholars, on fae magic and vampire lore.

Ryn heaved an annoyed sigh and reached for her spiced wine. Between the queen and the scholars, Ryn was spending far too much time learning. She took a deep swig of her wine. The spices tingled against her tongue and down her throat.

"Oh, this one must be for you," she said, fingering the faded lettering on the spine. "Vampire Royalty in the Silver Age."

Zain sighed. "That will be a task for tomorrow."

She returned the book to the stack. The kingdom knew Zain to be a vampire, but only a handful knew he was vampire royalty. Word would likely spread, but they would not help it along.

Sipping her wine, she noticed the red around Zain's eyes.

At her stare, he raised a brow.

"You skipped your tonic this morning," she whispered.

Zain swallowed his whiskey, looking sheepish. "I, uh, must have forgotten."

"You forgot?"

"Okay, I didn't. If I'm not trying to hide what I am, I don't need a tonic as often."

"What if something happens?"

"I told Colby." Zain glanced to where his guard stood by the door, opposite of where Irene stood. "He is watching me."

Ryn sighed through her nose. "That makes me feel a bit better."

"And you only noticed now," he said, loosening his collar. He took a backward step toward his chambers. "You would have said something if I were acting strange."

He wasn't wrong. She hadn't noticed anything amiss with him. If anything, he seemed more at ease and comfortable.

"You didn't notice my eyes this morning either," he whispered with a sinister smile.

"In my defense, we were rudely awoken."

Zain chuckled, fangs peeking out from his lips.

Her eyes snagged on them, and he noticed. Desire danced through her lower belly. Oh, she knew what she would be doing tonight. She pressed her hand against his chest, pushing him toward his bedroom.

Colby let out a resigned sigh, and he and Irene remained by the main sitting room door.

"Are you sure about this?" Zain whispered. Guilt darkened his eyes, remorse hung on his words. "I almost killed you last time."

"The time before that, you didn't," she added. "You were in control, and you took what you needed. The second time you were starving." Swallowing, terrified about what she was about to suggest, she pulled her braid over her shoulder, revealing her neck. "You're in control now. And I can stop you if I need to."

Uncertainty rippled through the bond between them, residual from the night in the vampire cave, from his blind thirst and her fear.

But this was a hill they needed to conquer. Together.

Zain took slow, graceful steps to the bed, until he stood between her knees. "Are you sure?"

"Yes."

Zain lowered himself, his breath warm on her throat as the tips of his fangs scratched the skin over her pulse. He bit—with every suck and swallow of her blood, desire wound tighter around her bones. She felt him, his being, his soul, as if it were her own, and if her enchantment encompassed them both. She tangled herself within it, irreversibly tangled.

Her husband.

Her mate.

ACKNOWLEDGEMENTS

Every book I've written has come about in a different way. No other book has given me such a headache in the rough draft stage as the hot mess that would become A Bloodied Crown. I rewrote the outline three or four times, started a rough draft with three different premises, because I couldn't figure out who Ryn was or how Zain was going to enter the picture. One premise I tried had Ryn as the royal trapped in the castle and Zain as a vampire hunter who was secretly a vampire with a thirst for vengeance. Another premise had Ryn finding work at the castle and Zain the prince who takes an interest in her. None of those premises felt right. None of them worked.

Until I found the one that did. This one.

This book would never have seen the light of day had it not been for the amazing team at Authors 4 Authors: Renee, Rebecca, Brandi, and Lisa. Huge thanks to Lisa and Renee and Rebecca for the amazing and insightful edits, for finding things I couldn't, and helping to turn this mess into something worth putting out there. Huge thanks to Brandi for the beautiful cover! I could never have made something so incredible, even in my wildest dreams. And of course, a big thanks for all the support, editorial and emotional, that you all have shown over the last few years.

I can say with utmost honesty that I have the greatest parents. You have been supportive of my dreams from day one, and have been among the first to buy each book, even if you never read it. From the midnight hailstorm that is my mechanical keyboard, to my bad habit of hoarding books until there's no room to walk through my office, to the time when I asked Dad to drill a hole in my floor and help me wire my PC to the router—you are the absolute best.

I've had a handful of jobs in my lifetime, but none have been more enthusiastic and supportive of my writing as the team I work with now, especially after I told them this particular book had a little bit of spice in it. Jackie and Kaylyn, you two are the best coworkers I could ask for. I love talking books with you, Emily!

And of course, I would be nowhere without all of you: the readers who gave this little author a chance. Without all of you, each and every one of you, who reposted, reviewed, liked and commented, none of this would be possible. Thank you from my whole heart!

About the Author

Beatrice B. Morgan was born and raised in the countryside of southern Illinois, where the fields and forests allowed her imagination to run wild. When she isn't working on a book or reading, she is playing a game or trying out a new hobby or cookie recipe, or adding another book to her endless TBR.

Follow her online:
www.bbmorgan.com
Twitter: @BBMorgan_W
Facebook: @BBMorganBooks
Instagram and Threads: @BBMorgan_W
TikTok: @beatrice_author

AUTHORS 4 AUTHORS PUBLISHING

A publishing company for authors, run by authors, blending the best of traditional and independent publishing

We specialize in speculative fiction: science fiction, fantasy, paranormal, and romance. Get lost in another world!

Check out our collection at https://books2read.com/rl/a4a
or visit Authors4AuthorsPublishing.com/books

For updates, scan the QR code or visit our website to join our semi-monthly newsletter!

Want more romance? We recommend:

TONGUE TIED

by Brandi Spencer

When a cunning linguist comes to Carum Sound, Princess Conora sees an opportunity to regain control of her life and impulsively accepts his offer of marriage. But can she trust his seduction, or are his promises of passion and freedom too good to be true?

books2read.com/tonguetied